HALF CITY

HALF CITY

TITLES BY KATE GOLDEN

THE SACRED STONES SERIES
A Dawn of Onyx
A Promise of Peridot
A Reign of Rose

THE HARKER ACADEMY SERIES
Half City

If Not for My Baby

HALF CITY

HARKER ACADEMY: BOOK ONE

KATE GOLDEN

First published in Great Britain in 2026 by Arcadia
an imprint of Quercus
Part of John Murray Group

Copyright © 2026 Natalie Sellers
Excerpt from *A Dawn of Onyx* by Kate Golden © 2023 Natalie Sellers

The moral right of Kate Golden to be
identified as the author of this work has been
asserted in accordance with the Copyright,
Designs and Patents Act, 1988.

Book design and title page illustration by Jenni Surasky
Map by Alexis Seabrook

All rights reserved. No part of this publication
may be reproduced or transmitted in any form
or by any means, electronic or mechanical,
including photocopy, recording, or any
information storage and retrieval system,
without permission in writing from the publisher.

This book is a work of fiction. Names, characters,
businesses, organizations, places and events are
either the product of the author's imagination
or used fictitiously. Any resemblance to
actual persons, living or dead, events
or-locales is entirely coincidental.

A CIP catalogue record for this book is available from the British Library

HB ISBN 978-1-52944-368-4
TPB ISBN 978-1-52944-369-1
EBOOK ISBN 978-1-52944-370-7

Offset in 12.18/17.4pt Bell MT Pro by Six Red Marbles UK, Thetford, Norfolk

Printed and bound in Great Britain by Clays Ltd, Elcograf S.p.A.

Papers used by Quercus are from well-managed forests and other responsible sources.

Quercus
Carmelite House
50 Victoria Embankment
London EC4Y 0DZ

John Murray Group
Part of Hodder & Stoughton Limited
An Hachette UK company

The authorised representative in the EEA is Hachette Ireland,
8 Castlecourt Centre, Dublin 15, D15 XTP3, Ireland (email: info@hbgi.ie)

*For my mom,
Who raised me with unconditional love
and boundless imagination.
I think that might be all anyone needs
to become a writer.*

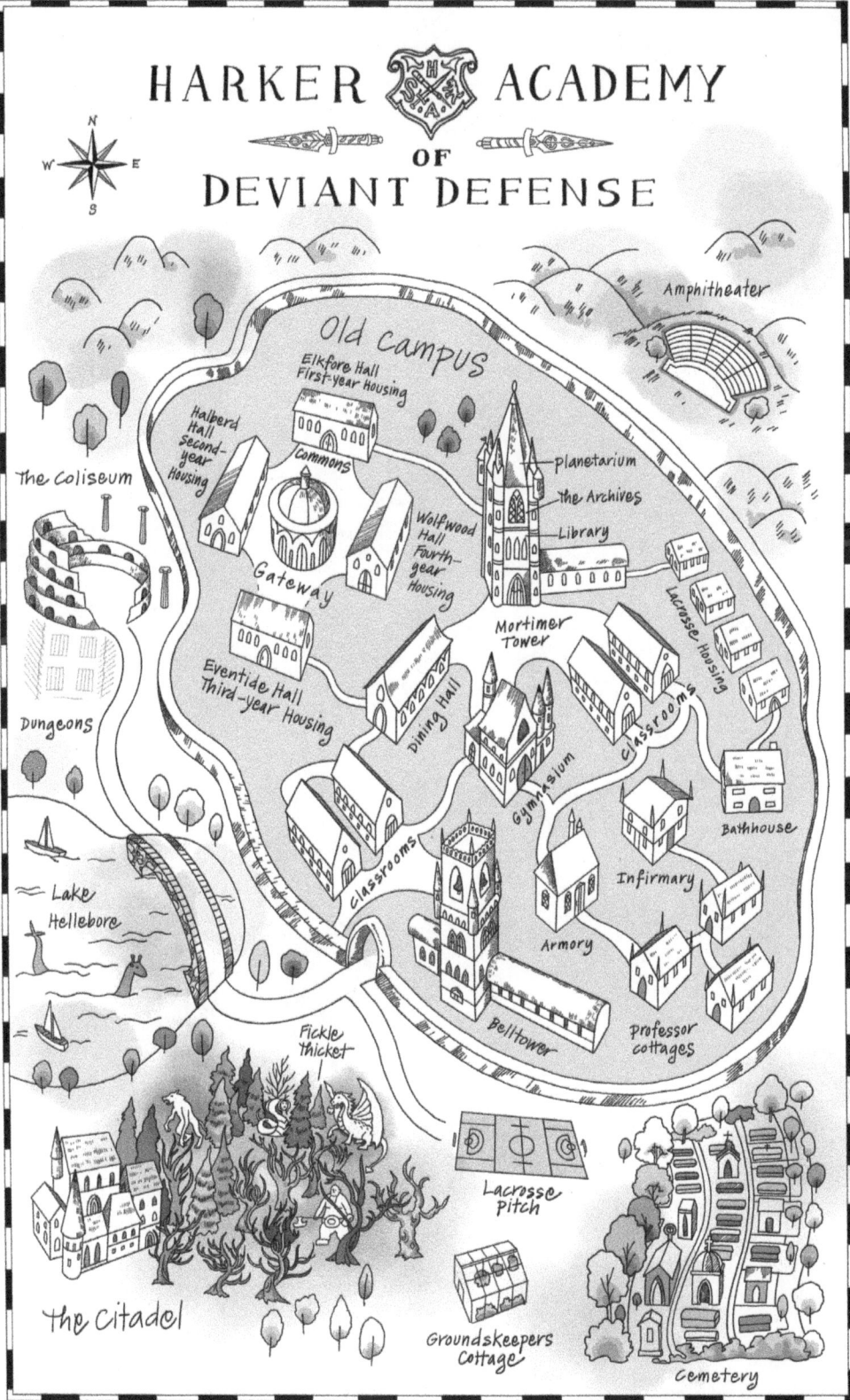

HALF CITY

HALF CITY

CHAPTER 1

ONCE, I CRUSHED a beetle with my bare foot.

Nora was faster than me back then. I was all limbs and joints, with little coordination between them. We'd been playing gymnasts on the sidewalk—cartwheels resulting in skinned knees and tumbles leading to bits of asphalt embedded in our palms—when the sun-drenched day bled into a dusk that turned our neighborhood downright menacing. Or at least, that's how it looked to six-year-old me. I peered up from one of my more impressive somersaults and realized Nora was already at the stairs of our apartment building.

I ran after my big sister as if the shadows yawning off the power lines were long fingers that could seize me where I stood. I didn't even see the bug.

When the shell crunched beneath my heel—innards spreading across my foot like jam on toast—I expected revulsion. Guilt. Horror.

But none came.

I bent down to inspect the gore, my fear of creatures that slunk out with the fading daylight forgotten. I couldn't tear my eyes away from the insect's shattered exoskeleton. The still-twitching limbs. My blood thrummed with morbid allure. A predator discovering prey and, with it, a sick, insistent desire.

A desire I've fought against every single day since.

Staring down at the once-blue, now-gray gum stuck to the heel of my loafer, I try to shake the memory. I don't have time to dissect my psyche this evening. I'm late.

"Thank you so much for calling—"

I nearly jam the phone into my ear canal. "Yes? Hello?"

"Your call is very important to us. Someone from the district attorney's office will be—"

The noise I release is less human woman, more exasperated hyena. A balding man in a crumpled shirt recoils from me, and I deserve it. The Astera subway at rush hour is terrible by anyone's standards. The Astera subway at rush hour *in the summer* is a stinking, sweat-drenched hellscape from which few emerge with their sanity. A hellscape made worse only by all the lunatics who call this city home, and tonight, to Crumpled-Shirt Man, I am said lunatic.

But there's no time to mutter apologies. I secure the phone against my shoulder and shove past him down the stairs into the bowels of the multifloored subway. A sardine in a sweaty, sticky, tin can of conference calls, nursing scrubs, and unsupervised teenagers. My bags, water bottle, wallet, and railway card are about as secure in my hurried grasp as a handful of eels. When I maneuver through a turnstile, a dog's yapping echoes from deeper within the subway, rising above the din.

Someone behind me, equally rushed, knocks my precious phone from the crook of my shoulder and I spy the endless depths of a grate beneath my feet. A mere second before disaster, I catch the phone between my chin and collarbone. *Phew.* I listen to the irritating melody over the line to confirm that my spot in the queue hasn't been compromised.

What kind of mother is more likely to answer her work line than her cell? I'm all for boundaries, but if I hear one more automated woman tell me how valuable my time is, I'm going to implode. While I wait for my train, the Muzak blares in my ear and that dog yowls again.

Every time a train thunders past, the entire tunnel flickers. One fluorescent light high above is missing a bulb. My stomach growls, and I wonder if every suit on the crowded platform can hear it over the rumble of the subway cars. I search through my leather tote—a designer bag my from my mother, which I hate yet carry daily out of some misplaced guilt—and find the soft pretzel I grabbed on my way to work this morning.

This morning.

Shit. I haven't eaten today.

My mother once told me that forgetting to eat when stressed is a superpower. I'm about to cram as much of the stale, salty dough into my mouth as I can in an act of fierce rebellion against such an archaic, patriarchal notion when I finally catch sight of the dog that's been barking for the last ten minutes.

Against the tiled wall to my left, below graffiti depicting white antlers on Caspar Harlock's ad for his burgeoning news network, sits a yowling, dark-haired mutt, not too unlike my own. He's barking mostly at his owner, a kid with matted hair, leathery skin from too much sun, and clothes that I can smell from here.

The boy's sign reads: **HUNGRY, ANYTHING HELPS.**

Astera—the Half City, the country's epicenter of culture, business, and politics, located on the glittering edge of the eastern seaboard. We must have the largest population of billionaires in the world—our graffitied Caspar Harlock over there and my best friend Penny Pine's parents, to name a few—and yet a seriously shameful percentage of the city is living on the street. And who can you blame for a cycle that never breaks? Those in government? Say, perhaps, our tough-as-nails district attorney?

Whose office I am *still* on hold with?

Even though she *birthed* me?

It's moments like these in which I almost understand my mother's obsession with marrying me off to James Pine like some tragic Dickensian wretch. It's the same part of her that gifted me this bag on my first day of work so I wouldn't look quite so *pedestrian*. She loves me. She wants me to be taken care of in this dog-eat-dog city. And even though I can take care of myself in more ways than she could possibly fathom, I do wish I had the means to pull a wad of hundreds out of my bag for this kid and his dog.

Instead, I offer him my squashed, cold pretzel. His eyes light up as he takes it from me, immediately ripping off half for his floppy-eared companion. The dog eats hastily, fragments of wet pretzel crumbling on the ground, before he quiets, snuggling next to his owner in satiated gratitude. The young kid offers me a similar expression.

I don't even realize my heart is in my throat until my mom answers on the other line with a shrill "Yes, Viv, what is it?"

I falter for words.

"Viv? Do you need something? I'm about to step into a meeting."

"Hi, sorry." I pull myself together just as my train arrives. "Your team left a box of Dad's things outside my place this morning?"

A pungent whiff of some guy's noxious body spray fills my nose as the crowd coalesces around the open doors. I can barely hear my mother's exasperated sigh over the tumult.

"Yes." She sounds distracted. "I'm trying to declutter."

I nearly take a model's bony elbow to the chin as I find a seat. "You don't want . . ." I can't even find the right words. "Anything to remember—"

"My assistant saw a drug exchange on your block when she was leaving the apartment. How many times do I have to say I don't like you living so far past the Chasm?"

I mentally pound my head against a wall. I want to ask, *Have you blocked out everything that happened before Dad died? You guys raised me around the corner from a brothel. The madam had to pick me up from school once.* But I go with "Babylon is up-and-coming."

"Will you at least have James stay with you? He says you never invite him over."

It's not her fault—she doesn't know how laughable it is to assume my boyfriend can protect me better than I can protect myself. I fumble for a response that isn't *No thank you, please.*

"Or I could have a home security system installed?"

"You're kidding, right?" Her silence is like a whip. "Yeah, okay. If you must."

"So much graciousness on this phone call."

I bite back my attitude. "I'm sorry."

"Is Fiona having you work opening night?"

My mom has hounded me about this new exhibit on the Chasm for months. I work at the Windsor, Astera's largest and most well-funded museum, gallery, and research institute, and our newest collection opens in November. To my mom, whether or not I am one of the assistants chosen to help wealthy old women in pearls and tweed-wearing historians up the stairs on opening night is the full extent of my worth as a human. "I still don't know," I tell her. I don't add that I told her the same thing last week, and the week before.

"Well, you've certainly put in the time. I'm sure she will."

"One can only hope," I deadpan. When I hear her irritated sigh on the other line, guilt swims in. "Thank you, though. For the faith."

"Mm-hmm."

"Love you," I add.

But the line is already dead.

After my dad died when I was ten, my mom traded in her grief for justice. She'd been a city councilwoman in Lethe, the lower-middle-class neighborhood where my sister and I grew up, but his death prompted her to get a law degree, spend her weekends championing local anti-crime legislation, and dig into my father's murder until it was branded a cold case and thrown into some cheap suit's file cabinet.

Only two years later, she got a fancy government job and moved Nora and me across the city in the same station wagon we'd used as his hearse. I went to bed one night in the dingy yet lovable five-story walk-up I'd known all my life and woke less than a week later in a luxurious, chillingly empty house over the hill in the Hesperides, enrolled in Belaire School for Girls—and yes, it was as bad as it sounds.

I allow myself a brief gut-deep sigh at the memories before taking a seat and rummaging through my three overstuffed bags—gym bag, tote, purse—and running through the work wear–to–cocktail dress transition in my head.

My dress can be thrown on over my blouse. Or Nora's blouse, which I've stolen to look presentable. Then I'll shimmy the blouse down and off. No, wait—it could snag on the dagger strapped to my ribs. Britannia silver would eviscerate the blouse, and Nora would eviscerate me. Luckily, only I inherited the hunter gene from my father, otherwise that wouldn't be a joke. I'll unbutton the blouse first and pull it through my dress's neckline.

Pants always come off last, even after shoes, meaning there will be an unavoidable period of time in which I am barefoot on the Astera subway.

Vile, but alas—the things we do for love.

Thankfully, by the time I'm ready for my acrobat-level quick-change maneuver, the railcar's crowd has thinned out a bit. Probably because we're heading farther and farther south toward the Chasm. Nobody from up here goes down to Babylon, the neighborhood where Penny and I live. Especially not at this hour—assistants at the Windsor rarely leave before eight.

After graduating from Belaire, I didn't quite have the GPA to attend a decent college. My mother was beside herself, of course, but it's not like I could tell her I missed half my finals because a vampire was drinking his way through the city's strip clubs.

After my gap *year* became gap *years*, I'd wanted to apply to entry-level jobs at photography galleries. There's a smattering of cool ones in Babylon, but—to nobody's shock—my mom was not jazzed about that idea. I think she said something like *I didn't spend every dollar I had on Belaire so you could look at other people's pictures for a living.*

However, Nora's wife, Fiona, stepped in a year ago and offered me a job as her assistant. She's the Windsor's head curator, which basically means she's a history buff who gets to travel the globe, say the word *gala* a lot, and wear high, clacky heels every day.

As the subway car moves over the Erebos Bridge across the Chasm, my bags begin to slide. Despite having a cocktail dress currently overhead, I save them from escaping with my outstretched foot, like it's a frog's tongue on an errant fly. For a rare moment in which my tampons and sweaty Pilates clothes don't spew onto everybody's shoes, I am awash in warm appreciation for my heightened hunter reflexes. Though I pray the second dagger strapped to my thigh didn't poke through my slacks. I can't afford another pair this month.

Eventually, the dress is on, loafers replaced by sensible heels, and there are no injured subway citizens to show for it. My eyes find my shoes, and I twist my ankle for a better look. In my head, my mom says, *A stiletto wouldn't kill you.* In-my-head-me replies to her, *Actually, it might. Have you ever chased down a demon in a six-inch?* Two sprained ankles have taught me that a platform heel is the only way to go.

I peer up at the remaining stops ticking away on the digital banner. Three more until Babylon. I check my hair using my phone camera and pull the long night-black strands into a low bun. Smooth my brows. Examine my teeth. The phone reads 8:51.

Dinner was at 8:00. I can probably be through the doors of Cobwebs by 9:07, which isn't too terrible for me. Maybe Penny won't even notice.

The smell of bacon pulls a growl from my stomach. A woman at the end of the railcar is munching a breakfast burrito with one hand as she holds on to a double stroller with the other. Her eyes are drooping closed as she chews.

A breakfast burrito at 8:00 p.m.—my kind of lady.

I reach into my bag and grab my half-frame camera to discreetly snap a shot of the mom and her burrito. There's exhaustion there but also the joy of a perfect bite when you need it most. It's incredibly human, and, as I often try to remind myself, so am I.

The train slows to a halt and a few more passengers file in and out. One stop left. Thank the lord.

"They're sleeping, so . . ." the mom says. When I peer back over, a man in a grease-stained jumpsuit is scooting closer to her, asking to see her kids. He's shifty—eyes darting here and there, scratching hastily at his arm. I hear the noise like his nails are inside my brain.

Scratch, scratch, scratch.

I try to tell myself he's just a poppy addict or a mugger from STC—South of the Chasm. But then shivers break out across my skin, and my heart sinks. I can almost hear kind, forgiving Penny ordering a red wine for me and saying to the waiter, "She'll be here any minute . . . She has a really demanding job." I wonder if they already sang her happy birthday.

But this scratchy, shifty man is no junkie nor mugger. I know it immediately, like realizing I've crushed a beetle underfoot. The vibration beneath my skin. The gut-twisting desire just as insistent as it was back then.

My stop finally arrives: 14 Babylon. I watch as the rest of the passengers file out.

Goodbye, you lucky bastards.

The metal subway doors close, and now it's only me, Burrito Mom, and a demon.

My two silver daggers tingle pleasantly against my skin, and I stand, grateful for my sensible heels.

CHAPTER 2

I TRY TO stretch innocuously as I stride over. My body hurts. Somewhere between hunching over a desk all day and the werewolf who kicked my ass two nights ago, I think I threw my back out. Is twenty-one too young to throw your back out?

The demon appraises me with thinly veiled irritation. He's so thin I assume he does have a drug problem, but by the look of those cloudy eyes and rotting teeth, it's not the high-quality poppy Astera is known for. His calloused hands and the black grease on his brow tell me he's some kind of manual laborer, though his improperly buttoned coveralls and variety of bruises tell me he's not the star of his field. Whatever he does, I don't think he's a member of the Brood.

Good news. I didn't have the energy for certain death tonight.

The Brood is like the mafia, but the soul sucking is literal: a savage cabal of demons and the lesser deviants they employ who all serve at the behest of the High Thane—the king of all deviants. Sycophants offering brute strength to their king in return for belonging, power, and the infliction of pain and the indulgence of pleasure in equal measure. And, like any exclusive society, the

Brood employs only the most clever and violent, so they're not easy to find and even less easy to kill.

Not for lack of trying, though. Watching a dozen of them murder your father right before your eyes tends to have that effect. Some might call it vengeance, but I prefer the term *pest extermination*. I'm just doing my part to clean up this city I call home. My mom went from neighborhood councilwoman to DA in his memory. How is my vendetta any less noble? Sure, mine comes with bloodlust, but she has to wear a pantsuit.

I'll give her this—my mom has a much easier time prosecuting the criminals she thinks killed my dad than I do fighting the Brood demons that actually did it. I feel a flash of relief thinking of how little my mother knows of her husband's death. Of the sick, menacing creatures she shares the city with. She, like every other mortal, has no clue that deviants stalk through the streets, feasting on human souls and blood and flesh. It's brutal out here, and I'm grateful my mother's none the wiser.

I eye the greasy demon once more and come to the conclusion that this glassy-eyed creep doesn't scream *elite evil*. They also brand their members when they take the mantle, and though I can't see the back of this guy's neck under his hair, I'm confident in my analysis. All I'm dealing with is your run-of-the-mill low-level demon hankering for a soul.

And I hate that inside me, a little thrill begins to bloom. That I want to save this mom and her kids—really, I do—but I might've missed Penny's birthday even if he was sitting on this train alone just for the chance to puncture demonic flesh with my silver. Rage swims inside me at my own nature. I don't only hunt to save lives like other hunters. I hunt because if I don't kill things, I'll crack. I'll get sick. I could kill humans instead.

Just like there are deviants—any and all creatures born from the depths of the underworld—there are also lymantrians. Beings with souls who have nonhuman abilities or appearances, living right here alongside the mortals. Hunters are one lymantrian species, but I'm not just a hunter. I'm an *aeon*—a type of hunter who has a second sight. Meaning I get a full-body buzz just being in the presence of a deviant. And a twisted, nagging craving for the kill.

According to my dad, we aeons don't really play well with others. Not that I would know; I haven't spent much time with other hunters. We're a solitary breed. I know there must be more—I've seen one or two dagger-wielding silhouettes slip through the shadows—but it's rare. For the last nine years, it's just been me and all the wicked things in Astera. That's okay, though. I like to work alone.

As I approach, the demon's eyes flash red. That bloody ring around both irises is the only way a regular hunter can tell a demon from a mortal. Unless they show you their clawed, winged form, but they so rarely do. It's part of why they sit at the top of the deviant food chain—demons are the most indistinguishable from mortals. Perfect example: Burrito Mom here has no idea the guy trying to inch closer to her drinks human souls like Gatorade.

When she looks up at me, her eyes shine with relief. She's in a sweatshirt that's been through the wash so many times the logo has all but faded and leggings with enough pilling to look fuzzy. I want to offer her a pillow and a sleep mask while I waste this guy.

"Miss?" I ask in my best customer service voice. "Do you know this man?"

"No, I don't."

"Aw, come on, lady," the demon croons. "I thought we were getting friendly—"

"Let's leave the woman to finish her dinner in peace, yeah?"

The demon snarls at me. It's always a little rush knowing deviants can't distinguish hunters from mortals. I love seeing that menacing swagger disappear when I reveal myself as their own personal grim reaper.

"Come on, sir," I cajole. "We can go to the next car over."

His eyes flash an even brighter red. He's pissed. Lucky me.

I'm already beginning to think of cover-up stories for Burrito Mom when he lunges for me, spitting, "I'm not going anywhere with a bitch like—"

I don't let him finish.

My daggers lash out whip-fast and almost slice him clean across the throat. Burrito Mom screeches like a banshee. I don't blame her—I'd probably do the same if some museum assistant in a cocktail dress whipped out two silver daggers and attacked a dude on the subway.

But the demon is quick and dodges before I make contact. He ducks again before I can land a solid blow to his heart or head. We struggle through the car, sliding around metal poles and sticky seats. I try to direct us away from the family. Burrito Mom's babies wail.

I lunge for his gut, but before I can get there, he's kicking me out of the way. My head smacks the reinforced glass window, and pain reverberates through my skull. He's stronger than I expected, and I'm winded and hungry. Not in my best form.

The demon moves for my blades, realizing I have two and he has none—better math than I expect from the guy. I maneuver both to my right hand and deck him hard across the face with my left. Two points to Viv: one for ambidexterity and another for hunter strength.

He howls as he holds his nose, now leaking blood. "You *cunt.*"

"Watch it," I snarl, out of breath. "There are kids on board."

I leap over a row of empty seats. My right fist, carrying both blades, drives toward his chest. But he dodges faster than I can anticipate, nearly tripping over a coat some passenger left behind. One dagger careens off the metal pole, and I hear every splinter as the ancient blade cracks, a shard snapping clean off.

Fuck. These were my father's.

Heat pumps through my veins. My fury alone is enough to ensure my next blow lands.

Right as the demon moves for me, eyes rabid, I grab the metal pole and kick the demon with everything I've got. He flies, cranium first, into a row of empty seats.

Heart racing, feet starting to ache, blade broken, I stalk over to him.

That hit might've killed him had he been mortal. But any hunter worth their salt knows the only way to kill a demon is with pure silver to the heart or brain. That or another demon's claws, but it's not like I have a pair of those handy. It's why I only wear silver jewelry. You never know when all that stands between your life and a demon's are the earrings your dad got you for your fifth-grade graduation.

The demon shakes his head like he's a cartoon surrounded by spinning stars. I can tell from his expression that he's had enough. Good thing too, because I'm running out of steam.

He yanks me toward him and I allow him to take me down. Burrito Mom behind us gasps in shock and horror, and I almost feel bad. She thinks she's about to witness the wrong ending to this brawl.

The demon's mouth isn't too far from mine now. Demons live forever down in the underworld, but up here, on our turf, they need a healthy dose of human souls to keep them alive and kicking. He opens wide to suck mine from my lips. To send me down to hell.

I have no doubt he would've found some decent sin in my tattered soul. Punishing sinners is said to be the reason demons have this ability in the first place, and I'm like one of those seedy watch peddlers with the trench coats full of stolen goods. *Any sin you want, I got 'em.* Envy for all those born without my aeon blood. Pride inherited from my egomaniac mother. Enough deep-seated wrath over my father's death to power a small, furious country.

But I don't give him the chance.

Based on the awed look on his face, he didn't know that, for a deviant, hunters' souls, blood, and flesh deliver not just more power, but more *ecstasy* than a mere mortal's might. His surprise at the scent of my soul offers me the upper hand I'd been banking on. I drive my still-intact dagger into his heart and am hit with my own rush of elation. Nothing feels as good as delivering that death blow. Not sex, not drugs. Not anything at all.

Inch by inch, my blade cuts beautifully through primordial sinew and muscle until I feel the demon collapse atop me. I wheeze under his weight and attempt to catch my breath.

Before I move, I shift him so I can get a good look at his neck. No demonic brand.

Just as I'd thought—not a Brood demon.

I push him off and stand, surveying the frazzled mom. Her burrito landed on the ground a while ago, and we both watch it slide as the train comes to a stop, leaving a snail trail of beans and egg across the rubber flooring. She's clutching her babies to her with such fierce protectiveness it stalls my heart. Her face isn't tear streaked. Her jaw isn't trembling. She's a picture of unflinching determination. Willing to throw herself between us and her children a hundred times over. She's looking at me like I'm as much a monster as the creature I just saved her from, and . . . she's right. Like an endless ride I can't get off, my triumph loops back into shame.

"Nothing to be alarmed by," I say as calmly as I can, though I'm still catching my breath. "I'm law enforcement. That man was a criminal we've been hunting for a while." I eye the station, the people lining up to jump on. "Please make your way onto the platform."

The subway doors crank open once more. One stop away from Cobwebs. I'll have to run.

God, I'm so tired.

The woman makes no move to exit the car. And there's still a dead demon body inside.

"Come on, ma'am," I tell her. "It's going to be okay."

She recoils from me as I approach her. "Is he dead?"

"No," I lie. "Just unconscious. Let me walk you out. I've already alerted the railway marshal." To my knowledge, there is no such thing as a railway marshal. But the mother is in so much shock, she just nods. I help her push the double stroller out onto the platform. "Will you be able to get home all right?"

She nods again, placing her babies in their individual seats. Sisters. Less than a year apart, I'd guess.

"How old are they?"

Finally, her eyes soften a bit on mine. "Eight months and eighteen months."

Warmth spreads through my chest. Despite everything, I'm glad I was here tonight. This is why my father taught me what he did. "I have a sister too. She's five years older, though."

She smiles weakly. I can see the exhaustion creeping in. "Thank you, Officer."

Burrito Mom rolls her daughters away in a daze, fading into the masses. I stay by the automatic doors, ushering people to a different railcar until there's nobody left. I'm lucky—not many are going deeper downtown from this stop. Through the glass, I just narrowly catch the demon's cold body decaying into a puff of ash. There and gone.

I'm about to leg it across the platform when hairs rise on the nape of my neck.

It's uncanny, the feeling of being watched. I don't think it's a hunter thing or even an aeon thing. Everybody's had that bizarre sensation of someone's eyes on the back of their head. But perhaps it *is* my hunter gene that allows me to swivel and instinctually find those eyes in the crowd. My gaze locks onto a figure one subway car over from the one I was on. I can't make out much in the shadows, but I know someone's been watching me. I can just feel it. The faintest prickle on my skin. Another deviant?

Before the train leaves the station, I swear the shadow waves.

I brush off the full-body chill as I hightail it for Cobwebs. I tell myself it doesn't matter what they saw. People get into knife fights South of the Chasm all the time.

CHAPTER 3

ALL THAT'S LEFT of Penny's birthday dinner are plates of half-eaten confetti cake and discarded bright green margaritas with salt crystalizing on the rims. Plastic silverware and faux–severed finger stirrers litter the tables.

Cobwebs is the best bar in the city, and I'll verbally fillet anyone who disagrees. Sure, Penny and I are biased: We live two flights of stairs above the place and the owner let us in even before we were of age. And yeah, our landlord gave us a discount on rent because of all the noise and permeating bar smells and the occasional kitchen fire, but we don't mind them one bit. It has the only karaoke machine this side of the Chasm, all-you-can-eat rubbery mozzarella sticks, and cozy, well-worn leather booths.

But the best part is that Cobwebs is kitschily made up to look like a 1950s Halloween party or an episode of one of those black-and-white TV shows about a family of spooky monsters living in suburbia. Peeling gothic wallpaper, a grandfather clock, stuffed owls, and hanging bats. Just the kind of dingy, divey decor that allows it to remain Half City's best-kept secret. Nobody comes in here but us, and how they stay open regardless is one of life's wonderful mysteries.

Penny and her gaggle of normal friends—some wealthy childhood pals, some coworkers from the elementary school where she teaches art—are singing a valiantly committed version of one of the birthday girl's favorite pop songs.

And Penny looks ravishing. She always does, but tonight especially. Her curled, straw-colored hair whips around as she sings into the karaoke mic; a dewy sheen of sweat dusts her nose and forehead from the balmy summer night and harmonious exertion. Her cheeks are pink from too many of those campy green margs—she'd never have the courage to belt a girl-band anthem before a dwindling crowd otherwise—and her generous curves are accentuated by her tiny, shiny light blue dress. I fish my camera out and snap a photo of her mid-belt, hand to her chest, eyes crinkled in joy.

It's all I could want for my best friend's twenty-second birthday. I just wish I hadn't missed it.

I suck in a bracing breath and sidle up to James as he pays the bar tab. "Hi."

When he jumps nearly a foot in the air, I remember once again that my increased speed, agility, and reflexes must be used on deviants, not my boyfriend.

"Hey," he says with an exhale, pressing a kiss to the top of my head. "We missed you." With his sister's same tawny hair and ivy-green eyes, James looks like the quarterback on a TV show about a small-town high school football team. Kind, harmless, blandly handsome.

"Wasn't the real birthday dinner the friends we made along the way?"

James cocks his head in confusion, and I wonder why I even try.

"Tell me she wasn't sad." I plop onto the barstool beside him and dump all my bags on the floor.

He turns his attention to his sister, and we watch Penny nearly faceplant into the faux spiderweb–covered jukebox as she picks out her next song. We both exhale audibly when she catches herself safely on the glass display.

"She wasn't," James says in the end, putting a reassuring hand on the small of my back. "She's having a blast."

That one hurts, but I guess it's what I wanted to hear.

"I wish I could get her out of this dump, though." James lifts his other hand from the bar and wipes whatever stickiness clings to his fingers on a cocktail napkin. "Both of you."

Annoyance zips through me. "We like our place. Penny doesn't want to live in a stuffy penthouse North of the Chasm that your parents pay for. You can't bribe her into moving out."

James's eyes widen. "I wasn't . . . I won't offer again."

Guilt pools inside me. "I'm sorry. I just got an earful from my mom about the same thing. She dropped off a box of my dad's stuff this morning too."

James rubs my back and nods in understanding. The music blares and I try to breathe through my anger. It's not his fault I'm like this. James is great. I'm trying very hard to fall for him. I have been for years. And it's not James, it's me, which is not a line, I swear.

It's all any dark, weird girl with a secret can hope for: that her best friend's catch of an older brother will fall head over heels for her and whisk her away from her miserable life. But here's what they never tell you in all the rom-coms and romance novels: It's not the best-friend's-hot-brother that's the issue. It's not that he's a player or a jerk who can't tell the offbeat heroine is beautiful until her glasses come off. It's the dark, weird girl with a secret who's the problem. She's incapable of romantic love! Probably because she's killed too many werewolves. Or lost too much blood over the years. Or because her family hates her and she watched her dad die.

I don't know, I don't make the rules.

All I do know is that when everyone, my mother included, begged me to give James a chance, there was nothing on planet Earth that sounded worse. But then he went to college, and I grew up, moved out, lived on my own. I met a lot of pricks, kissed too many frogs, lost out on good guys because I had demons to hunt and ghoul goo to wash from my hair.

And by the time James moved back to Astera and began asking me out again, I realized I'd probably never find love and I'd be lucky to land a man like James, who knew me well and still seemed to genuinely like me. Who had a stable job and didn't try to sell me Bitcoin. Who made my family proud to be related to me. Or prouder, at least.

The first dinner our parents had together that James and I attended as a couple, my mom was beside herself. She looked at me like I'd done something right for the first time in my life. At least, for the first time since the night the police brought me home without my father and I couldn't explain why I'd come back and he hadn't.

I'm ashamed to say what a high it was—to see myself like that, through her eyes. When I stood there, my dark nails clasped in James's soft, uncalloused hand. I hadn't seen her that happy in years. I've been chasing that feeling for about six months now, with mixed results.

"Viv!" Penny squeals.

"Happy birthday!" I cheer, feeling something like relief for the first time all day.

She launches herself at me and I am enveloped into the warmest, most joyful Penny hug. The scent of her gardenia perfume mingles with the tequila on her breath. "You made it!"

"I'm sorry I missed dinner. And singing."

"And cake," she slurs.

"And cake," I amend, tucking some sweaty blond strands behind her ear. "I am really going to work on the time management thing. It's one of my many birthday presents to you."

I also have a set of canvases and her favorite horsehair brush up in the apartment. Plus a new plaid bow for Hound, which he'll hate but she'll love, *and* I convinced our landlord to fix our pipe issue for free. Now we don't have to keep flushing the toilet and turning on the garbage disposal at the same time to get hot water.

"It's okay! I didn't really think you'd make it," Penny admits. "We are who we are. You know?"

If my smile slips, Penny doesn't seem to notice. I change the subject to ease the burn. "Where's Claude?"

"He couldn't make it." Penny pouts. "Stuck in Vienna."

James and I sneer in unison. Penny's art dealer boyfriend is universally abhorred by everyone but Penny. My protective nature especially does not take kindly to the way he walks all over her. "That guy is—"

"I love this song!" Penny throws her hands into the air with reckless abandon and bolts in her bright white Keds back to the jukebox.

I can't help my laugh. Thank god for Penelope Pine.

Penny was the only girl who talked to me my first week at Belaire after my mom got her fancy government job and moved Nora and me to the Hesperides. The only person who never looked at me with pity or judgment. And Belaire was tough: I wasn't blond and push-up-bra-capable—I was dark-haired, flat-chested, and *new money*, something I quickly learned was worse than having no money at all. I wasn't a cheery, pleasant tween, either—my father had just died. And then my loving, thoughtful mother had become unrecognizable. It was like in the span of one awful night I'd lost them both. All the while I had—and I guess *still* have—a vicious secret I couldn't share with anyone, which made me feel like even more of an outcast than I already was.

Despite it all, after Penny and I met, we were inseparable. When she left for college, it was as lonely as I'd ever felt. And when Penny's mom got sick and she dropped out, we moved into the shoebox above Cobwebs together. I don't know what I'd do without the girl.

Penny finishes her solo and slumps down into a booth with a friend of hers I recognize from Belaire. I don't want to interrupt, nor do I really want to talk to James, so I help clean up, gather people's purses, and cling-wrap the leftover cake.

After Penny belts one last song, James and I carry her up to the apartment and tuck her into bed.

"I'm tired enough for sleep now," Penny mumbles as I pull a blanket over her.

"You were a rock star up there."

"Only shattered one of my eardrums," James agrees, rubbing his left ear.

We both frown at him.

"I'm sorry again," I say even though I know she's too drunk to care or remember. I realize it's selfish and could bring down her vibe, but still I add, "I really wanted to be there tonight."

"Honestly," Penny says, pulling me close as if sharing a tidbit of juicy gossip. "I didn't even notice. Don't worry, for real."

I know she's only trying to help and I'm the one who pushed for it, but the words bite right through me. And this apartment is too hot and I'm starving and suddenly I wonder if I'm going to cry.

I hate the dementedly blazing summers in this cramped city. I hate thinking about that kid and his hungry dog. And Burrito Mom and her girls and what might have happened had I not been there or had I chosen my friend over my duty to this city. Over my compulsive need to kill. I hate my long hours at the Windsor and all the pressure that comes with them. I hate being late. I hate being a hunter and the fact that Penny and I aren't as close as we used to be. I think I might hate my boyfriend. I definitely hate myself.

"Viv?" James whispers. While I've been staring off into a stack of sketchbooks, bubbling over with self-loathing, Penny has fallen asleep. "You okay?"

When I nod, he adds, "Walk me down?"

We trudge down the scuffed stairs of the walk-up and back out into the night. Taxis speed by under a couple of hazy streetlights. One flickers jerkily, in need of a new bulb. The balmy heat whips at my skin as we stroll over to his sleek black sedan, which I can't stand for no good reason.

James is headed to his family's house in the Sewards tonight—the seaside town a few miles east of the Hesperides. He's going for the weekend with some of his fraternity brothers and their shiny, happy girlfriends. James invited me to join, but I can't seem to enjoy a lazy afternoon by the rolling, manicured seaside without thinking of deviants tearing into people while I work on my tan.

"You sure you don't want to come?"

"Too much work to do for the new exhibit. Sorry."

"You could work from the summer house. My bed makes for a very cozy home office."

"I just can't this weekend. Rain check?"

"Sure." James smiles softly and my stomach turns. "I'm proud of how hard you've been working."

I'm such a jerk—I can see how James is trying. "I haven't eaten today. Want to walk and grab a slice?"

"Er . . ." He glances around, adjusting his tie to give his neck a reprieve from the heat.

Spooky music drifts out of Cobwebs, likely empty for the night now that we've left. Up the sidewalk a bit, trash spills out onto the street—mostly plastic wrap and soda cans. A mouse scurries between the bags, and I hear the sound of its claws on asphalt like they're skittering along my scalp. Even farther up, a guy snorts something out of a plastic baggie, and another next to him bites into some late-night pizza. Gooey cheese and a slightly burned crust.

James shifts on his feet. He hates this street corner, our apartment, our little haunted bar . . . I save him the rejection of my offer. "It's okay. Rain check on that too, yeah?"

"Yes, please." He nods. "Be safe, will you? I don't like you out and about South of the Chasm without me."

Though his words irritate me, I just take a deep breath of city air. Aeons are prone to mood swings, something about our ever-hungry desire for blood. Meditation helps, as does getting enough sleep. Two things I never have time to do.

But what I really need is to hunt. To shake off the anger and frustration of the night. Just the thought of a solid kill is relieving tension across my body. "I'll be good."

I kiss him goodbye and head off. I don't tell him I can take care of myself just fine. Or that he couldn't protect me from a chicken potpie. He's just being thoughtful.

And he's right, I tell myself as I pass flashing neon signs that claim *Only a mile away from the world-famous Chasm!* The massive crevasse that bisects Astera and gives it the nickname the "Half City" is more than a third the size of the Grand Canyon—it also serves as a kind of safety demarcation. North of the Chasm, you'll find yuppies and politicians and finance bros—basically a bunch of James clones running around telling one another about synergy—as well as the pristine NTC (North of the Chasm) Park, the Windsor, and wealthy housewives paying people to water the plants outside their lovely limestone townhomes.

But down here, South of the Chasm, is where all the beatniks and poppy addicts and kids who can't afford anything live. In STC's defense, it's also where you'll find the kinds of parties they write exposé articles about, as well as avant-garde art galleries and the best wine bars for first dates. As long as you stay away from the depths of the South, you're unlikely to run into any slums or drug lords. At least, that's what they'll tell you on the Chasm tours tourists pay forty-five dollars for. Don't even get me started on the pricing of their **CHASMGASM** T-shirts.

I think of my dad explaining to me when I was seven that my elementary school teacher had been wrong. How what they tell you on those tours—that the gaping Chasm around which early Asteran settlers built the city is a geological anomaly that's been here since recorded time—couldn't be further from the truth. He taught me that there was more deviant activity in Astera than anywhere else in the world because the Chasm was ripped open many millennia ago by the then High Thane of the Brood when he released deviants from the underworld, making it the largest and oldest gateway to hell. Even though powerful lymantrians closed it shortly thereafter, the majority of freed deviants made this city their home. And over the years, all the vampires and werewolves they've turned or offspring they've birthed have done the same.

If only James knew I wasn't grabbing a slice but instead troll-ing the streets for deviants to kill to quiet my internal turmoil. If only he knew I do that more nights than I complete my skincare routine. But he doesn't, which means I have no right to be annoyed with him for being cautious. All he's ever done is look out for me. There was that one time Penny and I visited him at his frat and he punched a guy for pinching my butt. It was so sweet—his hand swelled to the size of an eggplant. Same color too. I wouldn't have even needed ice had I punched the loser myself, but James did it for me. That's worth something, right?

Passing parlors with women in red-glowing windows, I wonder for the hundredth time *why* he's always cared for me. I wish it didn't matter. Is it the chance to fix something that's broken? He does work in the highest echelon of PR. A literal *fixer*. The irony is not lost on anyone, least of all my mother. Or perhaps I provide an opportunity to rebel against his perfect parents by dating someone who isn't sweet and chirpy like his litany of socialite exes?

Or maybe—

I'm so lost in my own overanalysis, I don't even realize I've nearly walked to the notorious nightclub Fever Dream when my skin lights with the presence of a deviant.

"I'm not sure what was more impressive," a cool voice says, the low sound curling around the shell of my ear. "Killing a demon on a moving subway car or taking your pants off on one."

CHAPTER 4

MY FIRST THOUGHT before I turn around is that this is what I deserve.

For wandering so far South of the Chasm on a Friday night, like James warned. For missing Penny's birthday. For being what I am.

My second is that I was right earlier. I knew someone saw me slay that demon in the subway.

My third is relief. At least my prey came to me this time. Just the kill I need.

I fish my one and a half daggers out from under my dress, crack my neck, and spin around.

My first blow is aimed directly at his heart, and I can't lie, I'm impressed when he uses his bare hand to knock my dagger away without so much as a grunt. My second shot sails for his neck, and when he ducks with lightning speed, I'm already winded. Not good.

This far past the Chasm, everything is hotter and more stagnant, as if we're sloping toward hell. The air is thick in my lungs, the sweat still on my brow. Despite the fact that he's so cloaked in shadow I can't see his eyes, I can tell from the way he moves that it's a demon I'm fighting.

There are no cars to be found on this side street. No homes, either. Only warehouses and boarded-up storefronts and one dilapidated apartment building. It's quiet save for the low-decibel thrum of the music pumping out of Fever Dream a few blocks farther south. I suck in a breath and rush him again, but he dodges with seamless ease.

It's not until the demon backs into a pool of streetlight that I get a good look at him. It only takes me a millisecond—my hunter gene at work once more—to clock his neck. Peeking out from beneath the curls at his nape is a raised patch of long-since-burned skin. A brand—the seven-pointed star with horns.

A Brood demon.

And yet the ice-cold fear that slices through me isn't what shoves all the breath from my lungs.

This guy—this apex predator, the same breed as whoever killed my dad—is *gorgeous*.

Painfully so. Like those beautiful, serious actors who were made for historical roles. Timelessly handsome. Curled brown hair, high cheekbones, the chiseled jaw of a storybook villain. And piercing, churning blue eyes. The color of a starless dusk.

As he watches me gape at him, I wonder if I've ever felt attraction like this before . . . Or if perhaps I was drugged back at Cobwebs. What was in that green margarita? As the daughter of one of the most important people in the city, I've been to enough haughty, highfalutin events to bear witness to many good-looking men—and *still*, this guy is something else.

Of course he is, I tell myself. It's the same reason I can't land a blow on him. He's a Brood demon. A gorgeous Brood demon staring at me like my hunter soul is dinner.

I ought to just flee—trying to beat a Brood is likely futile. But I won't be able to sleep knowing he's loose in the city. More honestly, I won't be able to sleep if I don't kill something. Aeon bloodlust at its finest, ladies and gents.

I lunge with my daggers once more, thinking of my dad and the men who killed him—and my rage makes me faster. I nick the demon's rib cage, ripping through his crewneck sweatshirt. A passing shaft of golden light from a taxi up the street illuminates the grimace on his face. The demon takes a step back to duck my next swing and makes his first misstep, tripping over a broken curb. I pounce, daggers ready, footwork just as my dad taught me—

And land hard on my hands and knees.

The demon . . . he's tricked me. I didn't even notice his foot there. Didn't even notice the trap he'd set. The stumble over the curb—a fake.

But the handsome demon doesn't attack while I'm on my knees. He doesn't kick me in the ribs like I'm bracing for. Like I would do. He waits for me to stand. Patient, like he's behind an old woman in the checkout line. None of this is adding up. Why follow me all the way from the subway and pick a fight only to not hit me even once?

"What gives?" I pant, standing to catch my breath.

"I can't believe you fell for that," he says, studying his ruined sweatshirt.

Fury roiling, I charge at him and get my broken dagger within an inch of his throat before I realize he hasn't even flinched. I get a whiff of his bright, citrusy scent. Like lemongrass and evergreens and a bar of soap.

"Your dagger is broken," he says, Adam's apple bobbing against the razor edge of my silver.

"What?"

"You ought to get that fixed. One wrong blow and it'll shatter."

The way his jaw flexes as he stares at me . . . He's nearly too pretty to cut up.

Nearly. I press my dagger deeper, and his skin threatens to split around it. "How long have you been following me?" Maybe it's hypocritical, but I'm not a fan of being preyed upon by my own damn prey. "Tell me now, or I swear—"

"You have three seconds to remove that blade from my neck before I take it from you."

He says it calmly. Low and gruff, but calm. Unfazed. This guy's mesmerizing eyes haven't even shed their dark blue hue. Not a flash of hungry red to be seen. If my body weren't humming, I might mistake him for a human man. Clearly, if this demon wanted to kill me, I'd already be dead.

I snarl, lowering my dagger and backing up about six paces. This demon may be handsome, but he's still no better than a walking, talking chain saw, just waiting to rip into me. Any Brood demon knows a hunter's soul extends their lifespan to nearly triple a mortal's. But an *aeon's*? Filled with all our twisted sin? Downright delectable. If Broods are the lions of this animal kingdom, my aeon soul is catnip.

The demon leans against the brick wall of a warehouse and folds his arms across his chest. "I'm Reid."

"Tell me how long you've been following me."

His eyes sparkle, cold and uncaring. "Long enough."

"How *long*?"

"Heard your friend singing. That was worse than the screaming babies on the railcar."

My blood stops. He was near *Penny*. "Are you going to tell me what you want?"

"Vivienne, right?"

"It's Viv." I hate my full name. It's dated and formal. Vaguely French, which I am not. My mother insisted on it, and my father only ever called me Viv.

"I'm an instructor at Harker. We'd like to offer you admission."

My own bark of a laugh startles me—I'm not even sure which part of that insanity to question first. I go with "Harker?"

"Harker Academy for Deviant Defense," he says, stepping closer. "Exclusive, grueling, prestigious, and hidden right here in Astera. The only college in the world for hunters." Another step closer. "Just like you."

A taxi speeds by behind us and I realize my heart is thumping. I take a step backward. "I'd have to be brain-dead to believe anything that comes out of a Brood demon's mouth."

"What's that expression again? Something about books and their covers?" I sneer until he adds, "Do I look like I'm trying to kill you?"

It's what I was already wondering ... He hasn't even touched me.

I almost ask *Why now?* I've been hunting alone for more than a decade. But then I remember that regular hunters gain their abilities at twenty-one. Only aeons can hunt before they can ride a bike. And if my father taught me anything, it was to *never* reveal that we were aeons. Never. Other lymantrians hunted our kind to virtual extinction centuries ago. Not pure enough to be hunters, they said. Fell into the darkness too easily.

The better question might be why, if this "academy" is real, my father didn't tell me about it. He wouldn't have kept something like this from me. When the memory of his pained screams from that night sound in my ears, I can't help my flinch. Reid stares at me with mild curiosity.

"If *Harker* were real," I bite out, "I'd know about it. I've lived in Astera all my life."

"That's why they need a recruiter. To find the stray dogs."

"Real nice."

"You work at the Windsor, right?"

My eyes narrow. "So you've been fully stalking me."

"Take this." Reid pulls a coin out of his back pocket.

The small antique coin is dwarfed by his large hand and long fingers. I take it gingerly, even as my heart races, and inspect both carved sides. Caked in rust, engraved with lymantrian lettering . . . This coin might be a thousand years old. Fiona would flip. Reid must be able to tell he's gotten to me, because he takes one step closer, and I don't back up this time.

"On Monday morning, use it in the broken ticket machine in the utility closet off the lobby."

But . . . This is insane, right? There's no gateway to a demon-slaying collegiate campus in the middle of the most well-regarded museum in the country.

"I can't afford college." It's a very dumb thing to say, but my mind is stalling out.

"Harker is free for students. We have our own wealthy benefactors. The Citadel is housed on campus."

"The Citadel?"

Reid ignores me. "Orientation is Monday at eight. You don't have to do this alone, Viv."

I've been on my own a lot longer than he thinks. "I like working alone, I—"

"Fine. If you're going to fight for this city all on your own, don't you think you owe it to yourself to be the best hunter you can be? Isn't that your responsibility?"

My muscles tense. I eye the brand on Reid's neck.

But he only backs up toward Main—the street that cuts from STC all the way up to the Windsor. "Use the coin, huntress. See for yourself."

And then he's gone.

CHAPTER 5

WHEN I GET back to our apartment, it's nearly one in the morning and I'm drenched in sweat. The oppressive Astera heat does not abate at night, and the speed with which I rushed home didn't help. Hound greets me with such fervor I nearly topple right over him. Deadly deviant slayer overpowered by her own dog. Same as it ever was.

I try to calm him down, but he licks the salt from my face like it's his job, and I'm no match for the hundred-pound Doberman. I sit back and allow myself to be bathed in slobber.

"I know, boy." I scratch behind his ears. "I missed you too."

Penny and I adopted Hound only a few days after we'd moved into our apartment here in Babylon. We found him abandoned in a dumpster outside Cobwebs when we were taking out our trash. I said something like "Penny, we're going to be parents" to combat the lump in my throat. It only made Penny cry harder.

Sufficiently licked, I pull myself up with help from the edge of the kitchen countertop. I'm weak from the evening's battles and more than twenty-four hours without food. Not to mention everything Reid said still rattling around in my head. And the depth of his eyes. That kind of blue should be criminal.

I crack Penny's door open to check on the birthday girl, and once all toes and fingers are accounted for as well as one mop of blond hair fanned over her pillow, I kick my shoes off and head to the kitchen to make myself some goddamn dinner.

Hound trots in behind me and I allow my mind to wander. Reid was surely full of shit, right? But why? What's the end goal? What kind of trap is he laying? He had me in his clutches and passed up the opportunity to drink my soul so he could fool me with some tall tale about an elite deviant-slaying college? Perhaps Reid's some sicko who likes a long, drawn-out game of cat and mouse before he goes in for the kill. But a game that involves sparing the life of the intended victim? Feels like a stretch.

Hound's gentle whining pulls my thoughts back to the matter at hand—dinner—and I realize I've opened all our cabinets and put together a strange concoction of bananas, peanut butter, and stale cereal in a bowl. This can happen from time to time—hunters do pretty well on tactile autopilot. Sometimes I'll realize I've filed an entire cabinet at the Windsor while thinking about the best detergent to combat viscera.

I scoop up a fingerful and hold it out for Hound to enjoy. Then, despite my exhaustion, I stand over the counter and eat an entire bowl of whatever this is, turning my conversation with Reid over and over in my mind. It doesn't make any more sense no matter how I look at it.

Still licking a peanut butter–coated spoon, I slip into the bathroom and slide my daggers out from their sheaths. Under piping-hot water and a pump of hand soap, I scrub the silver and watch demon blood swirl down the drain. As I run my finger along the splintered crack, I find my light eyes and pitch-black hair reflected back at me in the polished silver.

Both daggers have antique cross guards carved from hilt to

end. One depicts a serpent twined around the pommel, the other a sleeping fawn in tall grass. I never asked my father where he got them, but there's something almost biblical about the engravings. Sometimes when I wield them, I wonder if these blades weren't forged in that same old world that yawned the underworld into existence. The same one that birthed pure lymantrians and, alongside them, our black-sheep aeon bloodline that can see wicked deviants for what they are.

But to be seen is to be known. And to know deviants . . . to feel them under your own skin . . . There's a reason aeons were killed off. When their thirst for deviant blood couldn't be quenched, they were said to have hunted mortals. Sometimes I think that the unholy darkness within me—that ferocious hunger for the kill—is as primordial as the blades in my hands.

All this time, I've fought the deviants and my own sickness alone. But if Reid was telling the truth—

"What are you doing?"

Penny's groggy voice shocks me so thoroughly I barely have time to toss the blades to the shower mat and cover them with my bare foot. Pain sears through my arch—one of them has sliced my skin.

"Just washing this spoon," I rasp, willing my eyes not to water. "Kitchen sink on the fritz."

Penny's hair pokes this way and that, mascara smeared down her sweet face. "I swear it looked like a little sword."

I laugh way too hard, pointing the peanut butter spoon at her. "You're still drunk. Back to bed with you!"

"I didn't take my makeup off," she says, eyes fluttering closed, leaning into the doorjamb.

My eyes land on my outstretched foot with the daggers hidden beneath. Blood is pooling on the bath mat.

"Who needs eyelashes? Sleep first," I tell her. "Makeup off tomorrow."

Penny nods as if that makes sense and trots back off to bed. I exhale mightily.

When I'm certain she's in her room once more, I lift my foot up and inspect the damage. It's a nasty slice, but nothing I can't slap a Band-Aid on and worry about tomorrow. Once I've done so, I wipe up the blood, rinse my daggers *again*, and make my way into my own bedroom, desperate for sleep.

My room is compact. It barely fits one full-size bed with no frame, box spring, or headboard—so a mattress with sheets, I guess—and a dresser Penny and I bought at the Babylon Bazaar, an open-air marketplace that sets up in our neighborhood every Sunday. There's also a string of low, glowing lights that eases my hunter senses. I've filled the walls with too many black-and-white photographs, some I've taken, some I just love. Annie Leibovitz, Ansel Adams, Robert Mapplethorpe.

The box of my dad's things that my mom's people dropped off this morning sits in front of my bed. The fact that she can clear all memorabilia of him from her home . . . The disrespect to the memory of my dad—the warmest, most loving person I've ever met—fills me all over again with the kind of rage that teeters on combustible. Aeon rage.

To calm myself, I use my unbroken dagger—the one with the serpent—to slice the cardboard open. I pull out my dad's college lacrosse stick and hang it on the wall across from my photographs, then place some of the framed photos of the two of us around my room.

I comb through the rest of the box, putting off the necessary high-quality crying. Moth-eaten sweaters that still smell like him, old vinyls that are peeling at the edges, and a silver locket. I recognize it as the one that used to hang from his keys. He told me he'd gotten it from his mother.

The inscription is fading and coated in dust. I rub my thumb over the words and give them my best shot. It looks like it reads, **For David. Harker Bound, Fall 1992**.

My breath stalls in my lungs.

Harker Bound.

Harker.

I never met my grandma, but she was an aeon as well. My dad told me she wore the charm every day for protection. I didn't know she'd had it inscribed before she gave it to him. I press my fingers into the groove of the antique oval but can't get the thing to budge. With my hunter strength that means it's probably welded shut.

I slip it around my neck in the quiet stillness of my bedroom and try to feel close to him. To remember his laugh. To think of the adventures we used to go on together, the safety I felt when he was alive. When my fingers find the pendant, the smooth Victorian-era silver is warm from lying against my skin.

I'm struck with a sudden sinister loneliness so bitter I can taste it. I have nobody to ask about any of this. I have nobody with whom to share all these questions burbling in my mind. What a relief it must have been for my dad to share his hunting with both me and his mother. I fight off a strange jealousy—she had him, he had me, and I have no one.

I'd give up just about everything to ask my dad a handful of questions. How did he deal with all the years of hunting by himself before me? Does he even recognize what's become of Mom? Why did the Brood go after him that night, twelve to one? Who was he talking to before he died? The words have haunted me every single day since: *You. After all this time . . . At least tell me why.*

I'd ask if there was any way I could have saved him. If this whole Harker thing is a joke. And if it's not, why he kept it from me.

At some point I fall asleep atop the covers with all the lights still on, Hound in my bed, and the only remaining artifact of my dad's secret life looped around my neck.

THE WINDSOR IS always beautiful, but early in the morning it's the staggering kind. By eight the lobby is a madhouse, crowded with students on field trips, scientists and historians, guests staying at the Maison Hotel across the street who want to pop by and see the enormous bronze fossils in the lobby. But at this pale, chilly hour, it's something else. Something breathtaking.

The Windsor is so far North of the Chasm it's practically in the clouds. Astera is built on a slight incline, from the slums to the hills that separate the city from the Hesperides, and the Windsor sits as far North as the Half City goes. The elevation up here means all the glass in the museum is illuminated just a few hours after dawn, when the sun can drift inside, while the morning fog still lingers below. The whole lobby glows with it; it's like being inside a chandelier.

And it's quiet. Blessedly, peacefully, *mercifully* quiet. Heightened hunter hearing means that's a rare find—sometimes, even at my desk, I can hear car alarms going off six streets over.

But for a moment, all I hear is my own Mary Janes clomping on the lobby floor. I stroll past all the water fountains and the ticketing machines. I don't allow my eyes to linger on the utility closet down the hall nor my mind to snag on the fact that there really *is* one there in the first place. Anyone could have known that.

I take the elevator up to the sixth floor and smell nutmeg and coffee. Fiona's always in before me, even when I'm in before everyone else. I don't know when that woman sleeps or how Nora puts up with her hours.

"Morning," I call out, wincing as I sit down at my desk. My back is still kind of killing me after the subway fight, and now my foot is sore too. Hunters have accelerated healing and strength—we can lose a lot of blood without passing out, wounds become scars pretty quickly, etc.—but the gash on my foot hasn't sealed all the way up quite yet.

"Can you come in here?"

I limp into Fiona's office to find her on the floor, surrounded by papers, a leathery book cracked wide open in her lap. Three discarded coffee cups have all missed the trash bin. Her slight nose and wide eyes are hidden behind some kind of antique glasses, and she's got her exhibit gloves on.

"What are you wearing?"

"Eighteenth-century bifocals. I'm trying to get this quote about them just right for the exhibit."

"Have you been here all night?"

Fiona stares up at me with a frown. She looks kind of like an animated bug in those things.

"This new wing is nearly five years in the making. It's not something that can be done within regular work hours. Maybe you should take a page from my book. I know how much it would mean to your mother if you worked opening night."

Perhaps Fiona thinks all assistants show up at seven in the morning, but I let it slide because she seems a bit jittery. "Copy."

Fiona removes the bifocals and sets them inside an antique case, where there's something golden and round wrapped in cloth. As she rubs the bridge of her nose and temples, I move to get a better look at it.

"Don't touch that," she snips, eyes still closed. "Christ above."

"Wasn't gonna," I breathe out. Sheesh. "What is it?"

"Gnostic censer. Just found by our archaeological team a few weeks ago around the rim of the Chasm. We've been looking for this piece for ages."

"Nifty," I deadpan.

Gnosticism is a little-known second-century religion. I have a sneaking suspicion that a lot of ancient religious artifacts in this Chasm exhibit—and in museums all over the world—are actually deviant relics, but I guess it's a good thing historians like Fiona will never know that.

"Viv, why do you think I'm always in the attic?"

She's not talking about the space between the ceiling and the roof. Those of us who work at the Windsor lovingly refer to the museum as Half City's attic due to its equal influx of dusty manuscripts and baubles no one wants.

"I don't know. Rough homelife?"

Fiona's sigh sends wisps of strawberry blonde hair fluttering. Between her long, lanky limbs, cheeks crowded with soft freckles, and hair the color of apricots, you'd think she'd be sweet as pie, but the glare she's giving me right now is downright sour. "You know you could never get away with saying things like that if I wasn't married to your sister."

I pick up her newest coffee and take a sip—mocha almond latte. Dessert in a to-go cup. "She is the worst, though."

"She loves you. She worries about you all the time."

I know it's my fault we've arrived here, but this is not a conversation I want to be having. "Why are you always in the attic?"

"I have committed to this role. I have a responsibility to this building. To the research. To the board. I take it *seriously.*"

Oh god. Not the responsibility speech again. Fiona gives me this schtick every once in a while because about a year ago she walked in on me poring over one of my dad's lymantrian scrolls with an ancient chalice in one hand and an amulet in the other. I'd been trying to do a ritual to trap a succubus inside the amulet, but I told Fiona I was praying for Penny to dump Claude. She asked me if I felt like Penny's happiness was my responsibility, which I guess I shouldn't have said yes to. After that she seemed to think it was her job to guide me or mold me or something, starting with getting me this gig.

And the worst part is I actually do hate disappointing Fiona. Somehow my sister-in-law is the only member of my family who cares more about how I'm doing than how I'm making them look.

"The work is important to me, Viv. Even when I'm exhausted. Do you think I'm *always* thrilled about gnostic censers?"

I answer rapidly. "Yes."

Fiona opens her mouth, only to close it again, rethinking. "Fine. But there are other parts of the job that tire me out. And I'm still here every morning and every night, away from my wife, because it's my responsibility. My duty. Do you understand what I'm saying?"

But my mind is elsewhere.

It sounds a lot like what Reid asked me. *If you're going to fight for this city all on your own, don't you think you owe it to yourself to be the best hunter you can be? Isn't that your responsibility?*

That's why my dad taught me all he did. Not just because we're from a lineage of aeons and we're burdened with the compulsive, visceral need to kill things with fangs and horns and claws but because of our *responsibility* to this city. I have followed in my dad's footsteps my whole life. Even long after he wasn't here to guide me. And now I have the chance to uphold my duty to him.

I allow myself, standing there in Fiona's office, to indulge this thought for just the briefest of moments: Harker, if it's real, will offer me the chance not just to walk where he walked, to study what he studied, to see the place that molded my father into the hunter he was—but also maybe to get some answers after all these years.

And perhaps Harker is fake. Perhaps I'll make a fool of myself trying to insert a faux-lymantrian coin into a broken ticket machine. And perhaps I'll never know why Reid the handsome Brood demon stalked me or let me live or tricked me into having hope.

But if Harker Academy for Deviant Defense exists . . . it might be the only place in the world where I can find out not only why my father kept this school from me but maybe who he recognized the night he died.

It's that possibility alone that sends me out of Fiona's office with a made-up stomachache and sprinting down to the Windsor lobby.

The morning's tranquility has been devoured by the expected 8:00 a.m. rush: Two security guards frisk a surly kid. A teacher attempts to corral an entire sixth-grade class. A shrill woman complains to guest services about the preorder ticket prices for our upcoming exhibit—*The Chasm of Astera: Crown Jewel or Jagged Scar?*

I turn down the hallway and find the utility closet. Inside I'm met with the smell of industrial cleaning fluid and mothballs. Before me, a single broken kiosk beckons. Reid's lymantrian coin is already warm in my palm . . . but there's no coin slot. Broken or not, this is a twenty-first-century machine, and there's only space for paper bills or a credit card. I step closer and squint at the payment mechanism, though I know it's useless—hunters have perfect eyesight. There's no crease, no divot, no space for a coin to slip into.

But I've come this far. I drop to my knees and look underneath, sliding my hands along the sides and curves. Nothing . . .

Until I feel it.

A tiny slot, like you'd find on a plastic carnival ride, tucked right under the lip of the machine. Too small for a quarter, too large for a nickel. The size of the coin in my hand. I slip it inside and am engulfed in blinding light.

CHAPTER 6

A FEW BLINKS desaturate a white sky back to blue.

I flex my jaw and fists—everything is wound tight, an instinctual reaction to gateways. I've only passed through one before, when my father took me to hunt down a powerful warlock who had turned to the side of the deviants. The warlock had enchanted a gateway that led from an Astera noodle restaurant to a gurgling bog somewhere halfway across the world.

I was only ten then, and this gateway is more jarring than I remember. Probably because along with the discomfort of having all my molecules scattered and reassembled in a heartbeat, almost everything I thought I knew for the last decade of my life has been proven false.

Students mill past me on both sides of a wide cobblestone path dotted with lampposts. A manicured lawn sprawls in all directions, spring green under the vast sunshine. No skyscrapers in sight. No scaffolding or whizzing taxis. Only vast oaks that flutter in the morning's breeze and the red brick of an old collegiate campus, complete with gray-tiled roofs and classical columns. Iron-crossed windows and stonework crawling with ivy. Sweeping towers, arches, and spires.

It's like I've been sent back in time. And space too—beyond the campus, all I can see are rolling green hills, rich with wildflowers and thick elms. I'm in a scholarly oasis of some kind. And yet it's modern: Students are in shorts and sneakers, blasting end-of-summer hits from handheld speakers as they gather grimoires and textbooks to race through the quad.

"Hurry," a mousy brunette in a navy **HADD** hoodie and yoga pants calls to her friend. "Orientation's already started."

Once again, I'm late.

I HAVEN'T EVEN reached the entrance to the amphitheater and already my thighs are aching. Three times a week I go to a cute Pilates studio down on Ambrosia Ave, and I routinely sprint through the city streets tracking demonic creatures from the underworld. I thought that was a pretty solid fitness routine. Based on the throngs of students trudging past me up this gargantuan grassy hill without even a wheeze, I was mistaken.

What I've gathered so far about Harker is this: It's nestled in a valley of hills somewhere, and while the majority of buildings are down in the flatland, surrounded on all sides by a moss-covered brick wall, the amphitheater, where orientation is being held, is up at the top of a grassy slope.

If I weren't so winded, it would be kind of remarkable. The higher I climb, the more of the expansive campus I can make out—the imposing bell tower, the placid lake, the wide stone courtyards. Even this hill—I can imagine students lazing about here between classes, tall grass swaying, a view of the valley and

Harker's gothic campus. Not a bad place to get a demon-hunting education.

But all I can feel is my stomach clenching so tightly I'm nearly folding in half. All these years I'd felt so violently alone, and this place has been here, waiting for me to turn twenty-one. How could my dad have kept it from me?

Sweat prickling under my arms in my Windsor-approved linen button-down, I finally crest the top of the hill and begin the steep decline into the outdoor theater. There are hundreds of students. *Hundreds*. I can't tell if I'm relieved or humiliated.

Someone is already speaking, her severe voice carrying through loudspeakers. Students angle their bodies for me as I push past to find an open seat. I nab one next to an intense-looking girl with hair as dark as mine and a lanky boy with sweet doe eyes.

Onstage, the female professor is addressing the masses. She's got mismatched earrings and a brightly patterned violet skirt. Horn-rimmed glasses and long black nails. "For the first years who don't yet know me, I'm Professor Gemeline Lisette, chair of Harker's Underworld Studies Department. First, allow me to welcome you to Harker Academy for Deviant Defense."

There's something haunting about the tenor of her voice. Something ancient. Foreboding. Even as the students clap for her, she doesn't smile.

"Over the next four years you will be taught everything from grueling physical combat to extensive knowledge of deviants and their vulnerabilities. Everything that a hunter might need to protect themselves, their fellow hunters, and, of course, the human race."

Students across the theater clap again with enthusiasm. They're . . . joyous. I can't remember being *joyous* about hunting even once since my dad died.

"And . . ." the woman says, adjusting her glasses, "let me warn you as well."

A tense quiet descends on the crowd. But not one of fear. This is a crowd of protectors. Of trackers and warriors. At the mention of danger, a tidal wave of ears collectively perk up. There's something destabilizing about it. For the first time in my life, I'm surrounded by people who can do the job I'd thought for years only I could do. All those nights out with Penny and family dinners I gave up . . . There were others who could have been saving the day. Nobody told me that community could make you feel so small.

"Thanks to the Elders, talented warlocks have warded Harker's Old Campus against deviants of all kinds for the last seventy-five years. Alongside the wards, both professors and Citadel hunters alike do everything in our power to keep our hunter students safe. But deviants so often have other plans. They crave bloodshed, cruelty, chaos, power . . ."

Students around me shift in their seats.

"It is for that reason we adhere to strict rules here at Harker. First and foremost, first years are not to leave the walls of Old Campus after nightfall. While the heart of campus is protected, the same cannot be said for Lake Hellebore nor the rest of the grounds. Second, no student, regardless of year, is to enter the Fickle Thicket. The creatures in those woods are as volatile as the forest's name suggests. Third, there is no hunting in Astera while you are enrolled at Harker unless supervised by a faculty member."

My eyes threaten to bulge from my head. *No hunting unsupervised?* Why even bring us here in the first place if we can't hunt? I look around at the sea of other students and don't find one ounce of outrage to match my own.

"Students must complete all four years of Harker academics and combat training and then pass final physical and written examinations in order to be stationed at any of the deviant hotspots across the world or, of course, to earn a coveted spot working at the Citadel."

The Citadel... Reid mentioned it being located on campus.

"These rules are for *your* safety. After all, you are the first and last line of defense between mortals and deviants, and as you well know, it is our job to protect those who cannot protect themselves. It is on *our* collective shoulders to stamp out any and all deviants that have infested our mortal plane."

This time, the students don't clap, and I find I'm relieved. They may not have been hunting for the last decade as I have—all their abilities having just hit them in their twenty-first year—but they understand the risks. They nod solemnly, some braced already for a looming fight.

As Professor Lisette continues to speak, I scan the row of what I assume to be other professors and instructors seated behind her. A refined white-haired man in a tweed coat, a brutish thug in his fifties with menacing tattoos, an elegant woman wrapped in colorful layers with pointed ears and wings. It's kind of a motley group. A staff of people who I can't imagine have one thing in common besides this shared mission. And at the very end of the row... Reid.

Hunched over, elbows pressed to thighs, broad, muscled back rippling under a thin athletic shirt. Strands of his brown hair fall gently over his forehead, but his eyes... Those ruthless, night-sky eyes—

They're staring right at me.

My heart stops. In this sea of students, Reid's zeroed in on me like a hawk, even from all the way down there. The sensation of his gaze boring into me does something floppy to my chest. I clear my throat against the sensation and get a sharp *shh* from the dark-haired girl beside me.

But I can't reconcile what a vicious killing machine—the exact creature Professor Lisette is cautioning us about—is doing sitting onstage with so many lymantrian teachers. How did he con his way into this job? Why do they trust him? What is his endgame here?

Onstage, Lisette wraps up with "A few final items: As you'll see on your maps, we have completed construction on the water tank in the dungeons for detaining aquatic deviant species."

Cheers sound. For a deviant dungeon swimming pool. I am surely in *The Twilight Zone*. I scan the crowd and find everyone studying a pamphlet I don't have.

"Here." The lanky guy next to me offers up his Harker brochure, folded to display the school's map. "You can use mine."

"Thanks," I whisper back to him.

The girl beside me whips her head at us. "Shh!"

"And," Professor Lisette continues as I study the extensive academy grounds, "we have adjusted the school's stance on battle-axes. They can now be borrowed from the armory by second years without a faculty signatory."

A section of students I can only assume are second years chatter excitedly about this while other students, older ones perhaps, murmur their complaints.

But all I can feel are my dad's two daggers, one broken, both worn from overuse, prickling against my skin. I've never needed a battle-axe to do my job.

"Now please welcome to the stage our dean, Edgar Driscoll."

The crowd of students applaud like their dean is the headliner of a music festival. I'm hit once again with the all-too-familiar feeling of not belonging. I don't know who this guy is or why he's worthy of applause. I don't know about gateways or why a college for hunters would need a coliseum, bathhouse, or planetarium. I've been hunting deviants since I was ten and have gotten along just fine without any of this fanfare.

And suddenly the sun is beating down too hot on the crown of my head. My dark pants feel sticky in the creases of my knees and I'm nauseous. Every time I look to the stage, I can feel Reid staring at me, and it's been a physical effort not to meet his eyes this entire time. I know what he's thinking—why did I even come? I don't fit in here.

I want to go back to my apartment and snuggle Hound. Hell, I'd sort exhibition permits in Fiona's office over being stuck in this over-the-top hunter cult. I'm in enough rooms where I feel less-than in my real life. I don't need to feel that way when I'm hunting too.

I move to stand, to sneak out of here and gateway myself back to Astera, when the girl next to me grabs my wrist, yanking me back down.

"You can't leave," she hisses. "Not before the dean speaks."

"I can, though," I snip, attempting to pry her fingers from my wrist. But like my own, her hunter grip is no joke. "Are you serious?"

"Just stay until he's done?" the guy who gave me the pamphlet offers. I can see the stress in his narrow jaw and the panic in those puppy eyes. He doesn't like us arguing. I wonder how he stomachs killing deviants every day.

"Fine, whatever." I sit back down and Super Grip Sally releases me to focus on the dean. She's watching like she's being graded on eye contact. Down on the stage, Reid's jaw has tightened at my failed escape attempt, and I curse my stupid hunter eyesight for its precision.

I wait petulantly for Tweed Blazer to take the stage and am surprised when the brute with all the scars and tattoos rises from his chair instead. He's no stately wizard nor wizened businessman. Belaire's headmaster was a retired Southern senator who wore polo shirts and called all the girls *doll*. Dean Driscoll is hulking. Mean-looking. He's got thick rings on his fingers, a scar down his chin, and another across his brow. He looks like he could fuck up almost anyone and probably does so on the daily.

When he gets to the front of the stage, the students throughout the amphitheater are still clapping. Dean Driscoll frowns and waves his hands at them to quiet down. "Unnecessary but appreciated," he tells the crowd. He has a gruff, honest voice. No bullshit from this guy. "Whether you're brand-new or this is your last year here at Harker, you should already know what I'm about to say."

I swallow the churning in my gut at once again feeling like I'm taking a test I didn't get to study for.

"Save lives. Don't turn. Don't die. Have a great semester."

CHAPTER 7

THE CROWD CLAPS for their beloved dean of few words, and people begin to funnel out of the amphitheater.

I'm wondering if I have enough film at home to go take some pictures at NTC Park, since I've already bailed on work for the day, when my narrow-eyed, dark-haired captor says to me, "Sorry about that. I didn't want you to get called out in front of the whole school. I'm Kitty, by the way. Kitty Briggs."

The leap in emotion from intensely focused to warm and chatty is very aeon of her. I narrow my eyes, assessing the sharp-featured girl. She's angular and focused as a fox. Could she be like me? "Why'd they all cheer like that for the dean? He barely spoke."

Kitty's eyes go wide. "You don't know about Dean Driscoll?"

"Nope." I want to tell Kitty, *I'm not from around these here parts*, but the puppylike guy she was sitting with jumps in, his overgrown hair flopping as he walks.

"He's a legend. Killed a high-ranking Brood demon back in the seventies and he's not even a hunter." Lanky Guy pushes his hair from his face with a grin. "He's a *warlock*."

Not a hunter? "How'd he end up at Harker?"

"Driscoll and some of his hunter friends saved an entire town from an ogre," Kitty tells me. "They championed the school to let him attend."

"He domesticated a wyvern while he studied here," Lanky Guy adds. "He told us about it when Kitty and I took his summer program on spells and hexes."

"And he's a great dean," Kitty adds. "Takes care of his students and keeps Harker safe. He's the only witch currently employed by the school, given their tendency to . . . you know."

"Turn," the guy supplies. "Unless you believe the old rumor that the groundskeeper's a warlock."

"Which I don't," Kitty says tightly. She kind of reminds me of Nora.

I'd imagine for most lymantrians, turning is as big a fear as death. But for hunters, whose sworn responsibility it is to kill deviants and not add to their numbers, it's far worse. And the risk is there for us as much as any mortal: A werewolf bites you? Turned. Drained by a vamp? Turned. A demon takes your soul? Turned and, worse, relegated to hell. The only kind of turning that also punishes you for eternity.

But witches are the trickiest—they can be turned by any of the above, but can also swear fealty to the High Thane and, through dark magic, turn deviant and gain immortality. Since they can do this to themselves without any fangs or werewolf bites, witches get side-eyed in even the most welcoming of lymantrian circles.

At some point as we amble down the grassy hill and back toward the main drag of Harker's campus, we lose Kitty to a squealing group of girlfriends, but the long-limbed, floppy-haired guy makes no move to abandon me, which I appreciate.

"Peter Roydon," he tells me, thrusting out his hand. "Kitty's cousin. I take it you're new?"

And while every instinct in my body is urging me to say something dry and disinterested, I can't find it in myself to be rude to Peter. There's something terribly earnest about him. And not in a pitiful way. It's like he's too good to be mocked. Like he wouldn't even realize you were mocking him, and *you'd* be the idiot for not taking Peter Roydon seriously.

I shake his hand. "Viv Abbot."

"How come you were going to leave mid-orientation?"

I debate lying, but the truth is, if I'm going to stay . . . if I'm going to learn enough about my dad's time here to find out who the deviant was who killed him, I need someone like Peter. Someone who can help me begin my search. "I've been hunting on my own for . . ." I'm about to say *years* when I remember only aeons develop their abilities early. "A bit. I'm almost twenty-two." Which is true. "Never even knew there were this many hunters in the world, let alone that this place existed."

Some guys are tossing a football back and forth down in the quad at enough miles per hour to crash clean through the brick behind them. They jump like dogs high into the air to catch the ball and smack one another on the backs in success. A fresh-faced girl is watching them as she sharpens a long sword dutifully on the lawn. "I'm just not sure this is the right fit for me."

"That's a bummer," Peter says easily. "I bet we could learn a lot from someone who's been doing this solo."

It's a kind thing to say even if it's lip service. I had no idea I cared whether anyone saw value in the way I hunt. "Thanks."

Peter shrugs a shoulder, and I follow him through an arched pathway because I don't really know where I'm going. "Want my two cents?"

"Do you know how few men ask that before they give advice?"

Peter's grin comes equipped with a sweet little snaggletooth. "Can you tell Kitty that for me?"

"What are your two cents?"

"My mom was the only hunter in my family and she passed away before she taught me about Harker. I was recruited by an instructor, Reid Graveheart. He'd found me in the spring trying to take down a troll with my newfound strength. It wasn't going so well . . ." Peter cringes at the memory. "I was on the fence too. It sounded daunting and dangerous and . . ." He shakes his head at himself. "It wasn't until I signed up for the summer program that they found me in the Citadel's records. Learned I had a cousin here who was as orphaned as I was." His eyes survey the bustling campus. The cobblestones and varied students. "You might realize you're also not as alone as you think."

"I doubt I have a long-lost cousin hiding out in Harker's bookshelves."

"All I'm saying is you might as well give it the day. See if this place surprises you like it did for me."

Peter's grin is so earnest, it pulls at my heart. But I'm not ready to commit nor disappoint him, so I pivot to a lingering question. "What's the Citadel? What kind of records do they have?"

Peter frowns and we resume our walk. "The Citadel is a massive palace well past the Fickle Thicket." When I show no sign of knowing what a Fickle Thicket is, he adds, "The woods that surround the campus. Basically, the Citadel is the White House for the Elders and everyone who works for them."

"Cool, cool. And what are the Elders?"

This time Peter just laughs. "The oldest living lymantrians and our governing body. Dispensing inter-lymantrian justice, regulating hunting, ruling on conflicts. That one's basically in the title."

"You seem to know a lot. You're only a first year?"

"Kitty and I both. Same grade and everything. Lived five miles away from each other in the Pacific Northwest but never met. How about you?"

"I'm from Astera, actually."

"No way." His eyes light up. "That must have been an exciting place to grow up."

I grimace, dodging his question. "So Harker students are from all over the country?"

Peter guides us back inside those mossy brick walls and down a cobblestone path. "Yeah. Harker's the only demon-hunting college that I'm aware of. Pretty sure all hunting roads lead here."

I get the impression that if there were another school for deviant defense, Peter would know about it.

"There are gateways across almost every major city to get *into* Harker," he tells me. "But the gateway here within Old Campus only leads out into the Windsor. Most hunting by students and teachers is done in your city, given the Chasm."

I clock it as odd that the gateway out of the school is set to lead to the exact museum where I work. I've never been a suspicious person, but it's a strange coincidence. Still, I don't know Peter well enough to tell him I've worked in that exact museum for a year, so I go with a different question. "What's Old Campus?"

Peter gestures to the walls we just walked through. "Everything within the old brick. It's all from the mid-thirteenth century. That's why it looks like the Basilica of Saint-Denis or Canterbury Cathedral."

He looks at me expectantly like I'm meant to understand thirteenth-century architecture references, and I'm too scared of hurting his feelings to admit I'm not his target audience. The phoniest nod ever spasms out of me, but Peter only smiles.

"The name 'Old Campus' would imply that everything else is

younger, right? But actually everything beyond the gates is *older*. The amphitheater, the coliseum, the Fickle Thicket. I think the campus was built under a Roman emperor, maybe Vespasian, and then the center of it was renovated in the thirteenth century, and then again every hundred or so years. That's why the commons all have flatscreens."

"So . . . where are we, exactly?"

Peter shrugs. "No clue. Maybe the old lymantrian plane." He tips his head up toward the heavens. When I was growing up, my father showed me some texts implying our ancestors once lived on a higher plane that was destroyed by the deviants when the lymantrians came down to seal up the Chasm. The whole concept is so foreign to me, I don't pry for more. "Wherever Harker is," Peter says, eyeing the lush hedges and gothic architecture, "it's the best-kept secret in these ancient walls."

Harker's entire existence is still a shock to the system, but Peter has certainly taken the edge off. I clock my own defensiveness and try to store it somewhere else. "That's pretty cool."

"Yes, it is."

We come to a stop under the ornately designed rotunda that the gateway spat me out of this morning. Carvings of warriors and winged beasts battle overhead. Next to the imposing steel gateway doors is a wall of relics, figurines, and war trophies from various deviant kills.

But I'm less interested in the fossilized werepanther claw or Van Helsing's original journals. On the far right is a grainy black-and-white photo of a cheering college kid, lacrosse stick raised in victory, being hoisted onto the shoulders of two other boys. They're all in the same checked jerseys, numbers displayed proudly on their backs. They look like the greatest of friends. I squint at the photo until tears grow hot in my eyes.

"Pretty moving stuff," Peter says on a reverent breath. "That's when the Marksmen were at the top of their game."

I don't tell him that's my dad they've got raised on their shoulders. I don't tell him it's the first time I've seen that photo of him. I don't tell him how much it hurts to have confirmation that the only person who ever really gave a shit about me kept an entire chunk of his life a secret.

Peter allows me to study the photo for a beat too long before I wipe my cheek and ask him hoarsely, "Where to next?"

Under lofted ceilings, we make our way into a building at the edge of the redbrick wall. Inside, we climb a creaky staircase that smells of old wood, and Peter says, "This is Elkfore Hall. First-year housing."

"Oh, I won't be staying on campus. I have an apartment . . ." But Peter's already wandering down a wood-paneled passage to find a chalkboard filled with names.

"There you are," he says with triumph. Sure enough, he's pointing at my name and my room number. **VIVIENNE ABBOT, SOPHIA VALENTINE—ROOM 314.**

"Sophia Valentine. You know her?"

Peter shakes his head. "Nope. Pretty name, though. Look, I'm just down the hall from you guys. Room 319."

I peek at his room number. "And in a single too. Lucky duck."

"I wonder where Kit is . . ."

As Peter hunts for his cousin's assignment on the board, I think of that photo of my dad. I can't find it in me to be angry with him. He looked so happy with his friends. *Hunter* friends. Hunter friends he never spoke of to me. Digging into his history at this school is going to be my best shot at finding out not only why he kept me away from this place but also whether anyone who knew him then knows anything about the night he died.

"Hey, Peter, do you know where I can find information on the school and its alumni? There's so much I don't know about Harker. I just want to get caught up before I fall behind."

Peter looks like he knows exactly what I mean. "The library has plenty of books in the Harker History section. It's in Mortimer Tower."

"And those records you were talking about?"

"Those are with the more classified resources in the archives. But that room requires a staff member's key card."

I store the information away for later. "That's fine, the library will work."

Peter's smile is so sincere I almost feel bad—for what, though, I'm not sure. I don't even know this kid. Or his cousin or any of the students here. None of them are like me. None of them can relate to what I've been through. None of them are at Harker only to figure out why they were never supposed to be.

CHAPTER 8

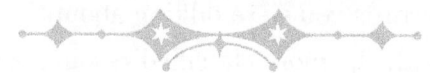

ROOM 314'S SLANTED ceiling, exposed wooden beams, and hazy bars of light make for a surprisingly cozy living space. Wide Victorian-era windows douse the place in sunlight, and luxurious, plentiful cream curtains surround them and pool onto the hardwood floors. There are a few tarnished gold frames on the walls—one encasing a mirror, the others, yellowed maps and pressed leaves. One leather armchair rests by a window, and beside it, a low bookcase with peeling white paint and an iron lantern perched on top.

Two scarred vintage desks sit on opposite walls, already stocked with everything your average college gal might need: wooden crosses, athames, bell jars with incense and herbs, and little vials I guess are filled with holy water and powders for exorcism and banishment. They're decorated with a few pillar candles and some ritual books, as well as a fresh set of number two pencils.

The two twin beds are on opposite sides of the room, wooden bed frames replete with bedknobs and carved headboards. Whoever Sophia Valentine is, it seems she's beaten me to our dorm. While one bed is empty, the other is already fitted with a mess of unmade sage-green sheets. There's even a lipstick-stained wineglass perched on the bedside table.

"Are you capable of shutting the fuck up for even two seconds?"

When I spin toward the source of the words, I find a drop-dead gorgeous woman plowing through the door, phone pressed right up against her ear as she shuts her eyes in frustration. I recognize the telltale signs of a hangover, and when she dumps her backpack on the bed, I clock a nightclub stamp on her wrist. Sophia Valentine, I assume.

"But it's not me! It actually *is* you," she says, kicking her cowboy boots and socks off—anklet and toe ring on full display—and unloading a mess of textbooks from her backpack onto the comforter.

She's got on jean shorts that show plentiful butt cheek, an oversized T-shirt of some band I've never heard of, and a handful of necklaces dangling from her elegant neck. Her cascade of long hair is coppery brown, but some sections shine golden when she runs her hand through it in exasperation.

"No number of vintage cars is going to make me want to fuck again, okay? It's getting weird. And can you please stop texting my mom?"

I feel my brows shoot up my face and stifle a laugh, turning to ignore the conversation and give her some kind of privacy. My fingers find a groove on the mattress of what I assume is my bed. I don't have books to put away or anything to move in. I should probably just leave the dorm, but I don't know where exactly I'd go.

"Are you listening to me?"

Maybe the armory. I do need to get my blade fixed. Probably easier here than finding a welder in the Half City and pretending to be a LARP enthusiast again.

"Hello? Spooky girl? I'm talking to you."

I whirl around. "Me?"

"Yes, you." Sophia's smile is broad—big teeth, full lips, a little gummy, but beautiful in an old-fashioned starlet kind of way. Her wispy bangs nearly fall into her eyes. "Who else would I be talking to?"

I make a face at the phone in her hand.

"Oh, him? Don't worry about him. Male hunters are idiots."

"Vintage cars, huh? Plural?"

Sophia turns back to the books on her bed. "The 1965 Porsche 911 was especially hard to part with." She rifles through her things until she finds what she was looking for—a crumpled piece of paper—and spits a wad of gum into it. "I was asking if you just got here."

"Just in time for that riveting orientation," I deadpan.

She gives me an assessing once-over. "I'm into your whole black-cat vibe."

"Black cat?"

"Yeah." Sophia slips her loose T-shirt over her head as she talks, and I realize too late she isn't wearing a bra. "Hot, bored, hair like the shampoo commercials, resting bitch face." I adjust my facial expression as Sophia digs through her things once more, and this time a little baggie of red dust falls out along with the thinnest white tank top of all time, which she slips on. "How are you not sweating? It's hot as balls out there."

"No, I fully am," I tell her, my eyes still on the baggie on the floor. I guess I should've assumed she was a partier. "I can't lift my arms in this shirt for the rest of the day."

Sophia laughs, big and loud. "Where are your bags?"

"I don't have any. I'm actually from Astera, so I have a place there—"

"Nobody's *from* Astera."

"What do you mean?"

Sophia pulls open the antique armoire and yanks out a pair of beat-up Birkenstocks. "Harker alums get stationed there, but nobody *lives* there. Not permanently. Hunters' souls give demons too much of a hard-on, and the Brood is based in Astera."

I bristle at what she's implying. "So?"

"*So* the Elders trust Harker professors and students to take care of most deviant action while living safely *within* Harker walls. If hunters were to live there, raise hunter babies there . . . Why serve up a soul buffet for the Brood?"

That explains why this school was here all along but I'd never seen many hunters gallivanting around my city. Also explains that no-hunting-without-a-teacher rule a bit more. "Well, I've lived there all my life and haven't been a soul buffet yet. And I have a mortal roommate and a job in the city too, so I probably won't be in the dorms too much. Don't want anyone back home to worry."

Sophia shrugs. "Fine by me. Word to the wise—you don't need your lymantrian coin to get in and out of the gateway in the Windsor anymore. You can just step through that kiosk anytime when you want to come and go."

"Oh, thanks." I pause, studying her. I thought students were supposed to stay on campus throughout the semester. "How do you know that?"

Sophia can't contain the hint of a smile at her lips. "Your deviant-infested city has better nightlife than anything happening on campus."

She says *nightlife*, but she means *drugs*.

"Anyway . . . you wanna borrow something?" She eyes my armpits. "For the sweat situation?"

"Nah, I'm used to it," I tell her. But between this girl and Peter, I'm kind of floored. Why is everyone so friendly? "It gets blisteringly hot in the city this time of year."

Sophia nods, fishing a lipstick from her bag and swiping it across her full bottom lip in the mirror. It's easily the perfect color to match her tan, freckled skin. She's like a seventies rock star. Or a mermaid. "I grew up by the ocean where it's way cooler. It's taking me a beat to adjust. What's your first class?"

I shrug. I'm not sure how to tell her I'm just biding my time until tonight, when I can get into that library and research my dad undisturbed. "I was late to orientation. Haven't registered yet."

"Perfect," Sophia tells me. "You can follow me and I'll sign you up for all the classes I'm in. Like a ride-along. I'm Sophia, by the way."

"I gathered that," I tell her. "Viv."

"What's it short for? Vivica? Viviana?"

"Vivienne."

Sophia appears vaguely disappointed. "Vivica would've been badass."

I can't help my laugh. "I agree, actually."

AFTER INTRODUCTION TO Aztec Weaponry, Lymantrian Beings I, and Western European Rituals and Exorcisms, I've amassed a twelve-credit course load before the second half of our classes tomorrow and enough books to weigh down a commercial airliner. And we still have one class left: Underworld Studies with Professor Lisette.

The classroom is in a basement that smells like cinnamon and sweet coffee, and I spy four used mugs on Lisette's cluttered desk. The annex has no windows, but it does have one wrought-iron chandelier lit with flickering candles and a black chalkboard spanning the entire back wall. The wooden seats creak when we slide into them, and when there's no space left, students take to the floor and cram themselves into the aisle in the back.

"Popular course?"

"Very," Sophia tells me, making herself comfortable cross-legged despite how cramped everyone is beside her. "Even though Lisette is impossible."

"Scoot down, Soph," someone says. When I look up from my new notebook, I see that the voice belongs to a guy with the rich bronze skin of a surfer and the build of a gym rat.

"Elliot," she says brightly. "This is my new roommate, Viv. Viv, this is my Elliot."

"*Your* Elliot?"

He grins, his teeth as pearly white as a dental brochure. "We've been told *platonic life partner* is a mouthful."

Elliot is just as cool as Sophia. He's jacked—more muscle than man—and boy-band handsome. The two of them exude a charm I'd thought reserved only for models and socialites. He squeezes past our entire aisle and plops down next to Sophia, tossing a casual arm over her shoulders. When I adjust to make some more room, I accidentally kick my stack of textbooks into the seat in front of me.

"Shit, sorry," I mumble. Only when I bend down to pile them back up, I see the student I've nearly taken out with my avalanche is none other than Peter. Kitty sits beside him, organizing her notes.

"Viv." He grins. "You stayed."

"Trust me, I'm as shocked as you are." But I know my smile betrays me.

"You find your roommate?"

"She sure did," Sophia butts in. "Sophia Valentine. Hi."

Something about what she's just said stuns poor Peter into another stratosphere. His pupils dilate, his cheeks flush. I can *hear* his brain go blank. It only hits me a moment later that it's not what he's heard but what he's *seen*. Peter is in literal awe of Sophia. And who could blame him? Her stunning body is practically on display in the world's littlest tank top and shreddiest shorts, her anklet and gold bangles drawing the eye to every inch of exposed skin.

"Hi," Kitty says in Peter's place. "I'm Kitty."

"Sexy name," Soph tells her, and Kitty awkwardly tucks a strand of dark hair behind her ear. "This is Elliot."

"'Sup," he offers. "I like your tattoo." Elliot is covered in traditional Pacific Islander tattoos of his own, which swirl up and down his carved arms.

Kitty's brows knit inward before she comes to some realization and shakes her head. "Oh, no, it's just a stamp from a bar." She rubs absently at the white antlers inked on the inside of her wrist, and I realize it's the same one as on Sophia's arm.

I shake my head. *Hunters*.

But a strange pang of connection hits me. I never got to go to college. I've never experienced this kind of academic camaraderie or shared anticipation for the year to come. It's . . . nice.

"The quiet one is Peter," I tell Sophia and Elliot. "Kitty's cousin."

Peter opens his mouth to say something, but he's interrupted by the irritated strumming of Professor Lisette's long nails on her desk. When a hush falls over the classroom, she lifts a brow. "No, please, continue. Mingle, chat. My time is meaningless."

I roll my eyes. It sounds like something Fiona would say. The candles along Lisette's desk flicker more vividly as she dims the lights and takes a seat on the edge of her desk. She lowers the horn-rimmed glasses from her head, where they were hidden among tufts of frizzy yellow. "All right, first years. Who can tell me why this course matters?"

Silence across the crowded classroom.

"Your enthusiasm inspires."

Sophia's hand shoots up, bangles jangling. "Because it's required to graduate?"

A few muted snickers sound. I expect Lisette to chew her head off, but she only presses her lips together. When her eyes find me beside Sophia, she glares like I'm a demon myself. I immediately swallow my laughter.

"She's not too far off," Lisette says, peeling her eyes off me slowly. "Miss . . . ?"

"Sophia Valentine."

"*Why*, Sophia Valentine, do you think mine is the only class at Harker you must take to graduate?"

Sophia chews her lip in thought. "So that we know the literal hell that awaits us if we turn?"

More hushed laughter. But Sophia is undeterred. She's got the kind of impenetrable confidence that is unaffected by being flat-out wrong. I can't think of anything that might embarrass her and decide it's an enviable quality and not an obnoxious one.

Professor Lisette grabs what appears to be the class syllabus from her desk and hands the stack to the first row to pass on. "To understand what is above," she tells us, "we must first understand what is below."

Peter and Kitty scribble this dutifully in their notebooks. Beside me, Elliot is scrolling through a feed dedicated to men doing CrossFit. I write my first bullet point on my new notepad—I have a feeling this is the only class that will matter for my specific purposes at this school.

"In the earliest days, deviants dwelled solely in the underworld. Born there, lived there, died there. Humans were safe here on the mortal plane, and lymantrians lived above. Until the High Thane used the darkest form of magic to split the earth."

The Chasm. Like my father told me. He also said the spell the High Thane had used drove him so mad that he carved out his own liver and ate it raw. Delightful information to receive at eight years old.

Lisette nods at Peter. "And then what happened, Mr. Roydon?"

Peter opens his mouth to answer, but Kitty replies for him. "Our lymantrian ancestors had to descend from their astral plane to protect the mortals and close up the Chasm. A great war was waged. The deviants took this opportunity to destroy the lymantrian homeland, and the lymantrians were forced to relocate here and live on the mortal plane in secret. Hunters became invaluable in fighting the newly freed deviants, and aeons were briefly brought back into the fold to help before they couldn't contain their hunger surrounded by mortals and were eliminated."

I shift in my seat at the mention of aeons. She makes it sound like we're some kind of fallen angels. Disgraced, a last resort. Bloodthirsty feral animals.

What eats at me is that she's right.

Lisette nods. "Very good. Though try not to steamroll your classmate next time, yes?"

Kitty's cheeks glow red and Peter shrugs at her as if to say, *Don't worry about it.*

"But," Lisette continues, "not all deviants were set free when the Chasm was split. Think of it like a crack in a frozen lake. Not a dam breaking. Millions still live in the underworld, deep down below our feet."

Sophia hands the stack of syllabi to me and I take one and pass the rest down. It's three pages stapled together—the first two contain dates for essays, research projects, and tests. The third is double-sided. The front reads:

STRATIFICATION OF DEVIANTS
High Thane
Demons
Born Deviants
Turned Deviants
Half-Borns
Beasts
The Undead

And on the back:

LYMANTRIAN ORDER
The Elders
Hunters, Pixies, Witches & Warlocks, Nymphs,
Mermaids, Shifters, Fairies, Elves, and Gnomes

I study the pages. Some of this I knew—my father taught me about the hierarchy employed by deviants, the cruelty by which each class subjugates and marginalizes those beneath their rank. He taught me that we're lymantrians, but . . . everything else is an onslaught of new information. I didn't know some of these beings even existed.

I'm hit with a jolt of sharp and unwelcome hurt. How could he have kept a place like this from me? Somewhere filled with information I could have used to hunt these last ten years? Perhaps

I'll learn things here that my dad already taught me, but after all this time, I can't recall them. I find the thought profoundly sad—that there are moments he and I shared that are now lost forever to the abyss of my memory. I hate that I'll never be able to ask him. I hate almost as much that Reid might have been right about Harker making me better at what I do.

I shake my head, still shocked that this school *employs* the very kind of demon it seeks to eliminate. And that's one of the many questions bubbling in my mind. I'm no Sophia—there will be no hand raising if I can avoid it—but I do lean over to her and whisper, "What's a half-born?"

Sophia takes the paper from my hand and writes next to *Half-Borns, Selkies, Succubi, Sirens, Giants, Djinn, Harpies, Trolls, etc. Not as human-looking as vamps, werewolves, or demons. Not as beastly as... beasts.*

I nod my thanks, then I write under *Turned Deviants*, Why are turned deviants considered lesser than born deviants?

IDK, deviants are species-ist assholes.

Professor Lisette addresses the class. "Questions on the stratification of deviants?"

One kid up front raises his hand.

"Yes . . . ?" Lisette prompts the student. He's still got a bit of baby fat in his cheeks, which gives him a disarming cherubic look, but I spot a mean gleam in his eye.

"Matt Peverell. Have demons always been at the top of the food chain?"

"Yes—"

"Why?"

Lisette's lips purse. "Despite the pride deviants claim to have for their kind, their hierarchy is entirely based on which hell-born beings appear the most human. That's why demons are so hard to root out and eliminate. They appear just like us."

Reid's face blooms in my mind once more.

"They're also the rarest of deviants you may encounter. Do you know why that is?"

Matt thinks a moment before shaking his head irritably.

"Does anyone?"

Peter raises his hand again. "When demons turn people, they wake up in hell. Not up here, like a turned vampire or werewolf would. So they aren't repopulating on earth with the same numbers."

"Very good," Lisette says. "Deviants take their hierarchy very seriously. Only a born demon can ascend to High Thane. No other species has been allowed to sit atop the Throne of Bael since its creation. And the throne offers extraordinary power to the demon who claims it—immortality with or without taking mortal souls, incomparable strength, unique abilities . . . Ever since the High Thane broke open the Chasm, he and his Brood have resided here, among the lymantrians and the mortals, blending into human society. A physical demarcation of their class."

Matt raises his hand once more. "So why don't we spend more time hunting the High Thane and his Brood and less on all his weaker, lower-class subjects?"

Next to me, Sophia blows her bangs out of her face with an annoyed breath, and I purse my lips in agreement. The High Thane is as realistic a target as the boogeyman. The title passes from father to son like a medieval monarchy, and the identity of their crowned leader is the best-kept secret in all of Astera. Sure, a few hunters throughout history have taken down one High Thane or another, but then someone new is crowned and the mystery begins again. One of many reasons a hunter's job is never done.

"If we knew who the current High Thane was, we'd have our most deadly hunters on him." Lisette takes two steps forward, and that eerie feeling seizes my gut once more. Like there's something off about her. "Harker *alumni*, mind you, not ineffectual first years who think themselves Rambo."

The class titters, but Lisette's lips don't even twitch. "Anyone else?"

Most of the other students shake their heads. Someone asks for a refresher on what constitutes a beast, which Lisette explains to be basilisks, dragons, wyverns, banshees, strzyga, ogres, and hydra. I knew about three of those and quickly jot down the others. For whatever reason, I cover my paper to make sure nobody besides Sophia can see all the things I didn't know.

She takes my list from me and adds *ghosts, wraiths, ghouls* under *The Undead*.

So born deviants means they were birthed. Not turned? I write to her.

Sophia writes, *That's what born means last time I checked.*

But Elliot steals the page from her before Sophia can write more. *No deviants or lymantrians can crossbreed, if that's what you're asking.*

Sophia writes back, *And they said you couldn't be smart and pretty.*

Elliot flashes her a cocksure grin, and I catch Peter in the row below us, watching them with mild curiosity.

I lean over Sophia and write, *So what happens if a succubus or a harpy has sex with a vamp or something? Nothing?*

Sophia and Elliot both nod, but Peter waves a hand at us and motions for the paper. Elliot hands it to him as Lisette talks about how beasts and the undead are given the most grueling positions in the underworld, due to their lower stature in the caste system, while higher-ranking deviants enjoy their roles as enforcers and torturers.

Vampires only procreate by turning others, Peter writes. I nod, reaching for the paper, but he hastily adds, *They don't have sperm.* Then he smiles at us, proud to have contributed.

I grab the paper and write back, *Thank you for that, Peter,* before flashing it at him.

Kitty motions for the list and we pass it surreptitiously over to her. She begins to write under my original question. *Nothing will happen if two different deviants fuck, EXCEPT with harpies. Since they are all women, they are the only deviant that can become pregnant by another species. But they can only birth more female harpies, and thus they are all considered "half." TLDR: deviants are SPECIES-IST!!!*

I stifle a laugh.

"Have you five completed the dissertation you're writing back there?"

Hot shame coats the back of my neck as the entire class turns to ogle us.

"We were analyzing harpy discrimination," Sophia says, clearly unbothered, while Peter, Elliot, Kitty, and I collectively span all possible shades of red.

"Wonderful," Lisette says. "That will make a strong topic for your first essay."

The class groans. Dirty glares are heaped upon us, and I force myself, through a will of steel, not to make eye contact with anyone.

"If I've learned anything in my many, many years at Harker, it's that a lack of focus is the swiftest way to get yourselves killed." She says this like she's in her eighties, but she doesn't look a day older than thirty-five. I wonder if she's an elf of some kind. She doesn't strike me as a hunter, but what do I know? This is my first day at hunter school.

"Each one of you needs to give this course—this entire curriculum—every ounce of focus you have. You must take it seriously if you intend to live through your four years here." A shadow crosses over Lisette's face. "Or more importantly, have any hope of protecting humankind. You are all they have, after all." Lisette takes her glasses off and stares at me until a shiver runs up my spine. "And on that hopeful note," she says, finally letting her eyes survey the classroom, "you're free to go."

CHAPTER 9

THE COURTYARD OUTSIDE Professor Lisette's basement classroom is dimly lit; it's too early for the lanterns to flicker on, too late for ample sunshine, but the heat has died down and the grounds no longer bustle with hundreds of students. I spy both the setting sun over the hills in the west and a sliver of shy moon cresting in the still-blue sky, and I feel the corners of my mouth tick up. I love when that happens.

"Dining hall for dinner?" Elliot asks Sophia, then looks to Peter, Kitty, and me, extending the invite to us as well. "I'm starving."

"You're always starving," Soph says, fanning herself with a notebook. "But I'll go anywhere with AC. I cannot take another minute of this heat."

"It's kind of brutal, huh?" Kitty asks, tucking her hair behind her ear. I get the sense new friends aren't common for her, either, and my heart gives an empathetic squeeze.

"Very brutal," Sophia agrees. "We could all watch something in the commons after?"

Kitty's brows lift with interest, and Peter eyes his book bag anxiously before nodding at Sophia with guarded enthusiasm. I fear Puppy Eyes may be a goner.

"We don't hunt in the evenings?" I ask the group. "Even with an instructor?"

"Very few first years are selected for Field Training," Peter says. "They want you to learn a bit before they toss you to the wolves."

"Literally," Sophia jokes.

"I already can't wait to graduate," Elliot muses, running a hand through his wavy hair. "Freedom to go take out deviants whenever I please."

"No babysitters," Sophia agrees.

"And a Citadel hunter salary," Kitty adds brightly.

Sophia and Elliot look at each other like that's a bit more ambitious than anything they're hoping to accomplish, and Kitty shifts on her feet. Peter just looks like the thought of hunting in general terrifies him.

"That what you want to do?" I ask Kitty without judgment. "Work for the Citadel?"

"I'd be happy to be stationed somewhere cool after this. Japan or Romania or Salem, Oregon . . ." These must be deviant hotspots. Places where the average alum is sent as an expert hunter after graduation. I nod along as if it isn't news to me. "But being able to work for the Elders, to help maintain order . . . to hunt in *Astera*. I think I'd be good at that."

She definitely reminds me of Nora. A classic type A with the ruthlessness of an aeon to boot. I can't imagine Kitty's childhood was an easy one.

"If anyone can do it, it's you," Peter tells her.

He says it like working for the Citadel—hunting in big, bad Astera, where the Brood lives—is an incredible feat. I almost want to tell them Kitty could kick ass at that *tonight*, before I remind myself I started hunting when I was seven, as did my dad, and his mom before him. Nobody I'm standing with has hunted on their own, except maybe here and there in this last year before school started. I also remind myself none of these people have the bloodlust I do. Maybe to Elliot it's a sport. To Sophia, an adrenaline rush. To Kitty, a challenge to excel at. But to me it's a razor-sharp need. A compulsion.

"Harker's laxer about people hunting back home during winter and summer breaks," Sophia adds, and I remember I'm the one who asked about hunting tonight. "Probably because they'll have taught us the basics by then. And because nobody is going home to a place like Astera." Sophia catches herself right as she says it. "Except you, I guess."

I'll just tack it onto the seventeen other reasons that even among a literal *school* of hunters, I'm still the odd one out.

"We could spar, though," Elliot suggests, eyes lighting. "In the coliseum. My brothers told me they never clean the blood from the floor after battles."

Kitty's nose scrunches. "That can't be right . . . or hygienic."

"Elliot's brothers are rarely either," Sophia muses.

"They went here before you?" Kitty asks him.

Elliot grins. "All five of 'em."

Peter says, "I don't think there are any classes being taught in there tonight. Might not be open."

"Do you have the entire curriculum memorized?" I ask.

"Of course he does," Kitty says. "He's like a walking registrar."

"Then the gymnasium," Elliot concedes. "We can spar in there."

After what has to be one of the longest days of my life, I was hoping to find that Harker History section of the library Peter was telling me about, but maybe sparring isn't a bad idea. If I'm going to stay enrolled at this school long enough to figure out more about my father's death, that means giving up hunting in Astera. Which means I need to take every opportunity I can get to let off steam.

Still, the thought of accepting this rule—letting deviants slither all over my city with nothing to stop them but some stationed Harker alums I've never met—goes down about as well as a doorknob, but I tell myself it's only temporary. That I'll be even better at what I do when I'm allowed to hunt over the winter break, less than four months away. Who knows if I'll even make it here that long.

"I'm in," I tell them.

"Sick," Sophia says as we amble toward the gym. "I got these new arrowheads last week—"

"Shit." I stop short. "I forgot. One of my daggers is broken."

"Which one?" Sophia asks.

I shrug. "My left?"

The look on her face is one of grave disappointment. "You haven't named them?"

"Named them?" My eyes cut to Elliot, Kitty, and Peter, but nobody seems to find this sentiment as absurd as I do.

"Most warriors and knights name their blades," Elliot tells me. It's strange to hear something so silly coming out of the mouth of someone so cool.

"And all the best superheroes too," Peter adds. "Thor named his hammer Mjölnir."

"Peter's obsessed with comics," Kitty says with an eye roll. "He can recite every *Spider-Man* issue alphabetically."

Peter opens his mouth and I wince. "Maybe some other time?"

"Go to the armory," Sophia tells me. "They'll fix your dagger for you in like twenty minutes."

Elliot's already walking again, a smirk on his face. "Don't worry, I'll save you an ass whooping."

"Want to bet on that?"

His entire face brightens with my words. "Twenty bucks says you can't get me to the mat."

I grin at him, a warm, excited buzz lighting in my chest. "You're on."

On my way to the armory, I stroll past low stone archways wreathed in decadent ivy and soaring buildings that resemble cathedrals, just as Peter said. My map from earlier leads me around classical columns and wide-open courtyards, tufts of soft hydrangea and quiet peals of student laughter. I find my pace quickening—try as I might to fight it, I'm eager to get back to the group. Today wasn't just manageable, it was . . . kind of a relief. No covering for broken bones or strange scars. No lying to people. And I actually made new friends. Something I haven't done since I met Penny.

Shit, Penny!

I fish my phone out of my back pocket and shoot her a quick text. Stuck at the Windsor under a mountain of work. Might just sleep on Fiona's couch tonight.

And suddenly the truck-size weight this afternoon removed from my chest returns, twice as heavy—the lies are going to increase tenfold now that I'm enrolled at Harker. If I'm really going to give this place a chance—at least until I get some meaningful answers—I can't half-ass it. These classes are no joke, the hours, the workload, the rules . . . And I haven't even done any physical training yet.

I'm going to have to come up with some kind of longer-term lie for Fiona, James, my family . . . But none of those will hurt as badly as lying to Penny. I don't think Penny's lied to anyone once in her life. Certainly never to me.

But it's not like I have a lot of options. Even if humanity wasn't better off not knowing about deviants—even if it weren't safer for society as a whole—I'd *still* never want Penny, of all people, to know how horrific the world really is. Her sunny outlook is a rare and precious thing. To wake up every single day and genuinely believe that people are good? That things will be okay? I'd yank out my own front teeth Novocain-free for that peace of mind. I never want to take that from her.

And more selfishly, when I'm not having nightmares about the docks where my father was killed or being turned against my will, I'm having nightmares about Penny learning what a monster I am. So I have to lie to my closest friend to protect her and our friendship. A lovely hunter classic. The most heartbreaking catch–22.

By the time I reach the armory, a shabby little cottage amid sturdy oak trees with a steeply sloping gray-tiled roof, my frustration's simmering. I'm irritated all over again by Harker's inane rules against hunting. If I could, I'd explain to the gruff dean that I need the fight—the kill—to remain stable. That I've been taking down deviants—and in Astera, no less—since before I could reach the top shelf of my pantry. But I know it would out me as an aeon, and we can't have that, now can we?

By the time I yank the armory door open, I'm looking for a fight.

And lucky for me, I get one.

Amid racks of glinting spears and sharpened long swords, rows of Harker-brewed oils and salves, I find the demon all these weapons exist to destroy. I'd have known even if I hadn't clocked his perfect loose brown curls or the wide expanse of his lean, muscled back. The way my body buzzes—alerting me that I'm in the presence of danger—would've been enough.

The armorer isn't here, but Reid is hunched over one of the

workbenches, tinkering with the chain of a spiked flail while a female student with a fair complexion and icy-blond hair watches with hearts in her eyes. This time, I know the hot feeling in my chest is pure, quality-guaranteed annoyance. Doesn't she know the man is a predator that needs to be put down?

"You really did a number on this thing," he murmurs, eyes still on the broken chain. "Dragon?"

"Giant, actually," she tells him. She's practically on her tippy-toes to inch closer. "Found him in the plains outside my hometown this summer. Killed him all on my own."

His response is quiet. Measured. "Well done."

I roll my eyes, wandering through displays of gleaming metal as I wait for the armorer to come back. It's all I can do not to nab something and swing toward the brand on Reid's neck. I try to count my breaths.

One. Two. Three—

My eyes catch on one of the sealed-off cases, locked with an ancient-looking iron padlock. Inside are several short swords—bejeweled and polished and sparkling like wet diamonds in sunlight. The smallest one, resting on a velvet cushion in the display corner, looks oddly similar to my own. It's cleaner than mine and has a different carving, not the doe nor the serpent. This one is of some kind of prowling jungle cat. A jaguar, maybe. It's savage-looking—narrowed eyes, bared fangs—but carrying a small kitten on its back.

"Don't get any ideas," a rough voice says behind me.

I spin to find Reid glaring at me. Curiosity and irritation war in his eyes.

"Any ideas about what?"

"You're not strong enough to break that glass. No hunter is. That's why they use it."

I gape at him until I find the words to express my outrage. "You think I'm *casing* the place?"

Reid only shrugs. "I saw you try to flee orientation. Here for a souvenir before you go?"

Shame coats my cheeks. Even worse, behind us, the pretty blonde is hanging around, clutching her fixed weapon, clearly pretending to browse the soldering machines as she uses her heightened hearing to listen in.

I should just leave. Fix my blade tomorrow. But I can't help myself. "I'm staying," I manage between clenched teeth. "I'm here to fix my damn dagger."

Reid's expression hardly changes. "The cracked one?"

"Yes. And why are you still hovering over me anyway? I came to your secret school, didn't I? You can stop stalking me now."

Reid's eyes twinkle in the low lantern light. "Stalking?"

"Yeah, you're, like . . . keeping tabs on me or something." I peer past the shelves and behind the countertop. In the back room, I can only make out a smattering of half-built swords and knives. Still no armorer. "Or are you just jonesing for the immortal energy drink you missed out on in that alley? Is it hard? Being surrounded by all the goods in a place like this?" I nod toward Blondie and find her stiff as a board. *Bet you never thought about that*, I think. *That the handsome Brood demon you're mooning over might crave your very soul.*

Reid says nothing, though his jaw has turned to granite. It seems I've struck a nerve. The fury in his eyes is like fire to the freezing—I want to stoke those flames and bathe in them.

"I don't take human souls," he snarls. "You think they'd employ me here if I did?"

I glare at him. "Then why were you watching me so intensely today?"

Reid folds his arms across his chest and leans against the wall. "You're hard to miss." He doesn't say it like it's a compliment.

Steam could billow from my ears. "Why are you always leaning against things? Are you very off-balance or something?"

Behind us, Blondie stifles a laugh that sounds a little like a gasp.

To my shock, a subtle smirk tugs at the corner of Reid's mouth. It's a look I haven't seen yet—not the smug grin or brooding boredom. This is . . . genuine amusement. Dear lord, I've made him laugh.

"Instructor?" the girl calls out in her singsong voice. "I think the chain is still a little loose."

Reid makes no move to leave. He only continues to stare at me, still and assessing.

I fight every urge to squirm under his brutal, ancient gaze. The desire to use any number of these weapons on him has not subsided. "Your groupie beckons."

Another twitch of his lips. He pushes off the wall and returns to the eager student without another word. I can hear their hushed conversation about the integrity of the iron chain as my eyes travel over mounted muskets surely loaded with silver bullets.

"Careful around all that silver," I warn as I round a shelf and arrive behind their workbench. "Wouldn't want you to burn."

Blondie sucks in quite the breath. Hand on her heart and everything. "Mr. Graveheart is the head combat instructor here, first year. You should mind your attitude."

"What do they say?" I tap my lips in thought and watch as Reid's eyes follow the motion. "'If you can't do, teach'?"

"Funny," he says quietly, eyes back on the metalwork. "I don't recall you being all that formidable."

That *fucker*. "I wanted answers that night, not blood. I could slice you, gut to sternum, right here, even with my broken blade."

Reid's gaze lands on me, crackling with a furious heat. My breath hitches.

"Sorry." The armorer, a plump, kind-eyed man, rounds the corner, welding mask on his head, thick rubber gloves in his grasp. "Was torching a claymore back there and didn't hear y'all. How can I help?"

Reid, Blondie, and I stare at him until he swallows thickly.

"Feel free to show me at the end of the week, huntress," Reid says evenly. "In the coliseum."

I don't allow myself to ask why I'll see him there or to question why the thought makes my stomach plunge. His arm barely brushes my shoulder as he pushes past, and I get a whiff of that citrusy scent. My nose crinkles.

And then he's gone. I take a breath, allowing my fists to unfurl. I fully lost my cool with him. This no-hunting thing is not going to be good for my mood swings. But if that monstrous, Brood-branded creep keeps trying to tell *me* how—

"Miss?" The armorer stares at my broken blade expectantly. "Hello?"

CHAPTER 10

MY HEAD SLAMS into the mat hard enough to see stars, but Elliot doesn't let his elbow crush my larynx, which I appreciate. Despite his size and strength, Elliot is surprisingly gentle. Like when Hound play-wrestles with a puppy. Unfortunately for me, gentle does not mean pushover. I may not be earning that twenty after all.

"Jesus," Elliot grunts when I flip around and drive my heel into his rib cage. "Your feet made of lead or something?"

Unfortunately for him, I am not a puppy.

Kitty, who's stretching on a dark mat in the corner, snickers. Sophia has Peter locked in some kind of tactical hold that he looks to be enjoying far too much. Neither of them has even noticed that I landed some decent hits on the strongman. A good thing too—I've been trying to keep my experience slightly under the radar. Pulling more advanced punches, dodging less deftly. Anything to make sure they don't know that I've been fighting actual deviants for the last decade.

"Sorry," I breathe, bracing my hands on my knees. Elliot's the best sparring partner I've had in . . . well, ever. I've never had a sparring partner before—me at ten against my aeon hunter father wouldn't have been much of a fair match.

"Don't be." Elliot grins. His broad, shirtless chest gleams like polished metal beneath the low gymnasium lighting. "You're even tougher than Soph. Don't tell her I said that, though. She'll prove me wrong. Painfully."

"Yes, I will," Sophia calls from across the room before her face smushes into the mat. Now Peter has *her* in a tactical hold. Elliot and I watch as he tries with as much gentlemanly courtesy as he can not to accidentally cop a feel.

"Damn." Elliot shakes his head at me. "I keep forgetting she's got the same hunter hearing I do now."

I've been this way as long as I can remember, but for everyone else here, all the heightened senses are largely unwelcome twenty-first-birthday gifts. "Sensory overload's intense, huh?"

"For real. I can see the blackheads on people's noses from across the room."

"I find twinkle lights helpful," I tell him, getting a sip of water from the fountain near the rows of students running on treadmills. When I go to hand him twenty bucks from my wallet, he only shakes his head. "We'll go double or nothing on the next round."

The wood-floored gymnasium is open-air, built right into the center of campus, spitting distance from the amber-lit turrets of the great dining hall. The treadmills sit before wide arches that face a shady alcove where a marble fountain gurgles with a few students perched around its lip. One is reading a worn copy of *Outsmarting Satyrs and Other Clever Beasts*. Another, *The Bell Jar*.

"Back to it?" Elliot asks. "Or, Kitty, you want in?"

Kitty hops up, her short black hair pulled into tight space buns on either side of her head. "Don't go easy on me like you did on Viv."

"Whoa there." But I'm laughing as I allow myself to stretch on the rubber mats and watch Kitty and Elliot circle each other. She certainly moves like she's been doing this longer than one summer program. But that doesn't mean anything for sure. She was likely raised by hunters before she was orphaned; they probably taught her how to hold her arms and plant her feet long before she gained her abilities.

But Elliot is something else entirely. Even though he's three times her size, he's just as quick. A powerhouse of physical strength and agility. When Elliot lands a fast, light hit on Kitty, she lashes out, fists flying, losing form. Temperamental, ambitious, controlling . . . My mind tries to put together how I could even begin to ask her if she's an aeon. I don't think there's any way to do so without giving myself away.

Somewhere, Peter howls in defeat. When the three of us turn toward the sound, we find Sophia with her thighs on either side of his head.

None of us shower before dinner. I learn quickly that despite the awe-inducing cathedral-style stained glass windows, lofted ceiling and rows and rows of endlessly long medieval tables, Harker's dining hall is less Oxford dinner party and more battle-worn fortress banquet. Hunters in all manner of athletic wear—navy Harker sweats, sports bras, leather fighting gear—eat and drink boisterously, sharing stories and lessons from the day. The hall is loud and oddly cheerful, with students milling in and out of the swinging wooden doors that lead to the kitchen, where, Peter tells me, talented gnomes cook all three meals for us each day.

Matt, the baby-faced kid with the chip on his shoulder who Lisette referred to as Rambo, is sitting with some students who look older, pounding beers, interrupting one another's gory stories. A collection of beautiful third-year girls who have the viciousness of assassins and cheekbones of NTC moms are whispering about the group of lacrosse players sitting down the table from them. One girl offers a delicate finger wave, and a good-looking guy mimes being shot in the heart and falls back into his buddies.

Across the hall, beneath a threadbare tapestry, sit a couple of the professors we met today, including Lisette, who is sharing a glass of wine with the fairy teacher with the gossamer wings. They eat and talk quietly, used to the chatter of excitable young hunters, I'm sure. And at the end of the table, beneath a wide, gold-framed landscape of a ship weathering rough seas—

My body tenses at the sight.

Reid. Sitting alone.

He digs silently into his dinner. No book, no phone out. No teachers or students—not even his blond groupie—anywhere nearby. A pariah, it seems. *As he should be*, I want to think. But the visual is unsettling. I know loneliness. I know it in my bones. In the roots of my teeth. And that's what I'm looking at.

When Reid's eyes cross the room to meet mine, I try not to take an obvious inhale. Those eyes, though . . . Like tracking missiles of cobalt blue.

I cut my gaze away and follow my new friends to a table a ways down. I don't spy a ton of first years, but I'd imagine a decent number of them are still struggling to withstand this many stimuli—the sounds of chewing and debating and raucous laughter, the flickering candlelight and airy stripes of moonglow turned lavender through the stained glass, the blended scents of roasted meat and starchy carbs, and the sharp tang of red wine.

"I don't know if I can eat in here every night," Peter says, rubbing his forehead.

"I think all my years of underage clubbing have desensitized me," Sophia says, digging into her roast chicken without issue.

I take a bite and find it's just as excellent as I'd expect. Gnomes are known for their craft—clockwork, baking, tinkering of all kinds. In fact, my favorite camera repairman in the city is a gnome.

"Same," Kitty says to Sophia.

"You like to party?" Elliot asks, mouth overly full and brow raised. "You didn't strike me as the type."

"How come?" Kitty says, a bit tense. "Just because I'm dedicated to my studies and want to hunt for the Citadel one day means I can't cut loose? People can be more than they appear, Elliot. Are you just a womanizing bag of hunter muscles?"

Sophia swivels her head to Elliot as if she deems this question interesting.

"Pretty much," Elliot says with an easy shrug and another large bite. Kitty can't help her laugh and the rest of the table snickers too. But I catch something in Elliot's eye as he chews. There and gone before I can make sense of it.

"I bet you like to party," Sophia says to me knowingly. "Like a raver or something."

"Not so much, actually."

"No, no," Sophia says as if refining her understanding of me. "I've got it. You like a weird little bar that nobody goes to."

Cobwebs and its taxidermy bats pop into my mind and I can't help but laugh. "That's kind of scary."

Sophia flashes her magnificent smile. "It's a gift."

"Do me," Peter says, sipping his beer. When he hears himself, his entire face flushes. "I mean . . . You know what I mean. Do that trick—the thing where—"

Sophia turns to Peter and narrows her eyes at him. He grins

back, studying the freckles on her nose, the clutter of gold winding up her ear as she tucks a copper strand behind it. "You don't like to go out at all," she says after a minute. "Maybe you play Dungeons & Dragons with your buds. No—World of Warcraft. No! Scrabble."

"Close," Peter says, unashamed. "The correct answer is all three."

Sophia cheers at her success, does a faux bow for the table. But something a little mournful passes across his face.

"What is it?" Kitty asks Peter.

Peter tries to brush it off, reaching for his beer. "Nah. Nothing."

"Nope." Sophia, stronger than him, slams his mug down. The table jolts and the students at the other end shoot glares in our direction. "You have to tell us now."

"The guys I used to hang out with . . . I don't think it'll be the same with them once I go back home. Not after being here."

The sentiment hits me square in the chest. I've been fighting that feeling my whole life. Trying to be a version of me that fits with Penny and my mom and Nora. Trying to be the version my dad hoped I could be. Realizing those Vivs don't even have the same taste in shoes.

"Those people will always be there for you," I tell him, because it's what I tell myself about Penny. "Regardless of who you become."

"And what you love about them won't change because of what you learn while here at Harker," Sophia says. "Badass hunters can still play D&D."

"And," Elliot adds, "you've got us now."

Peter grins at us, snaggletooth peeking out, and I can't help but grin back. We spend the rest of the night sharing stories about our lives back home, the classes we think we'll like, the ones we know we won't. I revel briefly in a version of me I haven't met until tonight. One who doesn't carry a backpack's worth of pretending to be something she's not everywhere she goes. I decide to go to the library tomorrow night. I'm too tired—surely I'd miss something.

And upstairs, in our dorm, I crawl into my twin bed across from a snoring Sophia and decide that Peter was right. I'm glad I gave it the day.

CHAPTER 11

THE NEXT DAY I wake just after the sun does. Wisps of light slant across my face, illuminating flecks of antique dust in our little cove of a dorm. It's early enough that I have time to make it to the apartment to grab some necessary clothes, bedding, and my half-frame, but late enough that Penny's already left for work when I arrive.

I give Hound some snuggles while I pack, allowing him to flop on top of me as if he's a much smaller dog. It's not like I won't come back once or twice over the entire semester, but not seeing his sweet eyes and excited butt wiggle every day is going to be a gut punch. When I'm back at Harker, I formally enroll in all of Sophia's classes.

I call Penny before my first class to tell her I'll be staying at Nora and Fiona's place for the next few months given how much work there is to do on the new exhibit. *I'll practically be living at the Windsor.* Not really a lie. She is, of course, completely understanding and asks if there's anything she can do to make my life easier. Gut punch number two.

I tell myself I'll tackle the Fiona of it all next week. For now,

I've told her my stomachache has become a full-blown stomach flu, but I'll need to come up with something better to take a break from the Windsor without losing my job.

I'm determined to make it to the library later tonight, but first I have to brave the second half of the course load Sophia and I share. Today we have Potions and Salves and Monster Identification I. Wednesday we have the same courses as Monday; Thursday is the same as today; and Friday are a couple of physical classes including Combat Training I with instructor dearest, Reid Graveheart. My body nearly crackles at the thought of squaring off with him again.

Sophia and I amble down the spiral staircase of Elkfore and past the preserved suit of armor in the foyer outside our commons. On the way to our first class, I take in even more of the campus—the white stone statues of past great hunters, the cobblestone courtyards and students playing chess beneath shady oak trees.

Our Potions and Salves classroom looks nothing like any of the ones we were in yesterday, especially Lisette's gothic basement annex. The velvet curtains and professor's jewel-toned desk chair in this classroom make it feel more like being inside a lava lamp than a historic castle like the rest of Harker. The twinkling blown-glass chandelier that hangs above casts speckled rainbow light on all the students' faces as they take their seats.

I recognize Professor Rosalind Dawnmere, our Potions and Salves teacher, as Lisette's gossamer-winged dinner companion from last night. Draped in layers of fluttering fabric, with pointed ears and skin as warm and brown as chestnut wood, Dawnmere waltzes into the classroom as if carried on the last wisp of a soft summer wind. She's taller than I expect a fairy to be—over six feet—and yet nimble and lithe and dainty beyond measure.

"Good morning, students," she says with a gentle smile, the slight edges of her lengthened canines peeking out. "And welcome again to Harker."

Her beauty seems to have stunned half the class, as the responses are croaked and awkward, if uttered at all. But Dawnmere doesn't look like she minds. She floats over to the blackboard and writes across it *salves, potions, oils*. "Let's start with something easy. An icebreaker, of sorts," Dawnmere says in a voice as light and sweet as meringue. "Which of these three would be best to use on your blade before you battle a siren?"

"A salve," a student in the front says without raising his hand. Matt Peverell, from Underworld Studies. "Because they're easier to brew and can temporarily remove a siren's ability to hypnotize you with their voice."

"Very close," Dawnmere says gently. "But sirens are sea creatures. So you're going to need something that won't be affected by the salt water. Oils, on the other hand—"

"I don't think you're right about that," Matt says, leaning back in his chair. "My dad's big on using salves on all his swords no matter the creature. Brews them at home with my mom."

The crystal chandelier overhead begins to shake ever so slightly. Sophia and I raise our eyes to it in concern.

"Well, Mr. Peverell," Dawnmere says, "there's absolutely a time and place for the right *kind* of salve, but oils—"

"My dad says oils lose their potency way faster than salves. Is that not true?"

"Mr. Peverell," Dawnmere warns through clenched teeth. "You might want to listen to the lesson before you—"

"But don't you think—"

Dawnmere's eyes glow a molten gold as the velvet drapes shudder with the weight of her fury. "Don't *interrupt me*!" she bellows, the chandelier above shattering, sending shards of glass raining down.

Matt blanches, ducking for cover. "Jesus Christ, lady—"

A goblet from the mantel launches on its own across the room toward his head. Matt dodges instantly—hunter instincts kicking in not a second too soon—and the goblet clangs against his wooden chair hard enough to knock the pens off his desk.

For a moment, the entire classroom goes as still as the dead.

"As I was saying," Dawnmere resumes lightly, tucking a lock of shiny hair behind her ear and releasing a slight giggle. "Oils aren't *soluble*, which means . . ."

Sophia and I sink back silently into our seats as the fairy continues, as effervescent and ethereal as a bubble floating through air.

UNLIKE THE JEWEL-TONED, gilded splendor of Dawnmere's class, Monster Identification is taught in a wallpapered room stuffed with bookcases, brass candleholders, and a hanging coat of arms. Professor Maxwell Crowley is already pulling a chair to the center of the room when we filter in, still a little shaken by Dawnmere's outburst.

"So, fairies are terrifying," Sophia says as we sit down next to Peter and Elliot. "Got it."

"Dawnmere?" Peter asks.

I nod, a bit too stunned to speak. When I pull my hair into a clip, a shard of glass tumbles out onto the desk.

"She's actually really sweet," Kitty tells us. "Just . . . don't piss her off."

"I will not be speaking at all in that class, then," Sophia says, opening her notebook.

"Wanna bet?" Elliot and I say at the same time before we share a surprised grin. Sophia only glares at us both.

"Good morning, class," Professor Crowley says. His voice is cool and light. He has a relaxed ease about him that I appreciate. Like the guy behind the counter in a tech store who helps you understand your phone. Between the dean's menace, Lisette's odd glares, and Dawnmere's outburst, the professors so far have been as fearsome as some of the creatures they're teaching us to battle. But Crowley's also got a mouthful of shiny metal, so who knows?

"How'd he lose all his teeth?" I whisper to Peter.

"Brood demon punched him so hard his entire jaw shattered."

"But apparently his teeth are now sterling silver," Elliot tells us. "So he can chew through any others who try to do the same."

Sophia nods her approval. "Sick."

"Monster Identification," Crowley tells us, sitting backward on his chair, arms slung casually over its back, "is going to be your simplest class."

Half the class chuckles; the rest seem nervous this is some kind of trap.

"I'll show you images and descriptions of all manner of deviants, and you'll take about six tests where you regurgitate the information. You don't have to brew anything, fight anyone, or analyze names, places, or dates. At Harker, Monster Identification is our math. It can get complicated, but one plus one is always two. If it's got fangs and drinks blood, it's . . . ?"

"A vampire," the class says in half-enthused unison.

"Beautiful," Crowley says with a quicksilver grin. "Killing it already."

I have to remind myself that every single hunter in this room is looking for their prey based on visual identification rather than an inherent sixth sense like I have as an aeon. The flash of red in a demon's eyes. The batwings on a succubus. The claws on a were.

Crowley explains how beasts and the undead are probably the easiest for a hunter to track down. Ogres, ghouls, dragons—they have no human form at all. Which means hunters can perceive them with eyesight alone. Vamps are pretty noticeable too, because, fangs. He goes on to explain how lycanthropes might be even more difficult to spot than demons. While demons' eyes will flash red with hunger or fury, Crowley says, we might not know we've got a werewolf on our hands until we catch one chowing down on a tentful of campers in the woods.

As Crowley continues to talk about how monsters are like math, the skin across my arms and legs pebbles. I swivel in my chair just in time to spy Dean Driscoll strolling in through a door at the back of the classroom, meaty arms crossed, with Reid in tow. He's in a Harker crew and athletic pants like an off-duty soccer player. I nudge Sophia and give her *What are they doing here?* eyes, but she only shrugs.

"Now," Crowley says, pulling an empty chair from the front row up beside him. "I'll tell you one way monsters are *not* like math. You can't get in the head of a fraction. Can't ask integers why they are the way they are. Or"—he shrugs—"maybe you can. I don't know, I'm not a math teacher. What I *do* know is that we have a rare opportunity here at Harker to speak to an actual deviant."

Some mild intakes of breath across the classroom. Students who, I'd imagine, don't yet know that a reformed demon (or one claiming to be) will be teaching their most important combat course.

"And not just any deviant, but a Brood demon."

"Ex," Reid says behind me. The entire room whips their heads in his direction. He doesn't even flinch. "Ex–Brood demon."

"Let's all give a warm welcome to Mr. Reid Graveheart."

The class claps mildly and Reid makes his way down the aisle to the chair beside Crowley. When he doesn't sit immediately, Crowley gives him an unreadable look until he does.

"Okay, rules are simple," Crowley tells us. "Don't be a dick. You ask something Mr. Graveheart or I deem inappropriate, you're out and I'll count your first test of the semester as a failure. If you don't think you can handle that for any reason, the door is right there, and you can return to class on Thursday, no harm no foul."

To my surprise, two different students from separate sections of the classroom quietly pack up their things and leave. I imagine at least one of them is just happy to have a free period, but when I see their faces, they don't look like they've gotten away with cutting class. They look scared. And ashamed, maybe, to *be* scared. One row ahead, I realize, a student's hand is shaking.

I guess it's entirely possible that none of these students have ever seen a demon before.

"Very well," Crowley says, turning to Reid. "Anything you want to say before we open it up?"

Reid's face is a mask of calm disinterest. "Nope."

"Didn't think so," Crowley mutters. "Who's first?"

CHAPTER 12

THE FIRST FEW questions are weak, in my opinion. What does being a demon feel like? *Tiring because I'm very old and have to deal with students with dull questions.* Do you have horns? *No.* Do you have claws? *Sometimes.* Can they really kill other demons just like silver? *Yes.* Why did you join the Brood? *It was what was expected of me.* Why did you leave the Brood? *Someone showed me a new way of seeing the world.* At that one, Reid's eyes find the dean's behind me, and I wonder what that could mean.

I'm not surprised when Kitty raises her hand. "What's the underworld like?"

Finally, Reid's brows lift. This question interests him. "Care to be more specific?"

Kitty frowns. "What is the average deviant's day-to-day in hell?"

Reid seems to think on this one for a moment. "No clue—I was born here on the mortal plane, just as you were, long after the Chasm was closed . . ." Reid's mouth twists as he thinks further about the question. It's as if he doesn't want her to go unrewarded for actually asking something brave. "But what I've heard from older deviants is that demons, at least, live quite well, despite the fire and brimstone. The lesser deviants and turned demons, not so much. You're either a torturer or the tortured."

A girl in the front row raises a tentative hand. "Why don't the highest echelon of demons live in their own domain?"

"Why would they? The underworld is a place of pain and suffering. And up here . . ." Reid looks out the window of Crowley's classroom, where leaves are just beginning to fall with the end of summer. "Deviants feed on life. Blood, souls, flesh. Sins, sex, drugs, violence, euphoria. It's all up here. There's a reason the lymantrians came down and, when the Chasm was opened, the deviants fled up. Everyone, on some level, wants to be as close to mortal as they can. Without ceding any power, of course."

The honesty surprises me. It's not too far-off from how I feel when I fall asleep wishing I could trade places with Penny.

A girl with a septum piercing raises her hand next to Sophia. "Could the demons even go back down to the underworld if they wanted to? I thought the Chasm was closed."

"It is closed. Demons are the only kind of deviant that *can* go back down to hell, but only with the body of the soul they've taken. A demon's purpose in the old world was to drink the souls of sinful mortals and shepherd them down to their fate. But now—after the Elders sealed the Chasm—even the High Thane and his Brood would be stuck in hell if they accompanied a soul down there. Not a risk anyone's taking just to see the old stomping grounds."

"Who rules down there, then? If the High Thane is on the mortal plane?"

"A sentinel has been stationed to keep order since the Chasm closed. Someone the High Thane trusts and, I'd assume, communicates with somehow."

"What's running the gauntlet consist of?" another student asks.

I whisper to Sophia, "What's the gauntlet?"

She leans over to whisper back to me and I get a whiff of grapefruit body spray. "Only way out of the underworld ever since the Elders sealed it up. I don't think any of the deviants who have attempted it have survived, so we don't know much."

Reid's answer is a similar sentiment. "I wouldn't know. Some research has pointed to it having something to do with the seven deadly sins."

But the student pushes, unsatisfied. "You don't have any friends from your Brood days who braved it and escaped hell?"

Something shadowed crosses over Reid's eyes. "No. I only ever met one vampire who had. Said it was a series of trials. That's all I got out of him. It . . ." Reid shifts in his chair. "He wasn't right, after that experience. Not sure it was worth leaving the underworld at all."

"So if deviants can run the gauntlet," Elliot says, when called on, "why do we refer to the Chasm as *closed*? Seems pretty open to me."

"Also looks pretty open," Sophia chimes in. "There's an enormous valley cutting through Astera, in case you missed it."

Some kids titter. Crowley doesn't shush them—in fact, a little slice of silver peeks out from his half grin—and I decide he's my favorite teacher so far.

"I'd imagine fewer than fifty deviants have made it through the gauntlet since the great war. That's not *open*. When the first High Thane split the Chasm open, it didn't look like it does now. Imagine a sea of fire running through Astera—rising tides of flame filled with deviants. This was the time of armadas. Not tourists handing out binoculars for five bucks a pop. *That* was open."

"So today, if your soul is taken by a demon," Kitty muses, "you'll be a demon condemned to hell unless you brave this impossible gauntlet, which ninety-nine percent of deviants who even try die attempting?"

For some reason, Peter's entire body tenses at Kitty's question. When she turns to him with an inquiring look, he only sinks lower into his seat.

Down in the center of the classroom, Reid nods, cold as ice. "Correct."

It's something my father warned me of many times. To be turned—reborn as a vampire or were—would be a fate worse than death. But to be sealed in the underworld for all eternity . . . a fate worse than anything at all. I try my best not to think of all the mortals and lymantrians who have had their souls stolen and are currently rotting away deep down below my feet.

"Are you saying heaven and hell are real?" one girl asks. "That our sins direct where we go after death?"

"I'm saying if your soul is consumed by a demon, you'll die and wake up in the underworld. The moral judgment piece hasn't played a part in thousands and thousands of years. Not since the old world. I don't know any more about that than your religious studies professors might."

"And what about when you die?" Sophia asks. "Or any other deviant?"

"When I die, I die," Reid says with a cold, unfeeling shrug. "Just like you. Nothingness. The void. No underworld. No heaven, either. But that's just what I believe."

"The true death," Sophia says, voice a little somber. "Since . . . you're all already kind of dead, right?"

"Do demons need souls to stay alive?" a cocky student in the back asks before Reid can respond. "Like vampires need blood?" His voice is smug, like he knows the question will make Reid uncomfortable.

But it doesn't. "Yeah."

More silence. A desk chair creaks.

Crowley grinds his silver teeth. "Maybe you can tell the students about the choice you've made, Mr. Graveheart."

"I don't take souls anymore," Reid says without an ounce of ego. He's not looking for a round of applause. "Which means I'll have a shorter lifespan. Thirty, maybe forty more years."

It's not a great loss, I tell myself. The guy's been around for hundreds already.

"And . . . ?" Crowley prompts.

"And I'm not as strong as I once was. As the demons you'll fight. Human souls grant an extraordinary amount of pow—"

One kid interrupts with, "Who's the High Thane?" My money's on Matt, but I can't see. A couple of his friends snicker. Crowley rolls his eyes.

"Who's the Zodiac Killer?" Reid says, gaze narrowed. "Fuck if I know."

"You never met him?" Matt presses.

"If I had, wouldn't I be hunting him down instead of sitting here, wasting my time with you?"

Silence spreads through the classroom. I wonder if I imagined Driscoll's gruff laugh behind us.

"Do humans see what we see?" The girl who asks is two rows in front of me and has already taken two full pages of notes. I look down at my blank page and purse my lips.

Reid weighs this one for a beat. "For the most part, no. Half-borns, beasts, and the undead cannot be seen by mortals. A selkie will look like a seal. A ghost, a ripple of wind. But turned deviants and demons who already appear like mortals can show their true selves to humans if they choose. Just as they can to you all. That's why there are humans who claim to have been bitten by vampires or chased by a werewolf in the woods." Reid crosses his arms and leans back. "Thankfully there are also humans who think they've been abducted by aliens."

"Can deviants sense hunters?" the same girl asks quietly.

"No," Crowley says just as Reid says, "Rarely."

Crowley shoots him a look, but Reid only shrugs. "I knew a demon once who could," Reid tells us. "He'd taken so many hunter souls, he said he could feel them coming a mile away. He's dead now, but . . ." Reid shakes his head. "Yeah, I don't know how he did it."

The words send a chill through me. A demon, or any deviant, knowing what we are would make our job next to impossible. And for some reason, the thought fills me with genuine rage. These are softball questions. This entire practice is only making these first years think demons are, at worst, grumpy, uninterested assholes. They should be *afraid*. For their safety, they should know what he's capable of.

My hand shoots into the air and Reid's eyes pierce mine. They are endless as they take in my face. My determination. He looks like he knows I'm going to skewer him. Good.

"Yes," Crowley says, motioning to me.

"Why's the dean here? I'm guessing he's not just big on Q and A's?"

Crowley stands, jaw tight. "Hey. I said—"

"The professors," Reid interrupts. "He's here because the professors didn't like this idea. Didn't want me on trial before the students. Or maybe they don't like me near the students at all. Dean Driscoll vouched for me and said he'd observe for the students' safety. That's what you wanted to hear, right, huntress? That I'm dangerous and need to be watched?"

Something about the nickname, said before the whole class,

turns my skin hot. If my question aimed to drag him through the mud, he took me down with him. I don't have time to think of a response before someone else has jumped in with their own question. But Reid's eyes keep sweeping over the class and landing back on me. It takes another two questions before I'm breathing evenly again.

When class ends, Reid leaves before the rest of the students. We're trudging up the stairs when I realize the dean is still standing by the door. "Viv Abbot," he says brusquely. "A word?"

Sophia makes an *ooh* sound, and I swat at her arm before I follow the dean down to the center of the room where Crowley teaches. I'm preparing myself to be kicked out of the class. It wouldn't be the first time I pissed off a professor. I chased down a changeling once at Belaire and knocked our algebra teacher over a cafeteria table. Earned myself a three-day suspension.

"Miss Abbot," the dean says. He's even more vicious-looking up close—those jagged scars, those tattoos you can't get anywhere but prison. "You don't have to like being taught by a demon, but you do have to show him respect."

"With all due respect to you, Dean Driscoll, I don't *have* to do anything. I didn't even know this place existed two days ago."

"But you're here now, and you're on my campus and in my classrooms. So you'll do as I say or you'll leave."

He's right, of course. But I'm not going to snivel my apologies, and I'm not going to tell him that looking at Reid reminds me of the men who brutalized my father, so I say nothing, hoping to end the conversation here.

"You don't think it's an advantage? To learn how to kill demons *from* a demon?" When I remain silent, Dean Driscoll only studies me, curiosity glinting in his nearly black eyes. "Can I tell you a story, Miss Abbot?"

"Is it about listening to authority?"

Driscoll can't help his chuckle. "The opposite."

"Hit me."

"I grew up in a mining town. Nobody there expected much of a kid like me, and I didn't give them much to expect. But I wanted to get out of that town something fierce. My father told me I didn't belong anywhere else but in the mines." Driscoll's eyes grow hard with the memory. "But I didn't want to be anything like my old man. How do you think he took that?"

I fold my arms across my chest. "Not great."

"He beat me senseless."

I chew my lip, the image of his childhood turning my stomach.

"But I had abilities. Abilities my father didn't have."

"You were a warlock."

"So I left. Even though they told me I'd never be anything. And years later, after being on my own for too long probably, I learned about this place. Once again, I was told the same thing. I'd never be a student here. I didn't belong."

I see where this story is going, but find I have no more bitterness left in the tank. The guy's been through some shit. I'd have known that even without story time.

"But I proved them wrong too. Joined in with a group of students here who became my best friends. Protected this school with my life. Won tournaments. Fought beasts. Became its dean. And still, you think the Elders treat me with the respect they employ toward their hunters? The other professors?"

"Of course not."

"Of course not," he echoes darkly. "Especially not when I vouch for an ex-Brood. People don't like people who make them question their own biases. They don't like looking their own judgments in the eye. But your job as a hunter, Miss Abbot, is to do just that. To make sure you have the right read on everyone you encounter. Good, evil, lymantrian, deviant, mortal. Your misjudgment of Mr. Graveheart isn't just foolish. It's making you worse at what you do. And I know you don't want that."

I have nothing to say in argument. I'm starting to see why the students cheer for this guy. "You're the person who pulled him out of the Brood, huh?"

Dean Driscoll stands from the desk he was perched on and heads for the exit. Halfway up the aisle, he says, "Why don't you ask him?"

CHAPTER 13

BY THE TIME Kitty, Sophia, and I finish doing homework in the Elkfore commons on Thursday, it's midnight. They trot off to bed, bleary-eyed, with pen ink in the creases of their hands, but I stay put. The communal room is empty—just me, the olive-colored sofa, a baby grand piano, and the crackling, dwindling fireplace. Streaks of soft moonlight float through wide windows and paint the commons' oxblood walls and overstuffed bookcases.

I'm so tired I could pass out right here on this oversized couch, but Peter told me a few days ago that the library is open until two in the morning, and this may be my best shot to look into my dad without running into any other students. This first week has been better—more *fun*, if I'm honest—than I expected, but I came here with a single goal in mind, and it's time I actually work toward it.

Thin leaves snap beneath my boots as I duck out of Elkfore and head toward Mortimer Tower. The moon shines blue against my skin, and the night air's got a bite to it. I'm not sure if that's due to the arrival of fall or the chill of Harker's crumbling stone walls. I haven't seen this much of the campus after dark. We've mostly kept to the dining hall, the commons, and the gym. All the shutters and curtains are drawn in the windows across the many buildings except those of the library, which glow like kernels of gold.

In the pools of lantern light beneath the rotunda, a handful of second years, led by Professor Crowley, pass through the gateway. They whoop and holler, presumably returning from a raid. A successful kill beneath their belts. Envy stirs in me and I walk faster, less tired than I was before.

The silently flickering oil lamps and the stretching shadows of looming towers have me wrapping my long coat tighter across my body. I'd kill for a scarf. Honestly, I'd kill just to kill. It's been almost a week since the subway demon. I'm starving for more, and it's only going to get harder to abide by Harker's archaic rules.

Which is the exact reason I find myself in the Lymantrian Biology section—not Harker History. Bathed in light from a Tudor-style desk lamp, the cramped text I select offers me nothing on curbing hunter cravings. Probably because regular hunters don't have these kinds of urges. Only aeons. Only me.

When I realize *Hunters: Through the Ages* isn't going to deliver jack squat, I peruse two other books beneath an arched window, moonlight gilding their yellowed pages, and come up empty. It's like every book with information on aeons has been removed from the library. Or moved to those archives Peter told me about, with the other classified texts. Something low and broken begins to coil inside me.

Not because there's no way to calm the bloodlust—but because none of these hunter books even take it into consideration. Like no lymantrians have ever wished to change the darkness within themselves. The loneliness of the thought isn't new, but it is cutting. *You're the only shitty hunter on earth, Viv. You're the only one who feels like you need to kill. You hunt for the wrong reasons. You aren't good.*

I'm about to put this musty old book down and get back to my original plan when my eyes land on seven little words:

Some dark magic can remove hunter genetics.

My mouth goes dry. Dark magic is not something I want to get involved in. For magic to be classified as *dark*, that means a sacrifice is required. I don't even want to crave the kill in the first place. But still . . . I scan the page for more, only to find nearly all of it blacked out in giant inky strokes. The book's been censored.

I slam the book closed, and the sound echoes through the vacant library, a cloud of dust coating my skin. I tell myself it doesn't matter. I came in here tonight to find more about my dad's time here, not how to curb my aeon instincts. I peruse the Harker History section for a yearbook from 1992, just like my locket says. Sure enough, I find it, as faded and weighty as I expect.

I flip past pages of smiling students, lacrosse games, heartfelt tributes to alumni lost, until finally I reach the first years. But there's no photo of my dad under *A* for Abbot. I look under *D* for David in case hunters do yearbooks differently, but no dice. Unease pooling, I start back at the top and read through all the names. There were only five hundred kids in his graduating class, and I've got nothing but time.

When I find the photo of my dad—my same dark hair and gray eyes but a warmer, better smile, which he got from his mom and I was not lucky enough to inherit—I think some hunter on the yearbook committee must have gotten themselves into serious hot water. They've put him in the wrong section, under *C*. Right there, beneath his photo, is his name. David. David Cadell.

Except that's *not* his name.

I've never seen that last name before in my life. My father's name was David Abbot. Cadell wasn't even my mother's maiden name. And I don't know what my grandmother's maiden name was . . . I read it again to be sure, but there it is, clear as the light pouring over the washed-out pages. *Cadell.*

Which means if this wasn't an editorial error . . . my dad must have adopted a new name either when he came to Harker or . . . after he left.

"Those are Broods," I say, voice shaking. "You told me to run when we see them."

My father's eyes crinkle with something I don't recognize. "And you should. Always. But I can't keep running forever, kitten."

I shake the hazy memory from my mind. The sound of the roiling sea. The salty tears on my lips. I always thought he meant he couldn't run from the Brood because he was a hunter, and hunters don't run from a fight. But maybe he meant something else that night he died. Maybe he was hiding from someone. On the run. Enough to change his name sometime after graduation.

"*You,*" he says. "*After all this time . . . At least tell me why.*"

My head begins to pound. I came here—to Harker, to the library tonight—for answers. Not more questions.

But I'm not giving up. Maybe I can search those records in the archives. The ones the Citadel uses to keep track of all the hunters out there. I'll look up David Cadell and see if that gets me anywhere. Peter said a staff key card is required to access them. I'll just have to get my hands on one of those.

As I'm clicking off the desk lamp, a woman's voice says, "Isn't it a little late for studying, Miss Abbot?"

My eyes snap up to find Professor Lisette hovering over me, flashlight pointed in my face. I hadn't even noticed all the lights had winked out hours ago. I bring my hands up to shield my eyes. "You're going to fry my retinas. What is that thing, nine thousand watts?"

She lowers the beam of light but only enough to guide it over the stack of books I've got on the antique desk before me. Hunter genetics. This dated yearbook. "Now, what class could this be for?" Her eyes bore into me behind her glasses like she knows I'm up to no good.

This woman gives me the creeps. Being around her feels like déjà vu or someone saying something aloud you know you've dreamed before. I throw on my coat, shoving my phone and dorm key into my bag. "Just trying to stay on top of everything in my first week."

I move to scoot past her, but Lisette steps directly into my path. She's in silky pants and pointed shoes, which might be pajama bottoms and slippers or a very expensive ensemble for a quirky professor's dinner party.

"I don't recall you taking Yearbook or Biology this semester."

"What is with everyone in this school shoving their nose into my business? Am I some kind of campus celebrity? *Look, it's the girl from Astera! She had no idea this school existed! She isn't in Biology this semester!*"

Professor Lisette doesn't look remotely amused. "It would behoove you to keep out of trouble, Miss Abbot. Danger tends to find hunters wherever they are. Only a foolish one would go looking for it."

Before I can wrap my head around her warning, Lisette clicks off her flashlight, drowning us both in pitch-darkness. When my eyes adjust to the faint moonlight, she's long gone, and I'm left with nothing but the fading thud of my heartbeat.

CHAPTER 14

BY THE END of my first week at Harker, the summer's heat has finally faded. When our little group steps out of Elkfore, my nose fills with the scent of moss and still-fresh morning dew. It's always colder at this hour, especially on a soupy-gray early September day such as this one, but even still, I wonder if the shiver down my spine can really be chalked up to the shift in seasons.

The lengthy walk to the coliseum on Friday morning takes us past that smiling photo of my dad and his teammates outside the gateway. It's like the locket around my neck—a reminder that he's always with me. Not only his memory but all I still don't know about him. I stare at the photo and try to reconcile the cheering twentysomething with the man who raised me. Who died to protect me. Who changed his name and was on the run and never told me why.

As we stalk past Harker's stonework bell tower—haunted and alluring, with horned gargoyles and spires atop it—I try to put thoughts of last night's discovery from my mind. I'm going to need every ounce of focus for the week's final class. Combat Training taught by Reid. Irritation tightens my chest.

Outside the walls of Old Campus, we stride away from the

wide, silent lacrosse field and sudden, sprawling cemetery wrapped in wrought-iron gates. When we cross the low stone bridge over Hellebore Lake, there's an early-autumn mist crawling over the dark, glassy water.

"Whoa," Sophia murmurs. She's bundled in some guy's oversized hoodie.

"Fucking. Awesome," Elliot breathes.

Kitty and I can't help but grin at each other. Peter gulps.

In the distance, the crumbling arena rises into the morning fog. Like the ancient Roman Colosseum, with sunlight slanting through columns and arches. A feat of human architecture, history, and bloodshed.

We tramp through wildflowers and over slopes of matted grass until the meadow becomes a footpath again. Wide, craggy planes of stone lead to the soaring coliseum and I crane my neck up as we walk in. The giant oval reminds me of Harker's ancient amphitheater. Now I see what Peter was saying: The gothic elements of the school—all the collegiate red brick and iron candelabras—are layered like a collage on top of a far older canvas.

Looming columns surround the space, with victory banners of navy and gold lining the edges of the wide-open ceiling. Sparring championships, hard-won team battles. There are no tools or training pads or equipment in here like there are in the gymnasium. Just the clouds high above and the chalky arena at my feet. At first I think it's sand, but upon closer inspection I realize I'm walking on fine pebbles. Stone that's been pulverized over many years. No doubt coated in hunter blood, sweat, and tears.

We file onto the lowest steps of the steep stone seating that wraps around the arena floor alongside the other students. There are only about thirty of us in this class by my quick count.

"Morning, students," a deep voice echoes through the vast stadium.

My heart pounds in answer. I've come to recognize Reid's masculine growl—a more-than-aggravating realization.

He's wearing loose athletic sweats and a sleeveless black shirt. With his charming brown curls and muscled biceps, he looks like a nineties heartthrob. I can't reconcile the way his sharp jaw and defined forearms make me feel with the brand on his neck. I try to imagine Reid in his demonized form—with barbed wings and claws and a tail. It doesn't really compute.

"In your other classes, you'll learn how and when and why to fight deviants," Reid says. "Here, you'll actually fight one."

Some students shift around me. I hear a few intakes of breath. Not everyone here is taking Crowley's Monster Identification class this semester. Some of them didn't know that Reid was a demon. It's not like his eyes are flashing red at the scent of hunter souls. He's better trained than that.

"Find a partner and come down to the arena floor."

Sophia quirks a brow at me. "Partners?"

"Sure." I turn to Peter, who's begun to sweat a little at his temples. Kitty's already paired off with a girl behind us. "Why don't you partner with Elliot?"

"Yeah." Elliot grins, biceps flexing. "I promise not to crush your glasses."

"I don't wear glasses," Peter mutters.

"Are you sure?" Elliot asks. "I feel like you should."

"He'll go easy on you," I say, remembering how we sparred.

Elliot grasps Peter by the shoulders and leads him down to the arena floor. "I'm a gentle giant. Scout's honor."

We stomp down after them and pair off. Reid strolls past the groups to give each a slip of black fabric. When he gets to Sophia and me, he hands one to her without looking in my direction.

"As hunters," he says to the class, "you're gifted with heightened hearing, sense of smell, agility, and one hell of a gut instinct. To hone those senses, you can't rely only on what you see. We'll start with one member of each pairing blindfolded at a time. For those without the blindfold, remember this is *sparring*. Don't go straight for the tap out. Give your partner a chance to adjust to their new senses."

I raise a pitying brow at Sophia. *I'll go easy on you, pookie.* She shakes her head like *Don't you dare.*

"All right, blindfolds on," Reid commands. "Get to it. And no weapons."

Sophia groans beside me. "This is so fucking dumb. When am I going to fight a demon blindfolded?"

"I'll do it," I tell her with a laugh, taking the fabric from her hands. I bend over to stretch my back before tying the strip over my eyes. The chilly morning winks out into pitch-darkness.

"You ready?" she asks. Without my sight, her voice takes on a more sultry, feminine rasp. I'm picking up on the pitch of her breathing, the shuffle of footsteps beside me, the sound of Peter's pained grunt, Reid's low chuckle . . .

"Gimme a sec," I breathe.

This is actually harder than I thought it would be. I try to focus. My meditation app mocks me from my phone. Maybe my dad was onto something with that.

"Any day now, huntress," Reid drawls. The low register of his voice slides up the nape of my neck. I shake my shoulders out until I've cleared him from my senses, and then I leap at Sophia, fists raised.

The sound of her exhale guides me left. I listen closely as her feet slide over the arena's pebbled floor. Dust kicks up in her wake and filters into my nose, the scent of chalk masking dried blood. Demon blood, maybe. Like Elliot's brothers said. Just flecks of iron now, after all these years.

My instincts send me ducking low as Sophia's fist flies overhead. I can hear her grunt when she misses me like it's being broadcast into my ear canal. I can taste her sweat in the air.

Somewhere, I can hear a student asking Reid a question.

When he doesn't answer, the kid asks again.

"Sure," he says. He sounds distracted, his voice pointed in my direction. He's watching me.

I dodge Sophia's next blow and swing my fist where I sense her hair rippling in the wind. I only make contact with the strands.

She laughs behind me. "You look like you're going after a piñata without the stick."

But when I drive my fist toward the sound of her voice, I catch her in the solar plexus. I remember her shirt barely covers her navel when my knuckles smack toned abs and the edge of a belly ring. "How does it feel to be my piñata?"

"Not excellent," she groans.

Somewhere behind us, Reid growls to a student, "You think this is funny?" The low, rumbling fury in his voice renders both Sophia and me still.

"I'm a hunter," some kid responds to him. "I'm taking any advantage I can get, right?"

I lift the blindfold from my eyes and the unfiltered sun blinds me. I squint and blink until I feel less like an ant under a magnifying glass, and the coliseum comes back into view.

Only then do I see Reid towering over Matt. In Reid's iron grip is the handle of a switchblade, and on the ground, Matt's sparring partner is clutching her bloody, dripping fingers.

"You knifed your blinded classmate through the hand."

"She should've seen me coming."

Sophia and I sigh in tandem. *Hunters.*

Reid nods to himself, taking in Matt's words. Then he hands him back the knife as well as the blindfold. "So you should have no issue seeing me coming."

Matt lifts his hands in defense. "Well—"

"No," Reid cuts him off. "Not a question."

When Matt takes his time standing up, Reid barks, "Hurry up."

No one resumes their sparring. In fact, a bit of a circle has formed around Matt and Reid, as if they're about to have a schoolyard tussle.

"Put the blindfold on and take me down," Reid instructs Matt.

"Can't really without my silver."

Matt's a prick, but I don't totally disagree with the sentiment. My aeon blood has begun to pump and whirl. I want in on this fight.

Reid doesn't smirk. His cheeks don't redden in fury. He takes another blindfold from his back pocket and ties it across his own forehead. Before he slides it down over his eyes, he orders, "Take me down."

Once they're both blindfolded, Matt sniffs the air like a dog, nostrils flaring as he tries to pick up Reid's scent. He flexes his fingers and then coils them into fists, adjusts his stance, and charges. But it's all wrong. He's barreling too fast toward his moving target. He's doing the opposite of the lesson—he isn't using any of his senses.

It happens so fast I could cough and miss it: Reid moves out of his way with ease, catches Matt by the scruff of his neck like a newborn puppy, lifts him up, and slams him down to the arena floor with a bone-crunching *smack*.

Sophia physically jolts at the sound. Kitty's and her sparring partner's eyes both widen in awe. Peter and Elliot behind us make twin sounds of sympathetic agony. *Ouch.*

But I'm sick, twisted. Always have been. Like the moment I saw that smushed beetle on the skin of my foot. My body tightens and my mouth goes dry. I can *feel* my pupils dilate.

I want in, I want in, I want in—

Matt moans into the white stones beneath him. *"Asshole."*

"Up," Reid says, rolling his shoulders, blindfold still on. "Try again."

"No," Matt snaps from the floor, ripping his blindfold off. "This is stupid. Allowing a demon to beat the shit out of us? I bet this is like some kind of kink for you."

My eyes crawl over the blood dripping from Matt's mouth where he's bitten through his lip. The sheen of sweat on Reid's shoulders. My daggers are calling to me from my bag in the stands.

"Well." Reid crouches down, inches from the kid. He can't see, and yet he knows exactly where he is. He lowers his voice. "That did feel pretty good."

Somewhere, I can just hear the heart of the girl who took Matt's switchblade to the palm absolutely fluttering. *My hero,* she's thinking. *My demon hero.*

Matt growls and moves to punch Reid square in the face. It's poor sportsmanship on many levels—he's no longer blindfolded, but Reid still is. Plus, the fight's clearly over. Still, his fist flies out and I suck in a strange inhale. In the split second before his fist connects, I can't tell if I want it to land or not. But it's not up to me. Reid dodges easily and stands, lifting his blindfold to glare at Matt.

"Anyone else?" Reid asks, arms open to the class. "I don't bite."

Was that a joke? Did perpetually broody Reid make a deviant joke?

For a moment, silence sails across the coliseum, the only sound from Matt's ragged breaths.

My skin is hot. Sweat is gathering behind my knees and under my arms.

"Me," I say, stepping forward.

Reid looks me over, from my dusty sneakers to my Harker sweatshirt and low bun. I know he's thinking about that night in the alley. "A rematch already?"

"I probably need my back realigned anyway." I shrug. "Do your worst."

Reid gestures for me to join him, and I try not to stare at his hand or his long fingers or the way the blindfold on his head pushes his unruly hair from his face. I pull my sweatshirt off and toss it to the ground. I'm only wearing a sports bra underneath, though I don't think I'm working with enough up top for it to look X-rated. Still, someone—my money's on Elliot—hoots when I stretch my arms overhead.

But I can't take my eyes off Reid. Or perhaps I can't take my eyes off the way *he* can't take his eyes off *me*. His gaze simmers—that fire-laced navy blue—as it crawls over my newly exposed skin. It's as if he can't help himself. My senses are so heightened I swear I can hear his breaths coming out tighter. I want to say something nasty—something that'll humiliate him in front of all his students—but I'm too caught up in my own shame.

How it feels to be turned on and bloodthirsty at once. How I want to drive my silver daggers into his demon flesh and feel him pump his fingers in and out of me. Maybe at the same time.

Wrong. *Sick.* So wrong and so sick, and this is why I need to get this fight out of my system. This is why Harker's rules against hunting were not made for my aeon kind.

I slip my blindfold back over my eyes. I square my feet and—

"Not so fast," Reid breathes across from me.

I stall any movements when I feel the pebbled ground shift as he walks over.

"There'll be no more cheating in my class."

"I'm not—"

But then his smell engulfs me. Lemongrass and male sweat and evergreens. His hands come around the back of my head, and he unties my blindfold only to tie it tighter. Every hair on my head that he touches tingles on my scalp. His body is so warm behind me. My breaths funnel in and out in a rush. Being this close to a demon and not hacking at him is sending my senses into overdrive. I wonder if it's the same for him with me.

"Whenever you're ready," he says roughly, rounding in front of me.

I don't ask if his blindfold is on. I know it is. I take one steadying breath. And then I move.

My fists drive toward that zingy evergreen scent. Crisp, like a summer wood. Peeling bark and lemon peels and spruce leaves. But I hear his sidestep, hear his fist snap out in my direction. I twist to the right just in time to listen as his knuckles connect with the stone column behind me. A low curse barrels from his mouth. His breath fans over my face.

My next strike is quicker, a jab toward where I think his ribs are, but I'm met only with empty air and then a swift kick from him that takes my legs out from under me. I fall to my hands and knees, pain singing through bones and muscle. That sense is heightened too—and the pain is nearly as loud in my ears as the gasps of my classmates echoing in the arena.

Anger drives me upward, and my next punch is a literal swing in the dark. He blocks me with his palm, and the sensation of our skin touching ripples up my arm.

Another blow, another block. My next kick slices into thin air.

He's too agile, too clever. He knows every move before I make it. He knows every move before *I* even know I'm going to make it.

"You were close, though," he breathes, as if inside my thoughts. "So close."

His voice is a little warm. A little playful. As if he's having fun as he dodges and ducks. Despite my sawing breaths, I've not made contact once.

Demon quick and Brood trained, even my hunter senses—my *aeon* senses—can't keep up with him. His next blow sends me down hard onto my shoulder. I know instantly the pain isn't something I'm bouncing back from quickly. It radiates through my entire arm, down my side, and over my back. I have no shot of dodging his next punch as I roll on the floor in agony, and I flinch behind the blindfold, bracing for the hit, only to hear it land with a crunch in the stone, inches from my head.

Breathless, I yank the blindfold off and find him panting above me. He lifts his blindfold, and those turbulent blue eyes drill into mine so savagely I forget to breathe.

Then he stands and rips his shirt off over his head in that one-handed way that men do. "Class dismissed."

I ease myself up and grab my sweatshirt, then hobble back over to the stands. My shoulder aches, and I clutch it as I limp to put less pressure on my spasming back muscles.

"You were badass out there," Sophia tells me, taking my bag so I don't have to carry it.

Elliot nods his approval. "Like a blind warrior queen."

Kitty's jaw is tight with empathetic frustration. "You almost had him."

The three of them look at Peter as if it's his turn. He only shrugs, sheepish. "I couldn't watch."

We gather our stuff, and I trudge toward the exit, touched to find my friends moving as slowly as I am rather than leaving with the rest of the class. We're nearly out in the dew-covered morning, where I can lick my shameful wounds in peace, when we're stopped by Reid's booming voice. "Valentine, Briggs, and Thompson."

Sophia, Kitty, and Elliot turn, tension in all their shoulders as if they've been caught with their hands in Reid's cookie jar. He's still shirtless and sweating, his face that same mask of cold intensity.

"I'd like you three to join my Field Training class."

"What?" I balk. I don't want to spend any more time with Reid than I have to, but I held my own out there with him and I don't get the invite to do what I've been doing since I was *seven*?

"Of course," Kitty says, standing an inch taller. "It would be an honor."

"I'm there." Elliot grins.

Sophia cuts one look in my direction, brows knitting inward, before she says, "Me too."

Peter looks down at his shoes.

But my blood is hot in my veins. "What about me?"

Reid's defined ab muscles contract as his gaze lands on my shoulder. "You're not ready."

"Not ready? I'm better than anyone here."

"Hey, now," Sophia says at the same time Elliot mutters, "Ooo-kay." I don't even dare to look at Kitty.

"You're thoughtless," Reid says. "You take too many risks. Fight with your heart. Not your head."

"What kind of bad action-movie bullshi—"

But Reid's already grabbing his bag from the stands, uninterested.

"God *damn* him," I breathe as we turn to leave. Sophia squeezes my shoulder in support and I wince.

We're a few feet from the exit when Reid calls out, "Huntress."

I turn, body rigid in both pain and frustration. I'm about to swing at him all over again.

"Ice bath for the shoulder. Arnica on your back." And then he stalks out, his lean muscles rippling as he walks.

I'm so surprised, I can't muster a reply. The bright morning chill seeps into my bones as I stand there, dumbfounded.

"Oh no," Sophia says under her breath.

"What is it?" Peter asks.

"I'm attracted to him."

"Soph!" Elliot says with a laugh, shoving her into me. My shoulder sings in pain, and I focus on the tall grass at our feet and all the weeping dewdrops.

"Trust me," she says, her copper-and-flaxen ponytail swaying in the September morning light. "I'm as disappointed as you are."

CHAPTER 15

AFTER THREE WEEKS of school with no luck snagging a professor's key card to access the archives, an impossible essay on harpies hanging over my head for Lisette, and enough sparring bruises to qualify me as a leopard, I find myself agonizing over—of all things—my outfit for dinner at the Pine house. I rub my shoulder as I study my shoes. Two ice baths and a trip to the infirmary for arnica later, my shoulder still aches, but at least it looks less like the plums you avoid in a supermarket.

I'm not stressing out over my attire because of James's parents. I'm stressing because of *mine*. My mom is going to be there, and nothing I've ever worn has pleased her. I've decided on sheer black tights, a miniskirt, and a cashmere sweater. Still in the dark colors I'm most comfortable in—maroon, gray, black—but hopefully achieving that refined old-money look my mom so appreciates. I opt for shiny black loafers, which match my slicked-back ponytail. My small gold watch is on display, and I make a note to tuck my father's silver locket inside the crew neck of my sweater.

"You look really nice," James tells me when he picks me up from the Windsor.

I wish Pen and I were driving together and could practice meditative words of affirmation. Granted, Penny doesn't suffer like I do at the hands of her parents—the Pines find our apartment in Babylon "quirky" and "bohemian"—but I'd appreciate the moral support nonetheless.

"Thanks," I tell James. "You too."

He's in a loden sweater and his hair is slicked back. James Pine at his Piniest. He looks good.

"My dad invited some friends of his to join tonight. Had to bring my A game."

Fabulous. More blue bloods.

We drive for twenty minutes, up higher and higher, before I see the freeway signs denoting that we're over the hill. I have the sudden urge to stick my head out the car window and feel the whipping air on my face. All I want is a ninety-mile-per-hour wind to wreck my hair and streak my eye makeup under that sliver of moon. I want to scream into the night until my lungs ache, knowing I'm moving too fast for any sound to carry.

But I don't, of course. I sit still and feel James's curious eyes on me. His driver takes the exit marked **Hesperides**, and I try to relax my entire body like my meditation app instructs. Vertebra by vertebra. When I give in and turn toward my boyfriend, the streetlights paint his encouraging face in menacing streaks of gold and gray. In this light he looks almost deviant. I know I'm sick, because I find myself reaching for his hand because of it.

I wish I could say the Pine house is a monstrosity. But it's neither garish nor over-the-top. It's as perfect as the rest of the lives in the Hesperides. Just the right amount of flawless, with enough homey touches to still classify it as a house and not a castle.

I follow James down the flagstone pathway, past manicured hedges and the fountain with the marble angels that squirt water from rounded cheeks. Penny's parents' security men nod their greetings—the Pine manor is about as well protected as the artifact room at the Windsor—and I get a good chuckle out of imagining any of these ex-Navy guys going up against a soul-hungry demon. We're let into a foyer full of neutral sculptures and suede furniture that's never been sat on—as well-designed as my mother's closet.

And speaking of—

Beatrice Abbot strolls in to greet us with the elegance of Grace Kelly and the warmth of an industrial freezer. Baby-blue sweater set, pleated white pants. Red nails, dark hair. She looks like an American flag, as I guess any aspiring politician should.

"James," she coos. Two kisses, one for each cheek.

"The case you won this week was something, Beatrice. Our whole firm is in awe of you."

Sometimes I can't tell what annoys me more: the sinking feeling that James is closer to my family than I am, or the fact that he'll take any excuse for more face time with my mom, including dating me.

"Hi, kiddos," Penny's mother coos, wandering in after my mom. With her barrel-curled hair, feathery lashes, and cheery smile, you'd never be able to tell she's battling MS. I give her a warm squeeze.

"We brought wine," James tells his mother, handing her a bottle of merlot that costs more than my rent.

"A great pick." Laura Pine nods, giving the wine to their housekeeper, Marta. "Open this for everyone, will you?"

Another cliché debunked—Marta didn't raise Penny. Her parents were present for all her soccer games and high school plays. Meanwhile, nobody was at my plays. Not my working mom, not my dead dad, not even me—I was ditching school to take out banshees and then making up stories about getting stuck in the dressing room before curtain call.

"Viv," my mom greets me, brushing a stray hair from my brow. "How are you? Fiona tells me you've been out sick for weeks. James tried to bring you soup, but you weren't home?"

Images of Harker's tall arches and textbooks labeled *Modern Ghoul-Hunting: No Ghostbusters Here* fill my mind. "I was probably at urgent care. But I'm actually feeling much better n—"

My mom's tight bob sways with the force of her shaking head. "You're never going to be asked to work the exhibit if you keep missing days."

She's right. It's time I figure out something more airtight than being ill for the next semester. "I know, I'm sorry."

"That skirt is nice on you, though," she says, as if appropriate style is decent consolation for physical illness.

Still, I'm rendered speechless. Like a teen with a crush, my heart wallops. "Really?"

She nods. "I know how hard it can be for you to put in this kind of effort."

There it is. "Thanks, Mom."

I move past her and toward the living room as she scoffs. "What did I say?"

The argument plays out in my head as it has a hundred times before:

Why do you have to insult me any chance you get?
How did I insult you? You don't like to dress up!
Why does it matter if I like to dress up?
I just want you to look presentable!
Why does it matter that I look presentable, though? These people are practically family.

Why are you always so sensitive, Viv? I can never say anything right around you.

I bypass the entire potential exchange and opt for a double pour from Marta instead.

In the living room, Vivaldi is playing and enough candles are lit to make me feel like I'm in a home goods store. The scent of sandalwood is actually so intense I dip my nose into my wineglass in an attempt at relief. My heightened sense of smell is good for tracking, not so much for overlit dinner parties.

"Might want to slow down," James tells me with a warm smile. "Alcohol isn't great for a stomach virus."

"I'm actually just . . ." What? Having a huntress sensory overload to his mom's Nancy Meyers living room scent? "Thirsty."

James gives me a curious look before signaling to Marta. "Would you mind getting Viv some water?"

"Stop," I tell him, mortified. "I can get my own water."

"So testy," Nora says, standing from the pristine white couch. My sister's perfect bone structure and cropped dark hair fill my face as she pulls me into a tight, quick hug. "You okay?"

No, I had to come here. "Yes, of course. Hi."

Fiona wanders in, and to my pleasant surprise, her wave from across the room doesn't come with commentary on how healthy I look or questions of whether I'll be back at work next week. Though I'd imagine that's because all eyes are on Caspar Harlock, the unexpected addition to tonight's dinner. In fact, James abandons me with my sister—the biggest of boyfriend faux pas—to procure some face time with the Harlock Group's CEO.

Caspar stands by the mahogany bar, listening as Penny's father, Stan, tells him a story I can guarantee lacks any point at all. Pontificating, hands spread wide, potbelly pressing forcefully against an Italian leather belt. Penny stands beside him, nodding dutifully, not an ounce of irritation in those big green eyes. Bless her.

While Penny's father is stout and round, Caspar is tall and broad-shouldered with the kind of lukewarm good looks I imagine all multimedia billionaires have. His heavy brows are graying along with his thick hair, and even in his loosened tie, grasping his tumbler of scotch, I can't imagine he's ever taken it easy a moment in his life. He was the most cutthroat baby in the nursing ward, I'm sure of it.

When you grow up around one of the richest families in the country, you meet a lot of Caspar types. But Caspar Harlock is the worst Caspar type—the most money, the least interest in helping those less fortunate than him. The fact that my own boyfriend can't see that does more than boil my blood. I watch James nod along with performative enthusiasm—honestly, he looks more eager now than when we have sex.

I hate it here.

When my mom passes by, Caspar pulls her into a greeting that churns my stomach. He's far too friendly and spending far too long telling her how *radiant* she looks tonight. Despite my mom never remarrying—or even really dating, to my knowledge—Stan Pine's been trying to set the two of them up for years. Thankfully, while my mom is half the woman she was before my dad died, at least she's not the kind of woman who sleeps with a powerful man for political gain.

Wish I could say the same for my boyfriend.

Fiona stops on her way over to us to say hi to my mom, so, for long, torturous moments, Nora and I are left alone by the couch in silence. I wonder if it might make a decent photograph—a family portrait, if you will: me observing my wine as if there's some wisdom to be found in the swirls of dark red liquid, Nora checking her

Rolex. We have nothing in common despite twenty-plus years of being sisters.

Seconds tick by with no reprieve from the discomfort. We are stranded on Conversation Island with no life raft. Penny, where art thou?

"How's work?" I manage. There we go—normal human interaction achieved.

"The foundation just secured a second round of funding for our Astera Fights Poppy initiative," Nora says, eyes lighting up a bit. "We've raised almost four million dollars toward helping the Astera PD take down crime lords like the White Stag."

Nora's a high-ranking executive at one of the most successful nonprofits in the country, the Astera City Foundation Against Crime, or ACFAC. My entire miserable black-sheep persona would be so much more righteous if my family weren't putting away criminals and taking care of the less fortunate. Charitable jerks.

"You're going to get poppy off the street," I tell Nora. "Mom will be thrilled."

When Nora purses her lips like she's doing now, she actually looks just like her. "That's rude."

"What?"

"Come on, Viv."

"I didn't mean anything by it."

"Are we not over the jealousy thing yet?"

My cheeks heat as I grip my wineglass. "I'm *not*—"

"I don't have the energy for one of your mood swings tonight." She sighs. "It's been a really long day."

My fury pulses until I hear a shattering sound. Only a second later do I realize I've crushed my wineglass in my palm and doused the white carpet in rich merlot. "Fuck."

Laura Pine's shriek could probably be heard in the underworld.

"I'm sorry," I mumble, kneeling down to pick up the glass.

"No, no," she says as she shuffles over. "You could make it worse. Marta?"

Poor Marta hurries over with an arsenal of cleaning supplies, and I back away slowly as if there's a gun aimed right at me. My mother offers a quiet apology to Laura.

"Don't worry," Penny says to her mom with warmth and ease. "I can get it right out. The kids I teach spill things far worse than wine every day." She ushers Marta off her knees and takes over, offering me a reassuring smile. "Look, baking soda cures all."

My pulse subsides a bit in my veins. I love that girl so damn much.

I hear James say something about how the glass must've had a crack in it. Nora's already back on her phone, disinterested, but my mother . . . She's staring at me like I'm the Antichrist. I get that feeling sometimes, like she knows there's something rotten inside me. It's not too different from the look she gave me the night I returned home without my father. Like maybe she hates me because she's afraid.

Dinner is a formal affair with perfectly sauteed vegetables and steamed fish with more garnish than I have accessories. Nobody speaks to me—not even my boyfriend, who's too busy telling my mother about his firm's latest PR crisis, involving some philandering news anchor. Penny's seated all the way at the other end of the table, though she does text me an image of an identical rug on sale at Rugs Plus for thirteen dollars with an eye roll emoji.

The ringing of a knife against crystal pulls my eyes from the encouraging text, and I find my mom and her prim smile gathering everyone's attention. "Caspar and I have some exciting news."

For a moment, I wonder if I'm going to puke. If they're dating or having a secret baby or—

"After years of friendship," Caspar says, "I'm honored to share that I will be financially backing Beatrice's mayoral campaign."

Stan and Laura beam their delight, and James extends his arm across the table to shake both my mom's and Caspar's hands. Fiona and Nora nod knowingly, like they already had this information, which is only the sixth most hurtful thing that's happened tonight. At least Penny's wide eyes find mine across the elongated table. I shrug at her as if to say, *News to me.*

"It's just exploratory at this point," my mom adds, beaming.

"Oh, Beatrice," Laura coos. "You're perfect for the job."

"You'll clean this city right up," Stan adds, leaning back in his chair to free his belly from the table. I want to grab him by the rounded cheeks and tell him drug dealers south of the Chasm are the least of Astera's concerns.

Caspar nods to his friend. "Beatrice's strong record on crime is already speaking volumes to voters."

My mother goes on to share all about her pre-mayoral campaign, including that she'll be announcing her candidacy at the annual Windsor Gala in the spring. She and Caspar think that with him as her first backer and all the high-ranking relationships he can draw in, she has a good chance of beating the incumbent. She's got a squeaky-clean record, the perfect-on-paper family, and the mayoral haircut to boot.

Despite the fact that the political bomb drop means few jokes are made about my clumsiness, the ruined rug, or my inability to pay to have it fixed, by the time we pick at the dregs of our gluten-free, sugar-free, dairy-free cobbler, I'm still about ready to beat the shit out of something with horns.

And the truth is, I hate myself for it more than any of them ever could. It's that roiling, restless darkness I was born with—that spiked, meaty growth inside my chest that allows me to murder demons in cold blood—that makes me feel so alone at this dinner table, not the run in my tights or the merlot on the rug.

It's also what makes me ask James on the car ride home, "Can you drop me at the Windsor?"

James checks his phone beside me. "It's nearly ten."

I planned to spend my first night off campus at James's place, but I just can't bring myself to do it. Not after tonight. I find, to my own surprise, that if I can't hunt in the city, there's nowhere besides Harker I really want to be.

"I have so much work to do still," I lie.

He doesn't even argue, and we ride the rest of the way in silence.

THE MOMENT I step into Elkfore Hall, the angsty nagging in my chest subsides a bit, and I'm not even sure why. It's like I've taken one of the meds Nora takes before flying, but without the loopy side effects. In the common area, some students are playing cards and drinking coffee from chipped teacups. Others laze on the deep-cushioned sofa while a French film from the sixties plays on the screen above the flickering fireplace.

One student is leafing through a grimoire in a nook filled with melting candles and peeling books. Something smells like popcorn and white wine, and I turn just in time to see Kitty and another girl walking in from the small kitchenette, glasses and a bag of puffed kernels in hand. They're both in checked pajama bottoms and big navy Harker hoodies. I feel a tad overdressed in my wine-splattered patent leather loafers and thick mascara.

"Viv." Kitty smiles. "You joining us for the movie?"

"I—" I'm about to come up with an excuse when I realize I don't have to. "I'm going to train in the gym a little. I had a rough night."

"Sorry to hear it." She shrugs. "We can fill you in on the beginning if you change your mind."

And then I realize why Harker is such a tonic to my nerves. It's the relief of being surrounded by people I don't have to lie to. People I can be myself around. *You're not as alone as you think.* That's what Peter said to me on my first day.

I'm hoping Sophia will be in our dorm when I get up there. I want to tell her about dinner and hear her outraged response. Both her parents are hunters, as are Elliot's, and even Peter's and Kitty's parents were hunters before they passed away. None of them know what it's like to hide their abilities from their families. It's almost as if, when I'm with my new friends, I can imagine what it would be like to not feel so ashamed of who I am.

But when I get up to our dorm, it's empty. Sophia's left me a note on our chalkboard: *Spending the night with that idiot. Maybe I'll get a 50s Chevy out of it—Text if you need me.*
XO Soph

I bypass my textbooks and grab my daggers from the weapons shelf in our closet. My gaze lingers on the newly fixed crack down my left one. I never christened the blades. But I'm here now and it dawns on me that I'm not going anywhere for a while. Not until I learn more about my dad's secrets, at least. I might as well give the blades some damn names.

I stare at the silver and think of him. How he used to wield them. The ease and effortlessness with which he hunted. How fun he made it when we bested the bad guys together. That version of me would never have tried so hard to impress all the jerks at dinner tonight. She would have given this school a real chance. What would Dad think of me today? Of the double life I've crafted?

For some reason, the thought sends all the fight out of me. I'm exhausted—eyelids heavy, feet sore. I've been working and hunting and keeping up appearances in such rapid succession for the past eleven years, I wonder if it's all catching up with me right here in this dorm room on one unremarkable weeknight. I put the daggers back in the closet and lie down on my bed. I tell myself I'm just going to close my eyes for ten minutes, and then I'll change out of my Beatrice-half-approved outfit and go beat up some demon-shaped body bags.

When my eyes snap open I am sure of two things:

One: I've slept far longer than ten minutes.

Two: I've awoken to what sounds like a massacre.

CHAPTER 16

IN THE HALLWAY, a massacre is exactly what I find.

Students are being slammed into walls, screaming in agony. The scent of blood and decay permeates my senses. I can *taste* the iron in the air. Swords and knives sing past me—

I'm acting on animal instinct before I can even take in what's attacking. I grip my blades, and I'm diving for creatures in hoods, my silver sinking through ancient bone and muscle. Glossy black blood spews, and the creatures moan, but nothing is dying and none of these deviants are slowing, and I don't know—

"They're wraiths," a familiar voice grits out beside me.

I spin to find Peter, long sword drawn like a medieval knight—if medieval knights slept in gingham boxers and Batman T-shirts. He's splattered in shimmering black blood, but a quick scan tells me that's the only blood on him. He's not injured, and I exhale roughly. If he's afraid, it hardly shows. "You need—"

I don't get the chance to hear the rest. A ghostly-looking creature in a tattered shroud shoots toward me and I barely dodge in time. With gnarled fingers, it wrenches open a dormitory door and glides inside. I'm already running when the scream sounds, and my blades are hacking through primeval flesh just in time.

"What is that?" the half-asleep student cries, slamming on the lights and clutching the fresh wound in his side.

I'm rendered speechless when I yank back the weathered fabric over its face and finally get a good look at the thing. I've never fought a wraith before. Call it good luck or bad luck—given the current situation, I'm not quite sure which—but I do wish I'd known to leave the shroud on.

Beneath the ragged fabric is a face devoid of features. Mottled gray flesh with no eyes, no nose, no ears. But I know it's a face because of the gaping mouth. Split from one side to the other, crowded with too many teeth. I don't have time to look for a tongue as its snapping jaws aim for my face. I drive my blade into the wraith's skull and scramble free, even as it chases me out.

In the hall, the specters are everywhere. There are more and more of them—

And the silver doesn't seem to be doing jack shit.

Dodging two students who are taking one down together, I realize these wraiths might require something more specific, like a vampire with a wooden stake, or a strzyga with fire. Surely most of these students know how to kill them—these kids have had hunter parents guiding them on what's to come for the last decade of their lives—but there's too much violence blooming all around me, too many untrained first years holding their blades wrong. Too much chaos and too many different weapons and too much goopy, black blood.

I've lost Peter in the fray, and as my blades cut into anything they can, I don't have a spare second to catch my breath, let alone to take stock of what's working. And these wraiths have got the numbers on us. For every student there are three faceless, mournful monsters attempting to rip skin from bones, turning the hallway carpet slick and red.

My dagger is carving through the torso of one when another takes me down to the ground. My tailbone sings in pain against the wood, but I've got bigger problems. It's gotten those bony fingers around my neck, and no matter how I slam my dagger into its side, the grip won't loosen.

I can't get in an inhale. I can't fucking *breathe*.

Shit, shit—

Kicking and clawing and choking, I recoil from that smooth gray face bare of features, that dripping mouth with all those decaying teeth—still suffocating, lungs still *burning*.

The wraith shrieks a sound like steam from an angry kettle and collapses in a spray of black blood atop me. Air rushes back into my lungs and, with it, the putrid scent of carrion. I gag as I shove the soggy fabric off me.

There, standing in a wide-open dorm doorway, next to a shirtless dude in boxer briefs, is Sophia. She's wearing a men's button-down and white panties, barefoot, with post-sex hair, and gripped in her hands is a mighty crossbow aimed right at us.

I fish the soaked bolt from the heap of black goo and stand. Her arrowheads can kill the wraiths . . .

"Thanks," I call to her, my voice a little hoarse.

But she's already slipping past the useless hunk beside her, descending into the chaos, firing her crossbow at two wraiths—headshots, both of them.

I scan the room for Peter before I'm even back on my feet. He's not only alive and well, he's watching a pantsless Sophia take out wraiths with the precision of a CIA black op. I fear the distraction may cost him his life.

"Look alive," I tell him, slashing down a wraith in front of us with Sophia's arrow. It spurts into a pool of liquid black. My maroon sweater is no longer maroon.

Peter shakes his head and drives his sword into another screeching creature. "She is something else."

He's not wrong. But so is he—and I refuse to let anything happen to either of them. I tell myself there'll be time later to analyze how fucked I am if I already care about these two. It's awful enough going through life wondering if sweet-as-sugar Penny is going to round a corner in Babylon one night and come up against a werewolf asking for directions. Now I have to worry about new friends on the front lines too? I've discovered the first weakness in befriending other hunters: Their lives are in as much jeopardy as my own.

"Why do her arrows work? My blades—"

I use the arrowhead once more as another wraith descends on us. Peter slides his sword just past my hair to get one behind me. "It's the salt, Viv," he says. "Sophia's arrow"—another slice—"my blade . . . they've been dipped in salt."

Of course. I'll feel hideously stupid later. For now, I make the mental note to get a jar of salt and add it to my personal armory in the closet.

Peter slices through two more sinewy gray-skinned creatures. We help a concussed kid into an open dorm room. Together we try to hack the wraiths back, farther and farther away from wounded students, but there are just too many of them. And they had the element of surprise—they've incapacitated more than half the floor. We're grossly outnumbered and confined to this narrow hall. And I'm fighting with one fucking arrow, and students are still screaming, and this school is supposed to be impenetrable, and why has nobody come to help us—

Like a gust of wind barreling through fog, every single wraith explodes in a puddle of black gunk.

I've still got my arrow poised, only the specter I was about to shank is now liquid at my feet. When Peter and I turn, Reid Graveheart is standing at the end of the hall.

He's in nothing but low-slung Harker sweats, with a severe case of bed head, and I can tell by the carved V at his hips that he's slept in neither boxers nor briefs. But Reid's perfectly chiseled chest and the spare dusting of brown curls below his navel are, shockingly, the least interesting sight before me.

He's holding a leaf blower.

"You guys okay?" he asks. He sounds winded, like he sprinted through the campus at four fifteen in the morning looking for a leaf blower to fill with salt.

The collective mumbles and groans sound something like *yeah*. The hallway is splattered with black like a colorless Jackson Pollock.

Peter says, "The other floors—"

"They're all fine," Reid tells him as pale green beings in uniforms hurry up the stairs behind him and into the hall to tend to the wounded. Pointed ears and slight features, quiet whispered words. Nurses from the infirmary, and . . . pixies. Makes sense, due to their healing abilities. Some do chest compressions, but others use glowing blue light from their hands and conjured ointments to seal up wounds and set broken bones.

I count at least three kids with life-threatening injuries—severed arteries, head trauma—and riotous nausea swells in my stomach. It's my job to protect people, and I failed because I didn't know about fucking salt.

Reid heaves a sigh. "We've secured the perimeter. The Citadel is already looking into this. You can all go back to sleep."

"Are you kidding me?" I say to Peter.

He frowns. "We're the only school that trains hunters. Deviants are probably always trying to break in and get their fix. Wraiths crave our flesh as much as werewolves do." When Sophia wanders over, still without pants, Peter clears his throat and averts his eyes.

"You both all right?" When we nod, she tells us, "Elliot's fine too. He's on the top floor."

"You're . . ." Peter swallows hard. "Bleeding."

Sophia touches her forehead where there is, indeed, blood dripping down the side of her face. "Oh, yeah."

And then she wanders back into the dorm room she came out of, dragging the shell-shocked beefcake in briefs along with her.

"I'm going to make sure Kitty's okay," Peter tells me, his eyes still on the door Sophia just closed.

As he shakes his head and walks away, I spot Reid heading back down the hall, and I'm met with new anger. There is wraith goo all over this dormitory. There are unconscious, bleeding students. We have an entire gaggle of pixies tending to the fallen like it's a World War I battlefield. And Reid, one of our professors, is returning to his beauty sleep? He's lucky nobody was killed tonight.

I'm stomping over to him before I know what I'm going to say.

"Hey," I snap at the hard planes of his muscled back.

I can see the bracing inhale he takes before he turns around. Talking to me requires all his energy, I suppose. When he does face me, I remember our height difference and try to stand a bit taller. I'm five seven, so for me to feel short next to someone is rare. I add this to the phone book–size list of reasons I can't stand the guy.

Reid's eyes run over me as if he's looking for something specific. The curve of my jaw, the side of my neck, the scrapes on my hands. I'm acutely aware that I'm drenched in oozing black blood and smell like the inside of a carcass.

"You can't just walk away," I tell him.

"You always sleep in a miniskirt?"

"How can you be so glib at a time like this?"

Reid's face hardens. "At a time like what?"

"Students—*your* students—almost died tonight."

"We teach these kids how to hunt. Death at the hands of deviants is in the job description." He moves to turn, but I yank him back by the arm. His skin is hot under my hand.

"How could you let—"

"I didn't *let* anything," he snaps, grasping my wrist just this side of too tight and removing it from his body. "And you'd be wise to get your emotions under control. I'm your instructor."

Shit. I take a slow breath in through my nose. Aeons are notoriously moody. The last thing I need is this fucking *demon* figuring out what I am. "Harker doesn't even let students hunt alone. They weren't prepared for this."

"I didn't make those rules." He says it like if it were up to him, he'd do things differently. But with his sigh he seems to think better of the notion. "Harker does the best it can to keep the students here safe. We can't allow kids to hunt down danger alone the first few years after they gain their abilities. Doesn't mean the danger won't come to them. We have wards and spells and hexes, round-the-clock hunters on guard . . . This was an anomaly. And one I just told you the Citadel is looking into. But if Harker's going to try so hard to insulate their students, incidents like this may be the only way for hunters to learn exactly what they're up against."

"You're wrong." My voice comes out reedy. Too emotional. I try to rein in my frustration. "This ability—this hunter gene—it's a curse. Nobody should have to learn this way. Nobody here asked for this."

I didn't ask for this. The words might as well be spray-painted on my forehead. Shame heats my cheeks.

Reid studies me, and it feels like he's looking beneath my skin. "Hunting is a privilege. Whether these students asked for it or not, they should be honored to fight. Even those with fancy museum gigs, miniskirts, and blond trust-fund pets are still hunters. They will always *be* hunters."

I want to tell him that something about feeling inadequate in every single way, trapped in the nebulous post–high school haze, can lead to all kinds of peculiar romantic choices that people hope will impress their mother, but I go with the far more mature, "Hey, that pet is my *boyfriend*."

"You need to make peace with who you are, huntress." My eyes focus on his, and I find them churning like a storm-battered sea. "Trust me. I know a thing or two about fate dealing you a hand you didn't ask for."

"Do not give me some sob story about being a demon. You joined the Brood. You're at fault for that, not fate."

Reid clenches his jaw, his ruthless gaze drilling into me. But he says nothing. And try as I might to remember the point of Dean Driscoll's story, I just can't buy into this demon's bullshit.

"You must get some sick satisfaction out of playing the good guy. Knowing you took probably, I don't know, *thousands* of human lives in your time, and now you get to dress up as a teacher, and cute blondes bring you apples for your desk. Don't kid yourself, Reid. Everyone here knows you're still a demon. You'll *never* be good."

Reid studies me for a beat. I fight the urge to shift on my feet. When he speaks, his voice is lower, quieter than I expect. "Do you think your words have any effect on me? You think I don't know the students, the professors, all feel as you do?" He exhales roughly, coming back to himself. "You can put down the daggers, huntress.

Focus on actually learning something here. My place at Harker isn't your fight."

He doesn't wait for me to respond before he walks through the hall and down the stairs.

But he doesn't get it. He never will. He has no idea what is or isn't my fight. That more often than not I dream of men with his same brand ending my father's life. He doesn't know the aeon rage that boils inside me, like a pot left over a flame until everything inside has evaporated into furious mist. Reid Graveheart doesn't know me. And he never will.

CHAPTER 17

MY FEET TRUDGE along the overgrown pathway, patches of foxglove and milkweed drooping toward my legs as Sophia and I wander back from Dawnmere's class "field trip" to the edges of the Fickle Thicket. We spent the morning studying rare herbs and flower petals, which Dawnmere thought might be soothing for the students who witnessed the wraith attack last night. When we catch up with Elliot and Peter on our way to Crowley's class, Peter's calling Kitty, and Elliot's brows are knit.

"What's going on?" I ask.

Elliot shrugs. "Kitty missed our lecture this morning."

Weird. It's unlike Kitty to skip a class. "You get ahold of her?"

"Nope," Peter says, pocketing the phone.

"Let's go by her dorm before lunch," Sophia says. "I bet she has a guy in there."

Peter's visible disgust makes us laugh as we hurry to Crowley's class and take our seats.

Afterward, we make our way to Elkfore Hall. The dean sent

out an email explaining that the wraiths were able to slip through a faulty gateway in Mortimer Tower that's rarely used, and that seemed to be enough for most students and their parents.

Thankfully, nobody died, and the students who were taken to the infirmary are all in stable condition. We're grateful for pixie magic this morning. I thought knowing Harker wasn't deviant-proof would have been a bucket of ice water on most of the first years, but I get the sense they're excited to finally be fighting real threats. Once again I remember that they don't have the experience I do. They don't know how afraid to be.

"If she's actually in bed with someone," Peter says as he knocks on Kitty's door, "this is going to be really awkward."

Elliot leans against the wall. "I've walked in on Soph like five times."

Peter's face falls, as if the mental image pains him.

"She's not your cousin," I say.

Sophia snorts. "Basically, though."

Peter's fist slams against the door one more time before it swings open to reveal a narrow-faced girl, eyes wet and ringed with concern. I recognize her as the girl Kitty was having wine and popcorn with last night. Immediately my heart begins to thud.

"What's wrong?" Peter's voice is tight.

Her gaze darts from Peter to me to Sophia and Elliot behind us. "Our roommate . . . she left school."

"Kitty?" Peter pushes past her into the room. It's a triple, just as adorned with antiques and vintage wood as the others. Soft light spills across the desk where another girl, a ruddy-cheeked blonde, sits anxiously, piece of paper clutched in her hand.

"What do you mean *left school*?" Sophia asks.

The blonde hands the paper to Sophia. I watch her face as she reads what I can only assume is a letter from Kitty. Sophia's eyes sweep across each line, worry carving her features. When she's done, she hands the letter to Peter. "She dropped out."

"No way," Elliot says. "She was obsessed with this place."

"Are her things gone?" I ask.

"All of them," the blonde at the desk says, dejected. "She even took some of my shoes."

"Do you think she hated us?" the first girl asks her roommate. "Why did you have to sleep with those weird videos playing?"

"I told you, it's called ASMR!" the blonde says before storming from the room.

The first girl releases an exasperated noise. "I'm Mila. How do you guys know Kitty?"

"She's my cousin," Peter says, studying the letter. "Did you try calling her?"

"Only seventy times," Mila says.

Peter nods. He couldn't reach her, either. "When did you see her last?"

"Last night. We watched a movie in the commons."

Kitty had invited me to join. I turn to Peter. "Did you talk to her after the wraith attack?" He'd said he was going to see if she was okay.

"She texted me saying she slept right through it."

"That's weird," Mila muses. "She wasn't here this morning. We both had a text from her saying she wasn't feeling well and went to the infirmary. But we asked the pixies. They never saw her."

"She was hightailing it out of here," Sophia says somberly, looking over the note again. "Says so right in the letter."

But the look on Peter's face is one of suspicion, not sadness. "Guess so. Thanks, Mila."

"Sorry we were such shitty roommates," she says, sitting down on her patchwork quilt.

Peter's mouth twists. "I'm sure it had nothing to do with you."

AMID THE HUM of the dining hall lunch crowd, Peter says, "The letter's got to be a fake."

A bang sounds as a round-cheeked gnome pushes a cart of pots through ornate wooden doors. Peter lowers his voice. "She would never leave Harker. She's wanted to attend school here her entire life."

I've gotten the same impression from Kitty in the few weeks I've known her. "Is it her handwriting?"

"I don't know," he says, looking at the letter. "We only met this summer. I'd need one of her notebooks to compare, but . . ."

"She's gone," Sophia fills in. "Along with all of her things."

"My notes from Lisette's class—" I yank out my bag and rifle through binders and notebooks until I find our scribbled-over Stratification of Deviants sheet.

Sophia and Peter compare Kitty's addition about harpies to her letter. Elliot finishes his bowl of fruit and then swipes Peter's and digs in. When I frown at him, he shrugs good-naturedly. "He's busy."

"They're different," Peter decides.

Sophia's lips twist, eyes still glued to Kitty's looped *o*'s and slanted *i*'s. "They look the same to me."

As if my body has become attuned to not only his demonic nature but also his evergreen-and-lemongrass scent, I spin just in time to see Reid brush behind us with an apple and a banged-up book and take a seat—alone—at a wide wooden table.

I have the errant thought that I hope I got all the wraith blood off me. Last night I scrubbed every inch of my body until I'd scraped away any semblance of a summer tan and was back to being as pale as a ghoul myself. At least now I'm a ghoul who smells like vanilla and rose. Not that I care what I smell like to Reid.

"Maybe she was depressed," I say to Peter quietly, just in case Reid's eavesdropping.

"Sometimes people just drop out," Elliot says. "Soph dropped out of high school."

I cut my eyes to her. "You did?"

"Briefly." She waves the question away. "It's a long story. Let me check the lettering again."

"I'm telling you, regardless of the handwriting, Kitty would never use the word *bummed*. She was an academic. She made fun of me for calling graphic novels *novels*."

Sophia snorts. "In her defense . . ."

"I'm serious."

"You sure you aren't just butthurt?" Elliot says. "Your cousin was, like . . . your only friend here, right?" Sophia shoots Elliot a nasty look and he adds, "Until you met us. Obviously."

"This isn't my ego talking. Think about it—she ran the night of the wraith attack? She stole their shoes? Why?"

I think of my dorm. The two individual armoires . . . and our shoes, tossed together, inside one closet. "If someone were to try and make it look like she left the school, they'd have to take her things. But if they didn't know which shoes were hers, they might have accidentally taken some of her roommates'."

"You think someone *took* her?" Peter pales with the words. "Why?"

I don't say that if Kitty was killed by a wraith, the school's response to the attack would undoubtedly be different, or that she wasn't even on our floor, and no wraiths were seen anywhere else on campus that night, meaning it's more likely somebody used the commotion as a distraction to sneak her out than that a wraith got to her. Instead I say, "I doubt they did. I'm just brainstorming."

Usually I'm inclined to follow logic. Penny once believed our apartment was haunted, and even though I spend most nights battling the creatures kids dress up as on Halloween, I just didn't buy it. Even when the cupboard clanked open on its own in the middle of the night or when we'd hear groaning in the abandoned apartment above us, I didn't bat an eye.

It turned out we had a squatter in the building's attic. Some poppy addict whose heavy footsteps shook our cabinets open. Penny was terribly relieved. I actually thought a ghost might've been preferable to the physical evidence of how bleak the STC living conditions were.

Kitty was a textbook overachiever and seemed prone to emotional outbursts. It makes sense that she felt overwhelmed by the course load at Harker—we've only been here three weeks, and even I think twenty-four credits is a lot. Still, I can't shake the sinister feeling seeping into my bones. "But we should look into it either way."

"We will," Sophia says. "Of course we will."

"We'll find her," Elliot says.

Peter only stares down at his missing fruit bowl and nods.

"WHAT A DAY," Fiona says, taking her oversized glasses off to rub her temples as she perches her tiny butt on my desk. Her bare feet swing as she discards her heels. "The board is being just impossible about the committee for this year's gala."

I discreetly minimize two tabs on my computer: one of Kitty's last social media post and another of a gossip site with a headline that reads **Media Mogul Caspar Harlock Seen on Romantic Dinner Date with Mayoral Hopeful Beatrice Abbot.** "I wish I could offer some advice, but I thought the board *was* the committee, so . . ."

Fiona purses her lips at me. "You're as difficult as your sister, you know that?"

"Gross. Don't compare me to Nor."

"Will you call her sometime? She says you haven't been answering her lately."

Now that she mentions it, I remember silencing a call from Nora during a particularly gruesome case study in Rituals and Exorcisms. I was late for Lisette's class after, and I guess I never rang her back. Normally I'm pretty good about that—my feeble attempt at pleasing the stony queen of type A older sisters.

"Speaking of," Fiona says, eyes up from her phone and suddenly very focused on me. "Are you feeling better?"

I'm too fair to get any paler, so I probably go white. "Huh?"

Eloquent, Viv, so very eloquent.

"After your stomach ailment."

"Well—"

"And the food poisoning after that, and the migraines, menstrual cramps . . ."

"Who says *menstrual* anymore? You aren't *that* old, Fiona—"

"Viv, I'm serious." She eyes me until I swallow hard. "If something—"

"It's my mom," I blurt.

Fiona studies me and waits. She's fantastically patient like that. Not a crease in her brow. Though that may be the Botox.

You know when you can tell you're on the precipice of something irrevocably stupid? How you can feel the words that will doom you rocketing up your throat and resting precariously at the tip of your tongue? Well, I do. I say or do something irrevocably stupid at least once a month. Last month it was probably enrolling at Harker Academy for Deviant Defense. The month before, trying—and failing—to stake a vampire with a Popsicle stick.

This month it's "She's asked me to help her with her campaign. Something . . . kind of private that I can't share with anyone. In fact"—I swallow—"she asked me not to tell you and just make something up, but I'm such a bad liar."

Bad liar? Wrong. I'm a *great* liar. And the big lie I needed to get me out of my Windsor job while I'm at Harker has just left the station.

Fiona's already-round eyes go even rounder. I can see white on all sides. "I see."

There's just no way I can continue to study at Harker and work full-time here for Fiona. At least, not without failing miserably at both. But Harker has a winter holiday break right after the Chasm exhibit in November. If I can just make it until then . . . "Yep. So I actually need to take a leave until the exhibit. If that's all right."

"You want to take a sabbatical? For the same pay? In a job a thousand young professionals would kill for?"

"It's for my mom. You know how she gets. Her campaign is everything to her, and I just can't bear to let her down." Okay, so the train hasn't just left the station, it's been hijacked.

"I don't know . . ." Fiona says, fingers drumming on her lips.

"I'm really sorry, Fiona. If my mom wasn't making me do this, I'd never miss a day." When she scowls, I add, "I do actually want to keep working here. For you. You can send me briefs to work through. Paperwork to handle. I can do it from my mom's campaign offices. But I'll miss being here. I've actually come to love all the ancient relics, the history and humanity. The stillness . . ."

To my surprise, I mean every word. I don't love working for

Fiona—getting her morning mocha almond sugar bombs, reminding her when she's forgotten a shoe before going into a meeting, the ungodly hours—but I guess I do like the Windsor. And wouldn't mind being paid a living wage to photograph the exhibits here one day.

Fiona's looking kind of moved, so I add, "And the AC, of course. My apartment was like an Aztec sweat lodge all summer."

Fiona makes a face, but I can see the amusement peeking through her downturned lips. "You jest, but I bet you learned about that here in this very building."

She doesn't know how right she is. "Nobody has said *jest* since moats were a thing."

Fiona hops off my desk with a rueful shake of her head.

"Are you ninety?" I call as she walks down the hall to her office in her clacky heels. "Just give me your dermatologist's number and I'll keep your secrets!"

Her door closes with a thud.

And actually, I exhale a sigh of relief. Train successfully brought to safety. Now I can maintain my meager salary to pay rent and eat on occasion and, equally as important, keep up appearances. Viv Abbot Darling Daughter will still be working her way up the corporate ladder toward an acceptable and socially pleasing job.

Meanwhile, I'll keep studying at Harker and looking into my dad. And Kitty . . . Viv Abbot Huntress Detective just needs a faculty key card to get into those archives.

Which means all I have to do is keep my mom from finding out I'm skipping out on Windsor days and keep Fiona from finding out I'm not actually helping her with a "sensitive campaign issue." And keep Penny and Fiona from ever discussing my sleeping arrangements. Luckily, Fiona travels so often, supervising exhibitions on loan from the Windsor and acquiring new antiquities, she doesn't have enough time for in-depth conversations with her own wife, let alone Penny or my mother.

And yeah, Harker classes are grueling and already leave very little time for doing homework, writing essays, completing research papers, and, of course, training, but I'll just cram those things into the evenings.

And I'll see James on the weekends to maintain our relationship.

And meditate between classes to keep a lid on mercurial aeon emotions and bloodlust and also for those nebulous mental health benefits I've heard so much about.

And I'll see my family literally whenever they ask me to, because I'm still fostering some insane belief it can be like it once was between us again.

And I'll do the things I actually *wish* I could, like go to Pilates and take photos and hang out with Penny and my new friends—though never together, of course—and bring Hound up to NTC Park and travel and meet someone I actually *want* to see on the weekends, all in some other lifetime, I guess, because that's the irrevocably stupid position I've put myself in.

CHAPTER 18

PROFESSOR CROWLEY'S SILVER teeth are glaring at me.

"Don't stare," Peter whispers.

My eyes slam down to the open book on my desk. The cursive ink is fading into the yellowed pages, the spine peeling from overuse, and the cluttered sentences becoming hard to follow. I think this book was written before punctuation was invented.

Professor Crowley hunches over a projector while a student dims the candelabras on either wall. The screen focuses on the words **The Undead**, and I spy a few candles lit on the shelves behind him. When he turns to face us again, his silver teeth gleam in the flickering light.

"Ah fuck, are we having a séance?" Elliot groans.

"I hope not." Sophia snorts. "I've communed with enough undead to last a lifetime."

"All right." Crowley grins. "Who knows the difference between these three?"

The projector clicks through three images. The first is an old photo of a filmy gossamer outline. A ghost in someone's basement, barely caught on film. I nod my head at the impressive photography skills. I've never caught one with my half-frame.

The second is of the gaping maw and eyeless, noseless face of the wraiths we fought just a few nights ago. One of the girls in our class turns her face away and gags. The third image is of a rotting skeletal body gurgling out of a murky river, severed hand in its mouth. Dad and I fought one of those on a family road trip to the Great Lakes. The ghoul almost ate my dad's arm. Good times.

Peter raises his hand high in the air. "Ghosts have no corporeal form but can manipulate physical objects. Wraiths have form but are not conscious beings, and ghouls are sentient creatures that feed on both the living and the dead."

Crowley's teeth glitter as he grins. "Right you are, Roydon. Ghouls and wraiths move through the world like you or me," Crowley continues in front of the projector. "But ghosts can only be summoned by spellcraft. That's why you always want to find the origin object with any summoning spell."

"Anything from Kitty?" I whisper to Peter when Crowley's moved on. It's been two days since we found her letter.

"Nothing yet," he whispers. "And the school told me they haven't received her textbooks. Students who leave have forty-eight hours to return them to the registrar."

Unease drips through me. Kitty was nothing if not responsible. I'm opening my mouth to tell him I don't like the sound of that when the darkened classroom fills with light and nearly fifty hunter heads swivel in the direction of the doorway.

"We've had a sighting." Reid's hair is slightly damp, like he's just gotten out of the shower. "A deviant in Astera. I need my Field Training first years."

Sophia and Elliot exchange thrilled glances before standing and gathering their books and pens.

"Very well." Crowley nods, but I can see the irritation flicker in his steely gaze. I guess this is part of the curriculum as much as his class is, even when he's not a fan of the instructor.

But my heart is spiking in my chest too hard to think about Crowley's disdain for Reid. Not only is there a deviant in my city that I'm not allowed to fight, but now two people I care about are going to battle it without me?

I don't think so.

Reid lets the door slam shut behind him, and when Sophia and Elliot hurry out of the class, I get up to follow them. I just make out Peter's hushed *Viv, don't*—but it's too late. I've already set my mind on the hunt.

Plus, this might be the best way for me to swipe Reid's key card off of him. I would've made a decent pickpocket if we'd stayed down in Lethe throughout my teens.

Reid's entire body stiffens when he notices me in the hall. "Huntress—"

"Let me come," I tell him. "I know this city better than anyone."

"No." He turns and heads for the doors to the rotunda. "Where's Briggs?"

Sophia, Elliot, and I exchange a look. "Not sure," I say quickly. If Reid doesn't already know she's dropped out, I'm not going to be the one to tell him. Not if something nefarious might be going on. "Let me fight in her place."

"I *said* no."

"I've been training for weeks."

"And like all students, you'll keep doing just that. You'll have plenty of Field Training opportunities once you learn the—"

"Cut the crap. I'm going with you."

Reid stops in his tracks. His voice is as razor-sharp as his glare when he turns to face me. "No, you aren't. I am your *instructor*."

"Doesn't mean you can stop me."

Quiet wrath simmers in his eyes. "I stopped you pretty well last time."

"I've got two silver daggers on me today and one less blindfold."

"Enough," Reid growls. "You're out of line."

I suck an inhale through my nose. "Please," I say, though the word burns. "Please. I want to help."

Reid's mouth tightens into a flat line. Torturous minutes pass, my heart laid bare before him. I fight the urge to squirm.

Finally he relents. "Observe only. Or you aren't going out in the field again the rest of the year, understood?"

I exhale all the air in my lungs. "Absolutely."

Zero chance.

IF I'D KNOWN the deviant in question was sniffing around Shiloh Asylum, I might have put up less of a fight. A tunnel ride away, on a little borough off the coast of Astera called the Idles, sits the only mental health institution South of the Chasm. North of the Chasm you've got your pick of clean hospitals, wellness facilities, and luxury retreats. This place is something different.

Half the windows are boarded up, so the setting sun only reflects in two panes of glass. If the raw wood was ever painted, it's long since chipped off now. Shutters hang askew, and all the potted plants along the driveway up to the front doors are fossilized. If I were to touch the leaves, they'd crumble to dust in my hand.

"It looks like the setting for a horror movie," Elliot notes, staring up at the towering building.

"Like the sixth one in the franchise," Sophia adds, chewing her lip. *"Impalement at the Insane Asylum."*

"It's just a run-down psychiatric facility," I tell Sophia, chilly wind biting at my skin.

"Sure." She nods. "With a deviant running loose inside."

"We got a call from a fairy mortician in the city," Reid says behind us, voice grim. "A body from the asylum showed up drained of blood." Reid hands us each a pristinely carved wooden stake.

"So it's a vamp," I say.

Elliot places his stake in his front pocket. "God, I hope so."

When we ease open the front doors, I peek my head in, expecting slaughter. A hellish creature that's devoured half the patients and staff. But inside, a crusty speaker system plays soft jazz, and a woman with graying hair mans the front desk.

"Hi." She smiles, eyes crinkling. "How can I help you?"

Reid wanders over to the desk, careful to avoid a skittering rat that moves across his path. I eye Elliot, but he doesn't flinch, debunking the storybook theory that big, strong men are afraid of mice.

"Hi there," Reid purrs. His cheek has an actual dimple. It's strange seeing him turn on the charm with someone. Despite his movie star good looks, I didn't think he was capable of being pleasant. "We're the pharmaceutical reps. We called earlier?"

"Oh yes," the woman mutters. "Right this way . . ."

But I can't hear the rest. My entire body has electrified.

The vampire's nearby. I can feel it.

All thoughts of being a team player or stealing a key card tumble out of my brain. There's a predator here, and I need to put it down.

While Reid charms the front desk lady, I walk backward, heel-toeing down the hallway and around the first corner I find. Sophia sees and follows suit, leaving the boys behind.

"Why'd you ditch?" she whispers as we pass a nurse rolling a young woman into a room with ample padding.

"Gut feeling."

We tiptoe quietly down the hallway, fluorescent lights sputtering above. The buzzing in my skin intensifies when we round a darkened corner. But Sophia's stopped to peer into one of the open doors. "There's a patient in there who's very pale," she whispers. "Vamp pale."

"No, this way." I have to keep following the fireworks in my veins.

Eventually Sophia catches up. "Care to clue me in?"

But I don't have time to explain. Nor would I really know how to. I've never hunted with anyone but my dad before. My heart rate is ratcheting up. My fingers and toes beginning to pulse. I'm close, I can feel it.

When I hear the sound of a bucket clattering to the floor, I take off running down the hall, leaving Sophia in my wake.

"What the— *Viv?*"

But I ignore her, the need to hunt snapping inside me. An insistent, violent pleading that must be answered. I tell myself I work better alone anyway—I can't be worrying about Sophia getting hurt.

She launches after me, but I'm quicker, leaping over empty rollaway beds and barreling down stairs, following nothing but the demanding sensation inside me. Around two corners, down another flight of stairs, and onto an abandoned floor, where I realize I no longer hear anything.

I curl my fists and wait.

And listen.

And study the unmoving dimness, one fluorescent light flickering.

At the end of the hall, a scruffy orderly barks at me. "Miss." His voice is like an out of tune harp. "This floor is restricted."

My body rings like the damn Liberty Bell.

"Gotcha," I hiss.

The orderly feigns confusion for a split second before realizing the jig is up. He drops the papers in his hands and takes off down the hallway. And I take off right after him.

We leap over a bin filled with socks, slide around equipment in our way. He shoves an IV stand at me with vampire force, and it clips my shoulder, knocking me down to the linoleum floor. I scramble back up and hurtle after him, past a cart of meds, where the orderly grabs something, though I can't see what—

The vampire cuts through a door that he jangled open with his keys, and I slip in behind him right before it can slam shut. If Sophia was chasing after me, there's no shot she's finding us now. The thought is relieving and terrifying all at once.

This corridor is darker than the last, and there's only room for one patient at the far end—a room with no door but rather bars like a cage in a zoo. There's a bed and a rocking chair inside.

Silence gutters in as I listen for the vampire. But all I hear are my own footsteps. And . . .

A voice. Coming from that solitary room at the very end. A woman, talking to someone. Low and whimsical. Or talking to herself? I'm a foot away from an answer when pain radiates across my jaw. I slam into the ground, the vampire lunging to land another blow.

I scramble up and away before he can make contact, grasping for my stake—

Only to find it gone.

My blood stops.

The fall. In the hallway outside. It must have slipped out of my back pocket—

Shit, shit—

Dodging the vampire's next blow, I bolt back down toward the door we entered, only to find it locked. I have no key to get out.

Need to find wood, need to find wood—

"I love it when they run," the vampire purrs, stalking toward me.

"That's my damn line," I huff.

I tug uselessly at the steel handle before I give up and scan the abandoned corridor. The orderly advances on me slowly, a malevolent gleam in his eye. He knows I'm trapped. *I* know I'm trapped. And with nothing but that padded cell, a discarded mop, and a bucket—

The mop.

Perfect.

I let the vampire draw nearer. He takes his sweet time, likely reveling in the scent of my fear. That's fine by me, though. It's the distraction I need. Something glints in his palm, but I don't have the time to dwell on it. I cut left and dive for the mop and bucket.

He's faster than any being should be, catching my foot and throwing me down, the floor rushing up to meet me. Though I try to claw myself away, he steps toward me, fangs protruding and gleaming under the fluorescent lights.

But I'm close enough now to knock the bucket over, and with it, the mop comes crashing down beside my head. I snap it in half over my knee and drive it up toward the vampire. His cold hand is still wrapped around my ankle as the jagged end of the makeshift stake plunges through his heart.

Relief and satisfaction ripple through me, but I feel a jolt of pain at my ankle too. Panting, I kick the dying, croaking vamp away from me and find a hypodermic needle shoved into the sensitive flesh above my sock.

"God damn it," I heave, pulling it out with a wince.

I eye the blood seeping from the vampire's chest wound. Am I desperate enough to heal whatever I was just dosed with? I've never drank vampire blood before . . . I read the label on the needle—just Valium—and decide not to start today. I whip out my lighter and set the vampire's body aflame by his scrubs. Hot licks of fire curl toward me as the body shrivels and burns before it dissipates into nothing.

"Vampire's feast," that melodic voice at the end of the hall titters. "She was almost a vampire's feast."

"What?" My head is tilting and whirling. Whose voice is that? "No. That was . . . That was a—"

"Crafty little kitten. Nearly a vampire's feast."

I walk down the corridor until I come to the cell and find a woman perched on the lone bed, facing the padded wall. Even as the world begins to wrinkle around me, I can tell she's elderly. Behind the gnarled, thin-lipped exterior is the serene expression of a kind older woman.

"Who are you?" A patient here who knows about vampires? Perhaps she's a lymantrian, or a mortal who's seen more than she's supposed to. Either way, she doesn't belong in this facility. I scan the empty wing . . . Maybe there's more to Shiloh than I thought. Maybe it's a question for future me, who isn't slowly growing more and more sedated.

"Into a vampire's feast was she nearly made. The words were cast, and though I fought, I'm the one who paid," she sings to herself.

"Okay." I'm so woozy I have to brace my hands on the wall outside her cell. That Valium dose was massive. "Ma'am, can you tell me—"

But a second later she's an inch from my face, her wrinkled, paper-thin skin pressed against the bars of her cell. Her eyes are milky, clouded with cataracts, her teeth broken and cracked. The woman cackles as I stagger back, my heart racing, my hands balled into fists.

"Beware, little hunter," the woman hisses. "Thane's coming for the last of 'em."

Everything is blurring. "Did you say *Thane?*"

"I had one of those once too," she warbles.

One of *what?* But I can't even form my next question around the dizziness. Somewhere far away I hear the door at the end of the hall slam open and the metal handle clang to the floor.

"Viv?"

That's Reid's voice. That's Reid—

For a moment my mind sputters. Wheels spinning in mud. Then, where fear and confusion and horror were swirling moments ago, only soft white clouds float. I breathe in a mellow, dopey breath.

"Viv," Reid says again, rushing toward me. He yanks me to face him by my arm.

"Oh. Hi." I have the funny feeling I was going to tell him something, but I can't remember what just happened. And Reid . . . Reid's looking really angry, which is making his dimple extra prominent. "What are you doing here?"

His brows furrow as he studies me. And then his entire face shifts into an expression I've never seen on him. "Are you . . . high?"

"Fought the vamp. He died. But he stuck me with that thingy." I point limply at the scorch marks on the floor and the discarded syringe.

"Fucker," Reid breathes. "Come here."

I step closer to him, and he takes my chin in his huge hand to study my pupils. My cheeks and jaw heat with the surprisingly gentle touch.

"That patient over there told me to look out for the High Thane," I tell him.

"Sure she did," Reid says. "Let's get you out of here."

CHAPTER 19

I MAY OR may not babble something about the perfect fit of his athletic pants while Reid guides me down to the subway platform. He tells me he sent Elliot and Sophia home for their safety as soon as he lost track of me, but I can't remember when or how he said it. Reid sits me down on the metal seat like a child, and when I begin to tip over, he takes off his sweatshirt and props it behind my head, keeping me upright. I try to say thanks, but it comes out like gibberish. My brain is looping and everything smells like lemongrass and cozy boy sweat.

Reid takes a seat two spots away from me in the empty railcar and hunches over to run his hands along the back of his neck with a sigh. I find his humanity kind of adorable and then want to smack myself face-first into concrete for the thought. But before I can look away, my gaze catches on the raised flesh of his brand. What an awful practice.

"Did it hurt?" I ask slowly. Words are a little hard.

Reid's eyes stay glued to his shoes, but I can tell he knows what I mean. "Yes."

"They brand you because tattoos can be removed, right?" It's a theory I've had for a while.

Finally he looks up, chestnut hair curling over his eyes. "They brand us because we're cattle."

"That's why I hate you, you know."

"Because I was in the Brood." It's not a question.

"Yeah." The world is whirling, the train we're on moving both too fast and too slow. "The Brood killed my dad."

Reid shakes his head. "I'm sorry."

It's a challenge to blink, let alone say thank you.

After a beat Reid mutters, "It was a different time in my life."

The railcar sways to the right and I brace myself against the darkened, foggy window. I'm so dizzy.

"Like a lot of people who take up with the wrong crowd, I was trying to please other people."

I open my mouth before I know what I'm going to ask. "Who?"

His laugh is a little bitter. "My parents."

"Wait." I jolt up with the revelation. "Nobody gets that like me!"

"Is that so?" His eyes are down on his folded hands again, as if he can't quite decide if he should be having this conversation.

"Yeah," I tell him, scooting closer. He's still not looking at me, so I tug at his arm until he turns my way. "My mom can't stand me. That's why I'm dating that guy you called my pet. She *loves* him."

Some tiny corner of my brain shrieks at me for sharing such personal information with the closest thing I've ever had to an enemy, but I drown out the noise with all the warm fuzzies from the sedative. Like pillows of ease I can stuff into all my most painful nooks and crannies.

"Sounds like a healthy thing you've got going."

"His sister is my closest friend. She matters more to me than anyone on earth, including my dog, which is saying a lot. The three of us were close growing up. Me and Penny and her brother—not me and Penny and my dog. My mom likes that he can take care of me. My boyfriend. Not my dog."

Reid's entire body stiffens with my words. Like something's hurt him, which makes no sense. "You don't need anyone to take care of you, huntress."

"That's what I think too!"

His dimple pokes out with his half smile and I fight the urge to lick it.

"Why can't your own mother stand you?"

"You would know. You can't stand me, either."

He runs a hand down his face in exasperation. Or maybe annoyance? I can't tell. I'm *floating*.

"Are you going to answer me?" he says quietly.

"When your friends murdered my dad, I was there. She thinks it was my fault." I sit back a little, swaying with the railcar as it rounds a curve. "I didn't save him, so I guess she isn't wrong. I don't know, she's never said that exactly. Just a hunch. Mostly I just don't fit in with the rest of them. I zig, they zag, you know?"

When Reid finally peers up from his shoes, he looks like he could crush the steel grab bar in front of him with one pinch. "Your dad died and your mom blamed you? When you were, what, a kid?"

"Yep."

"That's . . ." He pushes his hand through his hair. "She didn't take care of you when you needed her most. That's inexcusable."

His words stun me into silence. He's kind of got a point. I make a low whistle like a *day-um*, and Reid's anger melts into a smirk. "You're zooted, huntress."

"I don't do drugs," I tell him. "But I think I'm on drugs."

"Do I have news for you."

Why is he being so cute right now? "Stay right there," I tell him, fishing my camera out of my bag. I snap a picture of his incredulous smile before he has a chance to look away.

"What was that?"

"Just my half-frame." I scoot a bit closer and tuck my knees up onto the seat. "One day I'll buy a thirty-five-millimeter film camera. You know they make them out of silver?"

"I did not know that."

"You should probably steer clear."

He wipes a hand down his face to hide the precious grin, but I already caught it. "I'll keep that in mind."

"What about you? Do you ever do anything?"

"Do I *do* anything?"

"Yeah, hobbies. Like cooking or skateboarding or girls."

Reid stares at me for so long I begin to wonder if I even said the words out loud. Finally, he says, "I like memoirs."

Makes sense to me. "You like to step into people's heads."

"Is that why you like photography?"

"Kind of," I say around a yawn. "I like to step into people's lives."

And though I can tell Reid has no idea what I mean, that's the only real way to explain it. My eyes drift over the empty subway car. The scuffs left behind from kids climbing on tired parents, a smear of lipstick that serves as the only remnant of a date gone well, a wine cork from someone coming home from the most miserable shift of their life.

At my worst, being an aeon makes me feel more predator than person. More deviant, even. I can grow so dead set on the kill, on tracking, trapping, and murdering my prey, I find myself untethering from what it is to be human. Photography allows me to peer into the lives of other people. To see the beauty and the pain in everyday experiences. It grounds me. And it makes me remember that I'm alive.

I want to tell Reid all that, but I'm getting so tired, my head too heavy for my neck to support, so I allow my eyelids to droop and my jaw to go slack. *Just for a minute*, I think. Sleep will feel so good.

A jolt of electricity courses through me when Reid catches me with his body and props me back up. "Not yet," he says quietly. "We'll be home soon."

Home.

At Harker.

I'm shocked to find the word feels just right.

BY THE TIME the subway car gets uptown, I've thankfully sobered up quite a bit. Reid and I walk in awkward silence back to the Windsor, and I spend the whole journey battling shame at my multiple overshares. I think I may have asked him if he *does girls*. Gah. I want to wash my memory with soap.

Once we're through the gateway to Harker, I make a beeline for Elkfore without so much as a goodbye. I follow the haunting candelabra light from our commons entry all the way up to my dorm. My creaky wooden bed is calling to me: I've never needed a good night's sleep so bad in my life.

But when I crack open our door, I find a furious, scowling Sophia. "What the hell was that?"

My eyeballs ache with how tired I am. "Soph—"

"You *abandoned* me in that hallway."

"I like to hunt alone," I say, dropping my things on my bed and kicking off my shoes.

"And I like to masturbate when I wake up in the morning, but

I have a roommate now and have to share the dorm like an adult, don't I?"

"Sophia."

"Don't *Sophia* me. If I can learn to change my ways, so can you. We're friends now, Viv. And friends don't leave each other behind."

I stare at her enraged face. The lines carving into her forehead beneath her wispy bangs. The tension in her pursed lips. "I didn't want you to get hurt."

"Bullshit. You did it because you hunt first and think second. Which is a great way to get yourself killed. But let's just pretend you meant that, what about *me*? Huh? I was worried about *you*. We didn't know if you'd lived or died when Reid sent us home. Can you imagine?"

The thought of not knowing if some vampire had drained Sophia makes me nauseous. "No," I admit. "I'm sorry."

"Yeah. You should be. It's your weird abilities that caused all this fucked-upness."

My blood stops. "What weird abilities?"

Sophia sits back down at her desk and pulls her feet up under her. "No need to play dumb. Your secret is safe with me. Even when you're being a selfish little loner."

But I can't relax. It's not that I don't trust her, it's just that my dad never faltered on his very first rule: *Nobody can know you're an aeon.* "I don't know what you're talking about."

"Okay." She shrugs. "But I saw the way you followed the trail of that vampire. It was like you had a homing device in your brain or something. And don't give me some hunter instinct crap. I've seen you rely solely on your senses. It was like watching someone play Marco Polo in the Atlantic."

I'm so anxious I don't say anything. Nobody knows. Nobody

has known but my dad my entire life. And he's dead, so . . . Nobody knows but me. And now Sophia.

She seems to clock my anxiety, because her brows meet in concern and she quiets a little. "Hey."

"Hi." I might be shaking.

"I won't tell anyone you're an aeon. You have my word. I'll always have your back, Viv."

Sinking into my bed, I exhale a thousand sighs in one. "You aren't scared?" *Of me? Of what I could do?*

"Scared? I fight creatures from *hell*. Eerie girls with Victorian-era lockets don't frighten me. Even if they do crave the kill. We all have vices."

I close my eyes. "I'm really sorry about today."

"It's fine," she says, standing up and coming over to sit with me. She pulls me into a hug and pets my hair like my mom used to when I was little. "It was fun having the moral high ground. Doesn't happen to me too often."

"You're welcome, then," I say with a weak laugh.

"Are you . . . the last one alive?"

I shrug. "No clue. It's not like I've had anyone I can talk to about this."

I feel her nod beside me. "That must have been really fucking lonely."

Though I'm sure it's just the waning effects of the sedative, exhausted tears prickle at my eyes. It's been such a long day. A long life, honestly. "I've been so scared I'll hurt someone."

"You would never do that, Viv. Never."

We stay like that for a while. Sophia running her fingers through my hair. My eyes fluttering closed. Before I nod off, I make sure to tell her, "I'll always have your back too."

CHAPTER 20

I'M NOT SURE if it's the confidence I've gained from finally telling Sophia what I am or the relief that killing wraiths and a vampire in the same week has offered my aeon itch, but when we sit down for breakfast in the dining hall the next morning, sunlight pouring through the sky-high windows, I feel reinvigorated. Not only on my stalled-out key card hunt but with tracking Kitty down.

"What's new on the Kitty front?" I ask Peter.

"Nothing," he says around a piece of toast. "Service's been shut off on her phone. No response to any of my emails. I even tried a pager number that was definitely not hers."

"Jeez." Elliot takes a sip of his juice. "And she has no family you can call?"

"Nope. As parentless as I am. No siblings, either." Peter shakes his head. "I even went back to the registrar this morning to ask if those textbooks ever came in. Turns out she formally withdrew from all her classes."

"That's good," Sophia says. "Right?"

"Maybe," Peter muses. "But I pushed for the date. It was days *after* Mila got the letter."

"Why is that a bad thing?" Elliot asks.

"Kitty was a *t* crosser and an *i* dotter," Sophia says. "She wouldn't leave school and *then* withdraw from classes almost a week later."

"Exactly." Peter's eyes look pained. Ashamed, maybe.

"Hey." I wrap my hand around his across the table. "This is in no way your fault."

"Yeah," Peter says. "I know."

But I can tell he doesn't. "Why don't we go back to her room and search for clues? First thing tomorrow, after Elliot's big game tonight."

Sophia snorts. "Who are you, Scooby-Doo?"

"No," I say pointedly. *"All four of us* are the people here who knew Kitty best, and we also happen to have superhuman eyesight, senses of smell, and attention to detail."

"It's not a bad idea," Peter says to Sophia. "I'm not sure what else there is to do."

It only takes Sophia seeing the pain in Peter's eyes to change her tune. She swallows her bite quickly and nods. "Okay, yeah. Let's do it."

"You guys can go tonight," Elliot says. "You don't have to come to the game."

Sophia whirls on him. "You think we'd miss your first Harker lacrosse game? Not a chance."

Elliot's soft smile makes my heart warm. "Where else am I going to practice my heckling?" I ask.

He narrows his eyes at me, even as his mouth has curled up in a grin. "I'll hurl the ball right at you."

"We'll catch it and scream like rabid groupies," Sophia tells him.

"I have that study group tonight," Peter mopes. "For Crowley's class."

"Viv and I will act out every single play for you afterward,"

Sophia tells Peter, patting him on his back. "It'll be like you didn't miss a thing."

I will absolutely not be doing that, but I smile and nod anyway.

WHEN WE ENTER the coliseum for Combat Training, there's a large tarp spread across one-half of the stone stands we usually sit on. Gleaming against the dark plastic are short swords, long swords, crossbows, knives—a treasure trove of carnage. My blood thrums.

"Take a seat," Reid instructs. He's in another faded sleeveless shirt, this one a cornflower blue that makes his eyes gleam.

From my spot, I can read little labels beneath each weapon: VAMPIRE BLOOD, HOLY WATER, MERMAID TEARS, NAGA VENOM. And some more mundane: SALT, ASH, BUCKTHORN OIL. One blade is frozen solid while another is perched over a small, contained flame.

"Today's your first test. Only two grades: pass or fail."

Peter swallows hard beside me.

"As you can see, to your left, our armorer has been kind enough to loan the class thirty weapons, each coated in a different substance. I'll give you a deviant, you grab the right weapon and land it on me, and you pass. Pick incorrectly and fail."

I have the sinking feeling that Reid's not going to tell anyone they've failed until they're writhing on the pebbled floor in pain. But maybe he'll surprise me.

"Thompson," Reid calls out. "You're up first."

Elliot lumbers across the stands and observes the weapons. The fighting portion will be a breeze for him, but he's not in Dawnmere's Potions and Salves class with Sophia and me, so I cross my fingers that he gets an easy one.

"Wraith," Reid offers.

Jackpot. Reid might know Elliot wasn't there when they attacked our floor in Elkfore, but Sophia, Peter, and I told him all about the salt-filled leaf blower. And the low-slung sweats.

Elliot swipes the hunting knife dipped in salt with an easygoing grin. Reid's expression doesn't change even as Elliot leaps down into the arena and charges. Reid evades his first few swipes, but Elliot manages to land a quick nick of the blade against Reid's arm.

"Good." He's not even out of breath. "Pass."

Elliot nods, pleased with himself, and heads back up to sit beside Sophia.

By the time the next student has gone down—ghoul, arrows dipped in sage—the cut from Elliot's knife has already healed. That's why none of the weapons on that cloth are silver. Reid is in no danger today.

For Peter, Reid is a "vampire," and Peter picks a stake dipped in holy water. A layup for him. I wish Reid had given Peter something harder, given his encyclopedic knowledge of this stuff. At this point, sage, holy water, sugar, wolfsbane, graveyard dirt, and salt are all off the table, and things are looking more and more difficult for Sophia and me. I peer over at the items remaining—I've never even heard of a bunyip, let alone what its fat might ward against.

Peter struggles to land a hit on Reid, and eventually, when Reid's nearly pummeled him to the ground, gets a slice on his hand. Sophia, Elliot, and I breathe sighs of harmonious relief. A strange part of me wonders if Reid gave him the out. I'd never have let my palm get so close to someone's stake.

Matt makes the first real mistake of the class.

"Troll," Reid gives him. I know from Crowley's class that the answer is crowberry juice. It's an evergreen fruit native to Scandinavia, where trolls have migrated since the Chasm's split. Something to do with the abundance of caves and mountains. But Matt falls asleep in Crowley's class a lot. With utter confidence, he grabs an axe slathered in mermaid tears. Wrong. So very wrong.

I can see the amusement in Reid's eyes.

"So if I hack your arm off," Matt says, swaggering down to the arena floor, "will a new one just grow back?"

Reid doesn't even smirk. "Swing and let's find out."

Matt gives it all he's got. Spittle flying, muscles bulging. None of it matters—Reid slams him down to the ground with one smooth blow. The axe goes skidding across the chalky pebbles, and Matt coughs until air hits his lungs again.

"That's a failure, Peverell," Reid says, offering the sputtering kid his hand up.

Matt swats him away, storming back to the stands.

"Abbot," Reid says, ignoring him. He gestures to the arena as if to say *The water's fine.*

My body tightens. I have a bad feeling I know what he's about to say. "What am I fighting?"

Reid assesses me, something mischievous in those blue eyes. "Hydra."

I knew it. The answer was mermaid tears. Hydras are sea monster deviants thwarted by sea-dwelling lymantrian pain, the cosmic balance. But Matt's mistake screws all of us. Now I have to take something that serves its best purpose against something *else*.

My eyes survey the options. Hydras are in the serpent family. My father taught me to fight them on land as well as in water, which means I have a few weapons that just might work, but I don't want to pick anything that leaves another student screwed. I settle on a crossbow with arrows dipped in shattered mirror dust. As close to pixie dust as I can find, without actually *taking* the pixie dust-laced knife that I know someone will need when Reid tosses out "basilisk."

When I step into the arena, he looks impressed.

And I want to be irritated that he tried to stump me. That he set me up to fail. But after our subway ride last night, it almost feels more like a thoughtful challenge. Which is why when he studies me, that slight smile playing on his mouth, and mutters, "Well done," I can't help the flush that rises up my cheeks.

I combat the strangely prideful feelings by shooting at him with my bow until I pierce him clean through the shoulder like the nasty little aeon that I am. I even offer a curtsy as he glowers at me, yanking the bolt out with a subtle wince. "Pass," he grunts.

After another twenty students—most passing among a handful of miserable failures—Sophia is called last. Reid gives her "hellhound" and Sophia grabs the only weapon left. A long sword coated in buckthorn oil.

"This isn't fair," Sophia says, folding her arms. "Someone else took the blade that was on fire."

Reid only shrugs. I'd expected him to look a little worse for wear after being hit with so many weapons, but his demon healing has exceeded expectations. He looks as battle-ready as he did when he entered at the top of class. "Part of hunting is working in unideal circumstances."

Reid charges Soph without another word, and Elliot allows me to squeeze the ever-loving crap out of his forearm. All I can hope is that this will be over quickly. Ice baths for us all tonight. But Sophia's eyes are roaming the coliseum. I want to yell at her to *focus* on the ex–Brood demon hurtling toward her, but before I even open my mouth, she's taken off up the stands.

"What are you doing, Sophia?" I mutter to myself.

"Valentine," Reid calls, leaping after her. "Stay in the arena."

But she ignores him, bounding up to where a torch burns brightly at the very top row of seats.

"That's so smart," someone murmurs behind us. It might be the kid who unintentionally screwed her over in the first place by taking the flaming blade.

It's beyond smart. It's so Sophia—risky, outside the box. The sword she chose was coated in oil. All she needs is a flame.

But it's also dangerous.

"She could light herself on fire," Peter mutters as we watch Sophia race to the top, Reid hot on her tail.

Sophia reaches the torch and stands on her tippy-toes to dip the end of her blade into the fire. In an instant, the roaring flames lick down her sword and she swings it on Reid.

"Drop the blade, Valentine," Reid grunts as he reaches her. The entire class is now facing the top of the stands rather than the arena floor. "You pass."

"I have to land my hit on you," she says with a grin, bangs fluttering perilously close to the fire. She swings masterfully, and Reid dodges out of instinct, curls of hungry fire nearly swallowing his shirt.

"Valentine." Reid dives for her, though she moves away. "You've made your point. Put it down."

The fire begins to crawl down the length of the sword toward the hilt. Toward her hand. "Why? You scared?"

"Yeah," Reid says, eyeing the flames that are snaking toward her fingers. "Of you burning alive." Reid lunges for the sword, but Sophia swings it away. Students have begun to cheer for her.

And I know she isn't giving anything up. Sophia isn't just wild and hungry for a good fight. She's like a hellhound herself: reckless, impulsive. She acts first, thinks later. With drugs, with boys, with hunting.

Reid knows it too. He dives for Sophia, sandwiching the blade between the two of them and snuffing out the fire. I didn't need a hunter dad to teach me that one: stop, drop, and roll. It's exactly what they do, tumbling through the stands until they come to a halt.

It's so simple. But . . . kind of brilliant. Low effort on Reid's part—pretty sure he didn't even break a sweat—and the perfect way to give Sophia the win. The blade was pressed up against Reid's chest, and he made sure she never got hurt in the process.

When Sophia stands and raises her sword in the air, the class claps for her, and she beams her radiant smile at them. She bested the beast. Slayed the monster. Won for her fellow hunters. When she reaches our spot in the stands, Elliot pulls her into an impressed hug and Peter tries not to look like he just saw his life flash before his eyes.

When we're making our way down to the arena floor and toward the exit, I can't help but look back at Reid, gathering all the discarded weapons.

And as much as I hate to admit it . . . I'm impressed. Not because he stopped Sophia from setting herself on fire or because he keeps putting Matt in his place. Not because when he reaches for a short sword, I decide his arms were crafted by angels specifically for shirts without sleeves. But because he's actually kind of a good teacher. Demanding, cold, tricky . . . but fair. And if he truly abstains from souls as he claims, he's still whooping hunters left, right, and sideways with about a third of the juice.

As I watch him pack up, my heart gives a shocking, unexpected achy tug. Just as I can see blood in a demon's eyes when they're ready to devour a soul, I can see something pained in Reid's. I wonder if, even though he could best the whole class without a second thought, he'd rather be cheering along with us. Fighting as one of the good guys.

CHAPTER 21

I'M NOT SUCH a *rah-rah* kind of girl—I think my dark wardrobe and resting bitch face, as Soph so lovingly puts it, could tell you as much—but tonight's lacrosse game is decidedly kind of awesome. Though perhaps that's just because both teams are made up of superhuman hunters who are playing an already-contact-rife sport like they've been dosed with steroids. Maybe *this* should've been held in the coliseum.

When I was at Belaire School for Girls, the only sporting event we had was ballet, during which I got rapped on the knuckles more than once for falling asleep. In my defense, I'd grown up in lower-middle-class Astera, where I'd known as much about ballet as I had about nuclear fission.

Once again, I find myself enjoying the collegiate experience I never got to have. Cosplaying as a regular Harker student isn't the first thing on my figure-out-why-my-dad-changed-his-name-after-going-to-school-here to-do list, but until I can get my hands on a staff member's key card, I have no way into the archives. My current game plan is to swipe one off a professor tomorrow during weekend office hours. After we inspect Kitty's room Scooby-Doo-style, that is. So tonight there's nothing more I can do on either front but watch the game.

On the field below, amid a pleasant fall chill, Elliot funnels his whip-fast predator speed into a stunning tackle that results in another goal for the Bat and Blood team. The crowd stomps on the bleachers, and the power of thousands of hunter feet pounding shakes the earth like a seismic event. The stadium lights glow against the swirl of violet sky fading into black, and I inhale salty snacks and freshly cut grass and think of my dad. Now I know why this was his favorite sport—he was a champion here.

Sophia lets out a rowdy whoop at the next point and throws her hands in the air.

"Why do you think hunters love lacrosse so much?" I ask her over the roaring crowd.

Sophia turns to face me, and I notice that at some point during the game, she borrowed someone's face paint and now has navy lines drawn across her cheeks. "It's like football, but you get to wield a weapon?"

A brutal takedown results in a foul, and the entire crowd boos. "No other sports?"

"I'm looking forward to the regatta on Lake Hellebore in the spring. Rowers' arms are . . ." She fans herself in mock lust.

"And everyone's rooting for Bat and Blood?" Lacrosse teams at Harker are like secret societies in the Ivy League. Generations old, each with its own distinct personality, recruitment system, and track record. The players even live in the same houses on the same avenue like frats on Greek Row. Elliot moved out of Elkfore as soon as he was accepted onto B-and-B. From what I've gathered, the Strikers seem to be the golden boys, while the craftier Bat and Blood are tonight's underdogs.

"Kind of. I'm rooting for a good game and don't really care who wins. But it's always satisfying to see Bat and Blood hand the Strikers their asses. B-and-B's the only team that recruits first years."

Sophia and I scream for Elliot to score as he barrels down the field until our voices are raspy. He could have been Division I at a real college. "Do they teach anything academic here? Like math or science? None of these kids ever get to go to legitimate universities."

"Eventually we'll have to read *Gatsby* and *The Catcher in the Rye*, don't you worry your little prep school heart." I make a face and she laughs her sparkling, open-mouthed Sophia laugh. At least two guys in the stands with us can't help their stares. "My mom says we'll even have career day."

"Career day?" I can't imagine all these hunters taking aptitude tests to see if they'd be better nurses or marketing execs.

"Yep. To help us to find the best job to hide our hunting. Overnight security guard, web developer. Nothing that's nine to five or requires too much personal info shared. You get the idea."

When Bat and Blood slams another goal into the Strikers' net, I'm convinced the game is over. The scoreboard reads 10–2, and the crowd is chanting, "Batty, bloody, batty." It's practically a slaughter.

"Where should we take Elliot to celebrate?" I ask Soph, motioning for her bag of chips.

"I'm sure the team will have a party tonight." She takes a sip of her soda, which she spiked with vodka before we left. "First one of the year. Here's to things getting *wild*."

I raise a brow at her, my mouth full of salty, crunchy heaven.

"I don't know what that face means."

"Yes, you do," I say, though it comes out like *hes hoo hoo*.

"Not wild like *that*. I'm not into Elliot. Never have been, never will be. Now that we're best friends, you have to wrap your perverse mind around that."

I clutch my heart in faux horror. "Perverse?"

"Yeah. You're a little freak, I can tell." Sophia tosses a few chips into her mouth. "You have all the makings of a sexual degenerate." She begins to tick items off on long fingers tipped in red polish. "Self-loathing, beauty, surly avoidant energy, trauma from probably both mommy *and* daddy issues . . . I get your whole thing, Abbot."

I swallow dryly. The chip grease coating my tongue is like slick oil. I haven't told Sophia about my parents. I certainly haven't told her about the things I want in bed that I'd never ask James for. I've never told *Penny* that stuff—even before I was dating her brother.

Sophia stares at me with fiendish delight. "I'm right on the money, aren't I?"

I debate brushing off the question. I've kept everything about my dad a secret from my friends just in case anyone at the school knew he was an aeon and could link me to him. But Sophia already knows what I am, so . . . "My dad was a hunter," I tell her. I think of the picture of him and his teammates in the rotunda, the scoreboard announcing the win for the Marksmen. "He was on a lacrosse team here too. And he died when I was ten."

Sophia's rich brown eyes shutter. This time when Bat and Blood scores and the entire crowd becomes a sea of cheers around us, she doesn't flinch. "That fucking sucks."

"And then my mom funneled her heartbreak into putting people behind bars. She had been a volunteer councilwoman in Lethe, where we grew up, trying to better the neighborhood and stuff. After my dad died, she worked her way up, eventually ran for district attorney. Fancy new job meant fancy new town, so she moved us over the hill to the Hesperides, and now she might be dating Caspar Harlock."

"Caspar Harlock? Like, the guy who owns all the news networks? When he's on TV, my parents throw the remote at his face."

I wish I could throw things at him in real life. "He's funding my mom's mayoral campaign. Which my sister, Nora, is helping with now too when she's not running this massively successful, fancy nonprofit. My whole family is stock photo perfect. Her wife, my boyfriend . . ."

"'Perfect' sounds like code for 'medicated.'"

I snort. "They're just all so . . . normal. And successful. And happy."

Sophia pretends to fall asleep and then jerk awake. "Horrible. A fate I wouldn't wish on the vilest of deviants."

"Your turn," I tell her, messing with the clasp of my locket and brushing some crumbs off my tights. I'm a little embarrassed by my overshare.

"Grew up in a kind of religious small town by the sea. Young hippie parents were rebels and had me—*gasp*—out of wedlock. They weren't like everyone else's parents, and that was on top of being hunters. I'm sure I had some shame around that . . ." Sophia shrugs and her long hair cascades off her bare shoulder and down her back. "But they love each other a nauseating amount. Probably more than they love me. We weathered the storm and people got over it. I spent so much time on my own because they were always hunting together. If I have any trauma, it's my fault, not theirs."

I don't push, because I wouldn't have wanted her to push on my sob story, but I am curious. What kind of trauma could she be talking about?

Another merciless tackle on the field sends the crowd to their feet before Sophia can say anything else. I try to see what's happening but can't quite make out who took down who. Multiple lacrosse sticks have been tossed aside, and players from both teams hurry faster and faster toward the commotion. I search for Elliot's large frame and wavy hair but come up empty.

"What's going on?" I ask. A brawl, maybe?

Sophia doesn't say anything, eyes locked on the field below. That should've been my first sign. Note to Self: When Sophia is worried, you should worry.

Instead, I don't feel my hackles rise until a harrowing scream slices through the night.

Then it all happens at once—someone two rows below us is knocked over, and their fall knocks over about six other people. Chips and cans of soda burst into the air like confetti from a cannon. Sophia and I both duck on instinct, and on the field I can hear the roar of students and teachers instructing kids to evacuate and protect themselves, but it's drowned out by a chorus of groans from something else. Whatever it is, it sounds like there's hundreds of them.

"*Run*," Sophia tells me.

Addendum to Note to Self: When Sophia is worried, you should *get the hell out of Dodge.*

When I was a young and overzealous little hunter—probably just thrilled to know the relentless violence inside me had not only a name but also a purpose, and that purpose came with something special I got to do with my dad—he'd tell me time and time again: *You gotta know what you're fighting to fight it.* Professor Crowley puts it even more clearly: *The first step in hunting is research.*

However you say it, Sophia and I have the same instinct—we take off at breakneck speed. Not down toward the chaos to help—if there's anything I'm not worried about with Elliot, it's whether he can fight—nor away to save our skins but up the bleachers to get a better look at what exactly is going on. Yet all I can see on the field below is a war zone. Blood, limbs, bodies—

At first I think at least fifty students are dead. I picture the High Thane using his cloven hooves to crush Elliot's skull like hard candy and nearly vomit.

Sometimes, amid calamity, mortals can't take in everything at once. It's impossible to see and hear and speak—there's too much adrenaline in their systems. Their bodies only have space for one sole focus: Survive. But hunters have a different sole focus: Kill.

And that means I take everything in both quicker and slower. I can scent the iron-rich tang of blood in the night air mingling with spray paint on the field and hot dog buns. I can hear the screams of agony, the grunts of effort as swords are swung, the tight breaths pumping in and out of Sophia beside me. And I can see clearly the stream of corpses hurtling toward the lacrosse pitch from the Harker cemetery not ten yards away.

Those bodies are *not* students. They're reanimated dead folk, dying once again at the hands of Harker's skilled hunters. I spy Elliot driving his lacrosse stick into an armless corpse until the Bat and Blood coach pries him up and helps him get away from the field.

But I've studied deviants for four weeks now, and a whole lifetime before that, and zombies are *not* deviants. *The undead* only covers ghouls, ghosts, and wraiths, as Crowley has taught us. Deviants are born in the underworld, not in graves here on the mortal plane. "Did I miss something? Are zombies—"

"They're not," Sophia says, reading my mind. "Must be a spell."

Right. Which means instead of hacking up the rotting flesh of legacy students and tenured professors buried on campus, Sophia and I need to find a way to end said spell. We must have the idea at the same time, because we both start for the cemetery before we realize we can't make it past the chaos in the bleachers without losing valuable time.

"This way," I tell her, and fling myself over the bleachers' edge without a second thought.

I hit the grass hard and the impact sings through my ankles and knees.

Sophia and I bolt through the night-drenched campus, her bow raised, my daggers grasped tightly in my hands. We don't stop in the foggy courtyards or along the torchlit path to catch our breath. We don't stop until we reach the source.

Hanging lanterns flicker and sway over Harker's cemetery. Wrought-iron gates surround the rolling, grassy hills, low stone benches, and trickling fountains shrouded in mist. Among the hunched weeping willows and vines of creeping Jenny are classical monuments, stately mausoleums, and crumbling tombs. And crawling out from them all—

Hundreds of moaning, reanimated dead.

CHAPTER 22

"HOLY SHIT," SOPHIA breathes.

The ornate iron gates to the cemetery have been wrenched open, and the zombies inside are dragging themselves out of open caskets and patches of earth. They slip and crawl over the hills and intertwining pathways doused in curling fog. Sophia raises her bow, but I pull her behind a towering oak tree, out of sight of the creatures. We watch as the zombies converge like ants on spilled syrup, their singular focus on the lacrosse pitch beyond the gates. Snarling, yowling, groaning their senseless need for flesh. They aren't fast, but together, they're strong.

A blood-chilling scream carries over from the field, and Sophia shudders beside me. I can't think about what's happening back there. The way students and teachers are battling monsters with faces they might have known, friends and colleagues they may have mourned. If Elliot's gotten to safety. If anyone's been killed. I have to have faith that older students and professors can defend themselves while we stop the spell.

"We need to find the origin object," I whisper. "Like Professor Crowley was saying in class yesterday."

But unlike the minor rituals hunters can perform, spells and hexes must be cast by witches. And I don't see any living beings around here but us. No dark figures. No cauldrons bubbling or incense burning or animals sacrificed on a hearth.

Sophia's eyes scan the hills and tombs of the cemetery. The weeping willows and babbling fountains. I can read her furrowed brow. We have no idea where to begin. The object that anchors the spell could be anything. It could take days to find, and we don't have that kind of time. Every minute, another zombie climbs from its resting place.

"The gates," I whisper at the same time Sophia quietly says, "We could block the exit."

We exchange a brief smile—great minds—and then bolt toward the entrance. A snarling, hulking, long-since-dead hunter hurtles toward me and I slice both my daggers clean through his neck before he can make contact. Groaning noises and shuffling feet threaten to overwhelm me, but I tell myself it's like the blindfolded sparring session. I only need to focus on one sense at a time. We just have to make it to the gates.

Sophia gets there first. The wrought iron's been ripped from its hinges. She shoves as hard as she can, but the parts don't fit together like they did before, and they're heavy even for her hunter strength. After three agonized attempts, I come to the same conclusion she does—there's no way to close them. No way to stop the reanimated creatures from spilling out and into the school.

"We just have to take them out as they reanimate," I breathe. But there are so many of them.

"Shit," Sophia curses as she shoots a crisp arrow into a decaying man whose lips have been ripped clean off. Another claws toward her ankles. My heart is between my teeth as I lunge with my dagger, but another one yanks me back. Sophia screams. The scent of rotting flesh races up my nose—

In two flashes of bright light, the corpses spring off us like we're electric to the touch.

I spin, breath sawing out of me, to find Dean Driscoll, hands raised, sweat and blood on his brow.

I've never seen magic like that before.

"Dean Driscoll." Sophia gulps.

"You two need to get out of here." The dean's face steels, and he raises a hand. Another flash of white light sparks in the corner of my eye, and two more zombies drop. *"Now."*

A mournful festering woman stumbles out from behind the massive oak and toward the dean before we can respond. This time, she halts, caught in midair by the throat. The dean's eyes narrow to furious slits as the fight is squeezed out of her. His power wrings her neck. She shrieks—a desolate, sickening sound. The scars and tattoos on the dean's muscled arms bulge as he holds his hands out in her direction until her rotting head pops clean off and rolls toward a squawking crow wreathed in fog.

I swallow hard, my stomach churning. "We're trying to fix the gates. To lock the zombies in here."

But the dean has closed his eyes, his hands raised toward the cemetery behind us. The scent of strange herbs and biting spices fills my nostrils as Sophia and I slice through any undead who wander toward him, groaning and stumbling, looking for flesh. The dean doesn't wink an eye open. His body tenses, the wind shifts, and a foreboding chill snakes down my spine.

When the dean opens his eyes, grim and bright with fury, he says, "The object of origin's down there." Sure enough, we follow his eyeline to see a crypt door flung wide open, muddy footprints trailing down the darkened steps. In the mist-coated night and in all my panic, I didn't even notice. "I can destroy it, but not if you two are in danger. You both need to get to safety."

He eyes the dead who continue to break free from their graves and slink toward us. More and more and more of them—

"We're not going anywhere," Sophia says, reading my mind.

"Get the gates closed, then," he says, voice baritone and resolute. Not one to bicker when student lives are at stake. He sidesteps the pool of congealing zombie blood on the ground before adding, "And do so without dying." Then he conjures a jagged, gleaming hunting knife from thin air and carves his way through the dead standing in his way.

"You heard the man." Sophia shoves at the gates again until her bangs are matted against her forehead with sweat. I try to help from the other side, but these hinges have clearly been broken by something far stronger than us. Magic, maybe. The same magic that spelled the cemetery.

My own breathing is too loud in my head. The more we bang the gates, the more we draw the dead toward us. Something grabs at my dress from behind, and I plunge my dagger back, but then another one is at my heels, and I can't reach, and his fingers—those cold, dead fingers—are trying to tear into my flesh, and when I turn around to stab . . . they're both dead. Arrowheads in their skulls.

My eyes find Sophia, crossbow raised, dead zombies lying between us. "Told you I'd have your back."

We watch as two more stumble over the fallen dead, trying to cross toward the field. But they can't surmount the lumps of rotting flesh at their feet. Bones breaking, they collapse to the dirt.

I'm opening my mouth to thank her when an idea slams into me.

"They can't climb," I murmur. I survey the wooded cemetery. "There. We can knock that tree down. Block their path."

Sophia looks up at the towering oak we'd hidden behind earlier. "With what army?"

But that's exactly it. I gesture to the snarling dead around us. "This one."

Digging my foot into the bark, I use my daggers like ice axes on a frosty mountain ascent to scale the tree. Sophia uses her arrows to do the same, and we make quick work of the climb. The view of Old Campus from the top of the oak would be hauntingly beautiful—all the swirling mist and gloomy, glowing windows—if there weren't a bloodbath on the lacrosse pitch to our left.

"Ready?" I ask her.

"Are you kidding?" She grins. "This is going to be awesome."

But adrenaline is coursing through my limbs so hard they're shaking. "I'm glad you feel that way."

Sophia screams as loudly as she possibly can. Despite every corner of my being telling me *Do not do this*, I follow suit. Our screams rival those coming from the pitch. Crows flee from trees around the cemetery, screeching in the air.

The dead below come slowly at first. Recalibrating their direction. Moving toward the sound. But the more we scream, the quicker they get the message. Like any herd, they have a pack mentality, and once a few come, so do the rest.

Only then do they attempt to scale the tree to get to us. Swarming, grunting, throwing their rotting bodies at the trunk. Arms and legs break off as a pileup begins to form at the base.

"It's working," she breathes. "Look."

There's no way down from the tree now. They have us surrounded. The roots begin to snap one by one. Hunter senses firing on all cylinders, I can feel them breaking as the tips of my fingers clutch the peeling bark. The tree leans and sways.

"Relax," Sophia says. She must notice my white knuckles gripped around a branch, because she adds, "It's like a roller coaster."

"Now, that's your horror franchise," I mutter, trying to brace myself for the fall. *"Zombie Roller Coaster Six."*

"The fourth one was better," she jokes. I don't think she's even afraid.

"You're out of your mind, aren't you?"

The herd gives one last shove and the trunk rips from the earth with a crackling *pop*.

Shit, shit, shit—

The ground flies up to meet us. The mob of undead moans and whines at a low, rumbling decibel. I hold on to the tree with my entire body's strength and then, a second before impact, let go to avoid being crushed underneath its weight. I go flying, rolling over trampled grass and mud. A jagged tombstone catches my hip and pain ripples through me.

For a moment, it's all I can do to lie still. The wind's been knocked out of me, the air stopped in the depths of my lungs.

Panic seizes me. I can't *breathe*—

But then the inhale dislodges and I suck in air by the lungful.

When I look up, I see Sophia's landed in a barrel roll on the ground. A rabbit flies from the bushes to avoid being crushed, and the oak tree comes crashing down onto rocks and mud and headstones. Debris splatters both of us. But when we stand . . .

The mighty oak has fallen over mere feet before the gates, trapping all the dead within the confines of the graveyard. They whine and groan, clambering on top of one another, trying to get out. Trying to reach the battle still being waged on the brightly lit pitch. But they're immobile, spinning their wheels.

Sophia and I exchange a look of exhaustion and pain and triumph before we begin to hack away at the masses. My daggers cut through rotten flesh and drying bones, sagging throats and empty guts. I swallow down my dry heaves. Sophia dry heaves at the stench. But we're making progress, taking them out with the kind of tactile precision only hunters have.

I'm about to tell Sophia we've done enough here and should go to the pitch to help when all the lights wink out.

Every single one on campus.

The lanterns in the cemetery, the fluorescent stadium lights from the lacrosse field, the little lamps that line the cobblestone path outside. The entire school is drowned in suffocating night.

There are no visible stars amid the too-thick fog. But the moon hangs in the sky like it's weighing it down, wider and yellower than I've ever seen it. The darkness only amplifies its enormity—imposing, punishing as it dominates the night. With the campus drenched in liquid black, my other senses perk up. My nose fills with the earthy scent of mushrooms and moss mingled with the musk of rotting human flesh. An owl hoots rhythmically above.

I've spent half my life prowling in the darkness, hunting things that make the nighttime their playground. Still, it hasn't hardened me to that intrinsic human pull toward light and warmth and people. The groaning sounds of creatures that want to devour me, their fingernails scraping like claws, the glowing eyes that blink and skitter in the brush . . . My blood pumps too loudly in my ears and I have the humiliating instinct to reach for Sophia's hand as if I'm five years old and she's Nora or something.

And then the screaming stops.

And the moaning.

And the sound of metal slashing through old, worn flesh.

When the campus lights click back on, all the zombies are dead bodies once again. Piled on the ground, sloping atop one another at strange, unnatural angles. And Dean Driscoll, walking toward us—

I nearly jump a foot in the air at the sight.

He's covered in cobweb and ash, and he's got a serious gash down his tattooed arm, which he's stanched with fabric ripped from his shirt. He's holding what looks like the remains of a crushed human skull. The object of origin, I'm sure.

He takes in the felled tree. "Good work."

"Thanks," Sophia breathes. "It was Viv's idea."

"Some first month you kids are having." Driscoll frowns, looking to the object in his hand, and then lets the skull crumble to the ground, wipes human remains and blood on his shirt, and extends the hand to each of us. "We're lucky to have you both. You saved lives tonight."

I get the sense his big, scary warlock thing might be at odds with a quiet, lonely, perhaps even awkward man.

"Dean Driscoll," a shrill voice calls from the other side of the tree.

Professor Lisette, wrapped in a cloak, climbs over the fallen oak and the mounds of corpses with a twist of her mouth. "Christ above," she mutters.

"It's over," Dean Driscoll tells Lisette. "Viv and Sophia here saw to that."

Lisette narrows her eyes at us, and suddenly I feel like I'm in grade school, about to be sent to the principal's office. The way she looks at me . . . A strange tension coils in my body. It's too familiar. Being a disappointment.

"Time for you girls to leave," Lisette instructs, face grim under the dim lantern light.

Sophia's face slackens. "But—"

"Go," Lisette snaps at her. "You've done enough."

"Professor," Driscoll says in warning.

But she's not deterred. She wraps her cloak tighter around herself. "Both of you girls, back to the pitch. Help bury the dead. Or . . . rebury."

"Yes, Professor," we mumble.

I drag Sophia with me until we're stomping down the cobblestone path under that enormous harvest moon, back toward the lacrosse pitch. Students are crying, whispering, limping in the darkness back to their dorms. In the distance I can see the glow of healing pixie magic, professors in pajamas and coats, students helping one another up or icing injuries. No body bags, but I'm not convinced yet every student made it through the night.

Before I can even open my mouth to ask about Elliot, Sophia spots him. "There." All the breath leaves her in a rush. His white uniform is coated in blood and guts, his caramel-brown hair streaked with sweat and dirt, but he's eyeing Sophia and me with pure relief, and I'm overwhelmed with the same exact feeling. Another person I never want to see get hurt. Fantastic.

We're halfway across the field to him when Sophia mutters, "Lisette's got such a stick up her ass. We saved people tonight."

My stomach twists. "There's something so strange about her . . ."

"Yeah, what a bitch she is."

"Thank god," Elliot sighs, pulling Sophia into a hug that lifts her off her feet. I'm smiling up at them both when suddenly Elliot pulls me into the hug too. My ankles dangle above the ground as my cheek is squished into his chest.

"Ouch," I mutter. Something is burning my skin. "Wait, stop, Elliot—" I struggle against them until Elliot releases us both.

Sophia's eyes widen. "What? What is it?"

"Shit," I hiss, fumbling for my blades. "*Shit.*"

I yank my blades out from their sheaths at my ribs and my thigh. They're scalding hot, the skin beneath already blistering. I let them clang to the ground and notice a faint burnished glow radiating from them, the grass beneath burning to ash on impact.

Elliot sucks in a ragged breath. "Does that happen a lot?"

I shake my head, still rubbing my burned skin. "No. Never."

CHAPTER 23

AFTER THE WRAITHS infiltrated Elkfore hall, I expected a morose haze to drift over the school, but everyone had proceeded like business as usual. It was an anomaly. A onetime occurrence. A faulty gateway. Something that's bound to happen eventually when you house all the young hunters across the world in one place.

But two students died last week at the lacrosse game. Harker students, ravaged by zombies. One was a third year on the Strikers who was eaten alive saving a first-year girl. The other was a kid whose name I recognized from two of my classes. They only found his arm.

So this is something new.

Harker is said to be impenetrable, but somehow wraiths broke in and a spell was cast on the cemetery that lead to two students losing their lives. The dean held an assembly. All nonessential classes—everything but Underworld Studies and Combat Training—were canceled for the week. We've only been told that they're looking into who cast the spell and why, and how a witch could have used magic on the school from outside our wards.

But it's not just that—it takes a lot to kill a hunter. With our accelerated healing, a wound that would be fatal to a mortal can cost us just a few days of bed rest. Still, a death blow is a death blow. Bullet to the heart. Decapitation. Removal of necessary internal organs . . .

It's tough to be reminded of that. To watch it play out in real time on a lacrosse field. To witness the grotesque, shredding, bloody end we'll all likely endure at the hands of a deviant. I'd say hunters do a pretty good job of fighting off the calling of that void. That despair at the inescapable. My dad did so with our family. Sophia, with drugs and drinks and boys. I do pretty well with denial. But watching a classmate be disemboweled by zombies would knock anyone back a few steps.

"Morning, cutie," Sophia says softly as we trek up the coliseum stands toward Peter. He's sitting front and center, as he always is, five minutes before class starts. A pink flush crawls up his cheeks at the term of endearment.

"Mila willing to let us into Kitty's room today?" Sophia asks, plopping down next to him.

She was injured in the attack and told us she'd need a few days before she had visitors. "Nope." Peter shakes his head in frustration, staring down at his hands until Sophia interlaces hers with his in comfort.

Now that the horror of the reanimation spell is starting to fade, I was going to ask our walking library of a friend if he has any idea what the hell happened to my daggers last week, but I stow the question away. Just for one more day. I know how scared and alone Peter feels right now. Not only is it starting to look like Kitty really isn't coming back, but the school he felt so safe at has been compromised twice in our first semester here.

My phone buzzes in my bag, and when I fish it out, there's a text from James. Dinner tonight? I'm getting drinks with the guys after work but could meet you somewhere North for a late bite? I miss you.

It's kind of good timing, since so many classes have been canceled. And James and I haven't had a proper date night since I enrolled at Harker, and my Windsor exhibit excuse can only last me so long.

Sure, I write back. Sounds fun.

Can't wait, he texts a nanosecond later. I'll make a res at Abattoir for 9:30. Apparently they let you kill your own lobster. I frown. A second later he writes, I'll handle yours for you, of course.

"You look like you're going to puke," Peter says. "Who are you texting?"

"My boyfriend." The words come out like *my executioner.*

When Reid walks in, I'm surprised by two things. One, that he's beat to hell—bruises like spilled port bloom up and down his arms, and he's got a nasty gash in one brow, a split lip, and what looks to be a slight limp on his right side. And two . . . that it bothers me.

Just a month ago I would have gladly inflicted those injuries on him myself. I didn't think anything had changed, but seeing him now . . . A protective urge aches in my limbs. He got those injuries saving people's lives.

"How's everyone holding up?" he asks.

Grumbles sound across the stands. Nobody's in the mood to whale on one another today, it seems.

"Anyone want to channel their sorrows into swordplay?"

Sophia chews her lip. Someone coughs. Even Elliot, sitting next to us, just runs a hand through his Adonis hair. If *he* doesn't want to swing a weapon around, you know spirits are low.

I brace myself for demon-level vitriol. Reid's about to skewer us for being afraid and weak and timid. None of us are behaving like hunters today.

But all he says is, "I thought as much. So I brought a friend with me."

That has us sitting up from our mournful, slouchy seats. Reid doesn't have friends.

Reid signals to someone waiting in the passage that surely led to gladiator quarters centuries ago. Instead of an oiled-up Russell Crowe, we are surprised to see Professor Crowley walk out, wheeling in a crate covered with dark canvas.

Immediately, goose bumps scatter across my skin.

"Good morning, students." Crowley grins, his metal teeth shimmering in the torchlight. It's still early enough that the sun has yet to crest overhead. "A little surprise for you today. For those of you in my class this semester, maybe less so."

And I already know. We experimented with different tonics on werewolf venom last week. The cage behind him rattles and clangs. Low snarls echo through the arena. My heart rate quickens.

Reid folds his arms across his chest. "Who wants to take a stab at Teen Wolf?"

My body hums with the allure of it. To sink my silver into matted, coarse fur. And after being excluded from his sacred Field Training nights, I'd love to show Reid just how *ready* I am to tackle anything he throws at us. But if my dad taught me one thing, it was that as much as we aeons crave the fight, you never make unforced errors. There's no reason to put myself in the line of danger out of ego or to scratch a bloodlust itch. We fight deviants to save lives. This is something else entirely.

However, the rest of the students seem to have received a different memo. They shoot their hands up across the stands, eager to prove their worth, to forget last week's horrors. Reid's unforgiving eyes scan the crowd. Every hand is raised but mine . . . and Peter's.

"Roydon," he says. "You're up."

Peter blanches beside me. Sophia's hand darts out to his shoulder on a reflex. But he stands, jaw tight, and pushes past her to jog down to the arena floor.

"You ever seen a were before, Peter?"

My stomach twists.

Peter nods at Reid, his throat bobbing with a swallow. "Watched my mom slay one once."

He's seen one *once*? I've fought at least thirty werewolves and still find my muscles clenching.

"Damn," Elliot whispers to us. "I've never seen a were."

"How?" I whisper back. "They're everywhere."

"Not by the ocean."

"Even in the winters," Sophia adds. "We don't really get lycanthropes where Elliot and I are from."

I guess that makes sense. I don't know many wolves and panthers who like sand and surf. "Astera's packed with them."

Elliot rolls his eyes. "Your city is built on top of the Chasm. Astera's packed with everything."

"Get it?" Sophia half grins. "*Packed?*"

Down on the arena floor, Reid offers Peter a veritable buffet of weapons, polished and laid out nicely on the same kind of rack you'd find weights on in a gym. He opts for a silver short sword, which is the right move. Obviously Peter's done his research: Werewolves are like demons—silver to the heart or head results in a surefire kill. But *unlike* demons, werewolves can die from natural causes too. When it's not a full moon and they're just regular people, an Astera taxi rounding a corner too fast can take one of them out just like the rest of us.

In fact, that might be the source of my queasiness. I'm all for taking out beasts and ghouls. Mindless, sinister monsters set on killing innocents? No problem. That gets me going more than my own boyfriend. Vamps and demons too. While they walk and talk and look like humans, they're only interested in soul taking and blood drinking, and that's a no-go in my book. Even worse, when they *aren't* using humans as their protein shakes, they're delighting in the worst humanity has to offer—violence, cruelty, hedonistic depravity. That's why I struggle to buy into Reid's I-don't-take-souls, I'm-one-of-the-good-guys act. It's just not in his nature.

But werewolves, windigos, all other lycanthropes—they have a purely human form. Some have been turned against their will and have had to reconcile their new fate with their past life as human. I don't actually *know* anybody like that, but my father once told me he knew a turned werepanther. He'd chain himself up every full moon and lived a relatively normal life as an insurance broker the other twenty-nine days of the month. Of course, some aren't turned. Some are born deviants. And those fuckers shift not only with the full moon, but whenever they damn well please. The problem is, you just don't really know what kind of were you're fighting until you do—which means I only kill them when there's a human life at stake. No unforced errors, remember?

"Ready?" Reid asks Peter.

He nods, gritting his teeth. His fear is plain across his face as he stares at the rattling cage, and my stomach flips again.

Reid nods to Professor Crowley, who studies Peter himself, as if he doesn't trust Reid's judgment.

"Any day now, Maxwell," Reid drawls.

Crowley doesn't even sneer at him. He just locks eyes with Peter and says, quietly, "You up for this, kid?"

Peter nods, steadfast even as his hands shake, and Crowley yanks the dark sheet off the metal cage. Inside, as expected, is a full-grown werewolf, foaming at the mouth. Werewolves don't look as much like wolves as *Twilight* has led us all to believe. Weres walk on thin, sinewy hind legs, with glowing-yellow beady eyes and an arm span longer than a dining table. Their faces and chests are hulking and hairy and yet still humanoid, in a blend of man and animal that even as a hunter I've never gotten used to.

And they certainly don't look like hunky teens with CGI abs when they've shifted back. Sometimes you're just left with the gutted corpse of a portly older woman who you recognize as your local librarian. Can you imagine how disorienting it is to realize you've just impaled the woman who helped you check out a book on your changing body?

The were I'm staring at looks mean too. Patchy brown fur, dripping fanged maw, scars, and bloodied nails that tell me he's been in a few of these fights. Crowley flicks the crate open and backs away. But the beast has no interest in him or Reid's demon flesh. Not when there's a shaking, gulping hunter pointing his sword right at him.

The were sniffs the air. Peter holds his ground. The arena is excruciatingly silent.

Until the werewolf charges.

Some of the kids sitting around me scuttle back up the stands in case this goes sideways, but I'm glued to my seat.

Peter makes the first swipe with his blade. It's a technical, by-the-book jab, like when he fought the wraiths, and the stands break out in cheers for him. Instructions too. *Go for the jugular! Watch your side! Get his paws first!*

But to my relief, Elliot and Sophia are silent. I'd actually have pegged Sophia as a cheerer, but she's stone-faced as she watches Peter maneuver past the volatile beast. Maybe it makes us poor sports, but the three of us have grown to love our resident brainiac and don't want to see him fucking mauled.

Peter takes one claw to the shoulder, and his shout of anguish has me standing before I know why.

"Sit down," Sophia urges, yanking my sleeve.

But I can't. My aeon blood is wailing in my veins. Peter is getting pummeled by the thing. And he's making rookie mistakes. Only aiming for the heart and not focusing on incapacitating before killing. Meanwhile, the wolf is enjoying playing with his meal. Swiping his hideous claws down Peter's back and over his calf. Each yelp from Peter sets my teeth further on edge.

Reid calls out guidance that Peter struggles to follow. I cut my eyes to Crowley and notice he's starting to pace, his half-silver hand coiled into a tight fist. But his eyes only dart over to Reid, who watches the fight with folded arms and a punishing gaze.

How is this teaching anyone anything? All I'm learning is how to die slowly at the hands of a deviant.

Peter manages one solid slice across the wolf's matted forearm. He gets some rowdy cheers from the crowd, but it's not enough. He's only angered the thing. Wolves are very prideful creatures. If he was toying with Peter before, he's set on the kill now.

It takes the creature less than a second to pounce. He bulldozes Peter down to the floor in one fell swoop, and a grim thud sounds. Next to me, Sophia sucks in a breath of sheer horror.

Peter protects his chest by lodging his short sword between the werewolf's teeth, but his hands are shaking and his breaths are coming too fast. My fingers twitch at my daggers. My vision blurs scarlet red.

There's no more cheering.

And Reid is doing fucking *nothing*. Even after last night, when we lost *two* students. One from this very class.

"He's going to kill Peter," I breathe.

I cut my eyes up to the sky, but it's still a unified blanket of morning fog. No way to tell the time. *Shit.*

The wolf rears its head back and—

And I don't even mean to leap from the stands. But when the beast knocks Peter's sword from his hands, I'm already down on the arena floor, yanking the snarling werewolf back by his fur.

CHAPTER 24

"BACK OFF, VIV," Reid roars. "It's not your fight!"

I drive my elbow into the beast's kidneys. "It's always my fight."

Peter scrambles free and crawls for his sword, one hand pressed to the wound in his side. Had that been inflicted by the wolf's teeth and not his claws, he'd be turned. Too fucking close.

The werewolf whirls—fangs mere inches from shredding my skin—and unleashes a howl from the depths of his lungs. He lashes out, and one swing of that mighty arm into my side knocks me to the ground. My bones shriek with pain, but I'm already up, daggers out and flying as I force the creature back inch by inch. A slice here at his paw. One there behind the knee. A slow inflicting of injuries that weaken the thing but not enough to kill.

The creature roars its frustration and I'm treated to a noseful of pungent raw meat and carrots.

But not rancid.

Not the scent of human flesh and blood that the weres I kill reek of.

This creature has been captured and fed for the sole purpose of being studied in Crowley's class.

I may have an aeon's bloodlust, but that doesn't feel fair to me.

My eyes find the sheet of gray sky above us once more. A sliver of pale sun is beginning to poke through. It's got to be almost seven by now. And the moon—it was nearly full Friday night, presiding over the horrors of the undead. Which, if I remember when the game started, was at seven in the evening . . . I've fought enough werewolves to know those twelve-hour windows are pretty airtight. Which means any minute now—

The next time the wolf lunges for me I don't drive either blade toward him—I run.

I can hear the crowd of students suck in confused inhales. Shock, concern—

I bolt for the stands on the other side of the arena, letting the creature chase after me on all fours. *Faster, faster.* I pump my legs as I formulate my half-assed plan. I'm not going to be able to outrun the beast, but if I'm right, all I need are a few more seconds—

The arena is a blur of screaming students and decaying white stone. I jump from bench to bench, higher and higher. And then back down to the soft ground. We careen around the rack of weapons and speed past the creature's cage. I can feel his hot breath on my ankles. Hear the gnashing sound of his fangs. I dig my dagger into my palm until it draws blood, then coat the silver in red and splatter it across the dusty stone floor.

The werewolf, like any canine, thinks with his nose first. My quads are on fire with each pounding footfall. The werewolf has stopped to scent the air. I don't look back. I don't stop running. I race up the stands to the top of the coliseum, putting as much distance as I can between me and the wolf. Running out the clock—

But I've used up whatever time the blood bought me. He's charging for me now, angry and hungry and feral. I'm tripping over the stone seating, twisting as I crane my neck back to see the snarling, spitting creature, fisting my daggers as I near the top of the coliseum. If this doesn't work—if he's a born werewolf, not a turned one—I'll have nowhere left to run.

Suddenly the snarling is replaced by a howl of bone-deep pain. I whirl to find the beast crouched behind me, wailing and thrashing. Changing under the hot, rising sun. It's 7:00 a.m. Twelve hours after nightfall.

Backing away, I breathe as best I can despite the way my lungs burn and the wound in my hand pulses. Coarse fur smooths into skin. Yellow eyes grow dull and watery. And crouched in the fetal position is not a beast but a man. An adult male, naked, scarred, and coughing to catch his breath. I don't have enough air myself to heave out a sigh of relief.

Only then do I realize that the students on the other side of the arena are cheering. Clapping and whooping. Stomping their feet in the stands. Sophia and Elliot are the loudest of the bunch. Even Peter, who I thought might have been shamed by my unplanned rescue, offers me a grateful smile, his hand thrust into the air in triumph while a pixie presses a glowing compress into his side.

Reid's already jogging up the stairs to me. I'm ready for the look of fury on his face. I, of all people, ruined his lesson plan with my altruism. But when his chin tips up I see it's not an expression of anger or impending discipline . . . It's one of fear.

And before I can make sense of why, I'm falling—

My bruised kneecap pounds into the stone seating behind me. The man, snarling and spitting, has me by the hair and drives his fist into my stomach before I can even grab my daggers.

"Fucking hunter—" He raises his fist in the air and I brace for impact. "Keeping me locked up! I'm going to fucking kill—"

But it's over quicker than it began.

The man gurgles and spurts in shock before rolling off me.

Blood dribbles from his mouth onto the stone seating as he falls to the side. His meaty, bloated body is in a heap, a silver sword lodged in his back.

I scramble away, eyes wide. Reid is standing over me, catching his breath. He swallows hard. His hand is blistered from holding the blade.

The arena is still once more.

"Class dismissed," Reid calls out, terse and definitive. His eyes don't leave my face.

One student clears his throat and asks, "Actually . . . I had a question about the were—"

"I said," Reid roars, *"class dismissed."*

They clear the space in ringing silence. Crowley included.

I can't take Reid's ancient blue eyes on me a moment more. Not when there's so much anger there. Anger and something else. Something agonized. Like that was too close for him.

Wincing, I push myself up and hurry down the stands to grab my leather book bag on the other side. I need some ibuprofen and a hot bath.

He sighs, prowling down the steps behind me.

"What?" I grunt.

"That was quite the performance." His voice is as cold as the frigid morning air.

"Hunting's not a performance. It shouldn't be treated as one."

"Is that what you thought this was?"

Yes, I have an underlying, near-constant, burning desire to kill, but I don't *like* that about myself. I don't even want to murder my own lobster for dinner. I don't believe in slaughter for the game of it, even if my instincts tell me to annihilate things on the daily. "Don't ask questions you don't want the answers to." I swing my bag over my shoulder carefully, but the weight still makes my knee scream. I'm about to have a very unexplainable bruise. Maybe I'll tell James I've traded Pilates for jujitsu.

When I face Reid, he's studying me with quiet interest. "Why didn't you kill the turned when you had the chance?"

The turned. "That whole species-caste-system thing is horrible. Even among deviants. You're all equally vile."

"Don't change the subject."

"I kill to save lives. Not for sport."

"You didn't kill him, even though he was a deviant. Who was trying to kill you."

I wince as I move to limp past him. "Some werewolves don't know what they're doing. Some are shocked to see what they've done when they're turned back."

"Even if he's a perfectly fine mortal, a turned deviant will always kill eventually. Always."

I stop in my tracks to narrow my eyes at him. "And yet when I apply that logic to you, it seems to annoy."

"I don't care what you think of me, huntress. I just want you to do your job and do it right. Kill deviants when you're supposed to. Stay out of it when you're supposed to. Stop trying to be a hero so you think you're worth something." He says the words like they're a mere observation. Devoid of bite or sympathy.

But a hot, sticky anger licks up my insides just the same. One that's reckless and curling, because the quicker it moves, the less time it has to linger on the fear that there's truth to his cruelty. "I couldn't just sit there while—"

His eyes heat. "I wouldn't have let anything happen to Roydon."

"Well, you have more faith in you than I do."

Reid says nothing as his eyes sweep across my bruised body and back up to hold my eyes. "I saved *you*, didn't I?"

As infuriating as it is, he's got a point. I stuff my fisted hands into my pockets and inhale sharply. He can think whatever he wants about me, but I'll be damned if I give him the satisfaction of being right. I can't leave this arena until I clean my side of the street.

"Thank you," I grit out. "For not letting me die."

Reid ignores me, walking over to pick up Peter's discarded sword by the leather pommel and wiping the blood on his pants, up by the thigh. I bite my tongue until it hurts, then stomp over to where he stands, even as my knee throbs.

"I'm serious," I say, grabbing his forearm. His key card dangles from the pocket of his track pants. My heart hammers under my shirt. "Thank you."

Reid's eyes snap to my hand on his skin like I'm poisoning him. Then his eyes, ringed in desperate, ravenous red, slice up to my own. The sight takes my breath away. I all but choke on air. I've never seen him hungry before.

"You need to stop doing that," he says so low I can hardly hear him. I'm so shocked, my hand doesn't move. None of me does.

He holds my gaze with lethal calm as he pries my fingers from his skin. One and then another and then another. That red still glowing. Still staring at me.

I come back to myself in time to realize the opportunity I have here. I hold his predatory gaze as I slide the key card that hangs off his belt loop into my pocket. His red eyes have not left my face.

"Time to go," he tells me through clenched teeth. None the wiser. Too interested in my soul.

I lift my hands and back away. I don't need to be told twice.

CHAPTER 25

PETER'S STILL LIMPING when we cross through the brick walls back into Old Campus. I'm not in much better shape with my aching knee, but I have the key card now to get into the archives, which means my bruised body will have to wait. A question's been nagging at me, though. "Why didn't Crowley kill that werewolf?"

Peter looks up at me. His eye is starting to swell. "You mean, why keep it in the dungeons after we'd finished our lesson last week?"

Elliot's hazel eyes light up with mischief. "Does Harker experiment on them?"

"Like Frankenstein's lab?" Soph says, wiggling her fingers at him. "Someone's getting into the Halloween spirit."

"I'm serious," Elliot says, pulling his sunlit strands into a man bun. "Maybe they run some kind of turned deviant rehabilitation program."

"Actually," Peter says, "in Kitty's and my summer program, I did my final paper on syrabraxas, and in the rare cases where they've been cast, the counterspell that removes them has taken some abilities with it. Maybe the Elders are studying the dark magic to see if a syrabraxa can strip a deviant of its deviantness. Or— Viv?"

Peter must notice my stunned silence. I scramble for words. "What did you just say?"

"Strip a deviant of its deviantness?"

There's something out there that can render a being mortal? The guilt rushes in almost as quickly as the idea does. What kind of hunter even thinks about being free of their responsibilities? "Syrabraxa." I shake my head. "What is that?"

"It's a type of spell. The most powerful form of dark magic," Peter says. "The kind of power that can break the planes of existence... It curses all who wield it with unendurable madness."

Like the first High Thane who wrenched the Chasm open. His liver eating has not been forgotten. "That's what was used to split the Chasm? A syrabraxa?"

Peter nods. "And like all dark magic, it must be cast by a turned witch."

"So any witch who crosses over to the dark side can learn this spell and end life as we know it?" Elliot asks, a little spooked.

"No, no." Peter rubs his swollen eye. "Syrabraxas are unique. They require complex ingredients to be brewed along with the incantation. And we're talking about ingredients that could take centuries to gather. On top of that, the deviant witch needs a host to put the spell *into*. The brewed potion is imbued into their skin."

"Okay, now I think we're *too* into the Halloween spirit," Sophia says.

"It gets worse," Peter tells her. And I know what's coming. All dark magic requires a sacrifice. "The power of the spell is granted to whoever *kills the host*. Sometimes it's called *blood magic* or *host magic*, but the technical name from the Old World is *syrabraxa*."

I knew about dark magic that could be brewed and cast by

turned witches that killed innocents, but I didn't know anything about hosts being used as human vessels. "What does a syrabraxa have to do with experimenting on deviants?"

Peter only shrugs. "It was just a hypothetical, not a feasible experiment. Not only would you need a turned witch to cast the spell, the syrabraxa can only be removed by the same witch who cast it in the first place. Harker would never work with a deviant witch on school grounds."

"Right," I nod, chewing my lip.

"And there's only one recorded instance of this even being possible," Peter continues. "Outside of the Chasm, of course. The one I referenced in my paper was from hundreds of years ago. A syrabraxa was implemented into an aeon and removed before they could be killed, and apparently the removal spell took the aeon's powers with it. They were rendered human—but it was ancient Egypt, and I'm not sure how accurate the hieroglyphic translation was . . ."

But my mind has stalled out. It's just as the lymantrian biology book from the library said. *Some dark magic can remove hunter genetics.*

I'm not a do-gooder like Fiona or Penny, Nora or my dad. Or a legacy hunter like Sophia, Elliot, Peter, or even Kitty. I'm not motivated solely by responsibility and honor. I hunt because *I have to.* Because I harbor a repellant, constant, *compulsive* need for the kill. But if it's somehow possible to be rid of my aeon gene . . .

I think of being able to actually live my life. I could stop thinking about everything in relation to my imminent gory death. Stop waking up in the middle of the night with crippling bloodlust. Free myself of torrential emotions. Be a real friend to Penny, not someone who is constantly making up lies and being called away from birthday dinners to stab things in dark alleys. I could be an even better friend to Sophia, Peter, and Elliot. I could be *their* Penny. Mortal, happy, *whole*. I could pursue photography—one of the only things that actually makes me feel *human*. Maybe I could even have a real relationship with someone. Maybe it would be James, or maybe it wouldn't, and that would be okay too.

And yeah, the thought of losing one of the only tethers I still have to my father cuts right through my insides. So bad I nearly keel over with the hurt. But he isn't here. He never will be again. And he lied to me, kept this entire world from me. Kept his real *name* from me. And if I were mortal, maybe my mother—the parent who's still alive and kicking—might actually care about me again. I'm not sure how that's related—it's not like she knows I hunt deviants—but still . . . It feels like not slaying monsters could only help things between us.

I wouldn't be bound by duty. Nor by a desire to kill.

I would be free.

"How do you brew one?" I ask, trying to keep the desperation from my voice.

Sophia eyes me warily.

"No idea," Peter says. "That kind of information isn't exactly made available to students. It would be like asking how to build a nuclear bomb."

I breathe out with an easy smile. I'm normal. I'm fine. "Of course."

Satisfied, Peter continues to stride toward the commons.

The bell tower chimes, echoing mournfully through the crisp campus, as unwavering as my new resolve. All this time, there *was* a way. Not an easy way. Not one I can attempt anytime soon or without risking my life. But a way nonetheless. A slim, nearly impossible death-wish-level decades-long-waiting-list way. A sliver of hope has slipped under my skin like a splinter: It's everything I've never let myself dream about, and I've found it here at Harker.

"Okay, Mr. Encyclopedia," Sophia says. "We have another question for you."

She nudges me and I pick up on the cue. He's in better spirits despite his injuries. Educating us seems to have that effect. Time to dig in about the blades.

"Peter, do you know what might cause my daggers to suddenly start . . . burning?"

"I already told you to get that checked out by the pixies at the infirmary," Elliot says with a smirk. "And always wear a sheath."

Sophia snorts.

"What do you mean *burning*?" Peter asks.

"After the zombie spell, I was just holding them, and suddenly they became hot as coals. They glowed like them too. It was a full two minutes before I could pick them up again . . ." I eye the ancient silver at my waist. "But they've been fine since."

Peter lifts a brow, intrigued. "Can I see?"

Even with his swollen eye, he inspects the silver with care, noting the carvings on the hilt. His lips turn down at the corners and I can tell he's noticed something strange.

"What is it?"

"I'm about to blow your mind," he mutters, eyes still on my blades. "Follow me."

I want to tell him I've had enough bombshells for one day, but I follow him dutifully away from Elkfore Hall, Sophia and Elliot in tow. We wind around bleary-eyed students still recovering from last week's trauma until Peter pushes inside the storybook-style doors of the armory.

There are a few students already in there, some sitting at workbenches, one getting help from the armorer with his scythe. My gut already knows why we're here. Peter guides us through the cluttered back shelves, over to that glass display. The double-paned casing hasn't been touched or breached in any way. No cracks, fissures, or fingerprints. But there, on the little velvet cushion, the dagger with the carving of the jaguar is now gone.

"Fascinating," Peter says.

Sophia cocks her head, confused. "Explain, please."

"Your blades are a set of three," he tells me. "The Demon's Dagger, the Lymantrian's Dagger, and the Aeon's Dagger. They're antiques."

Sophia goes stiff beside me. I clutch my blades tighter in my hands.

The Aeon's Dagger.

"Yeah," I say tightly. "They were my dad's, and his mom's before him."

"Most historical accounts will claim hunters of the old world fought with two daggers, just like you do. One was usually decorated with deviant imagery—to remind the hunter of what they sought to kill—while the other was a reminder of the good they swore to protect."

"My father's have a serpent on one and a doe on the other."

"Exactly," Peter says like I'm a very good student.

"She still hasn't named them," Elliot mutters to Sophia.

"No respect," Sophia sighs.

"But," Peter continues, "it's believed that aeons fought with a third dagger too. Often kept in a hidden holster and used when one of their other weapons had been compromised. And that dagger—"

"Was a mix of the two," I finish for him. "The light and the dark." I remember the carving on the missing dagger. The jaguar—a wicked, bloodthirsty beast—was protecting its cub.

"A-plus for Viv." Peter smiles. "Yours might be the last complete set in existence. The three of them are tied together through ancient magic. If one of them is destroyed, they all have a reaction. You said they got very hot?"

"Like they were in a furnace."

Peter purses his lips in thought. "Maybe the Aeon's Dagger was burned or melted down that night."

"Why? By who?" I don't ask him my last question: *Why was my father's other dagger on display at the school he went to in the first place?*

"No clue," Peter says. "Let's ask the armorer."

"Why didn't he notice my blades were antiques when he fixed them for me my first week here?"

Peter gives me a slight eye roll. "Most of the weapons in here are antiques. This armory's been collecting holy weapons like those since the thirteenth century. Not every armorer is going to catch every engraving like I can. They don't call me Mr. Encyclopedia for nothing."

"I don't think Soph meant it as a cool new nickname," Elliot advises.

"You don't know that," Sophia says, crossing her arms. "Knowledge is sexy."

Peter chokes on nothing.

"Let's just ask where the third one went," Elliot offers. He's a foot away from the armorer when I have a terrifying thought that sends me scrambling past a hanging set of greaves and yanking him back by his thick forearm.

"Wait," I breathe, my hand wrapped around his arm. Elliot narrows his eyes at me in confusion, and I don't blame him. But I can't have Elliot telling the armorer that the Aeon's Dagger used to belong to my family. It doesn't necessarily paint me as an aeon—anyone can own an antique—but I don't want the information somehow tying me to my father. Just in case someone at the school knew what *he* was.

Still, keeping this aeon secret from my friends is almost as difficult as keeping my hunter secret in my real life. And I don't want to live like that anymore. I don't want to live not trusting anyone.

"We can't tell the armorer . . . or anyone, that the blade used to be in my family."

"Why not?" Elliot asks.

But I can't say the words. My heart is in my esophagus. I'm like a kid with stage fright. It's all I can do to cut my gaze sidelong to Sophia. When her brows knit in silent question, I give her a slow nod and she and Peter wander over.

"She's an aeon," Sophia says so quietly I almost don't hear the words.

Silence drowns the four of us. But Elliot and Peter don't gasp. They don't widen their eyes or take trembling steps away from me.

"That's how you landed a hit on me when we sparred in the gym that first day," Elliot says eventually, as if it's been bothering him. But there's still warmth in his eyes, and I'm so relieved my knees could buckle.

"How . . ." Peter's voice is a rasp. "I didn't think there were any left."

"Just me," I say weakly. "That I know of, at least."

"Nobody can know," Sophia reiterates. As if they don't know how dangerous I am. How much danger this knowledge puts *them* in.

"We'll protect your secret with our lives," Elliot says. From anyone else, it would feel dramatic, but when he grasps my hand, his calloused palm warm around my knuckles, I know he means it without an ounce of hyperbole. "You can bet on it."

"Thank you." I laugh, swallowing a lump of emotion as it rises in my throat.

When I look at Peter, he's still a little shell-shocked. I try to hide the pleading in my eyes, but he must pick up on it anyway, because he says, "Viv . . . You—all of you guys—you're my family. The only family I have left, maybe. I'd never tell a soul." He nods to himself as if to get his mind back on track, though I know he'll be doing copious amounts of research on aeons later today. "But you really should ask the armorer where the dagger went. Maybe say you want to check it out? That's what the blades in this section are for. It's like Harker's version of renting high-tech equipment."

"Okay. That's a good idea," I tell him, pulling myself together too. "I'll be right back."

When I get to the counter, I do just that. "Hi. I wanted to check out the dagger in the glass case that has the jaguar on it, but it seems to be in use already?"

The armorer greets me with an easy smile. Not the look of someone who thinks a prized piece of Harker weaponry has been destroyed. "That was checked out a few days ago."

"Oh shoot." I feign casual disappointment. "Can I ask by who?"

"Let me check the logs." The armorer flips through a massive leather tome, and I wait, foot tapping until I force myself still.

"Here you go," he says.

Finally. "Who was it?"

"Kitty Briggs. She was good with her rentals this summer. Will be back within the week, I'm sure."

A trickle of dread slips down my spine. "Great. When did she check it out?"

"Looks like . . . Friday night."

The night of the zombie spell. And that's . . . not possible. Kitty had left school long before then.

His brows crease. "You okay?"

"Do you remember opening the case for her?" I will my voice not to tremble.

The armorer scratches the back of his neck. "I don't, actually. She must have been with a faculty member. Most of them have keys to that case."

A rushing sound fills my ears. "Oh well," I say with as much false ease as I can muster. "Thanks anyway."

"You want to check out a different one? There's a beautiful Argentium silver dirk that—"

It's all I can do not to sprint away from him. "No thanks."

I'm sweating by the time I make it back to my friends.

"You solve anything, Sherlock?" Elliot asks.

"Actually," I say, dragging them out with me, "kind of the opposite."

CHAPTER 26

WHILE THE LIBRARY is a dark academia wet dream, replete with antique windows and creaking wooden desks, the archives might actually be where all the fun is found. The Harker archives are housed in the same building as the library, Mortimer Tower, but on the second floor from the top, just below the planetarium, which Peter has told me twice now is the highest point on campus.

The view of Harker from the archives is nothing short of breathtaking. On a dreary, mist-shrouded autumn afternoon such as this one, I can see the heavy clouds as they roll in, casting long shadows over trees as they shed copper leaves onto the quad. The thought of torrential rain sends my heart sailing. A much-needed cleanse.

And maybe a good omen for the quest at hand.

"You *stole* a professor's key card?" Peter hisses as Elliot shuts the archive doors behind us. His voice is hushed even though we're the only people in here.

"Borrowed," I correct as we push past cluttered bookcases and shelves stuffed to the gills. Locked file cabinets and encoded books press up against wood-paneled walls under a low aged-brass chandelier. Its candles are coated in the same dust that pumps in through the vents with the heat. An antique carpet stretches underfoot. Something about the design—black and cream and winged—is both comforting and haunting.

Sophia drags a finger across a dust-caked tome on a shelf beside her head. "Who'd you swipe the key card from?"

"Reid." Something about saying his name twists my stomach, but I bypass the emotion. There's too much at stake right now for me to feel guilty about taking advantage of our charged moment this morning.

"My spooky little thief." When I look up, Sophia's gaze sparkles with mischief. "He's going to be livid."

"He's not going to find out."

"Maybe he'll spank you. He seems like the spanking type, doesn't he?"

Elliot snorts.

"Sophia. Focus. We're here to look into a stolen Harker antique." I brace myself to tell them the last piece of the puzzle. But the thought of hurting Peter . . .

"Why'd you take it off Graveheart?" Elliot asks, opening a closet to peer inside. "Class was before we learned about the missing dagger."

"Look who's Sherlock now," Sophia says, impressed.

"I wanted to know more about my dad. About his death." I take a seat at a wooden desk that's been shoved into the corner—the only furniture in the room. All that sits atop it are a quill, a crystal inkwell, and an antique leatherbound book with embossed golden filigree but no lettering. Inside, all the pages are blank.

When I turn to face the three of them, my palms are sweaty on the back of the ornate desk chair. "It's kind of the only reason I agreed to come to school here. My first week, I found out he changed his name to Abbot after graduating from Harker. I took the key card to search the Citadel's records for his real name. But now..." I steel myself. This is why I brought them here. Peter needs to know. "The armorer told me the Aeon's Dagger was checked out the night of the zombie spell. And the person listed as borrowing it... was Kitty."

A breath rushes out of Sophia.

Peter goes chillingly still. "But she was—"

"Gone then. Yeah. The armorer didn't even see her. He assumed a faculty member opened the case for her."

"I told you," Peter says, shaking his head. "Something happened to her." Sophia opens her mouth to argue, but he continues undeterred. "The blade went missing on Friday, right? The day of the attack on the lacrosse game. And Kitty wasn't seen after the wraiths broke in... What if both incidents were actually distractions? Orchestrated so nobody was in the dorm to see Kitty disappear or at the armory when the blade was taken?"

"That's sort of what I was thinking." I swallow hard. "That's why I thought this"—I wave the key card—"might be helpful. Maybe we can look into what someone might want with both Kitty and the dagger?"

"Unless Kitty's the one who stole the dagger," Elliot muses.

All three of us cut our eyes to him.

"I'm just saying what we're all thinking. Maybe she faked leaving school, broke into the armory case with a teacher's key like you broke into the archives..."

"Then she would have put a lot more effort into making her 'disappearance' look legitimate," I say. "Starting with answering Peter's calls."

Peter nods. "Her roommate's missing shoes, the imperfect handwriting..."

"I guess you're right." Sophia perches on the side of the desk. "What are the odds that the same night wraiths get into Harker, Kitty decides to flee the school and nobody can reach her in any capacity . . . and then, while a psychotic spell is cast on the lacrosse game, your grandmother's rare antique weapon is taken and destroyed and Kitty's listed as the one to check it out?"

My jaw tenses. "I'd say zero."

"You really think someone *kidnapped* Kitty?" A little trepidation has snuck into Elliot's voice. "Who would do that?"

"I don't know," I tell him. "But to use Kitty as a scapegoat in the armory log . . . Someone must know she isn't here anymore."

"Should we not go to, like . . ." Elliot scratches his neck. "The dean or something?"

"Not if someone really did take the dagger and forge Kitty's name," Peter says. "Only professors have the keys to the cases, like you said. If someone who teaches here is in on it . . ."

He doesn't have to say the rest out loud. If Kitty can be made to disappear, so can every one of us.

"How does this thing work?" I ask Peter, motioning down to the book with empty pages.

"It's a compendium."

All three of us stare at him expectantly.

Peter sighs. "An enchanted search engine. Write what you're looking for and it'll direct you to a section, shelf, or drawer in the room."

I lift the quill from the ink and stare at the blank page.

"What are you going to search?" Sophia asks, hovering above me. "*Who kidnapped Kitty Briggs? Where's my dad's aeon dagger?* It's a filing system, not a crystal ball."

"But that's not a bad place to start." I write *Aeon's Dagger* and watch as the ink fades away like drying water. On the other page, cursive begins to scrawl on its own, naming hundreds and hundreds of files and books across the room. I shake my head and try *uses for the Aeon's Dagger* instead and am met with the same result. Still too wide a net. I drum my fingers on the desk.

"You said the blades got hot, right?" Peter asks, coming to stand behind me. "Try *melted Aeon's Dagger alloy.*"

Fifteen results etch themselves onto the page. Bingo.

"You genius," Sophia breathes. Peter grins beside her.

We divvy up the hits among the four of us and pick through the room. Peter decides an article from a 1948 issue of the *Harker Herald* is a good place to start. The paper is filed somewhere between spools of film marked **Chaplin Original, 1914** and a demonic text that looks older than Stonehenge.

After he insists we put on the gloves used to handle antiquities—a man after Fiona's heart—we open the newspaper clipping titled **HARKER'S PENCHANT FOR RARE GOODS**, which describes the long list of collectors' weapons, rare books, and restricted potions found on Harker's campus. Everything from the Tang dynasty wallpaper in the third years' housing foyer to the medieval wand framed in Dawnmere's classroom is mentioned in the piece.

"Here," Sophia says after a minute. "Found it."

She points to a paragraph and begins to read aloud. "'There were never many aeons to begin with. By the turn of the century only four bloodlines remained in the Citadel's records. So it's no shock these Aeon's Daggers have great financial value. Even more so when the complete set, including the Lymantrian and Deviant daggers, is intact. However, the Aeon's Dagger is not merely a valuable collector's item. Centuries of being wielded by the deadliest hunters in existence mean the weapon is imbued with the spirit of great battles, kills, and triumphs. When the blade is smelted, the remaining alloy can be used in many dark rituals and spells.' So someone on campus is really trying to ace Rituals and Exorcisms?"

I stare at a shelf stuffed with paper thin enough to be tissue. The wheels in my mind are turning so hard I can feel them. *Dark rituals and spells.*

Peter and I look up and lock eyes.

He hurries over to the desk and writes across the page, *syrabraxa ingredients.*

Elliot hovers over his shoulder beside me. "The spell you were just telling us about?"

Only one result appears in that fine, enchanted cursive. An old grimoire, kept in the far corner of the room. Peter stands, sliding his gloves back on. "Let's just see."

But unease has spread through my limbs. That uncanny feeling of being on the precipice of something you know you'll regret. Opening up WebMD when your head has hurt for four days straight. Downing the final drink you know will seal your fate hurling your guts up the rest of the night.

And clearly I'm a glutton for punishment. I follow behind Peter and help him pull the decrepit book from the tallest shelf. The scent of decaying paper fills my nose with each turn of the page. We find the syrabraxa section quickly. It's been marked by three different *CLASSIFIED* stamps.

The first passage only tells us what Peter already has—

> . . . *a caveat to syrabraxas, which makes them unique from other spells: The syrabraxa's power is not granted to the host but instead to whomever kills the host. That power is more than any being can stand—mortal, hunter, demon, or otherwise— and drives them mad. One historian describes an instance in*

which the wielder was a king at war with a neighboring country. After having his most trusted turned warlock brew and cast the spell, the king killed the host, used the power to destroy his enemy's armada, and then set his entire crew on fire before drowning himself in the high seas—

Fighting a shudder, I let my eyes skim as I flip through the pages.

"Wait," Sophia says, hand shooting out. "There."

And sure enough, like your great-grandma's recipe for blueberry muffins scrawled into the margins of an old cookbook, there's a handwritten list of ingredients to brew a syrabraxa. The only spell that could help me shed my scaly huntress skin and emerge a beautiful human-woman butterfly.

It's all in Lymantrian, but it's been translated into English in the footnotes.

> *Liquified blade of the third*
> *Celestial bloom*
> *Eye of the conjuring witch*
> *Aeon's blood*

Sophia has gone as rigid as a corpse beside me. I wonder if we're both staring at those last two words.

"Wait a second," she says, going back to grab the newspaper clipping. The one on rare goods found at Harker. "'The asphodel, known by lymantrians as a holy celestial bloom, grew only on the lymantrian plane until its desecration. However, the Elders were able to save a few spare seeds of the highly sensitive flower. Now the asphodel grows in a light- and noise-restricted garden kept on Harker's Old Campus,'" Sophia reads. "'The exact location of these haunting blooms is unknown by even the majority of Harker's own staff.'" When she stares at me, real fear crests in her eyes. "You don't think . . ."

I thought I'd give anything to know how to brew the spell that could free me. But now . . . "Someone at Harker is collecting the ingredients for a syrabraxa."

Sophia's swallow is audible. "Kitty?"

"I don't know."

"Why now?" Peter muses aloud. "If the ingredients have always been here on campus?"

I chew my lip. "I don't know that, either."

"Do you think *eye of the conjuring witch* means the literal eyeball of the witch who casts the spell?" Elliot asks.

"For Viv's sake," Sophia says, "I hope nothing on here is literal."

We all stare at that last line on the page. *Aeon's blood.*

"I thought there was a chance Kitty might have been an aeon," I admit to the group. "She has some of the qualities we're known for—fluctuating moods, intensity . . ." I look to Peter. "Did she ever mention coming into her abilities before turning twenty-one? Maybe being able to sense deviants before seeing what they are? Like a full-body vibration?" I can't bring myself to ask about bloodlust. I couldn't stomach the fear in my friends' eyes.

But Peter just shakes his head, taking a seat at the desk. "I don't think so, but . . ."

They hadn't known each other all that long.

"We need to find that garden," Sophia says. "See if the asphodels have been taken."

Elliot doesn't look as convinced. "And if they have? I'm all for breaking into secret rooms and shit, but I really think we need to go to a professor if someone is trying to brew a spell that can . . ." He cuts his eyes to Peter. "What did you say? *Break the planes of existence?*"

But I'm with Peter. "My father never wanted me to come here. He kept this school a secret from me all my life. Changed his name when he left. And then he was killed by the Brood, and his last words..." Rage funnels through my body, and I shake off the memory of that night. "He knew the deviant who killed him. Maybe through someone he met here at this very school. And now it looks like a student is trying to harness the darkest magic known to man. I don't think we can trust anyone at Harker with this just yet."

"Jesus," Elliot mutters. "Fine. Okay. How do we find these flowers?"

All three of us look at Peter.

"I'll be in the library," he says, grabbing his bag. "I'll text you guys when I find something."

"We'll keep thinking too," I tell him.

It's not like I'll be able to do anything else. *Aeon's blood.*

Sophia rests one hand on my shoulder. "Nothing is going to happen to you, okay?"

She really does have a skill for reading people. But I don't want to dwell on the subject. "Don't you guys have Field Training soon?"

"Shit." She checks her phone and looks at Elliot. "Yeah."

"Go." I nod at them. "We're not solving anything tonight."

Elliot tosses me a supportive nod, and Sophia offers one last squeeze before they bound off, leaving me alone in the quiet of the archives. I put the grimoire and newspaper clippings away and toss my artifact gloves. Then I take a seat at the desk and face the wordless pages once more.

I know the mysteries around my dad's death need to be put aside for now. Kitty might have been kidnapped to serve as some kind of ingredient in a syrabraxa stew. Between that and the wraiths and the zombie spell and the missing dagger... I should be focusing on Harker and how to protect myself and my friends.

But what if my dad knew something sinister about this school? Something that scared him so much, he made sure I would never have a chance of attending? My fingers tap on the wooden ridges on the desk as I watch the sky outside fade from gray to a dark, bruised blue.

I'm here. In the archives. Probably for the last time, as I'll need to toss Reid's key card sooner rather than later. It'll only take a second to look my dad's name up. Then I'll leave before I can be caught.

CHAPTER 27

AS PROFESSOR DAWNMERE would tell us, with any good experiment, you need a baseline first. I write *Peter Roydon* across the faded pages of the compendium, to see what a normal entry in the Citadel's records looks like.

Sure enough, many hits come up—Harker's first-year roster for this year, his paper on syrabraxas for that summer program, a small-town magazine from a decade ago that describes his *Iron Man*–themed science fair win—but only one sticks out. The Citadel's list of all recorded hunters. I try *Sophia Valentine* and *Elliot Thompson* as well. Both times the book scrawls back their histories, their family members' names—Sophia's parents, Elliot's many brothers—and directs me to that same Citadel record book located in the back of the room.

Then I try my own name. *Vivienne Abbot.*

Just the one result. First entered in August of this year, when I was admitted. Not a single mention of me before that date, and no family denoted, either.

I scrawl *David Abbot.*

No handwriting comes. I stare at the yellowed page, waiting.

Nothing. Not a single hit.

I try *David Cadell*.

The results are plentiful. His mother, Ada Cadell, who was a Harker alum too, and her father before her. His years spent playing for the Marksmen. His many trophies. His impressive feats in the coliseum—killing a hydra within two minutes, winning best precision archer in his class. My heart begins to swell as an entire life unfolds before me. The year he graduated. His marriage to an unknown woman. The birth of his first daughter, and then his second . . .

And then nothing.

It's as if he died then, right after my birth.

But he didn't—

He lived another decade after that.

I flip through the pages over and over, looking for more, but they're all blank. Devoid of—

"I thought I'd find you here."

I swear my body jolts out of my skin, and I slam the book closed, pressing a hand to my heart to stall its thundering.

Reid's standing in the archive doorway, freshly showered, in a clean shirt and loose jeans. With his dreamy dimples and a surplus of healing injuries, he looks like an Abercrombie model who's had to fight off a herd of salivating teen girls. I wonder if Reid has ever actually sustained injuries protecting himself from rabid women. Seems unlikely, but I wouldn't be surprised.

"That's what stalkers say." I'm still a little breathless.

"No, it's what people say when they've tracked down a thief."

The blood drains from my face. I grab my things and walk over to him, key card in hand. "Oh yeah," I say, faux casual. "You dropped this."

Reid's lips fuse into a grim line. "Do you understand I could expel you for this? You stole an instructor's key card and broke into a restricted area."

I make a face. "Huh. I thought I just got lost."

He glares, those blue eyes swallowing up every inch of me. I'm sure he's going to snap. But he only exhales a mighty breath and drags a hand down his face. "Get out of here, huntress."

The change in his tone sends a jolt of surprise through me. "That's it?"

"Consider us even. After my . . . behavior this morning."

The memory of how he warned me away from him still hangs between us. I take a careful step backward, which he watches with something like distaste. "How'd you find me up here anyway?"

"Realized my card was gone after you left the coliseum. Tried every professor-only access spot on campus. This was number six."

I don't say anything, but I do note that he knew I had his key card all day and made no move to have me punished. My stomach does a somersault.

"You should leave, though. Before Lisette finds you. This is her domain."

"Lisette oversees the archives?"

Reid nods. "She's our resident historian. I help her with the artifacts sometimes."

"You wear a lot of hats," I tell him.

"And in this one, I tell you it's time to get going. It's almost eight."

I didn't even notice the candelabra flickering to life on its own. I take in Reid once more. He looks different in his street clothes, but I can't put my finger on what's changed. Maybe it was our last exchange or his leniency about my theft. "It's weird seeing you out of your training gear."

Reid's brows lift. "Weird?"

"I just didn't realize you owned jeans."

"Like how you don't own anything that isn't black."

I narrow my gaze at him. "If not black, then what?"

His eyes simmer. "You'd look nice in red."

It's by far the most complimentary thing he's ever said to me. I realize that somewhere between me getting high at the asylum and him nearly feasting on my soul this morning, the sharp edges of our interactions have been filed down a bit. Replaced with something else that I'm not quite ready to name.

It appears he, too, has no desire to name it. He looks like he's let something slip he shouldn't have. Like his self-control is untethering. He's my teacher and he's imagining me looking *nice* for him. In *red*.

My heart thuds and I decide to conduct an experiment. "What would you say if I asked for your help with something?"

He opens his mouth, then seems to think better of it. "Is this a trap?"

"No." I chew my lip. "Not yet at least."

Reid's eyes are glued to my mouth. I release my bottom lip.

"Go on," he says.

"You're a professor here."

"Combat instructor."

"Apologies, you're a *combat instructor* here. Can you help me find a secret garden hidden somewhere in Old Campus?"

Reid doesn't miss a beat. "No."

My blood heats. He's so difficult for no reason. But snapping at him would ruin the experiment data, so instead of telling him that there are more words in the English language, I go with "I'm serious."

I can see the muscles tense in his jaw. He clears his throat. "The place you're talking about . . . It's not accessible to students."

"And what a shame, I don't have my handy-dandy key card anymore."

"*Huntress*—"

"But you know where it is?"

"No," he admits. "I don't. And I'd be breaking about a dozen faculty rules bringing you there if I were to find out."

"Would you, though?"

He frowns at me. "Why? What do you need?"

The moment of truth. Was Elliot right? Should I confide in a teacher? Do I trust Reid enough to tell him someone at his precious school is trying to brew a syrabraxa? No. Definitely not. "It's for a research paper."

"So ask your professor."

"Okay," I tell him, hoisting my book bag up my shoulder. "Will do."

I can feel him eyeing me, but I don't give him the chance to indulge his curiosity. I'm already hurrying out the archive doors when he calls out, "Wait up."

I stall, lies already forming like a spider's web in my mind. Ways to cover what I've asked for, rude barbs to get us off topic—

"What are you doing tonight?"

My eyes bulge. Whoever is manning the desk in my brain has fled.

Reid bites back a gorgeous quasi grin. "Do you want to join Field Training? Starts at eight. It's a two-credit class."

Oh. I'm a moron. "I thought I 'wasn't ready.'"

A moron who's still bitter about not being picked weeks ago, it seems.

"You weren't then. Now you are. See how that works?"

Moron flashes in neon lights inside my empty head.

I have dinner with James tonight. Lobster-killing dinner. And no desire to spend more time than I already have to with Reid's evergreen scent and all-knowing eyes and the washboard abs I know are hiding under his Harker crewnecks.

Mostly, though, I like to hunt alone.

Which is why I'm shocked when I say, "Sure."

See? Nobody manning the desk up there. Just those neon lights, I swear.

But the truth is, while a hunter loves to hunt, an aeon *needs* to hunt. And like most prowling predators, we have egos that need stroking. I prefer to hunt alone, but I also crave the experiences I used to have with my dad. The praise one gets from hunting with a pride. Returning from battle, dinner proudly clenched between teeth dripping blood. Disgusting, really.

"Meet us at the gateway under the rotunda in fifteen? Bring your daggers."

"Don't go anywhere without them."

Reid's eyes simmer. "Good girl."

To my utter horror, I flush hot everywhere.

He's already gone when I get my phone out to text James. Sorry, something came up at work. Going to be stuck here late. Rain check?

At this rate, no amount of rain in Astera could make up for all the times I've let my boyfriend down.

CHAPTER 28

IT'S POSSIBLE SOME rain god was listening to me, because it is absolutely bucketing tonight. Not the cute kind of rain that sprinkles your eyelashes and just the pretty front pieces of your hair but the kind of rain that seeps into the padding of your bra. That leaves you shivering well after you've gotten into a hot shower.

And I'm in *heaven*.

"Shouldn't we be staking out farther south?" Sophia asks, whipping her wet hair away from her face. "Where all the criminals are?"

The blond groupie from the armory, a second year I've learned is named Ingrid, pouts. "Only if you want to get knifed by one of the White Stag's thugs."

I recognize the name as someone Nora's nonprofit raises money to put behind bars.

"What if I do?" asks Lyra Roth, a second year with gray eyes like mine and even paler skin. "Then Reid will excuse me from Field Training and I can go see the Chasm."

"I will?" Reid asks, scowling.

Lyra ignores him. "I heard people BASE jump down there." As we walk, her soaked dark braids tap rhythmically against the battle-axe strapped discreetly beneath her shirt.

"If you BASE jumped into the Chasm, I think I'd have to marry you," Elliot says, megawatt smile slick with rain.

Lyra flutters her eyelashes at him. Reid ignores them as we stroll around a pristine NTC town house and cross a freshly painted crosswalk, glowing yellow under the sideways-slanting rain.

He looks more like a demon tonight, the glow of the streetlights harsh on his wet brows and cheekbones. Like someone I'd fight in an empty park or an abandoned bodega. More dangerous than when he's in his unassuming athletic sweats, surrounded by eager students and soothing, swaying elm trees. More dangerous tonight and, somehow, more alluring.

"Maybe our instructor here could go first," Lyra says. "Wave hello to his old buds."

The laughs of the other second years rise over the rush of water in the gutters at our feet. But it's not a cruel sound. More like they've been hunting alongside Reid for long enough to stop fearing him and get a kick out of annoying him instead. It makes him even less hateable, unfortunately.

"I don't think people actually BASE jump," I tell them. "But there is a bar at the edge."

"A bar? At the Chasm?" Lyra's eyes go wide, and I realize that for a lot of these Harker students, even second years, Astera is a place of myth. The birthplace of the Chasm, the earliest and largest gateway to the underworld. I've always kind of taken it for granted that I grew up hunting at the pinnacle of deviant phenomena. And even though I'm not in my own neighborhood, it feels good to be back. It's been too long since I've been in the city. Seen Penny or Hound or even James.

"It's called Rock Bottom. I've never been, but we could go after this."

"Or we could go clubbing." When Lyra brushes rain from her eyes, I notice the fading white shimmer of a club stamp on her wrist.

Sophia's eyes light. "Hell yes."

"Or you could pay attention to the hunt," Reid says gruffly.

But Sophia ignores him. "I haven't gone out in forever. Let me have this."

"You go out in the city all the time," I snort.

Sophia frowns. "Well, I didn't get to do anything fun all summer. I'm making up for lost time."

"Because you were grounded all summer," Elliot clarifies.

Lyra looks impressed. "What'd you do?"

Sophia sighs dramatically like the story is too painful to share. Elliot tosses an arm over her shoulders and pretends to cover her ears. "We don't talk about the swim meet incident."

"The *swim meet incident?*" Learning about Sophia's past is like digging into a multilayered dessert created by a six-year-old. One bite, chocolate. The next, lemon. The one after that? Fritos.

"I came into my abilities like a week before this dumb swim meet Elliot's younger brother was competing in. The school had a selkie problem. I handled it. End of story."

Ugh, selkies. According to Professor Crowley, they're part of the changeling family—which means they like to steal or swap personal items with the mortals they prey on in the hope of disguising themselves and luring unwitting victims into the water.

Elliot smirks. "Sophia ended up topless in front of the entire swim meet crowd, and her parents grounded her until she got to Harker to teach her about *responsible hunting*."

"You're the one who trapped the selkie in the locker room," Sophia says with a shove.

"Yes," Elliot concedes. "But I didn't flash half the water polo team."

"She took my shirt!"

"Wear a bra!"

Sophia throws his arm off her. "Never!"

Lyra and I snicker with some of the other students, but Reid's stony expression doesn't change.

"I fought a selkie on a family cruise as a kid," Lyra tells us. "She appeared to guests as the entertainment director and coerced them into conga lessons. And then threw them overboard and ate them."

Sophia nods in thought. "I actually don't know if that sounds worse than conga lessons."

But my mind has snagged on something Lyra's said. She was hunting as a kid? As in, came into her powers early? I study the second year—another aeon? Or maybe she just meant helping her parents or watching them fight . . . I scan the rest of the small group. Nobody else seems fazed.

"Enough chatter," Reid interrupts before Lyra can tell us more. "Hunting requires focus."

"First you make us walk for an hour in the rain," Lyra whines at him playfully. "Then you deprive us of Astera's famous nightlife. Now we can't swap war stories. What's next on this journey through hell?"

"Don't knock the rain," Reid says quietly.

I lift my head to feel it splatter across my face. Inhale the cleansing smell of wet pavement. "Seriously. Throw in a dip in the ocean, and this could be a perfect night."

After my dad died, I swore the inky-black waters of the sea surrounding Astera would call to me. A twisted way to be close to him somehow. To be where he last was. To feel what he felt as the waves tugged him under.

Ingrid gasps beside me. "The ocean? At night? In this downpour?"

I can't even hide my smile.

Elliot stares at me like I'm an alien. "You're into some weird shit, huh?"

Reid's chuckle sends a jolt of heat through me. It's such a rare sound, hearing it feels like I've won something.

"It's nice," I say. "It's like . . ."

"Being inside something bigger than yourself," Reid supplies. "Water around you and above. Darkness so vast you can't tell where you stop and everything else begins. Sounds like peace to me."

"Yeah," I manage. "Exactly."

"Oh god," Sophia says. The trees above her rattle, battered by the downpour. "You're both gonna drown."

"No night swims tonight." Reid's eyes are on the dripping awnings and blurry, rain-flecked streetlights. "Focus on the hunt."

"Fine by me," Lyra hums. "It's been too long since I sliced and diced."

I cut my eyes sidelong at her. It sounds like something I might say.

For a while we heed our orders. We scan the streets North of the Chasm looking for anything out of sorts. I feel a bit like a cheat, knowing that if there's a deviant nearby, I'll sense it long before everyone else.

It's quieter up here than it is down in Babylon. The air smells better, the rain bringing out scents of jasmine and fresh coats of paint. I think that's the NTC altitude, but also all the trash has been tucked away, so there are no ripening dumpsters like there are down where Penny and I live. No graffiti, no peeling posters or vandalized signs, no people living on the street.

"How long are we gonna wander this fancy neighborhood until we call it a night?" Sophia asks Reid.

Ingrid nods in solidarity. "We haven't seen anything in a while."

"It's Astera," Reid tells them. "There's always something."

After we've passed a wrinkled woman tending to her plants under an umbrella and a socialite Sophia recognizes walking her dogs, I'm inclined to agree until my back breaks out in shivers like a rusted nail is sliding along my spine. When we prowl around the corner, I see her.

Lurking beneath a golden pool of light from a lamppost is a woman watching the rainy street like a bear over a stream rife with salmon. She's hunting too.

"There," I say quietly. "At the corner."

Reid's voice is just as low as we slow our pace. "What is it, Thompson?"

"A vampire, right?"

"Close. Valentine?"

Sophia cocks her head, assessing. "A demon, I think."

"She's a strzyga," I tell them. "Her proportions are a little off—legs too long, head too large. She's starting to shift into her deviant form and needs to eat quickly to stave off the transition."

It's not their fault. Vamps, lycanthropes, and demons look identical to humans until a hunter catches them in the act of killing or right before it. Some hunters at Harker have claimed to have a sixth sense about these things, clocking demons from across a crowded restaurant with nothing but a gut feeling, but they're full of it. Nobody who's an aeon would ever out themselves as one.

Reid looks like he's about to say something, but he doesn't get the chance. A wicked crack of lightning illuminates our strzyga right as she zeroes in on her prey. Under a briefly violet sky, a couple on a moped swish by over rainy asphalt, and she takes off after them, gangly limbs moving at odd angles. It won't be long until she's on all fours.

Thunder rumbles in my bones as we hurtle after her. I'm the fastest—dodging speeding cars and taxicabs in the pouring rain like a flitting hummingbird—but once we slip down an alley and out of sight of the busy avenue, Sophia's able to land a few solid shots with her crossbow. Nothing damaging, though. Not enough to slow the beast. When I catch up to her, I choke on horror.

The strzyga's already taken out the couple. The moped has crashed into a building, rainwater pooling in dents and cracks. The woman is unconscious, the man's leg torn into with ragged teeth. It's a gory display of ripped tendons and white bone where the strzyga feeds. She takes off when we rush to the couple. I breathe through my nose to quell both wrath and nausea. The air is rich with iron and wet asphalt.

Reid curses under his breath before kneeling to check the man's pulse. Lyra and Ingrid slide to their knees and do the same for the woman. The couple must be alive, because Reid takes off his belt to tie a tourniquet around the man's nearly severed leg, and Lyra starts chest compressions on the woman.

Elliot is already backing up Sophia, slicing into the deviant woman with his rain-slick sword, one stab after another, as powerful and agile as a titan. But it's too late. She didn't get her dinner, and she's begun to change. The strzyga's legs lengthen, as do her arms, until she's like a spider—torso compact and tight, clothes shed, eyes drooping and yet severe. Her mouth splits from ear to ear, her hair, soaked and dark, covering half her face. The strzyga hisses through her serpentine grin. Licks inhuman lips. And lunges for Sophia.

My scream catches in my throat as Sophia stands her ground, aiming her crossbow right at the thing.

I move swiftly, throwing my dagger hard into the creature's neck, but no blood spurts.

"We need fire," I grunt, yanking it back out as she shrieks and swings at me.

Elliot palms his sheaths and holsters before pulling out a compact flamethrower, but the rain is pelting us. Nothing is going to stay lit in this downpour. We have to drive her indoors somehow.

I try to say as much before the beast unleashes a screech that sets my teeth on edge. She whips out a spindly arm and tosses me into the wall. My head slams into expensive masonry, teeth crashing together.

"*Viv!*" Sophia shouts.

Sirens sound in the distance. Someone in our group has called an ambulance for the couple.

"Fall back," Reid tells all of us. He's still trying to stanch the bleeding from the man's leg. Lyra and Ingrid are doing CPR on the woman. "Let her go."

No chance.

I stand, a little dizzy as I touch the tender spot on the back of my head. My hand comes back red before the heavy rain washes the blood away.

"Huntress," Reid warns, but the man is somewhat conscious, rambling about an insane woman who bit into his leg. That's how she'll look to any mortal: like a strange, off-putting human, even in her deviant form. Same goes for all lower-level deviants, like Reid taught us that first day in Crowley's class. A wraith might have appeared to this couple like a veil of mist, a hellhound like a rabid dog.

"You didn't see anything," Reid tells him in the most luxurious voice I've ever heard. His eyes are glowing white. "You crashed because of the rain."

Reid repeats the words, his voice ebbing and flowing like river water over smooth, timeworn rock. It's like a lullaby but more seductive. Like a come-on but more subdued. He's glamouring him. A rare skill only some demons have. I've never seen it done before.

"The rain . . ." the man repeats in a daze.

The sirens draw closer. Flashing lights paint the falling rain like red-and-blue snow. The strzyga is already galloping off on her hands and feet toward Main Avenue.

Where far more people are.

So I take off.

Someone curses low beneath their breath, and then footsteps thunder behind me. Too heavy to be a woman's. Too nimble to be Elliot's.

"*Viv!*"

But I'm not falling back. I don't care that he's my teacher.

This is my city.

Main Avenue is quiet because NTC is always quiet, and it's late and it's raining, but there are more cars here than on the residential streets we were patrolling. The woman-beast dashes across the road, flitting between the swish of taxis in rain, causing cars to screech to a halt and bumper-car into one another as I lunge after her.

The strzyga stops to sniff the air and then takes a sharp left toward the only two busy spots on the street. A bar frequented by finance bros and a quaint Italian restaurant where a mediocre chicken piccata will cost you forty-nine dollars. She scuttles into an alley behind the restaurant and I move even faster.

I snake through oncoming traffic and am nearly flattened by a furious woman in a Range Rover. But I don't stop moving until I'm swinging open the door to the Italian restaurant and screaming, "Everybody out, there's a gas leak!"

That's what I like to call quick thinking, because when I blow the place up, this will make for an airtight story, and a much easier insurance claim for the owners. What can I say? I'm a hunter of the people.

The restaurant is a classic NTC affair—dark wood, low lighting, white tablecloths. Patrons gape at me across their candlelit meals with expensive silverware clutched in bejeweled hands.

"Miss," the maître d' hushes, "you cannot just—"

"Hurry," I pant, ignoring him. I wave my hands like a lunatic. "You only have seconds. Please!"

A couple put down their wine, gather their things, and speed past me and out into the rain. Then there's a clattering of silverware and porcelain plates as something careens into the back of house.

Not something. The strzyga. But it works in my favor, because it scares the shit out of everyone else in the restaurant, including the pissed-off maître d'. They funnel out just in time for me to—

"Viv, what are you doing?" Reid has his huge hand wrapped around my arm and the contact sends sparks of electricity through me.

"Let me go," I warn. "It's in here."

"Then you need to leave. I gave you orders to fall back—"

"Where are the others?"

"They *listened.* They stayed with the—"

Pots and pans clatter in the kitchen. My heart is so high in my throat I could chew on it.

Reid's grip tightens to the point of pain. "It needs fire, and our equipment, with the rain—"

"I know. I have a plan. Now, *let me go.*"

I'm prepared to fight him, but the minute the strzyga crawls out from the kitchen into the empty restaurant, he releases me. "What do you need?"

"Distract it," I tell him. And then I lock the door behind us and turn the sign on the door to **Closed**.

Like the night we met in that alley, Reid doesn't fight with a weapon—he *is* one. He engages the strzyga like a beast himself, that low demonic growl sending shivers up my spine. Deep red scales I haven't seen before shimmer down his arms. His fingers elongate and grow night-black claws.

While he lunges at the thing and takes it down alongside sailing glassware, I grab a steak knife from a toppled table and hop onto the bar. Amid lemon wedges and plastic straws, I search for an electrical cord. The wiring for the bar-top lighting will have to do. I begin scraping the rubber tubing away with the knife and ignore the grunts and hisses that sound from the other side.

Hurry, I tell myself, *hurry*—

Finally, the wire's frayed. Electrical fire, here I come. Now I just need heat.

The kitchen's too far and I don't know how to transport a flame from the stove out here without it snuffing out. I think about trying to carry a lit birthday cake and the frustration of all the candles winking out before you reach the table. There's got to be something faster.

I scan the bar. Margarita mix, maraschino cherries, no, no—

"*Huntress*," Reid grunts—

He careens over the bar and right into me. We topple back, his elbow in my sternum, the strzyga hissing, wide teeth inches from our faces. Reid's not moving, so I roll us both to the side a second before she lunges. Bottles shatter and douse all three of us in a boozy mix of vodka, whiskey, and rum.

Wait, that's it.

Not an electrical fire, then.

I scramble back over the bar, dodging the monster as she takes off after me. My fingers just narrowly swipe a box of matches off the maître d' stand, printed with the pretty cursive name of the restaurant, **Maria's**.

Sorry, Maria.

I duck under the beast's clawed swing and hurtle back over the bar. Reid is coming to, bleeding from his nose, the gash over his brow from the zombie spell reopened. Slipping my hands under his arms, I drag us back as much as I can, but the strzyga is too fast and too hungry, and there's not enough time, so I light the match and toss it toward the bar, throwing myself over Reid as I do so.

And then the whole place blows.

CHAPTER 29

I WAKE TO the smell of burning hair and flesh.

The grip of panic only subsides when I realize it's the strzyga burning down with the rest of the restaurant and not *my* burning hair and flesh. Or Reid's. We are in the eye of a hurricane of flame, though, and I can feel the heat cooking my skin. Or maybe that's Reid's singed arms, which are looped beneath my thighs and back, scooping me up.

"Come on," he urges, coughing.

He carries me through the kitchen. The smoke is thick in my lungs and eyes. I bury my face into his sweater and hack until I smell citrus again. Lemongrass cooked on a grill, charred to a crisp. My eyes water as I gasp.

Out in the alley, Reid slams the kitchen door closed with his foot and deposits me against the opposite wall with heart-wrenching gentleness and then takes a second to kneel on the ground and catch his breath. I do the same. The brick of the bar next door is cool against my back. The rain has stopped, and all I can smell now is smoke. Somewhere a siren sounds. First responders work fast up here.

"Are you hurt?" he asks after he nearly coughs up a lung.

I eye the blisters rising on the back of my right hand and up my forearm. "I could use some ice."

When Reid stands, I can see he's been burned too. Some of his cheekbone and brow, but that's not the worst of it. His sweatshirt and the tee beneath are seared through to his shoulder, and the skin there is black and still sizzling. I reach for him without thinking, and when my fingers touch the curve of his skin, he winces.

"Sorry," I breathe, remembering his instruction, *You need to stop doing that.* This morning when he uttered the words, all I wanted was to know what he was fighting to keep himself from doing. How much it killed him not to act.

Reid studies me but says nothing. I wonder why we've both forgotten how to speak. There's an immense sorrow in his eyes. Perhaps because someone got hurt on his watch. But he's said time and again that's our job, right?

"You glamoured those people," I rasp.

His nod is grave. He doesn't like it any more than I do.

"Have you ever glamoured me?"

Reid studies my face, a shadow of hurt crossing his eyes. "Demons can't glamour hunters."

Like taking souls, glamouring is another primordial power that harkens back to the old world and keeps demons at the top of the food chain. Just like the power that allows them a beastly, demonic form ... A chilling thought runs through me. Those scarlet scales on his arms and hands. Those black-as-night claws sprouting from gnarled fingers ... "You really don't have horns."

"Legend, mostly." His voice is low. "No wings, either."

For a moment we just stare at each other. Ash and blood and rain and barrels full of liquor between the two of us. And something else.

Dean Driscoll was right—I misjudged Reid Graveheart. This demon saved my life tonight. Twice now, actually. And though he isn't kind per se, he's . . . virtuous. A believer in right and wrong. Capable of more good than I gave him credit for. It's a shock to the system: Not all demons are purely evil. And like it or not, I need his help.

"I lied," I blurt.

"What?" He sounds a little hoarse.

"Earlier. In the archives."

A faint smile. "No shit."

"I think something strange is happening at Harker. Something . . . dangerous."

His eyes narrow, but he remains silent. Smoke is still curling off his skin.

I swallow, throat dry. "A first year named Kitty Briggs is missing."

Reid doesn't react immediately. "I know. She was supposed to be in my Field Training class. I was told she dropped out."

"She left the night of the wraith attack, and there were . . ." I try to think of how best to phrase it. "Inconsistencies with her disappearance. Then a dagger was stolen from the armory during the spelled lacrosse game—"

Reid's gaze narrows. "Something was stolen from the armory?"

"It was 'checked out with professor approval,' and the name used to check it out was *Kitty's*, even though she'd been gone for days beforehand. I looked into a few things in the archives . . . The garden hidden on campus I asked you about houses this flower . . ."

"Yeah," he says, tense. "The asphodel."

"Right. That, along with the blade that was taken and Kitty's blood, if she is what we think she is . . . they're all ingredients needed to brew a syrabraxa."

Now his face hardens. "You think someone on campus is trying to brew the deadliest magic on earth?"

"Maybe they don't know the power it holds." But I know how ridiculous the words are as I say them. To find the recipe, to go to all the trouble—to be working with a turned witch and possibly other deviants too . . .

Reid rubs a hand down his face, ash and sweat and rain smearing. "I have to talk to Driscoll—"

"No. One of his teachers could be involved—"

"Lisette, then."

"No," I tell him. "She gives me a bad feeling."

Reid raises an incredulous brow. "You're cover-judging again."

I swallow hard, thinking of all that I assumed he was the night we met. All that's changed since then. "I just want to see if the flowers have been taken. If everything is fine, I'll let all of it go. Maybe the blade will be returned and Kitty will get back to us and I can chalk it all up to paranoia." I try to breathe through the tension in my chest. "Nobody else needs to know just yet."

Torturous minutes tick by. I can practically hear the wheels in his mind turning.

"Fine," he relents. "I'll try to figure out where the garden is. But I'm going to look into Kitty first. A student going missing isn't something I can ignore."

I heave a grateful sigh. "Thank you, Reid."

For a moment he just studies me. It's the first time I've ever called him by his name.

And something about this moment makes me brave. We aren't just teacher and student anymore. "Why didn't you recruit me for Field Training that first week?" I didn't realize how much his judgment was nagging at me. My gaze finds the pavement at my feet.

"You'd seen me fight. You knew how good I was. That I'd only take risks if I had to. To save lives."

His voice is a bit strangled as he says, "I think that was what scared the shit out of me."

When I look up, his eyes are sweeping over my face. My mouth, my neck, my injuries. He smells like embers and evergreens. Energy crackles between us. I'm holding my breath.

"Come on," he says in the end. "I know a place around here with the best ice in town."

My laugh relieves tension across my body just as a group of guys who reek of beer exit the bar next door and barrel right into me.

"Watch it," I say before the finance bro turns, and I find myself face-to-face with my own boyfriend.

"Viv—" James eyes the soot on my face. The burns on my skin. "Jesus. What the— What happened?"

"I— It's—" I am an excellent liar. I've been lying my way through all my relationships for over a decade now. But this is a tough one. I told him I was working, and here I am, burned to a toasty golden brown, with some gorgeous guy outside a bar. I draw a complete blank.

"And who is that?" James glares at Reid. "Did he do this to you?"

"No—" Oh god. I'm so screwed. I whirl to look at Reid and find him practically snarling at James. I plead with my eyes. "No, he . . . he—"

"Your girlfriend saved me, actually," Reid says. "There was a fire next door."

My eyes widen a little. He's a good liar. If I didn't know for a fact that wasn't true, I'd believe him. A relieved breath sighs out of James. I offer Reid a look of immense gratitude.

"He's a colleague at the Windsor," I add. "Reid, this is James.

James, Reid. We were getting something to eat before going back to work."

"Sorry." James shakes his head. "I . . . didn't mean to bite your head off."

"Don't worry about it." It sounds like Reid's going to say something else, but he doesn't.

Behind us, James's friends are whispering. Nasty, snickering murmurs. They're making jokes—I guess it's emasculating to find your girlfriend performing heroic acts while you get shit-faced after work on a weeknight. My cheeks heat with embarrassment.

James scratches his neck. "My family would be happy to pay you for your discretion."

I can't help my wince.

Reid's brows shoot up his face. "My discretion?"

James's protective hand lands on my shoulder, and Reid's eyes don't leave the spot. "Viv's mother works in some very high places. Any press is bad press, I'm afraid."

Reid's snort is cutting. "I tell you she saved my life, and you want to pay me off?"

I can feel James stiffen. "I'm just looking out for her."

"You're *ashamed* of her heroism—"

"I'm protecting my girlfriend and her family. Come on, man, don't make me get my security team involved. I'm sure you know Fiona Hyde is Viv's sister-in-law."

God damn it. James is threatening Reid's made-up job at the Windsor, and Reid—who *does not* work at the Windsor, and thus *does not know* who Fiona is—has absolutely no shot of reacting the way I need him to, which is chastened. In fact, I can't imagine Reid being chastened about anything, ever.

"I don't need your money." Reid's voice is cold as the night air. "Or your poorly concealed threats."

James balks. "Threats? All I—"

"Let's just go," I tell James, tugging on his sleeve like a little kid. "Reid, I'll see you at work tomorrow?"

Reid studies me. I can't tell if he's disappointed or resigned. "Are you sure you're all right?"

James rolls his eyes, but Reid pays him no attention. It's all I can do to nod at Reid, the intensity of his gaze carving right through me. I open my mouth but find no words feel right.

Reid stuffs his hands into his pockets and offers me one last look before he heads out of the alley, past all of James's snickering friends.

"What a dick," James mutters once he thinks Reid's out of earshot. But I know his demon senses hear every word. James cradles me into his chest. "I'm so glad you're okay. Let's get you to the family doctor, yeah? Brent," he shouts to one of his buds, "have the driver bring the car around."

I don't hear Brent's response or anything else James says to me. Something about suing Maria's or asking why I reek of vodka. I'm frozen, watching the shape of Reid's back as he walks down the alley, hands in his pockets, until he rounds the corner and disappears into the night.

CHAPTER 30

FALL ARRIVES IN earnest, bringing with it gloomier twilights that bleed into darkness all too quickly. The air on campus is thick with chimney smoke and the gentle spice of nutmeg. Book bags grow heavier, papers clutter the commons, and leaves litter the grounds.

Even from the moody, insulated library, where Elliot and I scribble notes on our essay for Lisette's class, the last dregs of sun fight for our attention. Peeking through colored glass windows, gilding the iron candelabras, casting Elliot's bronze skin in a honeyed glow.

"I can't work anymore," Elliot laments, dropping his pen. "Soon it's going to be too cold to do anything outside. Let's swipe some chips and beer from the Bat and Blood house and hit the lacrosse pitch. I'll race you around the track. Twenty bucks says—"

"If every time we try to study together without Peter and Soph we end up racing or eating or betting on how many books the librarian can carry—"

Elliot shakes his head. "That woman is *strong* for her age."

"—we will never pass Underworld Studies." I keep my eyes on my notes as I speak. If I don't look up, I won't see the way the soft, autumnal sunshine beckons to us.

Elliot scoots closer and lowers his voice. "Any day now, whoever is trying to brew that spell is going to succeed and wreak some kind of havoc on the world. Maybe wipe us out of existence completely. Who cares about passing Underworld Studies?"

I hate that he's right. Even though the lacrosse schedule has picked back up and the armory display case has been rearranged to look as if nothing is missing and the zombie and wraith attacks have been pinned on a disgruntled ex-student with access to the school, I can't shake that gut-deep knowledge that something terrible is coming. That another attack will seize Harker. That another student will go missing.

I allow my gaze to meet Elliot's chocolate eyes. "We're not going to let that happen. I told you—I did what you said. I asked Reid for help, and he's going to find us the location of the garden. Then we'll know more about what's really going on. And maybe how to find Kitty . . . Until then, there's nothing else we can do."

And it's true. While I've been waiting for Reid or Peter to find the location of the garden, I've had to swallow the thought that any student I pass might be the one attempting to break open another gateway to hell. I've been so used to being able to *sense* a threat coming my way. But another hunter like me—a professor, even—plotting something so sinister? Working with deviants? It's almost more unnerving than the demons themselves.

And yet despite the sense of foreboding that hangs in the quiet, darkened halls of Harker, I'm . . . grateful to be here. I study creatures in decrepit books, spar in the coliseum, read in the quad with Peter and Soph—all of us bundled against a crisp, woodsy chill.

Sometimes Elliot drags us to a party at his lacrosse team's house, and I sip mugs of spiked cider with people I don't have to pretend to be someone else around.

My photos have taken on a dreamy quality—fewer lonely portraits and abandoned bus stations, more peaceful shots of Hound sleeping under twinkle lights when I go home on a free weekend or hot tea steeping on Sophia's desk or trees with no leaves in the foreground and the lights from the bell tower glowing in the background amid the foggy sky.

Not only have I yet to be fired from the Windsor despite barely doing anything outside of a few projects Fiona has emailed to me, but everything I'm learning at Harker is actually making me a better museum assistant. Fiona was positively ecstatic when an archaeologist on a recent call couldn't think of the word *debitage* and I supplied it. And amid it all, I'm actually honing my hunting skills too. Last week I bested two of the stronger kids in our class in the coliseum and witnessed a rare satisfied nod from Reid. Butterflies? Never heard of 'em.

"Well," Elliot muses, leaning back in his chair. "He have any updates?"

I check my school email again, legs fidgeting beneath the library desk. "Not yet. But I know he'll come through."

"Even more reason to blow off this paper on harpies. Once we save the world, Graveheart can put in a good word for us with the dean."

"You know, every time you flunk an assignment, you make yourself into a bigger cliché."

"You sound like Peter. I don't mind being a dumb jock." Elliot flexes his enormous biceps at me in an effort to lighten the mood. "I'm comfortable with who I am. Now, let's go race already."

I can't help my laugh even as other hunters in the library shush me. "You know I'll whoop you."

"I'm the fastest out of all my brothers back home."

I study him for a beat, a golden gladiator in a gothic library. It doesn't quite fit. "You don't talk much about your family. Are your brothers cool?"

Elliot shrugs. "They're like me, but on steroids."

"Aren't *you* on steroids?"

"Come on, Viv." A begrudging smile. "You don't want to rile up your competition like that."

"So, what, they're a supermasculine bunch? Muscles on muscles? Abs on abs?"

Elliot begins to pack up his backpack. "Pretty much. Fort Bragg's not too far from our town. My dad's a drill sergeant there. Even before we got our abilities, he raised us with plenty of respect for the craft. He calls us warriors, not hunters."

"Is he mean?"

Elliot's hands still as he thinks about the question. "No. Cold, though."

"So you get all that warmth from your mother?"

He smiles at me, proving my point with the softness of it. "Actually, I credit Soph with that."

"What do all these warrior brothers of yours think about your platonic female best friend?"

For the first time in the two months I've been friends with him, Elliot falters. "They, uh . . ." He clears his throat, gathers the rest of his papers, stands to leave. "They think she's hot. Are you coming or what?"

"Yeah." I pull my things together, a strange feeling nagging at me, like I asked something I shouldn't have. "Elliot, if I—"

"Where are you two going?" Sophia asks, bounding over to us. Her bangs flutter as she moves, her loose T-shirt ripped along the side to show off her toned stomach. "Peter and I just finished a *mountain* of work for Cryptozoology."

"She means *I* finished a mountain of work," Peter tells us, coming up behind her, still stuffing books into his bag. "While she researched classic cars and vintage band tees for sale."

"Sue me," Sophia relents as they follow us out of the library. "Life's too short for multiple-choice questions."

Outside, dusk is slowly slipping into early evening, and the sky looks like a painting from the Renaissance. Lanterns flicker to life across the campus and gild Sophia's copper hair. My eyes scan the chimneys dotting weathered roofs, pumping out tufts of warm smoke into the chilled air. Leaves like flecks of amber litter the drying grass.

"Viv and I were going to race around the track," Elliot tells them with a grin. "Wanna watch?" Whatever shift I noticed in him is long gone now.

"Sure," Sophia says. "I always wanted to be a cheerleader. Did you have those at your fancy all-girls school, Viv?"

But I find that my throat is kind of tight. These people—Elliot, Sophia, and Peter—are the reason, despite all the horrors we've faced, all the mysteries brewing, that Harker feels more like home than anywhere else I've ever been. I knew getting close to other hunters would be as painful as it was rewarding for this very reason. The more we look into Kitty, this school . . . the more at risk they are. What if tomorrow one of them is gone, leaving nothing but a forged note? Usually my nightmares are of the night my father died, but just last night I dreamed of finding Sophia's twin bed drenched in blood and woke with tears in my eyes.

"What's with you? You've been looking at me strangely all day," Sophia says. "You been dreaming about me?"

That Sophia intuition, man. It's no joke. I clear my throat to say, "Only nightmares."

"I'm serious," Sophia says, more concerned than playful. "You've been staring at me like I almost died or something."

"Maybe I'm obsessed with you. Would that be so wrong?"

Sophia snorts and throws an arm around my shoulders, appeased. "We'd make the cutest couple."

"Need a third?" Elliot asks.

"Sure," Sophia says and licks her lips. Beside me, Peter chokes on his water. "Can we get Halloween costumes this weekend?"

"I was going to spend tonight in the city, actually." And by *was going to*, I mean I just decided right now. I haven't seen Penny or Hound in weeks, and I need a little distance. Some self-preservation. I was a lone hunter for a decade, and now I have three new people in my life whose losses would tear me to shreds.

"Oh." Sophia's face falls. "Okay."

The way her disappointment makes me feel is exactly why I need this time alone.

On my way home, I call Penny to ask how work was, and she tells me she's going to a business dinner with Claude and will likely stay at his place tonight. I'm glad we're on the phone so she can't see my grimace. He's always using her as wealthy blond arm candy and never shows up for her in return. I debate going back to school, but I haven't been to the apartment in a minute, and I could use some warmer clothes. Maybe I'll take Hound on a moonlit walk through buzzy Babylon.

Once inside, I kick off my boots, give Hound dinner and lots of kisses, toss my daggers under the loose floorboard in my room in case Penny comes home unexpectedly, and make a comically large cup of coffee. Our apartment is cold—the frigid, starless night seeping in through our flimsy insulation—and I miss the toasty fireplace and heaps of thick blankets in the Elkfore commons. I crank up the heat and offer my eternal devotion to the god of working thermostats.

On the couch, I curl up under a pool of light from our single lamp and pull my limbs beneath a blanket with my weaponry textbook. Hound jumps up next to me and rests his head on my legs with a satiated sigh. A yawn seizes me and I stretch my sore limbs and look out the window.

Through the cool glass, the Babylon streets are alive with the sounds of Friday night. Up-tempo music swimming out of Cobwebs downstairs. Taxis honking, dogs barking. Girlfriends screaming at one another in greeting. Tonight, that familiar lurch in my chest is nowhere to be found. I don't want to be down there, experiencing my twenties through bad dates and worse booze. I really am grateful for Harker. And a lot less lonely than I used to be. Do I really want to go back to how I used to be? Plus, it's my favorite time of year, and there's no better place to soak in the All Hallows' Eve delights than Astera.

I open my group chat with Elliot, Sophia, and Peter.

Do you guys actually want to get costumes in the city tomorrow?

There's a Halloween shop down the street that opens in a vacant hardware store every October like Brigadoon.

Peter responds first. Yeah! Can we do Half City sightseeing?

For sure. Meet at my place around 10? Penny's sleeping at the Frenchman's.

We get to see your home? Sophia writes. Shall I bring my finest china?

Shit, Elliot writes. My Dior suit is at the dry cleaner.

I stifle a laugh. MY APARTMENT you dummies.

But that reminds me of the other half of my life: I text Fiona next to reiterate how much I still want to work the Chasm exhibit despite this "secret project" I'm doing for my mom. I'm attacking everything from all angles. Super Viv is in full effect. I even debate texting Reid and asking him if we should meet up next week to brainstorm the garden's location, but I don't have his number. My heart gives a dejected thump, which I choose to ignore.

Instead, I pry open my textbook. Once I drain this coffee, I'm going to be revved up and ready to tackle the dense, crinkled pages ahead.

I'm still feeling positive and assured I can do it all when my eyes droop closed.

"STAY PUT," MY father whispers. "Don't move no matter what you hear. You swear?"

He's crammed me into a storage container. I can feel the slickness of spilled oil. Taste the brine in the night air. Hear the horns of the ocean liners mooring at the docks.

"Those are Broods," I tell him. "You told me to run when we see them."

My father's eyes crinkle with something I don't recognize. "And you should. Always. But I can't keep running forever, kitten."

"Dad—" It comes out like a plea. Please don't leave me, I want to say. Please stay here.

"You swear?" he repeats, more urgently this time.

Tears are brimming in my eyes. I tighten my hold on his daggers. "I swear."

He gives me a kiss on my forehead. "You are everything to me."

When he closes the container, I begin to shake. From the cold, from the fear, from my sobbing. I can hear the ocean waves lapping furiously at the piles outside, trying to drag them free of the seabed. Seagulls squawk their hunger. Mildew and exhaust fill my nose.

I miss my dad already.

I hear low voices arguing. Men. Slithering, hissing, bellowing. Deviants. My whole body is electric with the certainty of it. My dad's daggers wail in my palms to be used.

Dad said stay put, *I think.*

And so I do.

Even when the sinister voices rise to a fever pitch. Even when I hear my dad begin to fight.

But as the grunts and cries grow louder, I can't help myself. I press my face to the metal to try to hear more and find a crack in the container wall. A sliver I can see through—

Blood. Flashes of silver. Twelve demons against my lone dad. It's not a fair fight. And they all carry the mark of the Brood.

He's screaming as he drives his sword, bleeding from his ribs and neck . . .

I know he needs me. But no matter how hard I pry at the container door, it doesn't budge—

I wake to the shattering of a porcelain cup and the scent of my coffee dripping onto the floorboards. My skin buzzes. My eyes, peeled open, take in the reality around me—my cold apartment, the couch against my face, the spilled caffeine—when the floor creaks across the living room.

My eyes snap toward the sound.

But there's nothing there. Just dark shadows cast by headlights and neon signs outside projected on the walls.

Still, I climb gingerly to my feet, heart in my lungs.

My daggers are beneath the floorboard of my bedroom. I walk heel-to-toe toward the kitchen drawers, which are closer. All our flatware is sterling silver—the only home goods I've ever splurged on. How did something get into our place? I've been home this whole time. Unless it's been watching me. Lying in wait?

Another creak. Longer, deeper. Like the stretch of a bow across a violin.

My pulse is ratcheting. My skin prickling. The feeling warps my terror into something with a sharper, finer point. My grip tightens on a utensil—

And then a shadow crawls out from Penny's darkened doorway, snaking across the floor . . .

I grit my teeth, and thrust my silver toward—

Hound.

Stretching sleepily with a pleasant yowl.

"Jesus," I tell him, sagging against the kitchen counter as I shut the silverware drawer. "I almost butter-knifed you."

Hound trots over and licks my leg.

The prickle in my skin fades. Perhaps it was residual adrenaline from my dream . . . or a demon who's a block away by now. Kneeling down to hold Hound close, I stare out at the city lights, hands stroking through his coarse fur, my heart still slamming in my chest.

CHAPTER 31

AFTER NEITHER PILATES nor my hot shower does enough to quell last night's unease, I do something I haven't done since I lived with my mom and Nora—I tidy for company.

Every surface has been spritzed with cleaning solution and wiped with a rag. Hound's dark hair has been vacuumed up and Penny's oil paint stains covered strategically with rugs and pillows. Penny's and my collection of front-door shoes have been sorted into their respective closets—black loafers, heeled boots, and patent leather Mary Janes in mine; straw sandals, vintage ballet flats, and white Keds in hers.

I'm doing dishes that were already clean when the knock sounds at the door and Hound howls so hard he nearly hurts himself.

Sophia's weekend style isn't too different from her school attire. Loose wide-leg jeans, a curve-hugging tank, one too many necklaces. Elliot's unsurprisingly in gym clothes that still smell like the morning's sweat and body spray. Peter's the only one who looks like he put effort into his outfit for our first off-campus hang: Instead of his usual Henley, he's gone for a suede jacket and a white button-down, which makes him look a bit like a professor himself.

"Wait, it's so cute," Sophia tells me, taking in the hanging plants Penny keeps alive, her easel, and the little paper lanterns we've hung off the fire escape. She kneels to the floor and gives Hound the nuzzles he craves, and I can see hearts form in his eyes.

"He's never going to leave you alone now," I tell her.

"That's all I could have hoped for," she says into the top of his head.

"Does he bite?" Peter asks, wary. And that's fair. Hound looks like he could tear your leg off. He probably could, but he won't, and that's what matters.

"Not unless you neglect to give him pets."

Peter doesn't laugh until I give him a pointed look, and then a relieved chuckle escapes him. "Good one."

"These are cool," Elliot says, pointing at the moody photographs that line the living room wall.

"Thanks." I debate saying I found them at a thrift shop but decide I don't care. That maybe I'm done caring. I actually don't think my new friends have any intention of judging me. "I took them, actually."

"I didn't know you did photography," Peter says. "Are you taking a class at Harker on it?"

I keep forgetting Harker teaches regular classes and electives. I can't imagine cutting out early from Monster Identification to make it to Intro to Pottery on time.

"It's just something I do for fun."

"You should do it for money," Sophia says, squinting at a photo I took of a little girl on an STC swing set. "This one makes me want to cry."

When the front door swings open again, four sets of hunter eyes snap to it like hawks spotting prey.

"Oh!" Penny nearly drops the overstuffed paper bags she's

holding in her arms. "Hi! Viv, I didn't know you had"—she takes in Sophia, Peter, and Elliot—"people over."

Shit, shit, shit—"Sorry, these are just . . . my friends."

Penny is too kind to raise a brow, but I can see the confusion in her eyes. I don't have other friends.

"From work," I add as Hound trots over to Penny excitedly. "New friends from work. Guys, this is my roommate, Penny."

I give all three of them my best *don't say anything weird* eyes.

"The famous Penelope Pine!" Sophia says with her pure-charisma smile.

Penny squeezes the paper bags closer to her like safety blankets. "Hi."

Sweet Pen. I hope Sophia's attempts at friendship don't scare her. "I thought you were at Claude's," I say.

With that, Penny's face falls. In fact, her eyes go a little glossy as she sniffs. "I upset him, I think. He told me we needed space."

I am going to have this art-dealing fuck drawn and quartered. Especially now that there's a chance a deviant was in our apartment. I want Penny here as little as possible.

"Yikes," Sophia says.

"He wanted me to come to Paris with him this week for work, which was really generous and all . . ." She drops the bags on the counter and begins to take out her Babylon Bazaar haul. Fresh marigolds in plastic, two bumpy-skinned gourds, some carrots, and a head of berry-red radicchio. "But it's the Harvest Festival at the school where I teach. The kids look forward to it all year. I told him I couldn't miss it."

"Sounds fair to me," Peter says with a comforting nod. "He didn't understand?"

Penny turns on the faucet to wash the produce. "He just wants me to prioritize our relationship. I know he's more hurt than angry."

Sophia shakes her head. "What are you, Mother Teresa?"

Penny blanches. "No, I—"

"Sounds like he wants you to prioritize his penis," Elliot says like it's helpful.

I wince. "Elliot and Peter are also part-time relationship therapists, apparently."

Penny dries her hands. "What do you guys do at the Windsor?"

Well. Now we're fucked. Sophia shoots me look of concern and I blurt, "They're interns. Unpaid interns."

"Why do we have to be unpaid?" Elliot mopes, falling back into the couch.

"It's a cruel world," I say, but my eyes tell him, *Shut up.*

"Don't get your sweaty clothes all over Viv and Penny's couch," Sophia scolds.

"Fine." He shrugs before pulling his shirt off, displaying a flawlessly chiseled eight-pack.

"Oh my god," Penny breathes before spinning around to shove the vegetables—and her head—into the fridge.

"Elliot," Peter says under his breath. "You've scandalized Viv's roommate."

"Wait," Soph says, looking at her phone. "Stay like that for one sec." She rounds the kitchen counter and takes a picture of Elliot's torso as he's sprawled across my couch. "Now you can put your shirt back on."

Elliot shakes his head as he yanks his shirt overhead. "Is this what being a sex slave feels like?"

"I think you need to be having sex to be someone's sex slave," I say.

"What's the picture for?" Penny asks quietly, eyes intent on her flowers and their vase.

Sophia makes a disgruntled noise, bypassing the stool next to me to climb onto the countertop and pull her legs up under her. "This guy I used to sleep with won't leave me alone."

"Vintage car guy?" I ask.

"No, this other guy." Sophia shows Penny and me her phone, where we see a depressing string of unanswered messages. The last one reads I can't stop thinking about you.

"He seems nice," Penny says, and the twisted thing is I know she means it.

I shake my head. "Oh, Pen."

Sophia replies to Sam's last message with the faceless photo of Elliot's abs. From this angle it looks like they've just wrapped up some decent a.m. couch sex. "There," she tells us. "That should do it."

Elliot laughs from across the room, but it's Peter's expression I'm hung up on. He looks like he's just realized the puppy he was hoping to adopt is rabid. I'd give him a pat on the shoulder if it wouldn't embarrass him. Better he learns now that Sophia is no man's peace—certainly not his.

"Should we head out?" Elliot says. "I want to get there before all the gladiator costumes are gone."

"You're a gladiator every year," Sophia says. "How about something with a shirt? I'm sick of you drinking your weight in alcohol to stay warm."

"That's the best part of the costume!"

"We'll be back in a bit," I tell Penny. "Then movie night?"

Penny nods, smoothing down her blond ponytail. "Sure. Have fun."

"Or you could come?" Sophia says, throwing on her coat. "We're going to get Halloween costumes."

My body goes rigid at the thought. This morning has been like a tightrope walk. A successful one so far, sure, but I have little desire to see the rope extended through the afternoon.

Penny mulls the offer over. "I wouldn't want to impose . . ."

"Stop it. You're coming. It'll help you get your mind off of Klaus."

"Claude," Penny corrects morosely.

"See, I'd already forgotten."

"Do you mind?" Penny asks me. "I know you guys are having a work hangout."

I couldn't deny Penny if she asked me to drink bleach. "Of course not. Don't be silly."

Sophia loops an arm through Penny's and drags her out the front door.

"Classic work hangout to get Halloween costumes," Elliot says behind me with a laugh.

"Didn't you know?" Peter says quietly as I lock up. "That's a fake unpaid intern's favorite activity."

"I'm going to fake fire both of you."

A short walk through leaf-strewn Babylon later, we arrive at the costume store before the afternoon rush. Halloween is next weekend, so we're lucky the place hasn't been completely picked over.

Elliot drags Sophia off to find his gladiator costume, and Peter asks one of the store associates to point him in the direction of the superhero section. Penny sticks by my side as we wander the aisles, "Monster Mash" playing from the loudspeakers. She's quiet, her hands grazing plastic bags of costumes but her eyes never sticking on anything too long.

"I'm sorry about Claude," I tell her.

"It's okay."

"He just wishes he could take you everywhere. I don't blame

him." It physically pains me to have Claude's back, but I think it's probably what Penny wants to hear.

"Sure," she says.

"In fact . . ." I remind myself this lie is for her safety. "There have been some break-ins on our street this week. I'm going to keep staying at Fiona's since the exhibit is so soon . . . Will you stay with him? Once you make up? Just until the guy is caught?"

"Oh," she says, frowning. "Okay. Sure."

I stop in the middle of the sexy Disney aisle. "Penny. Is something else wrong?"

Her eyes shift from my face, down the aisle, and up to the ceiling.

"Penny," I warn. The girl is not one for conflict. "Tell me what's up."

Her voice is quiet as she says, "Why didn't you want your new friends to meet me?"

And I thought supporting Claude hurt. Upsetting Penny is as bad as it gets. It's like stepping on your dog's tail and knowing they don't understand what you're saying when you apologize. "I didn't— I wasn't trying to keep anyone from you. I just didn't know if you'd like them is all."

"Who have I ever not liked?"

Penny is everything I'm not—happy, warm, friendly, *good*. We always say she's the sun and I'm the moon. In reality, I feel more like the pitch-black sky, but in Penny's eyes I'm the other side of her coin, and I'm not going to argue with an honor like that. And she makes a good point. In classic sunny fashion, Penny's never met someone she didn't wish well. It's as impressive an ability as my hyperagility. No, more impressive. Definitely more impressive.

"They're just different. They're"—*violent deviant-killing machines*—"interns."

Penny can't quite make sense of what I've said, but I can tell she's trying. She's too pure for this bullshit. "Well, I'm not judging anyone for where they're at in their careers. Certainly not as an elementary school art teacher."

"I should have known. Thanks for being . . . so open-minded."

Penny nods, satisfied. "I really like them. Sophia's great."

We round a corner and find Sophia coming out of a dressing room in a Medusa costume that leaves virtually *nothing* to the imagination. "Yeah." I laugh. "She's full of surprises."

Peter's messing with an animatronic skeleton. When he sees her, he turns as red as a thermometer in July.

"Can you zip this up for me?" she asks him.

His throat bobs as he tries to rasp out an answer, swiping his floppy brown hair from his face. The man is making an impressive effort to keep his eyes off anything remotely inappropriate.

"For sure," he croaks, eyes on the ceiling as if asking for mercy.

The song shifts to something with chains clanging and cauldrons bubbling. Elliot comes out of his changing room, as shirtless as expected, and I have to admit he looks good. Those abs are as flawless as they were on my couch, and his wavy hair frames a face perfect for beach volleyball.

He shakes his head at Sophia. "Soph, you look like a prostitute."

"Thank you!" She studies her stomach and thighs in the mirror as Peter watches on from behind her.

"Do you like this one?" Penny asks me, holding up a vampire costume. "Or this one?" In the other hand she's got a paisley hippie dress.

"That one," the four of us say in unison.

She nods to herself as if the vampire was a stupid idea anyway.

If Penny is the sun and I'm the moon, Sophia is all the stars in the sky, Elliot is a mellow haze of clouds, and Peter is the astronomer on the ground taking it all in. Set against the scent of fog machines and the sound of "I Put a Spell on You," I decide to reevaluate all my preconceived notions about keeping some kind of emotional distance from my new friends and keeping those new friends away from Penny. I want to store this moment in a frame like a beloved grainy photo. The kind you look back on and think *Things were easier back then.* The five of us together is kind of wonderful.

"What are you gonna get, Viv?" Penny asks. "Catwoman again? Or I liked your *Black Swan* one last year."

"Why are you allergic to color?" Sophia asks. Her boobs are staring at me in what is essentially just a snakeskin bikini.

"I can't hear you in that thing."

"What about this?" Elliot says, offering me a sleek witchy ensemble. "Feels you-ish."

"How about that devil costume?" Soph says, gesturing to a slinky red minidress hanging seductively off a mannequin. Open back, paired with sheer red thigh-high tights and red patent heels. And little horns, of course. I wander over to it and run the silk between my fingers. It's so vibrant. So unafraid of standing out—of looking wrong or evil or impulsive.

It's so *red*.

"It's perfect."

CHAPTER 32

I'VE NEVER FELT much like a sexual being. It's not that I don't enjoy sex. It's fine, I guess. A fine way to end a date, to know someone cares for you in physical, tangible way. We all know words from boys under the age of twenty-five are worth about as much as an expired nail salon coupon—most likely useless, but could surprise you on the rare occasion. And even then, I'm not much of a words gal. I'm a fan of action, and it doesn't take a genius to guess why. But just because I've felt desire doesn't mean I've ever seen myself as very desirable.

Mostly I've spent my whole life thinking I'm too tall, too flat-chested, my teeth too big, my black hair too harsh a contrast against my too-pale skin, my eyes too gray when I wish them blue. And that's before picking apart my personality. The way so few people get my sense of humor compared to someone like Sophia, who's so often followed by a cloud of chuckling admirers desperate to be in her orbit. How rarely people call me *warm* or *comforting* the way they do Penny. How unambitious I am compared to Nora or my mother . . .

And yet, my brain blares through loudspeakers—tonight I am hot as hell. Terrible pun intended. This costume must have been handsewn by the slutty Halloween gods. Not that the gods themselves are slutty, though perhaps they are. That's their prerogative. And tonight, those are the kinds of gods I worship. The gods who bespelled Sophia to force me at arrowpoint into wearing false eyelashes and putting sparkling red glitter on my cheeks and the bridge of my nose. The ones who sent me the last pair of red vinyl platform Mary Janes that were on sale (no, even on the sacred scantily clad holiday that is Halloween, hunters still do not wear pointy heels).

"You look like a demon's wet dream."

I roll my eyes as I finish blow-drying my hair, but honestly I agree. Even if they worship a High Thane and not an actual devil, there's probably something to the iconic red-horned, barbed-tail look that demons associate with their homeland.

"Any particular demon you're hoping to send to bed tonight with dirty thoughts?"

"I have a boyfriend," I tell Sophia as she applies wine-colored lipstick. "Who you are meeting in an hour."

"And I am so looking forward to making the acquaintance of Mr. James Pine."

I knew I would regret this. I've kept my worlds separate for so long. How could I have let one successful Halloween-shopping outing convince me this was a good idea? "Don't be weird. Not with James. He doesn't get weird."

"That sounds like imprisonment."

"He's just a serious guy. Please?"

Sophia stands and grabs her purse. She's in the Medusa bikini and snake wig, with heeled boots and a gauzy emerald-green skirt that flutters when she walks. Glitter shines off her skin. Thick winged eyeliner accentuates her already dramatic silent-film-star eyes. "I'm going to go find Elliot. Meet at the gateway?"

"Sure. You look wet-dream-worthy too, by the way."

She beams wickedly at me. "I know."

When I'm alone, I stare at my reflection and think about what she said. About demons and devils and wet dreams. My cheeks flush when brown curls and groans of pleasure fill my mind. Bad news.

Maybe it's this costume. Or the mischievous thrill of Halloween night...

Okay, I'm grasping at straws here. But it could be that James and I haven't slept together in so long. Not since I enrolled here, actually.

Things have only been worse with him since the strzyga. Perhaps we just need to spice things up. What would Sophia do? Probably show up without underwear and shove them in James's mouth.

My hand halts on the blow-dryer handle.

That's not a bad idea, actually. The first part at least. Before I can talk myself out of it, I slip my nude underwear down my legs and toss them into the hamper in our closet.

There. I'm fun. I'm girlfriend material.

The slutty Halloween gods have been appeased.

When I finish blow-drying my hair and go to grab my purse, my inner thighs rub against my sex, and I wince. Maybe this is dumb. We'll be in Astera tonight. What if I have to hunt? I'm going to attack a demon in a silk minidress and no panties? Ridiculous.

I'm halfway to the hamper to retrieve my underwear in shame when a knock sounds at the door.

I swing it open, already laughing at Sophia's reaction when I tell her how the devil costume ate my brain, and come face-to-face—or face-to-chest, because he's so damn tall—with Reid.

The look in his eyes as he drinks me in is knee-weakening. It's the image you'd find if you looked up *turned on* in the dictionary. It makes me clench all over, but mostly between my legs. I've never been certain if demons can actually scent things like fear and arousal—it's not like I'm taking Demon Anatomy this semester—but some corner of my mind knows the answer when Reid sees my legs pinch together and his hand shoots to the doorframe. The wood groans under the force of his grasp. I'm making a very similar noise in my head.

"You wore red . . ." His words are barely audible.

I swallow hard as I think of scarlet-scaled claws. "Happy Halloween."

"That it is," he replies. His eyes have not left my body.

Someone down the hall opens their door, and pop music swims out.

"What's up?" I manage.

Reid's hand abandons the doorframe, and I notice the wood has splintered in its wake. He pulls a paper out of his back pocket. "I, uh . . ." He clears his throat. "I spoke with one of our alumni stationed in Brazil. She's been hunting with Kitty."

That clears the attraction mist from my vision. "No way. Come in."

He looks hesitant. Like he doesn't quite trust himself around me right now. It should frighten me, that look, but I'm too greedy for more of the sexual torment swimming in his eyes. It's very aeon of me.

I usher him inside, closing the door behind us. Only then do I notice the state of our dorm room: Sophia's Maleficent horns from last Halloween on the desk, makeup bags stuffed with products gaping open, glitter dusting the hardwood. There's even a pair of butterfly wings poking out of the hamper, which I'm pretty sure aren't from anything Halloween-related. I feel a stab of embarrassment.

"What is that?" I ask him, kicking some of Sophia's clothes under her bed.

He hands the paper to me, still standing a bit farther away than necessary. "I printed the email exchange. Figured you'd want to see. Seems like she's safe, at least."

I flip through the emails as he speaks. The hunter confirms everything Kitty said in her note to Peter. The academic pressure got to her. She wanted to see the world. She wasn't sure about the way Harker taught hunting.

Relief sails through me. "So she's fine."

"Yeah." Reid sits down on my bed.

"Just like her letter said."

"Wait, Kitty left a letter? You told me she went missing."

"She did, the letter was weird . . . It was worth looking into. I promise." I drop the emails on the desk and take a seat next to Reid. "Any luck finding the garden?"

"What do you mean? Doesn't this—"

"Even if Kitty has nothing to do with it, someone still took the blade from the armory—"

"The Aeon's Dagger," Reid supplies.

"—and tried to cover it up with her name. And . . ."

Reid stiffens. "And what?"

"There might have been a deviant in my apartment last weekend."

His nostrils flare, jaw tensing. "Why didn't you tell me that sooner?"

"Why would I have? It's Astera; they're everywhere. I may have just been having a bad dream. But if someone knows we're looking into this . . . if someone wants to stop us . . . it means we have to find that garden before they do."

Reid sighs, his eyes lingering on the hem of my dress and my pale, bare thighs. "I haven't had any luck tracking down the location yet." His voice is a little raw. "You don't want me to talk to Lisette, and I doubt Driscoll would allow a demon, even me, to—"

But I remember how Driscoll stood up for Reid that day after Crowley's class. "You should try with Dean Driscoll. People's lives could be in danger. He trusts you."

Reid's eyes meet mine, and I am suddenly very aware of our proximity. I wonder if he can smell my vanilla shampoo. "Okay," he relents. "Okay."

"You two are close, right?"

Reid weighs the question. "He found me at my worst. Brought me here. I owe him a lot."

I guess I do too. I'm already leaning in when I realize I'm going to hug him. I catch a wary expression on his face, but he allows me to wrap my arms around his neck anyway. "Thank you, Reid. For helping me."

The hug is a mistake. Now I can investigate that zingy lemongrass scent—bodywash, I think—and the masculine evergreen. A bit of laundry detergent. And I can feel the hard planes of his back muscles under my hands, neck muscles against my cheek, pec muscles against my breasts . . . Everything is like granite. And everything is wound tight as a bow.

He is not hugging me back.

In fact, he isn't breathing.

I release him and look anywhere but his eyes. "Really, thanks."

"So . . ." Reid's register is a little husky. He stands, stuffing his fists in his pockets, averting his eyes from mine. "Where are you off to tonight? Lacrosse team parties?"

"Actually, we're going into Astera."

"All dressed up for your pet." But the barb is lacking his usual snark. He sounds kind of sad. I wonder if he gets as lonely as I do. Or did, before he brought me here.

"Do you want to come?"

Reid looks at me like I've suggested he shave my head. "What? Why?"

"For fun, Reid. Has nobody told you about fun?"

He makes a face, but I can see interest sparking in those stormy blues. Which are extra blue and extra stormy on this strangely triumphant Halloween night. "I'm not sure that's appropriate, as your instructor."

"Come on," I cajole. "We won't tattle."

"You mean your gaggle of hunter buds?"

"You know who my *buds* are?"

"I see who you sit with in Combat Training. The nerd, the jock, and the sl—"

"Don't," I tell him sternly. "Not when we're just becoming friends."

"Slob, huntress. I was going to say *slob*."

Reid and I both take in the state of the dorm, and I can't help my laugh. "How do you know *I'm* not the messy one?"

He studies me quietly before saying, "I think you like everything to be in its right place."

"What gave me away?" I can't keep the surprise out of my voice.

"Finding control wherever you can get it? Takes one to know one."

To change the subject from the fact that Reid's words have stripped me bare more intimately than anything I've done with my own boyfriend in months, I say, "If you're going to come, you'll need a costume."

He rubs the back of his neck. "I don't have one."

Is that a yes? Is Reid Graveheart agreeing to hang out with me on a weekend? Maybe he isn't lonely at all. Maybe he just wants to spend time with me. The thought is a dose of pure, shimmering dopamine. "You could just rock your own horns and tail." I gesture to my headpiece and try to quell the giddiness low in my stomach.

"Legend, remember?"

"Sure it is." I scope the room for inspiration, then have a stroke of genius. "Do you trust me?"

"Do I have a choice?"

CHAPTER 33

PETER AND ELLIOT both give me pointed looks when I arrive at the gateway with Reid in tow. He's got Sophia's butterfly wings on and the Maleficent horns on his head. He looks like a child's idea of a demon, which gave me a good laugh. Him, not so much.

Once Astera's pleasant chill curls around us, Sophia pulls me aside to ask why I've dragged the narc along if I'm not planning to seduce him, which I have no good response for. *He seemed lonely* only feels half-true. A more honest answer would be *He seemed lonely, and I wanted to keep hanging out with him.* My teacher. A demon. Both reasons why this is an utterly terrifying thought.

Regardless of my reasoning, when we get in line outside Cobwebs, I've come to the obvious realization that I invited our instructor out to party with us and that may not have been my finest decision-making moment. While Elliot chats with a group of buff Ninja Turtles and Peter helps Sophia with her bra strap, Reid stands in his makeshift demon costume, staring out into the night.

The Half City buzzes as it always does on Halloween. Jack-o'-lanterns and violet string lights decorate windows and fire escapes. The sidewalks are so concentrated with drunk twentysomethings in wigs and face paint that they spill onto Main, where cars honk in gridlock traffic. On Halloween it's always better to walk. It'll take you twice as long in a cab or on a subway full of masked teenagers with rolls of toilet paper stuffed in their backpacks.

"Hi, babes," Cobwebs' owner greets us at the bar's entrance. She's dressed as a fifties film star—cat eye sunglasses, beauty mark, and a polka-dot scarf around her head. "Your other half's already inside."

"Thanks," I tell her.

"Cobwebs' owner knows James?" Sophia asks, nose pinched in distaste.

I clock Reid's stony expression and shake my head. "She means Penny."

"I don't believe in friend jealousy." Sophia brushes a snake from her bangs. "But if I did, that would hurt."

Inside, Cobwebs is an undulating mass of skin and sweat and fake blood. "Thriller" blares through the speakers, and artificial fog hangs sticky and sweet in my lungs. I spot Penny past a punch bowl filled with something galactically purple. She looks like she's stepped off the set of a sixties variety show in her minidress and go-go boots. Her blond hair has been teased and sprayed to the high heavens beneath a white pleather headband.

"You might have been born in the wrong era," I tell her.

"Viv! Oh my god, you look so insanely hot." She squeezes me in a quick hug.

"She's right," a voice murmurs behind me.

Remember what I said about hunters taking things in all at once in a way that humans can't? Well, in this moment a few things happen at the same time.

I recognize James's voice, and an ocean wave of disappointment crashes over me. I have the shocking thought that I wish Reid were the one to say those words. He's the person I wore red for. Not James. It could never have been James.

And I come to the startlingly freeing realization that this isn't going to work.

I didn't think Harker had changed me much. Maybe I feel less alone, and my dagger technique is stronger than it used to be, or maybe I know more about arcane relics and how to wield them. But I didn't anticipate that it would change my outlook on my boyfriend.

Or, more honestly, my outlook on myself.

That's why I was dating James, right? Because it was important to my mother, and what she thought of me was important to how I saw myself?

For whatever reason, those tides have shifted.

And it's a relief to know that it's not entirely because I've developed a harmless attraction to my combat instructor.

"Thanks," I tell him, accepting a chaste kiss on the lips. "James, you remember my colleague Reid."

"Hey, man," James says, tucking me more closely into him.

Reid only studies me under James's arm. The look in his eyes is worse than annoyed or jealous—he looks upset with himself. Like he's not sure why he came. "Hey."

"Interns!" Penny squeals.

The pang in my heart only lasts a second before I see Penny absorb Sophia, Elliot, and Peter into hugs of their own. It's a sight that could make even a cold, hard aeon huntress shed a tear—my friends are becoming friends. I pull my camera from my purse and snap a shot of them together. Plastic snakes and paisley swirls.

"You guys look incredible," Penny tells them. "Wait! Peter, I have something for you." Penny fishes through her bag and pulls out a Spider-Man trading card in a plastic bag. "One of my students' fathers is a comic illustrator. Apparently he has a bunch of these lying around."

Peter nearly staggers back into the jukebox behind him. "It has the trademark corners from Marvel's first manufacturer . . . Is this an original from 1966?" His awe is palpable as he holds a card of the same superhero he's dressed as. "Thank you, Penny."

"God, Penelope," Sophia groans. "You're such a good person."

Penny only smiles earnestly at them both.

James makes no effort to hang with my new friends, and I'm grateful. I was nervous about Reid and James meeting again after the strzyga incident, but I've actually lost track of Reid in the crowd. My eyes scan over the throng of costumed revelers, but Sophia's repurposed butterfly wings are nowhere to be found.

My gut twists at the thought that maybe he's already left with someone. And not out of fear that he's drinking someone's soul but out of shameful schoolgirl jealousy. Maybe they're already pressed up against each other in the back of a dingy Astera cab. A little maniac in my brain is shouting *Hands off!* But I can't stop the train of thought. It's like pressing on a bruise. The pain bleeds into some kind of perverse pleasure, and I push harder just to explore what's there. I think about Reid's perfectly full bottom lip brushing over someone's thighs. Will he crave her soul the way I know he thirsts for mine?

"What inspired the switch-up this year?" James asks over the din.

I shake breathy moans and demonic grunts from my mind.

"They were out of Catwoman costumes. What are you?" He's essentially costumeless in his moss-green polo and dark pants.

"A billionaire, get it?"

"No," I admit. "I don't, actually."

"It's aspirational."

Wow, how did I wait so long to do this? "Can we talk outside?"

I don't wait for a response. James's hand is warm in mine as I yank him through the crowded bar, nurse hats and pirate hooks in every direction. I don't care if Reid's gone home with fifteen girls, I tell myself. I need to do this either way.

It's a feat to make it outside, where I inhale cool night air. I love Halloween, but I could do without the crowd it draws to our usually undisturbed bar.

"Listen, James—"

"I already know what you're going to say." He releases an accepting sigh. "And I'm not upset."

Relief breezes through me. "You aren't?"

"Of course not. I've known you since we were kids, Viv."

"I'm sorry." I take his hand in mine. "I wish it could have worked out between us."

James's relaxed features harden into an angry confusion. He yanks his fingers away. "What?"

"What are you—"

"I thought you were going to apologize for being so MIA lately. For embarrassing me in front of my friends. For all the weird behavior—"

"*Embarrassing* you? I saved someone's life."

"You know what I mean."

"Actually, I don't."

"Viv—"

"No, you know what? I am sorry. I'm sorry your self-esteem is so brittle."

"Come on, Viv. You're telling me this slutty getup isn't some kind of olive branch?"

Partially I'm upset that he's right. Some other version of me—one I feel all too divorced from now—was hoping to earn his interest back with sex tonight.

But I also wore the costume tonight for *me*. Maybe Reid gave me the idea of stepping outside my dark cocoon, but I liked how it felt to be bold. I liked that this one fucking year, I didn't dress up as something virtuous or benign. I'm dangerous, and this year I didn't try to hide it.

"We're done." There's an assuredness in my voice I didn't expect.

James doesn't miss a beat. "Penny is going to be devastated. And your mom."

"I'll handle them. But I think you should go."

"You know, everyone told me I was out of my mind to date you. That you'd cause me nothing but problems. Your own mother told me I could do better."

The words land like a slap across the face.

I guess I thought that eventually my mom and I could recover whatever closeness we had when my dad was alive. That despite how many times I've disappointed her, I could do enough right to earn her love again.

Clearly a fool's errand. "Guess you should've listened."

He shakes his head and one perfect blond lock falls into his face. He brushes it away like it's offended him. "You're a prickly, difficult person, Viv Abbot. I was nothing but patient with you, and this is how you treat me?"

"I must have left your Medal of Honor back home with my underwear."

His eyes flash with furious heat, and then he shakes his head once more before stalking off toward his driver and parked sedan.

Back inside Cobwebs, I find Sophia flirting with a shirtless fighter pilot. I tell her James and I broke up and that I'm going home early. She tries to leave with me, but I refuse to cockblock her. I just want to be alone anyway.

I search the crowded bar for Reid for ten pathetic minutes before I realize he's long gone, and I don't blame him. Visions of my jealous back-of-the-cab fantasy spin in my head until I feel queasy. So dumb on so many levels. I told him to come out with us and immediately abandoned him to break up with my boyfriend. I have nobody to blame but myself.

Penny's sitting in one of the vinyl booths, laughing with Peter and Elliot, trying on some girl's phoenix wings, and I can't bring myself to interrupt with bad news. It would be selfish anyway—I'm only trying to beat James to her so I can relay my side of the story first. But she's my best friend. Nothing is going to change between us over this.

I repeat the words like a mantra as I slip out of the bar and into the night. I plan to walk a little, maybe discern a real vamp from all the plastic-fanged ones, Harker rules be damned, when I spot Reid leaning against the wall on the other side of the bar. He's shed his phony wings and horns and is holding them thoughtfully in his hands. And that's . . . all he's doing. He's not on his phone or smoking or anything. Just staring out at the city like he was earlier. Taking in the merry and the macabre.

I walk over to where he stands and follow his eyeline over bustling Main Ave. Across the street, a cowboy is passed out against a busted window. On a basketball court behind a chain-link fence, I'm pretty sure a soldier and a cheetah are having sex. Down here it's a little dicey—everyone around us is decently fucked-up, and there isn't a child grasping fistfuls of candy in sight.

I think of Nora and me as kids down in Lethe, sprawled out on the floor in sugar comas. The two of us stuffing full bars of chocolate and bags of fruity gummies into as many cabinets and couch cushions as we could before our mother would inevitably stash the remains of our trick-or-treat haul away to be doled out over the coming months.

Only minutes later, my dad would steal the candy back for us—a heroic feat. I remember how my mom wasn't able to contain her laughter when we tried mightily to hide the smears of chocolate on our faces. How she carved pumpkins with us while my dad put on the spooky episodes of our favorite shows. How she looked bundled up in his oversized sweaters when the heat was finicky and the wind howled.

Sometimes it hits me like a sucker punch how much I miss it. Not just my dad but how we were when he was alive. Nora and me. My mom. That version of her would never have told James he could *do better*. His death didn't just break my heart, it broke our entire family.

"It's my favorite night of the year," I say to Reid, candy corn–scented memories fading.

Reid nods, watching a guy in a Ghostface mask scare the living crap out of a squealing Tinker Bell. "Only night they dress up like us instead of the other way around."

"Exactly." All these mortals, masquerading as things eldritch and occult. And tomorrow we'll resume our lifelong performance as mortal. Both Reid and me, demon and hunter. "How long have you been out here?"

"Long enough to overhear that conversation with your pet," Reid admits, eyes still on the busy street corner. "Or ex-pet, I should say."

"Don't sound so broken up about it."

When he turns to face me, the weight of his haunting beauty threatens to compress me into the sidewalk. "I'll never understand what a girl like you was doing with a guy like him in the first place."

"No, you won't."

Reid shakes his head, confounded. "The prick had no idea how lucky he was."

I don't know what to say to that, so I press my hands to the silk of my dress.

"And the shit about your mom—"

"It's fine," I say.

"It's not. She all but abandons you when your father dies, and then tells your boyfriend—"

"Really," I interrupt. "It's fine."

He shakes his head like it's all some great cosmic injustice. "Don't worry," he sighs. "I get it."

Our subway ride home from Shiloh comes back to me, fuzzy-edged and dosed in Valium.

Like a lot of people who take up with the wrong crowd, I was trying to please other people.

Who?

My parents.

And it's only now that I wonder if in some twisted way, Reid's broken from expectation too. I mean, he was a member of the Brood. And now he aids the enemy in defeating his own people. I'd guess by his family's standards, he's a traitor.

We stay there for a while, leaning against the graffiti-smeared wall, watching the wicked night creep on, lost in thought.

"So," Reid says in the end. "No underwear, huh?"

I erupt in laughter. It feels like emerging from the deep end, chlorine replaced by air. "I'm going to kill myself."

"And here I thought you were trying to kill *me*."

In the streetlight, his eyes are a navy so dark they're practically black. Wistful, hungry, isolated. He smooths a hand down his face in the kind of exhaustion I know too well. Wanting with no hope of having.

When he faces me again, he's not the demon I thought I knew.

"No, actually," I tell him. "Not anymore."

CHAPTER 34

THE BREAKUP SENDS the expected waves through both the Abbot and Pine families. Penny calls me three times, and when I finally ring her back, I'm relieved to find not only is she not upset, she's grateful her best friend and brother aren't dating anymore. *It was more stressful than it was fun,* she admits. I happen to agree.

The rest of the messages aren't as kind. My mother emails—*emails!*—me to say that she's sorry to hear about James and me and attaches the number of a highly regarded North of the Chasm couples therapist. She assures me she's already made an initial call and *filled her in.* Nora texts me to say she's around if I want to talk, which I don't, and I tell her as much. James and Penny's parents don't reach out, and I guess that's for the best, but it reeks of relief on their part, which doesn't feel stellar.

But it isn't all bad. Peter takes Reid's new information about Kitty surprisingly well.

"I'm so relieved to have some answers," he says, winded as he holds my kneepad for me. "And happy she's not dead or kidnapped. That we were wrong about all that spell stuff."

I don't tell him that I insisted Reid still look into the garden for me. That I'm determined to make sure nobody's touched the asphodels. He's been through enough. "I'm still sorry, though. About . . ." There's no right way to say *your only remaining family abandoning you.* "The way it happened."

"It's okay," he admits, eyes on Sophia as she pummels Reid's padding. "I have more people in my life now."

My phone vibrates in my pocket right as I'm driving my leg toward Peter.

"One sec," I tell him. He looks relieved.

When I dig it out, I'm surprised to see Fiona's name. I wander away from the sparring pairs, my feet crunching on the pebbled floor of the coliseum.

"Hey, Fiona." I cover the mouth of the phone so she can't hear Sophia's grunt of pain when Reid roundhouses her to the ground. "What's up?"

"Hi. How are you holding up?"

For a moment, I have to rack my brain: Does she know Lisette's essay on harpy discrimination is just a blank page with a cursor staring back at me? Does she know Dawnmere set the velvet curtains of her classroom on fire when Sophia's potion assignment was late?

"With the breakup?" Fiona adds.

Oh god, *duh.* "I'm hanging in there," I say with a sigh. I'm an asshole.

"Well, I'm here if you need anything. I know you're working hard on your mom's campaign, but I'm actually calling with some good news."

"Your punches are coming in too high," Reid tells Soph.

"Who is that?" Fiona asks.

I hurry over to the stands where Peter is catching his breath. "Uh . . . political advisor. When they go low, we go high or something. What's this about good news?"

"Even with the time you've had to take off for your mother's campaign, your past years of work here haven't gone unnoticed. We'd love for you to help with the *Chasm of Astera* exhibit tomorrow night."

"Holy shit." My mom is going to freak. I slap Peter's arm in excitement, and he gives me a *But why?* face. "Thank you, Fiona. I won't let you down."

"Eight p.m. Do not be late."

"When have I ever been late?"

Fiona doesn't laugh on the other line.

"Thanks again," I say. But she's already hung up.

"Care to share with the class?" Reid calls as Sophia limps over to her water bottle.

Students halt mid punch. I put the phone away and cross my arms. "I just got a very cool work opportunity, actually." Some of the onlookers offer mild congratulations and head nods. "Thanks, guys."

Reid frowns. Not the response he intended, surely. But there's a gleam in his eyes. "Why don't we celebrate with a rematch?"

He's picked the wrong day for a sparring session with me. I'm hyped up about a hundred things. A Windsor win and rare mother-impressing opportunity, solving the Kitty case, breaking up with James, looking good in a color (though I'm back in my black leggings and tank today; baby steps). Reid won't be fighting the same Viv he bested at the top of the school year.

I toss my phone in the stands and meet him at the center of the arena. Some students continue their one-on-one matches. Others take water breaks so they can watch. I bend over and feel the pleasurable ache of a good stretch. Stand and let my shoulders go loose. Shake my neck out to either side. "No blindfold this time?"

Reid's grin triggers that gorgeous dimple. "Thought you

deserved one less handicap. In fact"—he unstraps the padded kick shield and raises his fists—"there. Two less handicaps."

"Generous." I ready my stance, but he makes no move. "Any day now."

Reid's face shifts into a mask of fierce competition. "Always playing with fire."

"Come on, demon boy," I tell him. "Show me the claws."

Unfortunately, I'm not the only one with a competitive streak. Before I can make sense of what's happening, Reid's crimson scales are glinting under the chilled morning light. His fingers lengthen and stretch, the inky-black enamel claws at the ends as sharp as razors.

His words flash in my mind as I take in the beastly scarlet skin. *You'd look nice in red.*

Students suck in breaths. Disgust. Terror. Intrigue.

Where I expect to find horror within myself, there's only exhilaration. The thrill of the hunt sings in my aeon blood. My vision tunnels until I can see Reid's powerful body and nothing else. My lips pull back from my teeth and I leap forward.

My fists clash against ancient scales as Reid meets me blow for blow. I sidestep his swipes, block his fists as they fly. My kicks land ineffectually against his loose track pants or the length of his back in that sweaty sleeveless shirt . . .

Focus, Viv.

When Reid's claws slide past my side, I dodge right. When they brush so close—almost *affectionately*—against my neck, I duck neatly. My smile grows more triumphant on my face, and his, more lethal. I'm better now, after a few months here. A stronger fighter. More agile. Blending a lifetime of intuition and months of formal training.

With a hook kick, I take him down to the ground, my legs landing on either side of his torso. I nearly have my fingers around his pulsing neck, awaiting the sweet sound of him tapping out—begging me for mercy—when he flips me over him and into the ground, my arm held under his primordial hand.

He crouches atop me, snarling like a beast, and I wrench free before he can put me into a crucifix hold. My knee drives hard into his gut, and he grunts, absorbing the pain. I'm up and sailing toward him, breaths heaving, body alight with vicious, violent glee—

Until a jolt of pain sears through my upper arm. A spear of that curved nail carving through my flesh.

I tumble to the ground, knees landing hard, dust filling my mouth.

Reid curses above me. Low and hollow. Filled with shame. "*Fuck*, I'm sorry—"

I roll to the side, pain ripping through my bicep. "No, it's—" Reid reaches for me, but I stand up and back away, arm clutched in my hand. "I'm fine."

Students lean forward. Whispers swirl. Sophia stands from her seat.

"I'm fine," I repeat to nobody. To myself. I'm fine.

"Viv—" That look on his face. I could have gone a lifetime without seeing such agonized guilt in those blue eyes.

I bolt from the arena, clutching my arm, before Reid can say another word. Before anyone can see the blood oozing through my fingers.

NOT THIRTY MINUTES later a fist is pounding at the door of my dorm. Insistent. Worried. Even without the jolt that zips through my body, I know it's Reid.

I freeze in my bra and leggings, blood dripping down my arm

and pooling on the hardwood at my feet. My second attempt at stitches has only resulted in a mess of thread, gauze, and alcohol swabs littered along my desk.

The knocks pound again. *"Viv."*

My heart races. The gash bleeds more quickly. But I can't move. I egged him on. I made him hurt a student—the one thing I know he's sworn never to do. No different from my own fears of being an aeon. Of hurting mortals. Especially those I care for.

Shame is a hot, heavy sheen along my skin. Even as he continues to pound on the door, I can't bring myself to answer.

"I can hear you breathing in there," Reid barks. Then quieter: "I can smell the blood . . . Let me in, Viv."

But I don't.

BY TEN THAT night, the gash is still seeping through its dressing. When I peel the flimsy white layers back, the significant divot in my skin pours rivulets of blood down my arm. I rifle through our room's wooden first aid box and find I've used up all the gauze. *Shit.*

What I need are stitches, but the wound's too far around my arm for me to do it myself, and I'm not going to the infirmary. Even if the pixies could fix me quickly and painlessly with their powers . . . they log every injury down there. It would mean telling the school their own combat instructor was the one who sliced me.

Sophia is at Elliot's game, Peter has told me point-blank he can't even hold a needle let alone stick one into someone . . . and I'm starting to feel dizzy—not the greatest sign. Self-preservation may actually edge out my pride. Just by a hair, though, I think.

I rewrap the wound and stalk down the hall in my rolled-over Harker sweats, first aid box in tow. Outside, I realize it's way too cold to have left in just a thin black baby tee, but I'm already halfway across Old Campus, and I know if I turn around now, I'm not going to have the guts to bundle up and come all the way back. I have to capitalize on this blood loss–fueled conviction.

I rap once on the door of his cottage. When Reid doesn't answer on the second knock, I start to worry. What if someone found out he hurt a student and he's been removed from campus? What if someone learned he was looking into that hidden garden for me? Maybe it's paranoia taking root, but suddenly I'm knocking feverishly on the wood, so hard the lone lantern that hangs over his door rattles like it's alive and kicking. With no luck, I jimmy the door handle, yanking it this way and that until I hear a *snap* and realize I've broken the thing. Too late now.

Heart thumping like a rabbit, I shove my way inside.

Pools of watery moonlight paint the small space in pale streaks. The rickety table and two chairs. The simple wooden desk, bare aside from one dog-eared political memoir. A cast-aside pair of athletic shoes and the rushing sound of—

A shower.

He's in the shower.

Oh god, Reid's taking a shower and I've broken into his place like a sicko.

It's fine, I'll just step outside, and knock again in ten—

The water shuts off in the bathroom, and not one second later, a rush of steam billows into the chilly cottage. When it clears, there's Reid, in nothing but a towel, shock plastered across his face.

CHAPTER 35

REID'S HAIR IS damp and slicked back, his shoulders and abs glistening.

"I broke into your house." Better to just get it all out there, right?

The tiniest hint of amusement. "I can see that."

"It was an accident. I was . . . worried about you." It's hard to talk and have eyes right now. Reid's body is just so *male*. Every lick of tan, tight abdomen. Every curve from shoulder down to wrist . . . wet hair, the scent of lemongrass invading my senses. It's almost more than I can stand.

The humor fades from his face. His fist tightens on his towel. Now that I'm staring at him, he looks kind of wrecked. Like he's been pacing for hours. Or drank too much caffeine. His eyes soften when he sees my arm. "I've been waiting for you."

The words send my heart racing, but he turns toward his desk, and I clock his own first aid kit sitting atop it.

"I'm that predictable?" I shift on my feet. He's dripping onto the hardwood floor.

"It takes a lot to get me inside the infirmary doors. Unconsciousness, heart failure . . ."

"You know what they say: 'Stubbornness is next to godliness.'" I'm babbling.

Reid's brows meet. "Do they say that?"

"No, I don't think so." My eyes find the ceiling. "Could you put some clothes on or something?"

His voice is a notch lower when he says, "Are bath towels your devil costume?"

My eyes lose their battle, lowering to the slight rise where something long and heavy is pressing against the terry cloth. "Something like that."

His lips twitch and I'm hit with a jolt of giddy satisfaction. Yikes.

When he comes back from the bathroom in his athletic pants and long-sleeve shirt, he eyes the gauze on my arm once more. "Take a seat," he says, patting the corner of his desk like I'm a kid at the doctor's office. The implicit demand—his assumption that I'm going to do whatever he tells me to—makes my body hot. The idea of being at the mercy of his will. The *yikes* are plentiful this evening. I'm hoping it's the blood loss.

While I head over, he goes to lock the cottage door and inspects my handiwork. The minute he touches the doorknob it clangs to the ground.

"I'll pay for that," I say, cringing.

"Thought your job doesn't pay much."

"Who told you that?"

Reid looks up, caught. "I . . . asked around a bit about you. Wanted to make sure you were doing all right after . . . the weekend."

"The breakup, you mean."

He swallows thickly, eyes still on the broken handle. "Mm-hmm."

I tsk at him to hide what his concern does to my stomach. "Always stalking."

I'm perched on the corner of his spotless desk, so my feet dangle like I'm five years old. He washes his hands at his kitchen sink and then flicks on one dim light that illuminates only me. When he comes over, he unwraps the old gauze on my arm, and his closeness gives me a head rush. My eyes find the moon through the window over the sink. Anything but his chiseled, dementedly handsome face.

Reid grabs a clean cloth and holds it tightly to the wound. When I wince, his eyes follow the subtle movements of my body. His hand brushes up my forearm soothingly, lingering at my wrist a moment too long.

"No coat? It's thirty degrees out there."

"I run hot." It comes out like my voice is pure steam.

His has gone a bit hoarse too. "The anesthetic will take some time to work."

"No need, just stitch it up." I have to get out of here before I do something dumb like bite his earlobe. When he stares at me, I add, "Please."

They weren't kidding about that being the magic word. Reid looks like he can't decide which sounds more miserable: hurting me or denying me whatever I ask. I remember how he caved and allowed me to join the asylum hunt the last time I uttered the word. *Please.* Like a spell.

All the more reason to speed this up and be on my merry way. I'm in dangerous territory, and not the kind I so often find myself drawn to.

As if he's waging a similar battle, Reid admits his own defeat.

"Fine." And pulls out a needle and surgical thread. I wonder what it says about me that Reid's tense jaw and slight frown as he inspects my arm make my heart skip a beat, but the sight of the needle that's about to weave through my skin has no effect whatsoever.

"Stay still," he instructs with a rasp.

"Yes, sir," I mock. But it comes out almost needy. We swallow hard in tandem. He's my *teacher*. What is wrong with me?

His fingers encircle my arm and my nipples pinch. His hand is so big, it loops around my entire bicep easily. I feel very breakable in his demon's grasp. Not afraid necessarily, just . . . fragile.

"I'm sorry," he says after a minute, so quietly I barely hear him. "That never should have happened today."

My heart lurches in my chest. "Really, it's okay. It was an accident."

"I know what you're thinking, though. Of course it happened. A Brood demon training hunters is like a cat babysitting a nest of baby mice."

"I think *I'm* actually the cat in this situation. *Hunter*, remember?"

My attempt at a joke doesn't seem to land. There's a thorough sadness in Reid's eyes as his needle slides into my flesh. Crisp pain splits through my arm.

"I'm your instructor, and I hurt you." The words come out like he could rip himself open for what he did. It twists my heart.

"Hey," I say, holding his eyes. My hand brushes his lightly and his needle stalls before my skin. "All that stuff I said about you was wrong. You're more than the brand on your neck, Reid."

Something about my words seems to shudder through him. He says nothing as he works dutifully on the wound, and I wonder if I've overstepped. But I don't regret the words. In fact, they're long overdue. Somewhere between the burgeoning attraction and the way he's helped me and my friends and repeatedly saved my life, I've stopped equating him with the men who killed my father. He deserves to know.

"Plus," I add, "nobody could tell exactly what happened. And I'm not going to say anything to anyone."

"You don't have to cover for me."

"If you get fired, who'll bully the students into becoming decent fighters?"

Finally, a dimple curves in his cheek. "That was almost a compliment."

When my heart stutters, I look anywhere but his face. Neatly made bed with one pillow through a doorway. Another nonfiction book on his bedside table. Even though his cottage is larger than my dorm, Reid's housing feels smaller somehow. Emptier.

"Where are all your things?"

"What things?"

"You know." I avoid his eyes and the way I know they'll devour me whole. "Unfolded laundry, bags of chips, framed family photos . . ."

Reid stifles a laugh, and the needle sinks back into my flesh. "I don't eat chips. And I fold my laundry."

"And the photos?"

"Nobody worth framing."

Ah. "So those parents you'd wanted to impress . . ."

"Dead. And they did not die impressed."

"Disappointing everyone in your life?" I wince at a tug around the edges of the wound, and Reid's thumb brushes against the inside of my arm to soothe me. It has the opposite effect. "I'm an old pro at that."

He smirks to himself. "Not as old as me."

Even though I can assume his job here has something to do with it, I still ask, "What'd you do to piss everyone off?"

Reid mulls this over, the methodical rhythm of his stitching more painful as we sit in silence. The rich tang of my own blood hangs in the back of my throat. I try not to fidget. Finally, he says, "I told you once to make peace with who you are."

After the wraith attack, when I snapped at him. "I remember."

"I was probably talking to myself as much as I was talking to you, that night."

He'd said he knew *a thing or two about fate dealing you a hand you didn't ask for.* That look of disgust when he admitted to glamouring the people attacked by the strzyga. The way I could practically taste his shame today when he hurt me.

I allow myself to look at him. He's close enough for me to smell the evergreen of his skin. To see the few freckles like constellations on his cheeks. "You don't want to be a demon any more than I want to hunt."

His eyes lift to mine, and in the depths of them I find only suffering. "Why would I?"

"Reid . . ."

"I've felt this way as long as I can remember. Probably because the man who raised me was a monster."

I want to cut the tension—to quip at him about monsters and reroute us to our usual destination. Somewhere safe and feelings-proof. But I've crossed some kind of threshold. I can't even tell when I took the step—coming in here tonight? Buying the devil costume? Trusting Reid to look into Kitty and the hidden garden? At some point I steered us too far past our stop. Now a new road winds ahead, pulsing, crackling, threatening to drop clean off.

All I can muster is "That bad?"

Reid's gaze finds my nearly stitched-up flesh once more. "My father was as barbaric as any demon I've known. My older brother too. I was never like them. I didn't *want* to be anything like them. But in the world I was raised in . . . they were the highest standard."

Nora's shining smile as she accepts a debate trophy and then one for gymnastics and another for academic achievement flashes in my mind.

"My father pitted us against each other, me and my brother. Wanted to see who could be more vicious or debase themselves more for his love. For his respect." He sucks in a ragged breath. "It was usually me."

I know the feeling so well it turns my stomach. It's like catching your reflection in a mirror and wondering how long you've looked that rough.

"Did you kill them?"

At that, Reid's eyes slam to mine. There's an anger there, though not at me. A regretful fury. His hand is firm around my arm.

"No." The evenness of his voice is at odds with the ruthless expression on his face. "But I probably should have."

I bite my tongue as he tugs a stitch tight. "How does a demon with family like that end up working at Harker? You said the dean found you?"

"Joining the Brood was important to my dad. It's the most exalted rank for a demon and all he ever wanted for us. I was so young then . . . thought it would change how he felt about me." Reid shakes his head. Clearly, his joining didn't have the desired effect. "I knew immediately the Brood wasn't what I wanted. Did things I can never take back. I wish I could tell you I left immediately. Or that I left even after I secretly stopped taking souls or when my father was killed and I had nobody left to live my life for. But by then . . ." His inhale is as sharp as the needle piercing my arm. "I'd been in for too long. It wasn't until I met Edgar that I had any idea where else I could go. What I could be useful for. I'd actually been sent by the Brood to kill him."

"Really? Why?"

"Warlock dean of Harker? The High Thane had a hundred reasons to take Driscoll out. Many of his men had tried and failed. But Edgar saw something in me. Maybe how miserable I was . . . He offered me an alternative. Convinced the Elders to hire me. Protected my cottage with a cloaking spell when the High Thane realized I wasn't coming back. I owe the man my life."

"That must have been . . ." I search for the words. Leaving everything you know behind—a brotherhood, even a cruel one—to be a pariah here at Harker. "Difficult."

"It was. At first it was almost unbearable. I was a traitor to my own kind. But as soon as I started working with the students . . . seeing real growth in them, seeing them put a stop to my depraved kind . . ."

I don't dare say the words aloud, but I wonder if working here at Harker gave Reid's life purpose after his father's death. After he did all he was asked and still never made the man, nor his brother, proud. The thought bites at me until I ask, "Whatever happened to your brother? Once your father died?"

"My father hurt a lot of people. My mother, his kids. And my brother learned from him. He killed"—the needle leaves my skin as Reid's voice lowers—"the woman I loved . . . and died shortly after that."

Reid releases me and wipes his brow with the back of his hand to keep my blood from his face. I am rendered still on the corner of his desk. It's all I can do to watch him clean his fingers with a cloth and put away the first aid kit.

My heart aches for him. This man I've come to respect. Come

to admire. Who's been so wronged. Wants so badly to be good and has to fight his inherent genetic makeup every day to do so. I know that pain because I've been living with it for years.

When I still haven't moved, he tells me, "It's okay. It was a long time ago."

"What was she like?"

Reid crosses his arms over his chest, and then, as if noticing his own defense mechanism, lets down his guard, hands falling to his sides. "She was good. Like you."

I can't make sense of what the words do to my heart. The way it sails and breaks at once. "How could he do that to you?"

Reid leans back against the edge of the sink. Whatever anger filled him earlier seems to have all washed out. "Jealousy, maybe. A show of power. Perhaps he just wanted to hurt me . . . I'm not sure. I try not to think about it."

I come down off the desk. "Do you miss her?"

"Not all these years later."

I peel a bandage and stick it on my arm. "Hundreds of years, right?"

Reid nods, pressing his lips together.

"Because you used to take souls."

His chin dips again, slower this time.

I know I shouldn't ask. Know there's no right answer for him. But I can't help myself. Not in the solitude of his moon-drenched cottage, just the two of us, finally talking. I need to know if we're the same. "Did you like it?"

His chest has begun to rise and fall faster than when he was sewing me up. "You should leave."

"Do you remember your first?"

"Viv." His voice has grown dark and husky. "I'm your instructor. It isn't right."

I take a step closer. "Do you?"

"Why would you want to hear of it?" His ask is almost a plea. "We both already know I'm not good for you."

And yet I only bring myself another step closer. The room is dense with quiet. Perhaps nobody else is on campus tonight. Reid's lips part. I wonder if he can taste my closeness the way I can taste his. Lemongrass and traces of my own blood. The animal inside me likes that last bit far too much.

"Have you thought about it?"

He knows what I'm asking. It's not about being his student. We're both consenting adults. It's about my soul.

"You know the answer."

His eyes are on my mouth. I take a step closer until I'm nearly standing between his legs. He's spread them for me a little. Wide and masculine and waiting. He's sandwiched between me and his kitchen counter. The hunter in me thinks, *You've trapped him well.* But it also says *Run.*

"Tell me."

His hands find my hips, and the heat there is like a furnace. I wonder if he means to hold me at a distance but can't bring himself to push me back. "Whatever you're imagining . . ." he says, so low it's nearly just a rumble in his chest. "Worse." His fingers curl around the thin cotton of my waistband. "So much worse." I wonder if we're even talking about souls anymore. "Does that scare you?"

I shake my head slowly. It's beginning to hurt, this wanting. How much I'm craving his mouth over mine. It feels like sacrilege—yearning for a demon's tongue against my lips and on my skin. Not taboo because I'm his student—though that gets me going too—but because of my shameful, sick desire for something born from hell. I've been put on this earth to eradicate his kind. Now I'm imagining his hands moving lower. Bending me over his desk and forcing me to submit to whatever pain or pleasure he chooses to inflict. It's wrong. I know it is.

"Do you want my soul?" I want him to feel as torn up and turned-on as I do.

His eyes have gone poison black. No more night-sky blue. His hands feel stronger on my body. He doesn't look away and neither do I. "No, huntress."

And I know it's a lie. I can see the pulse in his throat. Can imagine what years—hundreds of them, perhaps—without a drop of human sin has done to him. The longing it's left him with. A predator chained in a cage of his own creation. And here I am—wounded, needy prey. The best kind too—a hunter, the *veal* of demon meat. Offering myself up to him. All I can hope is that a different kind of hunger reigns in Reid. I really don't want to have to kill him. After today, I know I'd be able to, but not whether I could bring myself to.

His fingers brush my cheek, and every hair on my body rises. I lean into his touch, but he makes no move to close the gap.

"Then kiss me," I tell him, brushing my fingers down the cotton of his shirt. Feeling the muscle and bone and heat underneath. The way he shudders under my touch. "Please."

And he does.

CHAPTER 36

REID'S LIPS BRUSH mine more gently than I expect. A trial more than a kiss. At first I think he's testing me—do I really want this? Can I handle it? But as his hands slide up my back and pull me closer, I realize that's not it. He's testing *himself.* Seeing if he can handle tasting me. If he can hold himself back from drinking my soul.

That small realization—the agony he's putting himself through to kiss me—is more sexually gratifying than most actual sex I've had. I'm overridden with longing to push him to the brink. To toe that line between danger and desire. I slide my hands up his powerful chest and around his neck. My fingers twine in the silky curls at his nape, and his breath rushes out against my lips. Molten, merciless. Decadent, deep. I sink into him like a spoon in honey.

His lips part mine, and his tongue sweeps into my mouth. It's almost more than I can take. In fact, I'm leaning so far into him, if he were to move aside, I'd topple face-first onto the countertop behind him. He's anchoring us completely as his hand slides around my neck and into my hair and his mouth moves like the tides against my own.

I can't remember the last time kissing felt like this. I've lost myself in him and have no desire to return. Let me stay here, where Reid's sole focus is drawing pleasure from me. Here, where his tongue is brushing mine and his hands are grasping at my hair and the curve of my waist. Where I have to fight to stay upright and not moan obscenely. Both are beginning to prove difficult.

When I feel his hardness against my stomach, I fail to suppress a noise of eager need. His fingers scrape roughly along the length of my sides. Then he's gripping my hips and I'm licking at his tongue. Feeling his erection throb. I push my hands beneath his shirt. His skin is fire. I want to burn.

"Huntress," he warns. "I can't—"

"Shh," I murmur against his mouth. *Do not let this end.*

He captures my bottom lip between his teeth and bites until I whimper. His hands have found the curve of my ass. The closer we press, the more I can feel his heart racing. His pulse thrumming in all those masculine veins on his forearms. I want them caged over me while he pounds me into oblivion. I want to be choked by that demonic strength until every breath of mine is up to him.

My depraved thoughts must be manifesting in our kiss, because Reid releases a groan and drives us back, around his desk, and against the wall, his hand catching the back of my head before I'm knocked senseless. Like a switch has been flipped, he shoves the thin fabric of my top up until his hands span my ribs and his fingertips brush the underside of my bra.

I arch toward him. *More*, I want to scream. *More*. I haven't been kissed like this in . . . No, I've never been kissed like this. I've never been kissed by something as powerful as myself. I hope my stiches split.

He grasps me tightly as I release his mouth to lick the column of his neck. The involuntary choked noise he makes will play in my head every night for the next calendar year. I'll make myself come to the memory of that sound. I think of that as I suck and bite his skin. As he murmurs my name and presses his hand over my head to catch his breath. I can hear his soft groan as I push my body against that massive length. Feel it twitch as I kiss as close to his collarbone as his damn shirt will allow. As I search for the waistband of his pants to yank them down.

"*Viv*," he groans. "You're destroying me."

With his free hand, he pulls the cup of my bra down, and his calloused fingers graze the skin of my breast. Need pools in my core—I am slick and aching. I'm whimpering with every gentle brush of his thumb over my nipple, every scrape of his teeth on my neck, every grind of whatever part of my body I can fuse against him.

And then he pulls back with a low growl. When I tug at his shirt, he steps away, fists clenched, breaths hard and ragged. I survey him and my heart thuds like a war drum. His hair is waving in all the wrong directions. Shirt stretched out at the neck, face flushed.

"Why'd you stop?" I breathe.

He looks like he's barely survived a hurricane. "I'm not going to fuck you."

He'd better be a dirty liar. "Ever?"

Reid shakes his head, still catching his breath. His eyes are too dangerous, those twin sapphires shining. "That was our first kiss, huntress. Not our last."

WHEN I WAKE up, I'm still coiled tight as a wire. I know I slept, because it was night when I walked back to my dorm in a daze, and now it's morning, but I don't feel like any time has passed. All I can think about is seeing Reid again. In a very carnal, naked way.

I can tell from the morning light that it's going to be a gorgeous November day. Clear and the kind of icy cold that chills your lungs and wakes you up. Just what I need to shake off whatever caged-animal level of ferocity has overtaken me. I make all kinds of promises to myself to let this doomed attraction go, and then I check my phone.

I have a text from an unknown number that reads Get back safe? Butterflies take flight inside my chest, and I fight the urge to curl up into a vibrating little ball. It's a new experience, crushing this hard. I try to remember the last time I got anything resembling butterflies over someone and come up empty.

Who is this? I send back after adding Reid's name in my phone.

Ouch, my ego.

I stare at the phone until he adds, I palmed your ass last night? And gave you stitches?

Doesn't ring any bells!

Come back to my place. I'll ring some bells for you.

I snort and roll my face into my pillow.

"What's got you all moony?" Sophia rasps before unleashing a yawn. She always gets throaty the morning after she's been partying, but today is bullfrog level. Light trickles through the curtains and gilds her bed head like a golden goose's nest.

"Nobody," I say, before I realize my mistake. "Nothing."

Sophia abandons her bed and crawls into mine. I don't even try to hide the phone from her.

"Holy shit," she croaks.

We stare at the text exchange. "Yeah."

"Wow."

"Yeah," I repeat. "We only kissed."

"ONLY KISSED?"

"Soph," I whine, clutching my ringing head. "My ear."

"I can't believe you kissed a demon. Something even I have never done. That's an accomplishment few achieve."

I laugh despite myself. "What are you, some kind of sexual black belt?"

She sits up on one elbow, eyes crinkled with sleep. "That's right. And the student is not yet ready to become the master."

"I don't know what's worse—that he's a demon or that he's our instructor."

"That's half the fun." When I roll my eyes, she groans. "Come on, you've never heard of 'Hot for Teacher'? Plus, he's only like . . . six years older than you in human years."

"Where are you coming up with that conversion rate?"

Sophia shrugs. "One of the many things they teach you to become a sexual black belt."

With a begrudging laugh I roll right over her out of bed and search the closet for my black silk miniskirt and Harker crew. I have to catch Lisette before her office hours are over if I have any hope of not failing her class.

"What was it like?" Sophia asks from my bed. "Kissing a demon? Did he try to steal your soul?"

The first word that pops into my head is *intoxicating*, but that sounds like something a wino housewife dating the pool boy might say, so I go with "It was a normal kiss."

Sophia makes a tsking sound. "You lying slut."

"Jesus, Soph."

"I tell you all the dirty details of my sexual escapades."

I yank on my loafers. "And I'll be sending you my therapy bill for that."

"You love it. Where are you going?"

"I'm biting the bullet and asking Lisette for help on this essay. Lunch after?"

Sophia rolls over, closing her eyes. "You're a braver woman than I. I'll have noodles waiting for you in the commons."

I grin and step into the bathroom, where I examine my reflection in the mirror. I'm hunting for traces of last night, though I have no idea what I'm hoping to find. I want to look changed somehow. Find evidence on myself of being his. My lips are a little bruised, my slate eyes ringed in red from lack of sleep. My hair knotted where he held it. A shiver of pleasure runs through me at the memory. I brush the strands in a daze.

"Okay, all jokes aside, it was unlike any—" But when I come back out, Sophia's already snoring in my bed.

I FIND LISETTE in her classroom, sweet coffee steaming on her desk, shoes kicked off as she grades a paper.

"Hi, Professor," I chime in my best teacher's pet voice.

"Miss Abbot," she replies, eyes still on her desk.

"I had a few questions about this essay . . ." The essay I accidentally gave us all by passing notes about harpies on the first day of class. I could knee myself in the teeth.

Lisette still doesn't bother to look up. She only rubs absently at her temples as she reads through her notes. "You won't be permitted to turn it in late."

There's something pointed in her phrasing. As if she knows I have a habit of that, though she doesn't know me at all. I try not to scowl—I do not like this woman.

"I was going to ask if harpy discrimination among deviants might be related to their connection to the astral plane." This essay is proving impossible—deviant speciesism is as complicated as it is pointless. "They have wings like many lymantrian creatures, and a few of my texts describe harpies getting power from lymantrian flora and fauna, which I can only imagine deviants would look down upon—"

"They do have a penchant for collecting lymantrian florals. Lotuses, asphodels—"

The word makes my muscles tense. "Asphodels?"

With an exaggerated sigh she looks up, lowering her glasses. "Yes, Miss Abbot."

"And . . ." I will my voice to stay neutral. "Where do those usually grow?"

"As far from the underworld as they can get."

Something inflates inside me. The highest point in the school is the planetarium. Peter has only told me that fifty thousand times. I might have stumbled onto a new lead.

"Of course. My bad," I say, turning for the door. "See you tomorrow."

"Miss Abbot."

I spin, girding myself for the worst.

"What did I tell you about looking for trouble?"

"What? I'm not—"

"I've known many hunters like you. Rash, impatient, selfish—"

My blood heats. "Why do you have a problem with me?"

"The better question might be why do you have a problem doing what you are told?"

"I *don't*—"

"Hear me when I say this, Miss Abbot. Focus on your schoolwork and your training. I'd hate to see you harmed before you grow to your full potential as a hunter."

I bite my tongue until I taste iron. "Is that a threat?"

Lisette rolls her eyes, but there's something in her expression. A *knowing*. "Don't be absurd." She motions for the door behind me. "Please. I have papers to grade."

On my way out of Lisette's classroom, cheeks still hot with irritation, I text in the group chat: Noodles are off. Heading to the planetarium. Lisette let it slip the asphodels might be there.

Godspeed Nancy Drew, Sophia writes back.

I reply with She really doesn't give you guys a weird feeling?

You mean between my legs? Elliot writes. Because, yes.

I scowl at my phone. Nauseating, thanks.

Something's always nagged at me about her, but if she was a deviant of any kind, I would know, right? Peter, has it ever been possible for a deviant to disguise themselves around aeons? So they couldn't be sensed?

Sophia chimes in. No way Lisette is a deviant. Someone would have figured that out by now.

With very dark magic, it's possible, Peter writes. A powerful turned witch could mask themselves or others.

Ice runs through my veins. Is it possible Reid isn't the only deviant employed at this school? I briefly debate inviting him to scope out the planetarium with me. Nothing safer than a little demon backup. But after last night, a new layer has been draped across our already-complicated relationship. I'm not sure I want our first postkiss interaction to be steeped in Harker business.

Being inside the iconic dome at the top of Mortimer Tower is slightly anticlimactic. I click on the lights to reveal a circular theater only big enough to seat a class of forty, and judging by the smell of mothballs, one hasn't been taught here in some time. The walls are blanketed in soundproof insulation, and a rounded glass roof curves over the entire room. A sky view for every seat. I slide my finger along the back of one and come up with enough dust to fill a vacuum.

A garden is a strange thing to find in a planetarium, so without much to go on, I try a few locked cabinets, a control panel by the nosebleeds, a dead bolt on a glass case with moon rocks inside, but no dice. Then, even though I'm in a miniskirt, I crawl under the musty fold-down chairs until I know the silk is ruined and search for hidden keyholes or little doors beneath the seats.

I'm halfway beneath row *G* when I hear a rumble of a laugh. "So that's the view I've heard so much about."

CHAPTER 37

THE SHOCK SENDS my head smacking into the wooden underside of the chair. When I come back up, Reid's got a guilty half smile on. "Sorry."

"We need to get you a bell." I rub my head, cheeks scarlet. "What are you doing here?"

"Could ask you the same thing."

His eyes sweep over my bare legs and up to my hair, which is now a crow's nest after I crawled on my hands and knees across the dusty theater. A pang of anxiety hits me—a moment in which I debate lying to Reid . . . but he helped me with the Kitty part of it all. It was dumb of me not to tell him my plan in the first place just because we kissed. I need to get this crush in check. "Lisette mentioned the garden might be hidden up here. Haven't figured out where."

"Yeah, I brought Lisette some new pieces for the archives, and she asked me why a certain student of hers might be sniffing around about asphodels. Told me you could be here."

"Think how much time we might have saved had we trusted each other." I'm aiming for a joke, but we both look away in shame.

"Speaking of," he says, "I have a favor to ask."

I raise an incredulous brow. Reid digs something out of his backpack and walks down the aisle to meet me. In his hand is a vintage copper charm bracelet. So tarnished some of the trinkets that hang from it have gone seafoam green.

It's beautiful. "For me?"

"It once belonged to a siren. Imbued with the species' unique form of echolocation, it allows the giver to hear the recipient if they're ever in danger. It's called a lure."

"So a very pretty deep-sea rape whistle?"

The corner of Reid's mouth tugs up in that half grin that hits my heart like a supernova. "You could put it that way. After what you told me about your apartment . . ."

The way I was sure I was being watched. And now, with my concerns about Lisette . . .

"Thank you." Slipping the bracelet on, I examine the charms: a sailboat, an anchor, a fanged fish with sapphires for eyes.

When I look back up at him, Reid's watching me with something almost wistful.

I clear my throat. "I haven't had much luck. The whole room is just insulation. Why does a school for deviant hunters need a planetarium anyway?"

"We used to focus more of the curriculum on the old lymantrian plane. It's fallen off over time, but the planetarium allowed students to see where they came from. It informed Underworld Studies as well. I'm sure you're familiar with *as above, so below?*"

I nod, eyes rolling. "I went to prep school. So it's not even used anymore?"

"Not really," he says, eyeing the space. "It would be a nice spot for date, though."

My brows rise. "A date?"

Reid strolls farther down the aisle to drop his backpack in the center of the room. The clang resonates through the hollow sphere. "Hangout? Chill sesh?"

"Jeez. You really are old."

A begrudging laugh. I'm lucky he doesn't call me out on my hypocrisy. I barely even went on dates with James.

"The last time I went on a date, it was referred to as *calling on someone*," he says, walking across the theater floor. "You'd go to a woman's house and call on her. Usually, her parents were there to ensure nothing scandalous occurred."

The whole picture of him begins to make even more sense: the brutal Brood parents, the emotional weight of breaking from what they expected of him, the loss of the woman he loved . . .

Reid probably hasn't been on a date in two hundred years. Not that I blame him—if my family had killed my partner, I'd be hesitant to jump back in too.

But . . . he kissed me last night. So maybe he's not hesitant anymore. "This would really be your date spot?"

Reid looks like he's fighting a smile. "Subtle."

"I'm just curious. What would we do?"

"We?"

I nod, pulse thrumming.

"Well, I'd bring a blanket. Some wine . . ."

I walk down to meet him on the lecture floor. "Sounds cute."

"Cute?" He mimes shoving a knife into his heart.

"Sorry. Sounds panty-wetting."

"We'd sit right here on the floor." He gestures between us to the center of the theater. "And stare at the sky."

I follow his eyeline. "Does that thing work?"

"No clue. Not a whole lot of places on campus for an instructor to take a student on a date, though. Pickings are slim."

"Is the date we *aren't on* forbidden?" The sensual rasp in my voice is supposed to be playful, but Reid still swallows a bit too hard.

"Kind of."

"Because you're a teacher? Or because you have a rep for hating me that you need to keep up?"

"You hate *me*, remember?"

I fold my hands together. "Those feelings were misplaced."

He looks down at his own palms. "Well, I never hated you."

"You know what they say about liars' pants."

When his gaze finds mine again, it's flecked with something heated. "A very sexy huntress will try to pry them off you?"

The laugh that tears from me sounds like *HA!* I turn as red as my cheeks can go.

His eyes are warm. "If anything, it's *your* rep I'm trying to keep intact. Students don't get gold stars for dating deviants."

"Don't worry about my rep," I tell him. "It's been mutilated for years. I've made peace with it."

"What are you talking about? You're the badass self-taught huntress from Astera. Bested a werewolf and a strzyga in her first year."

I wrinkle my nose at the idea. "I'm not talking about here at Harker. I meant in my real life."

"This *is* your real life."

"You know what I mean."

"The work you're doing here is more real than your pet—"

"Whom I dumped—"

"—or your cruel mom or fake job—"

"Hey, I like that fake job." The defensiveness in my voice surprises me as much as it seems to surprise Reid.

"Sorry. I didn't mean anything by it." Reid heads toward the back wall of the theater.

"If I wasn't a hunter, maybe I wouldn't even be an assistant anymore," I admit, following after him. "I could photograph the exhibits. But being a student here full-time doesn't leave much space for a promotion."

Reid stops short of whatever he was striding toward, seeming to mull this over before he turns to face me. He looks like he's debating something until he says, "Let's start this date over."

Embarrassment seizes my stomach. "I didn't know we were on one. Am I doing that badly?"

Reid's mouth curves to one side and he shakes his head. "You're not a huntress. You're a photographer. And I'm a . . ."

"Planetarium expert," I say, catching on.

"Sure. And this is our first date."

"Okay." I can't help the grin tugging at my cheeks. Reid smooths his hair back and a laugh slips out of me. "Do planetarium experts not have unruly bad-boy curls?"

"I don't know what a planetarium expert has. I'm just trying to roll with it. Where's your attempt at human photographer?"

"Oh, I'm on it," I tell him, pulling my hair back into a low bun. "There. Classic photographer look."

"Perfect," he says, eyes skating over my face. He lingers long enough that I wonder if he might kiss me, but then he adds a husky "Ready?"

I nod eagerly.

"Reid Graveheart." He sticks out his hand. "Planetarium expert. This is my planetarium."

I slip my palm into his and try to not shiver at the warmth. "Viv Abbot. I'm a photographer. I've never stabbed anything to death before."

Reid wipes a hand across his mouth to stave off a laugh, and it's a rush I want mainlined into my veins. "That's actually what I look for in the photographers I date."

"Then we're off to a good start, aren't we?"

Reid takes me by the hand and guides me to sit on the floor like he described. My skin prickles with the anticipation of further contact, but he doesn't do more than look into my eyes. "Tell me about yourself, human photographer Viv."

"Let's see." I inch a little closer. "I grew up in Lethe. I never had to move to the Hesperides after the tragic death of my father. My mom and I are supertight—we get mani-pedis every weekend, and I teach her how to use the internet. How about you? Close with your family?"

He nods. "My father adores me. We used to throw a baseball in the backyard while our golden retriever chased us around the bases. Me, my father, and my brother, we're as thick as thieves and unlikely to inflict physical harm on one another."

"Just like Norman Rockwell intended."

"Now I'm employed here. An expert on all things planetarium."

"Which means . . . ?"

Reid seems to think seriously on the question. "I teach young minds about the solar system. Study the stars and the moon. I don't crave souls. I'm not struck daily by the memory of taking a human life for my own physical pleasure. I never accidentally gouge the flesh of a girl I'm hoping to kiss. I work from nine to five and go home to a simple NTC apartment with a deep-cushioned couch and a view of the park that would strip you right out of that little skirt."

It takes everything in me not to choke on pure air. "Oh."

"Yeah. It's something else."

"Well, I work nearby. At the Windsor."

"And what do you do there?" His voice has grown low and rough. His hand crawls over to brush mine. Electricity crackles.

Who would have thought the best date of my life would be with a creature born of the underworld who I've been biologically designed to kill? There is no happy ending here, and I know it. But if that means I'm supposed to be holding back or playing it cool, I missed that part of hunter orientation.

"Um . . ." I know if I look him in the eye, I'll drool, so instead I study my fingers on the curve of his wrist. "I get paid a very healthy salary to photograph the exhibits. But I also have gallery showings of my own work down in Babylon from time to time. I do Pilates in the mornings and have long dinners with my friends after work, and I wake up every day actually grateful to be who I am. I never sit in the bathtub with no lights on, wishing I'd been born someone else."

"Viv," he says faintly. His hand leaves mine, and I feel his finger slide under my chin. "Don't say that."

I'm hit so hard with the unfairness of it all that my eyes burn. I want that life more than I can articulate. I'm not sure how much longer I can take feeling like a disappointment. When Reid angles me gently to face him, his gaze brims with empathy. Not pity, but a deep understanding. And I know he gets it.

"Why can't we be them?" I ask quietly.

"Not our destiny, I'm afraid."

"You believe in destiny?" The moment is too charged to mock. And maybe I wouldn't even if it wasn't. Not with that look in his eyes.

"You live as long as I do, it's hard not to feel like it's all got to be for something."

And though my limbs are heavy with a bone-deep grief over all the life I'll likely never get to live, there's also an expanse blooming in my chest. A feeling of not being so alone. Even more than Sophia and Peter and Elliot make me feel—my friends may understand my struggles as a hunter, but all three of them grew up with accepting families. Reid knows exactly what it feels like to be homesick for a life you never lived.

"Reid . . ." I start. But I'm not sure where to go.

His eyes darken. "I love the sound of my name on your lips." His fingers go still under my chin, then brush down my throat. My whimper is a noise of pure need. I'm intent on something but too scared to admit what, even to myself. But Reid knows.

He brings his hand around the back of my neck, and every muscle in my body tenses in anticipation. But all he does is pull my hair from its bun. The strands cascade down my back and into my face, and the scent of my vanilla-and-rose shampoo blooms over us both.

"That's better," he says, nearly hoarse.

My lips press to his in a rush. It's a little sloppy, a little quick. But he kisses me back with the same desperation, and we fall onto the floor. A vision of us in that other life plays out in my mind: Reid the planetarium expert is kissing my mouth. He's coaxing it open with his tongue, soft and yet demanding. His hands are molding to my hands, my sides, my neck. His breath in my mouth is drugging, and I'm slipping into something darker and hungrier. He is no longer human. And neither am I—

No, this kiss is pure creature. Two predators used to getting what they want. I'm clawing at him and he's letting me. He spreads my knees apart and hikes my skirt up, settling himself between my legs.

"I didn't sleep last night," he breathes against the shell of my ear. "I was going insane thinking of you. I was this close to knocking down your door and dragging you to my bed like a caveman."

"Demonic," I breathe out. I'm not sure which of us I'm talking about. His hands are everywhere. I can't think straight.

"No kidding."

I roll my hips, trying to gain the friction I know we both crave. Reid's mouth slides down my chest as he shoves my shirt up.

"I wish you had," I tell him.

He squeezes my body beneath those beautiful hands. My ribs, my hips. Long fingers slide over the outsides of my thighs. His teeth find the lacy band of my bra and he groans into my skin. A guttural noise that makes me shiver.

I pull his face back up to mine. His eyes are hazy and blown out as if he's done the finest poppy in Astera. "Fuck, Viv—"

My nipples are aching against the lace of my bra. My body twitches and jolts with every touch. His hands cradle my face as he drives his cock against me through our clothes.

"Please," I beg, knowing what that word does to him.

A sigh of near agony. His hair is a mess when he lifts his face. His mouth swollen and pink like he's been using it to make me come. "We shouldn't."

Adrenaline courses through me. "Let me suck you off."

Every muscle in his body tenses. "What?"

The ravenous look in his eyes makes me whimper. "You heard me." I'm hot everywhere and I need to be on my knees.

He shakes his head, fingers stroking softly over my breast and pinching faintly as if he's forgotten what I've asked him. "It's been . . ." His cock is so hard against his jeans, I worry for the integrity of his zipper. "Some time. For me."

I'm surprised someone as gorgeous and charming as Reid hasn't been fucking half of Harker—or Astera, for that matter—for the last hundred years. The thought of why he's been celibate so long only serves to remind me of the pain he's endured. The self-hatred and the loss.

We're both breathing so hard I wonder if we've fogged the room. "I don't care. Unless . . . Do you want to stop?"

But he doesn't answer. Only flips me over onto my stomach and pulls me back until I'm on my knees and elbows. The new position allows me to shove my face down into my arm, and I manage not to moan like a porn star when he pushes my skirt up and pulls my panties to the side. Thank god for little favors.

The room isn't that well lit—one or two bulbs on the wall are dead, and the rest are coated in a thin film of dust. But I am still keenly aware that Reid can see the full extent of my want. I'm surely dripping and slick and ripe as a peach. I'd be ashamed if I didn't know he's just as turned-on as I am.

"Fuck," he breathes. "You need it badly, huh?"

I whine like an animal and push myself closer to him.

But Reid takes his time, caressing my thighs, allowing his thumb to barely brush over my slit and the wetness pooling there. I hear his jeans unzip and wonder briefly if he's going to ask to fuck me. But I only hear the sound of him stroking himself as he spreads me and plays with my lips. He groans and sighs, and I do too. When he finally circles my clit, I can't help myself. I shove myself toward him to get more friction—closer, *more*—

Reid staggers back, knocking into the console behind us.

With a mighty groan, the ceiling opens up like a giant's eye blinking awake. The noise startles us enough to shake us from our lust. I allow my panties to slide back over me and pull my skirt down as I come up off my knees. Reid's hand grazes my lower back as we watch the ceiling breathlessly.

The lights wink out, and a breathtaking vision of the cosmos projects high above our heads. The pink of a summer sunset and purple like the punch at Cobwebs on Halloween. And vivid, stormy shipwreck blue. The blue of Reid's eyes. Reid falls back so he's sitting and pulls me into his lap, both of us in awe, silent save for our heavy breathing. Unable to do anything but stare at the psychedelic ballet of stars above us. The nebula cascading across the ceiling. The entire room swimming in softly moving colors. It's like we've been sucked into a black hole and spit out somewhere mid universe.

"What is that?" I murmur in awe. It's daytime. How can we see the stars?

Reid's voice is barely a whisper. "A projection of the lymantrian plane."

"It's beautiful."

He doesn't respond. When I glance up to find his eyes, he's studying me intently. There's an emotion there I can't place. Or maybe one I just don't want to.

Reid kisses me again. Slower, softer. His hands curving over my shoulder and cupping my face. He kisses my cheek. My eyelids. My temples. Pulls me in close to him as we watch a celestial kaleidoscope cast dappled violet shadows over us both.

I want to stay in this moment for eternity. I don't want to squash the static that's fizzing in my chest. I don't want to be reminded of the reason we're both here.

And yet—

"What were you going to do?" I ask him quietly. "When you headed for that wall over there?" Before we began our pretend date. And got carried away . . .

Reid pulls back, dazed-looking. As if our intimacy, our closeness, has left him spellbound. "Right," he breathes, voice tight. "Follow me."

Reid stands, and I remember that my chin barely grazes his collarbone. I have to physically shake off thoughts of him bowing over me, surrounding me from every angle, as he takes my hand in his and guides me toward the back of the room.

"I had the idea as soon as you said *insulation*," he says, brandishing one gothic black claw and slicing it through the dark foam covering the wall. "The flowers are sensitive to light and sound."

Before I can say anything, he rips back the thick layers. A whirring sounds in my ears. The noise of an electrical closet. Before us lies the outline of a door. Reid pulls out his key card and unlocks it.

Inside, we're met with a galaxy of blinking lights. Buttons, screens, sleek black keyboards, high-quality equipment, and—

At the center of the room is a small iron planter of glowing white flowers beneath a wide skylight, drenching their dainty petals in afternoon light. The barrier of intricately woven metal is illuminated by twinkling yellow bulbs. It's humid like a greenhouse, so the walls sweat condensation, and moisture already dots my brow.

"I know they have to be kept as high as possible, but . . . why in here?"

"It's not a room most students even know exists. And it's accessible by staff but draws no attention . . ." Reid studies the blooms, wiping the humidity from his chin. "Perhaps they like the ambient sound of the equipment."

My eyes crawl over the asphodels. They gently illuminate the buttons around them, their pointed petals stretching up to the skylight as if yawning under a hot morning sun. And there's a patch of them—just four or five stems—missing. Yanked from the earth. The soil dry and cracked where they were stolen.

Reid curses, following my eyeline. "We need to go to the dean. This is . . ." His jaw has gone to rigid steel. "You were right. The school isn't safe anymore."

The buzzing tickles my ears as I turn around in the small closet-size space. There's not much room between the monitors, the garden, the dimly lit lanterns, and Reid and me. No evidence of anything out of the ordinary. If a deviant broke in, wouldn't even one knob be out of place? I'm studying the stone walls and rough floor, looking for any kind of evidence that someone was in here who shouldn't have been, when Reid's phone buzzes.

"What's that?" I say, pointing to a small plastic baggie filled with red powder.

Reid leans over and picks it up. He opens the bag and sniffs. "Poppy."

But my stomach has plummeted. There's something on the other side of the bag. A set of white antlers. "I've seen that design before."

With the second buzz of his phone, I nearly jump, anxiety trickling through my bloodstream. "You want to get that?"

But Reid's eyes are unmoving on me. "Where? Where have you seen it?"

I can't remember. My heart is slamming and the room is humming and my mind is a blank and Reid's phone buzzes again and—

"Check it," I snap. I have a bad feeling that I pray is fake-first-date, stolen-asphodel, illegal-drug jitters and not my damn hunter instinct.

Reid frowns. "What are you worried about? We're the ones with the bad news."

"What if the school's been attacked again? Or another student has mysteriously disappeared?"

Reid hands me the bag of poppy to search his pockets. "We solved the Kitty thing, remember? Nobody else is going to disappear, I promise."

He digs his phone out and reads the incoming texts. Even under the soft glow of the machinery and the filtered skylight, I can see the color drain from his face.

My heart stills. "What is it?"

"Lyra Roth. She's . . . gone missing."

And then I remember where I've seen the symbol.

CHAPTER 38

UNLIKE KITTY'S DISAPPEARANCE, Lyra's is schoolwide news. By the time Reid and I make it to her dorm, it's like all the paparazzi have been called to the scene of a pop star's DUI. A swarm of students attempts to peek into a room blocked off by teachers and Citadel hunters. The latter are formidable alumni in dark navy uniforms, gear strapped across their chests and arms. It seems the Harker alumni have been called in.

Amid anxious murmurs and wringing hands, I spy Dean Driscoll, arms folded over his chest, conferring quietly with Professors Lisette and Crowley. I push past onlookers to get my own view of the dorm room. Inside is the unmistakable wreckage of a struggle: broken glass lampshade, speckles of blood, shattered window. The sight chills the blood in my veins. Lyra was a second year and a hell of a fighter. In fact, like Kitty, she struck me as having qualities similar to an aeon's. A hunger for the kill, the implication she'd had the abilities to hunt before turning twenty-one... Whoever took her had to have been worse than formidable. When I look away from the scene, my eyes lock with Professor Lisette's. My stomach dips with unease. If she's behind this, and now she's playing concerned teacher at the scene of the crime . . .

"What's going on?" Peter asks. I turn to see him and Sophia pushing their way through the murmuring crowd.

"It's Lyra—"

Sophia gets one look inside the dorm room and blanches. "Oh god." She turns to Peter to shield her eyes, and he cradles her head against his chest beneath his chin. I never noticed Peter was a full head taller than Soph, but he holds her like he was born to do just that. The longer Peter looks at the bloodstains, the paler he goes too. Only Reid stands stony-faced.

"How did the news travel so fast?" I whisper to them.

Elliot's found us too, his face a mask of sheer fury. "Her roommate heard screaming on her way back from a class. Lyra was gone by the time she reached the door."

I look at all three of them. Then to Reid. "We need to talk."

We make it to Sophia's and my dorm in record time. Elliot takes a seat on Sophia's bed while Peter just paces. Sophia studies me and then Reid, who's leaning against the wall beside my desk. "You two know something. Spill."

"The first day we met, after orientation, you had a stamp on your wrist from a bar or something. It was antlers, I think. Do you remember where that was from?"

Out of the corner of my eye, I can see Reid tense. Sophia plops down on her bed next to Elliot. "I go to a lot of places. That was months ago . . ."

"Really try to think."

"Was it Pomegranate?" Elliot offers. "Or maybe Finale?"

Sophia gets her phone out and begins to scroll. "I'll see if I took any pictures that night."

Peter stops pacing. "What does the stamp have to do with Lyra?"

I take a breath. Here comes my crazy conspiracy theory. Chances that my friends don't fit me with a tinfoil hat and send me right off to Shiloh feel slim, but it's all I've got.

"Kitty had the same stamp on her wrist when I met her. And Lyra too. I think it's a club here in Astera. Lyra said during Field Training that she liked to party. And Reid and I found a bag of poppy with that same club's logo in the room where the asphodels are kept. I think whoever took the flowers dropped it without realizing."

"You found the hidden garden?" Peter breathes.

Behind me, I hear Reid take a seat on the edge of my desk. I just know his arms are folded, forearm muscles coiled with tension.

"Some of the flowers have been taken," I tell them.

"I'm not following," Elliot says. "What do the missing flowers have to do with the club?"

I turn back to Reid, who looks lost in thought. Something is eating at him. All I can do is plow onward. "If the emails that claimed Kitty was fine were fabricated somehow, if someone at Harker really *is* brewing a syrabraxa . . ."

Reid's exhale is nearly a growl. He already knows what this means.

"Let's just think about their plan so far," I tell the group. "They let the wraiths in to cover for Kitty's kidnapping. They set up the zombie spell to cover their theft of the Aeon's Dagger. All their moves have been hidden by attacks on the school. But then they take Lyra in the middle of the day with no cover . . . I think something changed for them—suddenly they had to get Lyra and the asphodels quickly. Maybe there's some kind of time crunch. Maybe they're panicking, and in their rush, they dropped the bag of poppy from the club. It's a clue to who the person behind all this is."

Peter's brows lift slowly with solemn realization. "So Kitty being in Brazil..."

Sophia squeezes his hand. "We don't know anything for sure yet."

"We never heard directly from her that she was all right," I say.

"Why take Kitty and Lyra?" Elliot asks quietly. "What do they have to do with the spell?"

I suck in a ragged breath. I haven't told Reid what I am yet, and I don't know how to say *They were both prime candidates for being aeons, whose blood is required for the spell* without explaining that I only know they were prime candidates because of qualities I have myself. "I don't know," I lie. "But it can't be a coincidence that Kitty and Lyra frequented the same club as the person who stole the asphodels."

"Maybe Lyra and Kitty are working with a turned witch to brew the spell," Elliot suggests, his face propped in his hands. "But why make Kitty look like she left school and Lyra like she was attacked? And why—" His fingers rub roughly at his brow. "Never mind." He looks tired and miserable. I survey Peter's hollowed-out expression and Reid's and Sophia's grim ones. We all look wrecked, but Elliot wears it the worst. He's too beautiful to be exhausted. He needs a beer with a lime in it.

"I've got it." Sophia stands up to show me a picture on her phone of her and Elliot snorting poppy in the corner of some club. "Fever Dream. In Astera. I've been a few times. The stamp is a pair of white deer antlers."

Fever Dream. Of course. The infamous Half City haunt. Known as one of the most elite nightclubs in the world, it's impossible to get into if you aren't young and hot or richer than god, yet it's deep below the Chasm—as nasty and debauched as it is renowned. Stories are always circulating of celebrity scandals, legendary parties, and shady under-the-table deals. I've lived in Astera my whole life and have never stepped foot inside.

"Let's go tonight," I tell them. "See what we can find?"

"In," Sophia says. "I need a fucking drink."

"You can't go there." Reid's voice behind me is almost too low to hear.

I whirl around. "Why not?"

His eyes are colder than I've ever seen them. His jaw is granite. "It's not safe."

"Nothing that we do is safe." When Reid's lips don't move from their thin line, I take a meaningful step forward. "What do you mean?"

Silence rends the room.

"What do you know, Reid?"

For a moment, Reid says nothing. I can't tell if he's thinking or waiting for me to say more. Eventually he goes with "Just that the owner runs drugs and weapons out of the club. Assassins for hire, money laundering . . . The pinnacle of Astera crime."

I glare at him. "A nightclub with an owner who operates in high-level Astera crime *and* the fact that Harker students who go there end up missing? *And* the club's poppy was found in the room where the asphodels—one of several missing ingredients for the deadliest spell in existence—were stolen? And you're telling me *not* to go?"

"It's not up to him." Sophia's already pulling her compact crossbow from our utility closet.

"Don't confuse courage with recklessness, Valentine. I've seen the way you fight. You think you're brave, but . . ." Reid's glare is severe. "There's nothing brave about not giving a shit whether you live or die."

"Hey—" Peter snaps.

A gasp catches in my throat. "Reid . . ."

His jaw only tenses. "She's playing with your life here."

I bite down on my cheek to quell my fury. "I can take care of my own life."

Sophia nods to herself, arrows in her hands. "Hey, Reid?"

Reid turns to her, exhausted. "Yeah?"

"Fuck you."

Elliot chuckles. Reid stands from the desk, fists coiled.

"Okay," I sigh. "Let's all just cool our jets here—"

But Reid shakes his head like we're insubordinate children. "Harker has looked into Fever Dream time and time again. Not a trace of deviant activity. It's just not somewhere I want you—*any of you*—spending any time if students who go there end up missing."

"Fine," I concede. "Come with us?"

"Absolutely not. I wouldn't take you there if my own life depended on it."

"Oh, come on. That's dramatic."

He runs an exasperated hand down his face. "You're not going to save your father by saving these girls, Viv."

Sophia and Peter suck in twin breaths. Something inside me breaks a little.

Elliot shakes his head. "Everyone's taking hits today."

But my heart is racing, and the need to fight is building beneath my skin. "I'm going whether you like it or—"

"Can't you ever, just once," Reid snaps, "do what I'm asking you to?"

It lands like a roundhouse. I have enough people in my life telling me all the things I can't do or don't do properly. I know who I can and cannot save. I also know that as much as I don't want to lie to Reid, he's never going to let me pursue this lead.

I allow my face to shutter. Allow him to think his final words have shut me down completely. Then, quietly, I say, "You have to *swear* you'll look into it."

"Of course. Give me a couple days."

"Fine." I'm already moving for my bag. Time to get out of here. I bolt from the room without another word.

"Viv—" In the hallway, Reid's hand wraps around my upper arm, tugging me back. "Fuck, Viv. I *care* about you."

In spite of everything, my heart flips on itself. But all I can do is yank myself out of his grasp. I need to get away from Reid. Away from the sting of his words. From the guilt I feel about lying to him. "I just need some space, okay?"

The stairs of Elkfore surge up at me as I speed down them and toward the gateway. The news of Lyra's disappearance has sucked Harker into a tailspin. Students murmur and whisper amid a fog of panic. I check my phone to find an email informing me that all classes that aren't held within the walls of Old Campus are postponed indefinitely, which means no coliseum or Field Training, and all sporting events are canceled too. Nothing that might draw a crowd. Half of my professors are following up with emails reworking course loads amid calls from worried parents.

As I pass through the rotunda, my eye catches on the glass case.

I pass that photo of my father every time I enter and leave the school. Usually—despite whatever happened here or soon after that made him change his name—the picture spreads a comforting warmth through me. He walked these halls. He ran on these fields. He made friends here and learned and became the man who raised me.

But today the black-and-white photo carves something bleak and raw right through my heart. All I feel is shame. Reid was right: I couldn't stop Lyra from being kidnapped. I couldn't find Kitty. I couldn't save my dad. Someone at Harker is brewing a syrabraxa, and I haven't been able to do anything to stop them. I never even got to the bottom of who my dad's killer was, and that was the only reason I came to this school in the first place. Maybe if I hadn't spent so much time here making friends and learning to accept what I am . . . falling for a demon . . . I've been so selfish.

"You'd be ashamed," I mutter at the grainy image.

But my dad only beams, hoisted on the shoulders of two teammates: number fifteen and number twenty-six. Sweat and dirt coat his face, and he's got a lacrosse stick raised high overhead in that blind joy you only ever get to feel for a split second. The beat right after *Oh shit, I did it* and right before *So what happens now?* It reminds me of that photo in my apartment I love so much. The one of the girl on the swing moments before she leaps off. The triumph in her eye that she's made such a brave decision, a hair before the fear creeps in.

It's not an easy shot to get. Curiosity and perhaps a bit of envy drive me closer to investigate the photographer who captured it. I lean so close my breath fogs the glass and I have to smudge it away with my wrist.

I squint at the plaque beneath. DAVID CADDEL WINS HARKER LACROSSE CHAMPIONSHIP FOR THE MARKSMEN, 1994. ALSO PICTURED: NUMBER FIFTEEN, TIM HAWKINS; NUMBER TWENTY-SIX, EDGAR DRISCOLL. PHOTO BY STEVIE LANCASTER.

Edgar Driscoll . . . The dean? Was friends with my dad? Now that I think about it, that makes some sense. If my dad were alive, they'd be the same age. They have a similar demeanor. Tough but not unkind.

I study the image of him and Edgar grinning at each other. Maybe the biggest mistake I've made was never confiding in the dean in the first place. Knowing my dad purposely kept this place from me, changed his name after graduating . . . I was so hesitant to trust anyone here aside from Reid and my friends. But Reid trusted Edgar Driscoll in his darkest moments. And my dad trusted him too. A photo can tell you a lot. I can see the respect—the admiration—in both their eyes.

It's time I asked for a little help.

THE SUN HAS set and the air is as cold as a sleepless night when I reach the dean's cottage. My joints ache and my breath is coming in clouds of swirling steam. I knock on the dean's door once, and though I can hear the kettle singing on his stove, the dean takes his time answering. I have to rap my knuckles—already raw from windchill—a few times before he wrenches it open. His eyes are ringed red, his beard scrubby like untamed grass.

"Miss Abbot," he grunts.

"Rough day?"

He rubs his bearded jaw. "You could say that."

"I think I know where Lyra Roth is. Can I come in?"

His gruff eyes widen, but he steps aside and gestures for me to enter.

Inside, I take a seat on his cracked leather couch. His cabin is better decorated than Reid's. Larger, of course, and filled with potted plants and little herb gardens in windowsills. More ornate while still rugged, with animal pelts and thick thermal blankets and a pair of muddied boots by the door. A lacrosse stick is mounted on the wall, just like my dad's in my room. That kettle is still screaming on the potbelly stove, and he stomps over to turn it off before coming to sit down across from me.

"What do you know about a club in Astera called Fever Dream?"

Dean Driscoll leans forward an inch, a hint of a smile on his lips. "I knew you were bright."

My heart stumbles over a beat. "The owner—that crime boss—he's a deviant?"

"Not sure. The guy keeps a low profile. He's deep in the pockets of Astera's mayor, its CEOs and chairmen . . . They keep his identity well-protected. All the criminal operations are done under his alias, the White Stag."

The White Stag . . . Wasn't Nora talking about him being one of the biggest poppy dealers in Astera? All the white antler graffiti South of the Chasm . . . Hadn't Ingrid, another hunter from Reid's Field Training class, feared him?

"Even if we could find him," Driscoll says, "the Elders don't want us to take him out."

"What? Someone is running all number of illegal trade and business from an Astera nightclub frequented by mortals and hunters alike, and the Elders have instructed you and the Citadel hunters to keep him alive . . . Why?"

"Your guess is as good as mine. The Elders aren't the most forthcoming bunch. But if this White Stag were coming after Harker . . ." The Dean's face shifts into something raw with untapped rage. "I'd certainly press the issue."

I steel myself. I've come this far. "The night the wraiths attacked Elkfore, a friend of mine left school. Kitty Briggs. But her letter saying goodbye was suspicious—"

"Suspicious?"

I take a breath. "A lot about her disappearance wasn't as clear-cut as it seemed."

The dean grunts, bringing his head to his hands. "It just gets better and better."

I grimace. I don't envy the day this man is having. "Now today, with Lyra . . . both girls frequented that club. Fever Dream."

The dean's expression doesn't change as he listens, but his entire body has gone as taut as a harp string.

"I can't exactly tell you how, but I know someone stole the asphodels that are kept at Harker. Whoever did left behind evidence that they spend time at Fever Dream too. I don't know if this White Stag is infiltrating the school—"

"It's not possible. If he's mortal, he'd have no way of getting in. And deviants can't access the campus without the wards being adjusted—"

"Fine, then perhaps a student is working as his accomplice. Or a professor. It just all seems too strange to be unrelated."

The dean crosses his arms. They're as scarred as they are tattooed. And not lines of pale white—jagged gashes, uneven swaths of skin, burns and gouges. "Kitty's Peter Roydon's cousin, right?"

"The one and only."

I'm not sure the dean is capable of smiling, but his lips do twitch a little as he rubs at a scar on his neck. "He's a good kid. Smarter than every student here and braver than most too."

"I think he'd only agree with you on the first part."

The dean shrugs his large shoulders. "Better that way. If he knew how strong he was, he'd be insufferable."

A smile tugs at my mouth and I feel a strange pang in my heart. For all his gruffness, Dean Driscoll does remind me of my dad. Tough on the outside, and even tougher on the inside, but under *that*, perhaps a layer of something warm. Even knowing they were close, I can't bring myself to tell him his teammate was my dad. Old habits die hard, I guess, but until I figure out why exactly my father changed his name and kept Harker from me, I can't let anyone but my friends know I'm his daughter. Not even Reid.

Still, I can't help but say, "My dad played lacrosse too." I gesture at the dean's lacrosse stick on the cabin wall. "I have his stick on my wall just like that."

"I bet he's mighty proud of you."

The simple words squeeze my throat with emotion. I cough once to clear it and say, "He was."

I don't add what follows in my head. *Who knows if he still would be?*

But it's like Dean Driscoll knows from the expression on my face. "Wherever he is now, I'm sure he still is."

"I'm not sure I've lived up to his legacy. I'm struggling to . . . be what I think he wanted me to be."

"From what I can tell, you're doing just fine. Thank you for coming to me with this information, Miss Abbot."

I stand to leave. "What are you going to do about the White Stag?"

"Appeal to the Elders. Force them to change their stance on this guy so we can investigate Kitty's and Lyra's disappearances. Figure out if he's deviant or some mortal kingpin. Beat them senseless until they admit why they're keeping him out of our clutches." When I balk, he frowns. "Kidding, of course."

"They haven't listened to you before."

Driscoll scratches at his beard, then eyes me carefully. "I'll prove to them he was involved in these girls going missing, like you said. And the asphodels being stolen from Harker grounds . . ."

"Well, thanks," I say at the door, blood thrumming. I know what I have to do. "For everything."

But Driscoll stands. "Miss Abbot. You are not to go to Fever Dream. That's clear, right? It's *my* job to take care of these students. Not yours."

"I know," I assure him. "I wouldn't think of it."

His brows turn in. That gaze is brutal. "Miss Abbot—"

But I'm already out the door. I can find proof that Lyra and Kitty are tied to this club without even breathing the same air as this White Stag. I'm a proof-getting machine. When I bring that information back to the dean, the Elders will have no choice but to let him and the Citadel hunters take the fucker out.

And even if Reid won't go with me, I won't be by myself.

As I leave the cottage, I shoot Sophia a text: Still up for Fever Dream tonight?

She writes back a minute later. Def. Meet at the Gateway in 20?

We can go to my place in the city to get ready.

Aye aye captain. I'm bringing the white two piece set for you.

Fine, I write back, knowing better than to argue with the queen consort of clubbing.

A minute later she writes, Brace yourself. It has sparkles.

A sinking feeling runs through me. Of course it does.

CHAPTER 39

THE MINUTE SOPHIA and I enter the apartment I know something is off.

I can feel both our hackles rise. Somewhere, Penny is crying.

Loud, heaving sobs. Hound nowhere to be seen—

"Oh god," I murmur, horror eating at me as we both hurtle past the kitchen and toward her room. It's not a big apartment. I'm running for less than five seconds. Still, they are the worst five seconds I've had since I saw my father die.

I make it to her bedroom door before Sophia and I slam it open. There, on the bed, is Penny. Face mask on, mixing bowl filled with pasta clutched in her grasp, watching a movie with two people soaked by pouring rain, yelling about letters. When she sees Soph and me, both breathing raggedly at her bedroom door, she pauses the movie and wipes her eyes.

"Hi, guys," she sniffs. "Spaghetti?"

Sophia curses on an exhale, leaning on the doorway. "You cry like you're being axe-murdered, you know that?"

She nods quietly, lip trembling before more tears begin to crest.

"Oh jeez," Sophia sighs before bypassing me to crawl into bed with Penny. She takes the pasta bowl—larger than her head—and twirls herself a bite.

"What happened?" I ask. Penny was supposed to be staying at Claude's until I figured out if a deviant really did break into our place to scare me off the scent at Harker.

"Claude and I broke up. He met someone in Paris. The worst part is, she sounds really great. She works in fashion and has a poodle named Butter." Tears stream down Penny's face. "That's a great name for a poodle."

"Can you stop being so sweet for like five minutes?" Sophia asks, mouth full of spaghetti.

"I'm so sorry, Pen," I say.

"It's okay." She sniffs and Sophia hands the bowl and fork back to her. Penny spools another bite into her mouth. "What are you guys doing tonight? We could watch a movie?"

Sophia and I make eye contact, and I try to think of the easiest way to let her down. She's already so fragile.

"It doesn't have to be a romantic one," Penny adds, tucking her blond hair behind her ears.

"Penny, we—"

"Are going to Fever Dream and you're coming."

If my eyes were fists, Sophia would be laid out. "Penny doesn't want to go to a club."

Penny slinks deeper into the bed. "I'm not really club material."

My relief is tangible. "See?"

"Nonsense. You're young and smoking hot and newly single. That's the definition of club material. They make these places *for you*."

I'm going to strangle her. "Sophia, can I talk to you for a moment? In the hall?"

Sophia climbs from the bed with a petulant groan like she's

about to be grounded. She follows me down the hall until we're both standing safely out of Penny's earshot. "What are you doing? We can't bring Penny on a recon mission to fucking Fever Dream."

"Will you chill? It's filled with mortal girls just like Penny every single night. She'll be fine as long as we're there to protect her. Like you said, it's just recon. And maybe a little dancing."

"Do you care about anything? Harker has been compromised. Someone is trying to brew a syrabraxa. Two girls are *missing*—they could be *dead*."

Sophia's face hardens. "Yeah, and we'll probably be dead soon too. That's the nature of the job, babe. In the meantime, your best friend is hurting and needs you. You want to leave her here to sob through Nicholas Sparks movies and eat her weight in spaghetti? I hardly know the girl, and even *I* don't want to do that."

I hate that she has a point. I hate that I have far less time with Penny than she deserves. I hate that figuring out what's going on at this school means I'm likely to leave her and everyone else too early, the way my dad left me.

"We aren't sure yet if this White Stag is behind anything. We don't know if he's a deviant, or if he'll even be there," Sophia adds. "You think he hangs out at his own club every night?"

It crushed Penny when I almost excluded her from Halloween shopping. And now she's hurt and vulnerable . . . My gaze drops as I mull all this over. The lure Reid gave me sparkles on my wrist.

And an idea forms.

One that'll have to do for now. "Fine. But no poppy around Penny."

"'Course not. I'd never get fucked-up on a recon mission." She turns on her heel, and we walk back down the hall into Penny's room.

"Okay, no more moping," Sophia says. "We're going out."

Penny's eyes light and she puts the bowl of pasta on the bedside table. "Really?"

"Really. I have a gift for you too," I tell her, pulling the lure from my wrist and handing it to her.

She takes the delicate charm bracelet, eyeing each nautical trinket and dangling gem. "It's beautiful. A breakup bracelet?"

"A strength-when-things-are-hard bracelet."

Penny's teary smile seizes my heart.

"Up, up," Sophia cajoles, yanking back the covers on Penny's side. "Show me the closet. A rich girl like you must have a killer collection of high heels."

OUR CAB LETS us out nearly a block away due to the mayhem outside Fever Dream. Girls crowd the sidewalk in dresses as short as they are sheer and heels higher than my ankles could ever withstand. And the men—some suit-wearing, slicked-back old-money types I imagine will grow up to be little carbon copies of Stan and Caspar, others artistic, avant-garde, tattooed, and hair-dyed. High-profile DJs, artists on the cutting edge.

The line for entry wraps around the industrial-style building, which appears to be eight or nine stories high. Wannabe patrons spill out into the street, orange cones blocking the path of honking cars and fed-up cabbies who should know the city well enough to avoid this stretch on a Saturday night. The moon is high and wide and the air crisp with cigarette smoke and the tang of spilled liquor.

Sophia and I sandwich Penny between us, arms looped as we clop down the sidewalk in our heels. I feel a bit like a trio in a spy movie. Sophia with her endlessly long copper-toned tresses and gold hoops paired with wide-leg pants and a matching halter top.

Penny with her voluminous blowout, siren's charm bracelet, and baby-blue dress from the night of her birthday dinner. And me in Sophia's asymmetrical white skirt-and-top combo.

The skirt hangs off my hips at an angle, high-waisted on one side and sloping below my hip bone on the other. I don't love how the fabric is so sheer that you can see the white panties I've worn underneath, but the way it glitters is kind of extraordinary. Every streetlight and high beam sends the entire ensemble flickering with delicate rainbows like a flurry of bubbles in generous sun. And the top is the same—boatneck and sleeveless, cropped above my navel, sheer enough that every bra looked clunky underneath so I opted for Sophia's white heart-shaped pasties. One of the rare times I've been grateful for my Itty-Bitty Titty Committee membership. And Sophia's too, I guess.

When I try to maneuver the three of us to the back of the line, Sophia says, "Don't be silly," and drags us—even Penny, who doesn't "believe in the concept of line-cutting"—around to the front, elbowing our way past soaringly tall models and men in gold chains. We get enough dirty looks that I shove my hand into my purse to feel my daggers prickle against my fingertips. Without a whole lot of room to hide weapons in this nearly naked outfit, I stashed them in a sparkly black shoulder bag that I've tucked under my arm.

But Sophia steers us to the front with neither brawl nor cat-fight. The bouncer is a wiry guy with shoulder-length hair that's black as the night sky and nothing but disinterest in his violet cat eyes. My body hums in his presence. A vamp perhaps. *Not a trace of deviant activity*, my ass.

But alas, Lurch is not tonight's target. At least, I don't think. Sophia says something to him I can't hear over the crowd and the music pulsing from inside. Though the vamp bouncer's stony expression doesn't change, he stamps us with the shimmering white antlers before letting us in, red velvet rope lifted and all.

"How'd you do that?" Penny asks as the steel door is wrenched open for us.

"Baz and I go way back," Sophia jokes.

She must've never seen his fangs. I wonder what she'll think when I tell her he drinks blood instead of gin and tonics.

I don't know why I expected Fever Dream to be low-ceilinged and sleek. No amalgam of Half City nightclubs could have prepared me for what we find when we cross the threshold.

The building may actually be nine stories tall, but there are no other floors. Just this one room beneath a soaring, eye-weakening ceiling so high up I have to crane my neck all the way back to take in the whole thing. Carved concrete columns line both sides of the club, supporting arches that reach up toward the roof and surround the mind-numbed revelers. It's more like an industrial warehouse than a nightclub, but with something vaguely ancient brimming inside too. With the pillars and Grecian stonework and cavernous roof, it's like if you were to host a rave in the Acropolis. And at the center of it all is a stage for the DJ, raised too high for the patrons to reach, lit on all sides like a holy, glowing altar.

Sophia pulls us through the undulating mass of sweaty bodies grinding and swaying to insistent techno. The lights glow a deep, carnivorous red and then strobe black and white until everything moves like a flip-book. The scent of liquor and dope burrows under my skin. The thrusting rhythm seeps into my bones.

"Come on," Sophia yells, already swaying her hips and tossing her hair. The look of overstimulation bare on Penny's face has me concerned, but a minute later she's jumping with Sophia, and they're twirling each other, and I'm grateful we brought her. Sophia was right—she needed this.

"I'm gonna get us drinks," I tell them. When they don't hear me, I yell it twice more until my vocal cords ache.

The bar spans the entire leftmost wall of the club. There have to be fifteen bartenders holding down the fort on a night like this. The back bar is the same rough concrete of the floor and columns, bottles sitting on uneven shelves that appear to be carved directly into the original stonework. But the bar top is a glimmering celadon glass that lights up the space a little and draws partiers over like insects in search of nectar. My body tingles slightly, and I realize that somewhere in this thrumming, rapturous mass is another deviant.

"What'll it be, Snow White?"

It's not the first time my dark hair–pale skin–light eyes combo has earned me the nickname. When I'm not in Sophia's white gauze two-piece set and back in my usual black, I also get Morticia, Elvira, and Betty Boop.

"Original," I deadpan, turning from my scan of the crowd.

When I face the bartender, my spine buzzes like there are fireworks under my skin. The punishingly handsome man before me has dark skin, razor-green eyes, and the charming, winning smile of that guy in school you could never get to look at you. Though his neck is bare of any Brood mark, I've clearly found my deviant. Two, by my count, employed here alone. Either Reid purposely lied to me, or he doesn't know as much about this place as he claimed to. I pray it's the latter.

The bartender's lean muscles bulge beneath his shirt as he leans forward with a curve of his lips to say, "Did you want a drink, or . . . ?"

"Two tequila sodas," I manage. "And a white wine. Please."

The bartender nods to himself as if it's not the first time a club girl got lost in his eyes.

Maybe Fever Dream has long been a breeding ground for the nefarious and hell-born, under the radar of me, my dad, and all the Harker alums. Maybe what the dean said was truer than I realized—the Elders, for their own mysterious reasons, have allowed this place to continue its business, purposely leaving it unknown to even the hunters they train. Either way, I can't take down this bartender now any more than I could Baz the bouncer. I have bigger fish to fry. I need to find proof that Kitty and Lyra were taken by someone here.

While I wait for my drinks, I scan the place from this slightly better-lit vantage point.

Now I can see a few things I missed when we arrived: For one, behind the DJ, way in the far back, is a square pool glowing an otherworldly aquamarine. Even with my hunter vision, I can't tell if the people wading in it are clothed, but I can make an educated guess. Behind that, I spy a spiral staircase that curves around one of the sky-high pillars and disappears into the wall. Some kind of second floor built into the side of the building.

And in the other direction, at the end of the bar closer to the club's entrance, is an archway that's been funneling partygoers in and out. No red rope, no security to be seen, so nothing clandestine nor off-limits. Given the scent of weed and cigs emanating from the people who are coming through, I can assume it leads to an outdoor smoking space.

That's where I spot him. A man trying just a smidgeon too hard to look trendy. He's sweating, eyes shifty. Packing some kind of pistol in his leather jacket, with a briefcase I know from my Windsor days to be bulletproof steel. Not your usual clubbing clutch. It's as good a lead as any.

I'm off before I can pay for the drinks. Pushing through the crowd, I hurtle after him as he slips through the archway, down an echoing pitch-black hall and out a heavy stone door. The November cold licks up my skin, and my eyes adjust to the club's semicovered garden patio. Heat lamps help to dull the chill of the night air for the clubgoers who laze in antique Grecian chairs beneath hanging ivy and rough stone fountains. There are hookah pipes and cigarettes in every hand, the medicinal scent of smoked poppy in the air. A thick haze of drugs and tobacco stings my eyes, and I blink rapidly, but there are too many people back here, and I've already lost the man with the briefcase. God damn it.

I scan the crowd like a nocturnal beast. I pick up every bracelet glint and ice cube clink. And a door somewhere creaking closed. Hunter instincts send me toward the trimmed hedges, where I see one section of leafy green is moving. A false door in the organic garden wall. It's a calculated bet—that the briefcase man went in there, wherever *there* is—but I take it. Without thinking twice, I slide through the opening before it seals and hope I'm right.

I topple into a luxurious back office. Rough stone walls, like all of Fever Dream. Dim cast-iron lamps, a huge black leather couch. Concrete coffee table that I just know would take eight of me to lift. The scents of clove and dry tobacco mingle as if someone makes a habit of hand-rolling cigarettes on the broad, dark wooden desk in the center of the room. A literal man cave by way of Restoration Hardware.

And my body—my *bones*—are humming like I'm radioactive.

The only other person in the office is a hulkingly tall, broad-shouldered man in a white T-shirt, facing away from me. I know without a kernel of doubt that he's a demon. No lesser deviant has that kind of height and muscle. It's not the guy with the briefcase, but judging by the crisp white of this demon's hair and the debauched elegance of his clandestine office, I'm going to go out on a limb and say I found my Stag.

I take a few steps forward to get a better look and see he's standing in front of some kind of marble counter. I hear the twist of a cap and glug of liquid over ice and realize it's a bar and he's pouring himself a drink. Then I hear the tap of fingers on a screen. A sip followed by a low chuckle. He's texting someone.

"Why hello there." His voice is a deep rumble. Cruel and sensual and subdued.

I open my mouth, heart in my tonsils, but when he turns, clear drink swirling in hand, he's holding a phone to his ear.

He grins at me, and the beauty of his flawless face stalls the air in my lungs.

"*Hi, Daddy,*" a woman's voice coos over the line.

I fight the instinct to make a *yuck* face.

The riotously handsome, enormously tall demon motions for me to take a seat on the couch, as if a girl breaking into his back office is a common Friday-night occurrence. I do as instructed, grateful for the opportunity to buy some time.

"You know you're bothering Daddy at work, right?" he says into the phone.

If he really is the White Stag, he's younger than I expected. Of course, he's likely as old as Reid, but he looks about thirty-two. In fact, he looks like the type of criminally hot guy you'd find in a Babylon coffee shop: cigarette behind his ear, bleached-blond hair, plain white T-shirt, and loose black jeans with a chain on them.

On either side of his neck are two tattoos. Similar but not identical, both in some ancient text I can't read. There's something inherently foreboding about the way they curve down his throat and beneath his shirt. A silver chain, which I have to assume is actually white gold or some other metal, hangs around his neck beside the tattoos. I don't see any brand, but he's got to be the White Stag. And he's a demon. Which must mean he's in the Brood, right?

"I haven't been able to stop thinking about you," the woman on the phone purrs. *"Can I come over?"*

"Sorry, sweetheart," the demon says, gaze fixed on me. "I have an unexpected meeting."

I scan for my exit strategy. Besides the desk, the bar, and the couch, the room only has chic stone shelving with stacked decorative books in dark neutral colors. No windows. No other door. No way out.

"Remember our last meeting in your office?"

That gets a dark chuckle out of the demon and a dry heave from me as I scoot to the very edge of the leather couch. I will be sanitizing every inch of my body and burning Sophia's sparkling two-piece—sorry, Soph.

"Not sure. You'll have to remind me sometime. Bye, now." He ends the call before she can respond. The demon's moonstone blue eyes gleam as he studies me.

"I lost my earring," I say in my best drunk party girl voice. "Last time I was in here."

A quick, hot flash of red sparks in his gaze. "Is that so?"

"Yep," I hum before making a show of running my hands over the soft leather of the couch in search of it. I try not to think of all the human DNA I'm caressing. Did I say sanitize? I meant fumigate.

The demon only wanders closer, towering over me like scaffolding. He is offensively tall. His eyes sweep over my body. "What did you say your name was?"

I cross my legs in an effort toward casualness. I need to get out of here. Now I know where to come back and search for proof, but I can't do that if the White Stag kills me first. "Jenny."

Is that a common has-sex-with-nightclub-owners-in-their-offices name? Here's hoping.

"I think I'd remember you, *Jenny*." He says it like it would be a true shame if he didn't. The more my mouth twists in disgust, the more his curves in deadly amusement. "How about the truth?" When I falter for words, he adds, "Come on, sweetheart. Don't make me force it from you."

I fold my arms across my chest to put space between him and my racing heart. He already knows I'm lying. "It's Viv."

"There you go." He nods to himself, as if somehow that fits me better. "Vivienne?"

"Just Viv. But I really should get going." I stand on wobbly heels. "My friends are waiting for me."

I move to step around him, but he blocks my path just as smoothly. In fact, he takes one step closer, and I can smell the hints of black cherry on his clothes and the tobacco on his skin. My stomach flips over itself with unease. "What's the rush? You didn't break into my office just to chicken out, did you?"

Does he know I'm here for Lyra? Or does he think I've come to seduce him? That phone call notwithstanding, I get the vibe I wouldn't be the first girl who came here to get laid by the White Stag. But I think back to when Reid got the better of me that first night we met. Brood demons are another breed. And Reid doesn't even take souls . . . I won't be able to best this guy alone, and no way will he let me slip my phone out and call Sophia. Through the stone walls of the office, the beat from the club drifts in with a muted pulse. A death knell—I have to get out of here.

"I changed my mind," I say. "Not feeling it anymore."

He flashes a Cheshire grin. I get the distinct feeling that for him, this exchange is like finding twenty bucks in your back pocket: a skittish girl in minimal clothing for him to torment. "Well, now I know you're a little liar."

"Someone thinks highly of themselves."

That incredulous grin would be knee-weakening if his eyes didn't flicker with the promise of cruelty. "It's as if you have no idea who you're talking to."

I scowl. "The White Stag?"

His gust of laughter surprises me. "Now, that's disappointing. Another journalist with some tepid piece on Half City crime."

I try to swallow and find that I can't. He's given me a much better cover than a girl who came here to get laid and was disappointed by what she found. "What gave me away?"

"The outfit's a little try-hard." A filthy smile curves his lips. "But I'm not complaining."

"Shall I add sexual harassment to drug dealing and murder-for-hire services?"

His face hardens. A misstep. "Sexual harassment would be me demanding you get down on your pretty knees."

His gunmetal-blue eyes blink white. Like that night with Reid and the couple on the moped . . . He's trying to glamour me, but hunters can't be glamoured. He thinks I'm mortal—

And I don't have much time to decide between going along with the ruse or exposing myself as a huntress. But I'm here to destroy this fucker, certainly not to blow him, so I slide my daggers out of my bag in one smooth motion and drive them toward his heart.

CHAPTER 40

I DON'T GET anywhere near my target. My face explodes with pain and I fly backward into the couch. My entire eye socket pulses and my vision goes warped and spotty. I'm going to have one hell of a black eye if I make it out of here alive. When I scramble up, I realize he's laughing, still holding his drink, unspilled.

Shame and fury roil in my bloodstream. "You knew."

"You think I can't scent a hunter? With how many I've had?"

Had. Like hunter souls are notches on his bedpost. I know taking the soul of a hunter gives demons more strength, more power, but to be able to *scent* one . . .

I knew a demon once who could, Reid told us that first week. *He'd taken so many hunter souls, he said he could feel them coming a mile away.*

This guy must have killed hundreds of hunters.

Only then does it dawn on me. Secret criminal kingpin, operates under a false name, ferociously powerful, can discern hunters just by their scent. Maybe that's why he has no mark of the Brood. Because he *owns* them. I might be facing the fucking *High Thane.*

I take a centering, bracing breath. I'm probably going to die tonight. But my father didn't raise me to give up. Not ever. "Too bad you've had your last."

The demon rolls his eyes as if my taunt is boring and sets his drink down on the desk. "Save your cute little one-liners for sometime I can jerk off, will you?"

My grimace makes my already-swelling eye hurt. "You're depraved."

"So they tell me." He curls his fingers lightly in a *let's have it* gesture.

I leap from the couch and catch him around the middle, sending us both back over the desk. His drink shatters on the cold stone floor, and the scent of bitter liquor stings my nose. I drive my blades toward his back, but he rolls faster than I've seen anything move, tossing me clean off him. I land hard on my side and dodge before his fist can connect again. His knuckles slam into the stone, and tiny cracks fissure out like lightning.

When I snap my head up, he yanks me back by the shirt and gets ahold of my chin, brushing the curtain of black hair from my face as I pant. He studies me with lethal intensity. "My, my."

"Don't touch me," I spit, driving my fist into his rib cage.

He doubles over with a groan, allowing me to scramble back until I'm on the other side of the leather couch. He flexes his bloodied knuckles across from me, catching his breath, and I clock how close I am to the only door. I could probably clear it in one leap and make it out, but my body is *vibrating* for the kill. I wipe the blood that's dripping down my cheek from my busted eye and release a growl as I charge him again.

I swear I hear a low chuckle as he allows me to take him down to the ground and drive one silver dagger into his thigh. He groans in pain. My blood roars to end him.

"You're like a little hellcat." The words are bitten out through clenched teeth.

"I'm going"—I heave—"to kill you."

"Yeah," he says, shoving me off him in one push and yanking my dagger free from his thigh with a wince. "I got that."

The silver hisses in his palm, and he allows my blade to clatter to the ground. Slowly, his veined forearms ripple down to the fingertips with pale, moon-white scales. His nails grow into long night-black claws. He must see the horror in my eyes as I dodge his next swing and scuttle around the desk, desperate to put space between us. "How can you be the High Thane," I manage as I pant, "with no Brood on hand to fight for you?"

"High Thane?" The demon recoils as if I've insulted him. The first moment of real anger. It chills me to the bone. "I'd rather drown in my own blood then be dragged onto the Throne of Bael as some bullshit decorative joke of a king."

But everything the dean said . . . The power over the Elders . . . And Kitty and Lyra—"The missing students . . . They wore your stamp."

He's not even out of breath. "Harker huntresses partying when they should be studying? A crying shame."

This time he doesn't wait for me to regroup. He leaps over the desk in one smooth, powerful motion and catches me around the throat in a vise grip. The hand around my neck is shimmering with that corpse-pale scaling, his claws digging into the back of my neck to draw blood. I land a solid punch to his granite jaw and feel his bones crack. It's like poppy in my veins.

With a lethal snarl, he drags me across the room, knocking over modern art and glossy vases. He slams me down onto the stone coffee table until I lose my grip on my remaining blade. My spine sings with pain, my head throbs, every inch of me breaking—

His lips hover over mine, scenting the soul he's about to drink, filling my vision with his depthless eyes, and I'm running out of air, and none of my kicks are connecting, and even as my vision blacks out into merciful oblivion and I can't get one breath in, I can hear his sinister laugh in the shell of my ear.

"Deacon! Get your fucking hands off her."

That voice. The one that yanks me back from the darkness. *Reid.*

For reasons I wouldn't be able to fathom under normal circumstances, much less in my half-conscious state, the demon—Deacon, it seems—who's hovering over me releases my neck and lets me fall back onto the table in a heap.

Blessed air courses into my lungs, and I'm engulfed by lemongrass and the soft wool of Reid's sweater. He lifts me onto my feet and then tips my chin up to examine the pulpy mess I'm sure is my face. He curses, low and deadly. My fingers grasp his arms to keep myself upright.

"I'm fine." I sound half-dead.

"I'll kill him," he husks. "For touching you."

"Remind me," Deacon says, bored. "How did that go for you the last time?"

Reid snarls. A sound of white-hot rage. "You might not have died, but you suffered quite a bit, didn't you?"

When I peer past Reid, all the taunting amusement has drained from Deacon's cruel, carved face. He yanks open a desk drawer and then another. "Either of you have a light?"

Reid brushes his lips across my temple, and I nearly sway into him. I know I have a concussion. I'm usually the last one to say it, but I should get to the infirmary. Pixie magic is needed stat. Reid keeps me behind him in a painfully protective gesture as he says, low and steady, "We're leaving."

Deacon shuts the drawer below him with a real laugh. The sound is wicked. Wicked and shiver-inducing. When he looks up, his sky-blue eyes are on fire. "Never knew you to have a sense of humor before, but man, that is top-notch."

Reid stiffens. His fear fuels my own. I'm trembling and dizzy. Somewhere in the back of my mind, I wonder if I'm going to be sick.

"If you wanted to kill me, you could have. All these years . . ." Reid shakes his head, then repeats, "We're leaving."

"Just because I didn't care enough to hunt you down doesn't mean I won't rip your limbs off now that you're standing here in front of me, asking for it."

Reid doesn't even flinch. It's as if Deacon's brutality is nothing new to him. "Do what you have to. But leave her out of it."

"*Reid*," I breathe, grasping him tighter. "No."

His face shutters. "Viv—"

"Oh god, spare me," Deacon drawls, fishing a fresh cigarette from his pack. "Melodrama gives me the shits."

I sneer at him, and he glares right back at me, nostrils flaring. He cuts his ruthless gaze to Reid. "I'm almost proud. You finally decided to stop hiding from me." I wonder if I spy an ounce of pain in those astoundingly blue eyes. But it's gone as soon as I blink.

Reid bristles. "I didn't come here for you."

"Just for your huntress, then."

His voice is barely audible. "You were going to kill her."

Deacon's gaze shifts from Reid to me behind him. His eyes travel with lethal leisure from my split lip to Sophia's ripped top and my breasts underneath. He sucks his lip between his teeth. "I'm glad my reputation still precedes me."

"It isn't *happening*," Reid growls.

Deacon pops the cigarette behind his ear. "My guy. You know I can't allow hunters to come for me and live to tell the tale."

"It was a mistake," Reid says evenly. "She won't be back."

This concussion must be one of my worst, because I have the stupid instinct to say, "I'm not leaving without proof he took Kitty and Lyra."

Reid groans in frustration. "Viv—"

Deacon opens another drawer and finally finds his lighter. "I have no idea who those people are."

"Lying sack of shit," I snarl at him.

"Often, yes." His playful aggression has slipped into boredom. I can't tell if that's a good thing. "But I have no interest in Harker or your precious dean or philandering Citadel—"

It doesn't make sense. My stomach seizes and churns. "But the stamps—"

"*Viv*," Reid snaps, furious. "Enough."

Deacon stalks toward us, and I watch as dark red scales feather up the back of Reid's neck. I've only ever seen them on his arms. "Stay away from her," he growls.

Deacon ignores Reid completely, leaning around him to ask me, "What would I want with Harker students?"

It's not the question that stumps me. It's the honest curiosity in Deacon's eyes. He has no clue what I'm talking about. He wants to know more.

"Doesn't matter," Reid says. "You do what you want with who you want, hunter or otherwise. We're *leaving*."

I shoot my gaze up to Reid. That is not my stance on the matter.

"I can find your huntress, you know," Deacon purrs. "Anytime."

"But you won't," Reid says, backing us both toward the doorway. "I kept your secret for years. Until the day he died."

I open my mouth to ask *who* when I notice a twisted twinkle gleaming in Deacon's eye. "You owe me a lot more than that, brother."

Brother?

It's not the head injury that sends my vision tunneling, nor the shiver down my spine. It's shock—utter *shock*. I swallow it quickly, though. I refuse to give Deacon any satisfaction, and I can see the way he examines us. Looking for cracks—surveying to see if Reid's been honest with me.

Which he hasn't.

Reid doesn't allow the reveal to shake his conviction. "Way I see it, we're even now."

"Hardly," Deacon purrs. "If I ever see your girlfriend again, just know I'll be picking fragments of her spine from my teeth by the time you show up to save the day." Deacon runs his eyes over me one last time, and I desperately wish for more clothing. "Night-night, Vivienne."

"It's *Viv*," I spit.

And then Reid's hauling me out the door and into Fever Dream's smoking garden. Techno from inside pounds through my aching head. A fog of tobacco funnels from the open door into Deacon's office and paints his unreadable expression in a haze of swirling gray.

CHAPTER 41

MY BODY FIGHTS to keep me upright. All I can hear over the low din of the garden is my own thundering heartbeat. I still can't wrap my fuzzy mind around the fact that Reid's brother is not only alive and kicking, he's the White Stag. A demon the Elders have protected for reasons I cannot piece together. That he *let us go*. That Reid kept a secret for him for years until someone died.

We've not made it two feet from Deacon's office when his goons prowl toward us. My aching, pulsating limbs shimmer with the need to kill, and I recognize one as Baz, the violet-eyed bouncer vamp who let us in, and the other as the charming deviant bartender. The bartender's elongated canines flash in the dim garden lights when he opens his mouth to speak. "Stag wants you both out. And Snow White owes me for three drinks." Werewolf. Definitely a werewolf.

"We were just leaving," Reid growls.

Baz takes a purposeful step toward me, nostrils flaring as he scents the blood dripping from my face. Now that he's towering over me, I clock the same two symbols tattooed at the base of his throat as Deacon has on either side of his neck. "She doesn't have to pay for them with cash."

"Baz," the bartender scolds good-naturedly. As if drinking my blood would be as unfortunate as breaking a diet.

Reid's thumb tightens on my hip, pulling me closer. "Don't even think about it."

"We just need to find my friends," I manage around my nausea. *Infirmary*, my brain tells me. *Soonish*.

"You're in luck," Baz drawls, unenthused. "We kicked them out too."

Reid and I shove past both deviants and through the dark tunnel that leads back into the club. Leggy acrobats have descended from that cathedral-like ceiling and hang down with nothing but ribbons. The noxious smell of human sweat, breath, and spilled drinks has vomit rising in my throat. I need to get out of here. But the room is so dark, and I keep knocking into bodies, and someone in heels steps on my toe, and I can't even feel the pain because I can barely breathe, and Reid—Reid *lied* to me, and I almost died, and I just need to find Penny and Sophia, and—

"Whoa there," Reid says against my ear, catching me as I sag.

"Don't touch me," I slur.

He curses under his breath as if he knows he's in for it, but insists on picking me up and carrying me out of the club anyway. The late autumn night slams into me like a thunderclap, and even though I'm already shivering, I'm grateful—the cold has woken me up a little bit.

"Put me down," I tell him, and he does.

Penny and Sophia are standing outside, away from the line, huddled for warmth. Penny sees us first, and the look on her face makes me sicker than all the injuries combined. "I'm okay."

"Oh my god, Viv." She's at my side a second later. "What on earth— Who— How did this—"

"She's okay," Reid repeats. "She had a fall. I'm going to take her to the hospital."

Penny's eyes jump from him to me and back. "I remember you. From Halloween. James told me you were with Viv the last time she was hurt too. That fire at Maria's."

"Penny," Sophia tries. "It's not what you think."

"It's not Reid's fault," I say even though I'm furious with him and can't even look at his perfect wounded face right now. "Just bad timing."

"You show up here and Viv ends up injured again? I'm calling the police. I'm—"

"They're dating," Sophia blurts. "They met at Maria's the night of the fire. He would never hurt her."

Reid's eyes cut to me, and I can't stomach the guilt there, so I keep my eyes on Penny, willing her to let it go. Penny stares up at Sophia, and I wonder if this fucked-up night might just end here, but then a hurt confusion colors her face, and I realize the error.

"You told James he worked at the Windsor with you guys . . . that you'd been stuck there late. But if you only met that night at Maria's . . . Why would you lie?"

Sophia's eyes cut to me, wide and guilty, but I don't blame her. It's my fault for lying to Penny. It's my fault for thinking I could live all these different lives at once and never slip up.

"I'm gonna need you guys to clear out." The werewolf bartender has strolled out into the night and folds his arms as he appraises us. When his gaze lands on Penny, a gleam sparkles in those vicious olive eyes. "Except for you, buttercup. You can stay." He offers her a hand. "I'm Ward. You have plans tonight?"

"I do, yes. I'm so sorry. I'm not trying to be rude, but it's three in the morning. My plans have already happened, and honestly, they sucked. My boyfriend left me for a lovely Parisian woman. We were kicked out for no reason, and then my friend was assaulted at your club or fell down some stairs or . . . something. And"—Penny brings her hands to her face to rub her eyes, smearing her mascara—"and she lied to me. And nothing is making sense. And—I'm sorry, would you please excuse us? We are trying to have a private conversation."

For a moment, nobody says anything.

All I can think is that Penny has picked the *worst possible* moment to discover a smidgeon of assertiveness. While she has no idea she's just snapped at a werewolf who could have her face for dinner, the rest of us are plainly aware.

And I'm not that far off—Ward is staring at Penny like she's been left under his Christmas tree in the shiniest of gift wrap.

"Sorry to hear it, buttercup. I hope things pick up for you." Ward turns to Reid and me, and his warm grin drops. "You two would be wise not to come back here. Stag won't be so lenient again."

"Won't be a problem." My head is pounding and I want to dagger the creep.

When Ward leaves us, Penny looks as surprised with herself as I am. "Please, Viv," she says quietly. "Please tell me what is going on."

"It's . . . complicated."

Penny's eyes brim with tears, and I wish Reid had just let me pass out.

"I feel like I barely know you these days," she rasps.

"Penny—"

But she's already walking away, hailing a cab and climbing inside.

"Go with her," I tell Sophia. "I'll call you later. Just make sure she gets home okay."

Sophia nods, guilt clear on her flushed cheeks. "I'm sorry."

"It's fine," I tell her. "It's not your fault."

They climb into the car together, and when the cab melts into the night, I exhale the only sigh of relief I have coming.

"You never should have lied to her about who I was."

I glare at Reid. "No, really?"

He frowns, stuffing his hands into his pockets. "I just mean . . . Never mind. Let me take you back to Harker. You need . . ." His eyes travel over my split lip, my swollen eye, my bruised arms and torso. "A whole bunch of shit," he says with a wince.

"Thanks." I limp down the sidewalk toward the corner subway station, determined to get there on my own.

"Come on. Let me get you help and I'll call it even."

That spins me on a dime. *"You'll* call it even?"

He doesn't even have the decency to look sheepish. "I told you not to come tonight, and you lied to me, ignored me, and showed up anyway. I gave you a lure so I could protect you, and you didn't even wear it. Your stubborn, risky, loner bullshit nearly got you killed."

Two drunk guys stumble out of the club, and Reid watches with thinly veiled irritation as they ogle me lazily and without concealment, clearly unbothered by my head wound. *Men.*

"And you're in—" Reid eyes me up and down with exasperation. "What the hell are you even wearing?"

My swollen eye struggles to widen to show my true horror. "Are you kidding me? Reid. *You* lied to *me.* About, like, a thousand things. And now you're on me about my outfit? How did you even know I'd be here? Stalking again?"

"Are you kidding me, Viv? You'd be dead if I hadn't arrived when I did." The truth in his words seems to sober him a little from his fury. "I . . . I should have realized it sooner. You've told me you'd never run from a fight." I open my mouth to tell him that's exactly why he shouldn't have asked me to in the first place, but he cuts me off. "All I've ever done is try to protect you."

"Protect me? All you've done is *lie* to me. Not only did you tell me this place was deviant-free, you also said your brother was dead." I enumerate his indiscretions on my bloodied fingers in case he's unable to keep track. "Meanwhile, he's the very man I came here tonight to hunt."

"Which I told you *not to do*! Do you know how many people have tried to take him down? People a lot more powerful than you, Viv. If I said leave it be, there was a fucking reason."

"Yeah, one you kept from me. I asked you what you knew about this place. You told me some bullshit about the owner being a drug runner. And he was your fucking *brother*!"

I watch as Reid tries and fails to school the fury on his face. Stubborn as a bull, he can't pull it off. "My brother has taken more hunter souls than any demon alive."

Demons gain power with age and how many souls they've taken. Nobody lives as long or kills as much as those in the Brood. If he's taken as many hunter lives as Reid claims . . . To never have been recruited by them nor seen as a threat and killed off is shocking. To have amassed this kind of power and influence in Astera right under their noses is almost unfathomable.

I want to pry about how any of what Deacon's done is possible—why Reid was forced to join the Brood but his brother wasn't—when Reid adds, "He's more powerful than anyone aside from our High Thane, and he doesn't hate anyone as much as he hates me."

Reid spits out the words like they're bitter on his tongue. "Anything I said to you today was my attempt at keeping something exactly like tonight from happening."

But all I can think of is how he just said *our High Thane*.

He's a demon. He has been this whole time.

How could I have been so utterly blind?

He's been protecting his brother. Keeping his secrets. Maybe he even knows why the Elders have let Deacon operate out of Fever Dream all this time. He certainly knows more than he's telling me right now.

"I've avoided his path for longer than I can remember, Viv. Even knowing him—being known *by him*—is dangerous. For all intents and purposes, he was dead to me. The details outside of that are so complicated—"

"You told him *do what you want with who you want, hunter or otherwise*. You don't even care that—"

"Listen to me. I know you, Viv. I know you because I know *me*." He takes a breath and tries again with new resolve. "You're looking for a reason to kill our relationship before it can even exist. If you just give me a second, I can explain—"

And maybe this sinking feeling is realizing that the betrayal I feel right now has got to be nothing compared to how Penny felt when I gave her the exact same speech. I've only known Reid for a few months. Penny is my best friend.

Or maybe it's the ever-present self-hatred. Knowing I pissed everyone off. Failed Harker and the dean and all my fellow students. I have no proof of where Kitty and Lyra went. I failed everyone just as I failed my family. My dad.

Or maybe it's what's broken inside me. That angry, volatile thing. That aeon urge to slide my daggers into the supple flesh under Reid's solar plexus just as much as I want to slide my tongue against his lips. That predator within me that makes me violent even toward those I was beginning to—

Well, it doesn't matter now.

Whatever it is that makes me say it, I take a breath and tell Reid, "You don't have to explain anything to me. Whatever this is between us . . . it's done."

Reid's jaw grinds shut. "Fine by me. Just get your concussion looked at, okay?"

"I can take care of myself."

He shakes his head and fists his hands in his pockets. "You sure can."

The bitter night air has seeped well past my sheer skirt and pasties and settled into the marrow of my bones. I realize as I nearly tumble down the subway stairs that my hands have gone numb along with my toes and ears. I don't even care.

The way I laid into Reid, hurting him like I did when he'd put his life before mine tonight . . . I feel as cold inside as my skin is to the touch. Colder, maybe. My icy hand finds my swollen eye, and I hold it there until both ache.

Seated in the empty subway car headed uptown, I fish my phone out of my purse for the first time all night and scroll through the expected slew of texts and calls Sophia and Penny sent while I was being pummeled by Deacon. But I've also got three missed calls and two voicemails from Fiona. One from my mother as well.

My throat closes up as I check the time.

But I already know. It's past midnight.

I missed the Chasm exhibit's opening.

After releasing a string of curses I press the phone to my ear and listen to Fiona's voicemails. The first is full of genuine concern—*"Where are you? The guests are arriving. Please let me know everything is okay"*—but the second is composed of simple, resigned disappointment. *"You missed the event, and we have no other recourse at this time but to let you go. I'm sorry, Viv."*

The voicemail from my mother is worse than getting fired.

"Nora just called to tell me what happened. That you skipped the exhibit opening and Fiona was forced to fire you." She pauses to sigh. She sounds exhausted. Despite it all, tears of frustration bead in the corners of my eyes as I press the phone closer to my ear. *"Why..."* she asks quietly. *"Why are you this way?"*

That's the whole voicemail.

I play it three times, staring at the antlers bleeding white ink into my wrist until I throw my phone across the railcar.

CHAPTER 42

SNOW HAS BUILT up on all the windowsills like piped icing circling a cake. Flakes of it sprinkle the lawns like powdered sugar, tufts of the stuff making little cotton candy mounds out of all the campus shrubbery, and Lake Hellebore has frozen over into shimmering, reflective hard candy. Overnight Harker has become as picturesque as a gingerbread house. It should be the kind of sugary beauty I capture with my half-frame, but I have no desire to savor this moment. I hardly want to be inside of it myself—the campus has never felt so alienating.

It's too quiet. Half the students have gone home for their own safety. Some who have nowhere else to go or who felt for whatever reason that Harker was still safer than being with their families are hiding away in the campus's nooks and crannies, studying for next week's exams. You can threaten the most precious artifacts of the school—even the student body—but I guess we'll never come between professors and their finals.

At least fifty Citadel hunters in their utilitarian navy uniforms have been called to man the campus like soldiers in an occupied city. Harker used to be the only place I felt like I belonged. *Home,*

I called it that night coming back from Shiloh. Granted, I was high as a kite on Valium, but I really felt it then, and every day since. Now everything's changed. Students are wary and standoffish. Everyone knows something is wrong that the dean and the Elders can't seem to fix.

And I have to stew in the knowledge that on top of losing my job, disappointing my family, and breaking Penny's heart, I couldn't save Lyra or Kitty or anyone else. Couldn't figure out who is brewing the syrabraxa or what horrors they have planned. Have to fall asleep each night thinking of how stupid I was to think the White Stag—Reid's *brother*—had anything to do with any of it. How stupid I was to trust him, to let myself fall—

"Viv?" When I look up, Peter's frowning at me from the other side of the commons couch. "Contrary to popular belief, there's no final on the details of the fireplace."

We're the only two in here studying this evening, because even in the darkest times, we are still losers with no plans.

"Sorry . . . Just zoned out for a sec."

"Did you even finish the practice questions?"

"Yeah." I look down at my paper. "What did you get for number seven?"

Peter surveys his notebook. His faded *Iron Man* sweatshirt is folded in such a way that the playboy billionaire looks like he's melting. "I had *poison from a wyvern's fang.*"

"Hmm. I wrote *supermarket.*"

". . . Yeah, that's wrong."

I drag my eraser across the page. The hallway door opens, and Peter and I both look up to hear two girls clomp inside in their snow-coated boots, bags of holiday shopping in tow. Their hair is perfectly curled, cheeks flushed from the winter night. They burst into peals of laughter as they hurry up the creaking wooden stairs of Elkfore.

A scowl heats my face. "Annoying, no?"

Peter looks back to the hall where the girls were. Then back to me. "How dare they bring their shopping bags into our commons? They'll rue the day."

"Girls are missing. The school is being sabotaged. They could show some respect."

But he's already back to his notebook, highlighting a new passage. I've been insufferable this past week. I know it, Peter knows it, Sophia and Elliot know it. For some reason, they continue to spend time with me, which is more than I deserve. The fireplace crackles and snaps. Somber jazz drifts in through one of the speakers. I study Peter as he works diligently.

"Sorry," I say after a while. "For being on edge."

"No need to apologize. You're having a time."

"Penny and I call it the Big Oof." I finger the corner of my notebook where the color is fading. I miss Hound, and I miss Penny, and I miss our sappy movie nights.

Peter's soft smile warms the room. "Now that the exhibit's done, where does she think you've been staying this whole week?"

"I told her I'd sleep at Sophia's until she wanted to talk. In the scheme of things, it's one of my lesser lies."

"Maybe going out with them would have made you feel better?"

I think about Sophia and Elliot at whatever Astera bar they're at. Lately it feels like the city is safer than the campus. I wonder if they're drinking or laughing or dancing. Neither of them grappling with the kind of sharp, stabbing self-hatred that's eaten at me for years. I think of the conversation Elliot and I had in the library. About their friendship. "You think they've ever hooked up?"

Instantly I regret the question. Peter's face goes so pale he nearly glows in the dim commons light. "God, I hope not."

"Sorry. I'm sure you're right."

"I try not to think about it . . . any more than I already do." He winces a bit. "Which is just about every night when I'm falling asleep."

"Jesus, Peter."

"I'm kidding," he says with no conviction.

"Why don't you tell her?" Peter makes a face, and I make one back at him. "I'm serious."

"As am I. I'm a homeschooled orphan with a penchant for fictional characters. On what planet does a girl like that go for a guy like me?"

I guess I know what he means. Peter's eager, hopeful, too intelligent for his own good. I'd never call him a nerd, because I love him, and because *nerd* has a certain sniveling, academia-obsessed connotation, but maybe, lovingly, I'd call Peter a dork.

"Your mom homeschooled you?"

"She valued knowledge over everything else. Felt like she could educate me better than our 'crummy' public school system. Honestly, I think she just wanted to keep me close."

It's such a sweet sentiment, my heart twists. "I'm sorry you had to lose her."

Peter's gaze falls to his notebook. He doesn't speak for a minute as the fireplace snaps and licks. Then he tells me quietly, "It's my own fault."

His words drop a weight on my chest. "What? Why?"

"She'd taught me everything about hunting. And yet when she was staring down a Brood demon, when he was taking her soul"—Peter shudders out a breath and rubs his eyes—"I just stood there. Watched it happen."

"Peter . . ." I can't think of anything else to say. My stomach churns with a familiar pain. "How old were you?"

"Eight. I'll never forget his face. The sound of his claws clicking together . . . He let me go after. Told me living as a cowardly hunter was a worse fate than being a turned demon down in the underworld with her."

The image of a young Peter, grasping at his mother's lifeless body before she crumbled to ash, rips my chest in half. "You were *mortal*. You were a kid. There was nothing you could have done."

"Is that what you tell yourself? About your dad?"

"It's different." I lower my voice even though I know we're alone. "I'm an aeon. I had all my abilities then. I should have been able to help him. I should have gotten to him in time . . ."

"Can you imagine what it was like for them? To train us to fight, knowing they'd have to leave us one day? Knowing their job was to set us up for the same fate? At least you've done something with all your dad taught you. Fought deviants, saved people . . ." Peter's laugh is solemn and rueful. "I can't even tell a girl I'm into her."

As my heart twists, I wonder if on some level Sophia already knows how he feels. Anyone can see the way Peter looks at her. "She really cares about you, you know."

"I know. But honestly, Elliot was right that day when he said Kitty was my only friend. Ever since she . . ." His mouth turns down. "Left, or didn't leave . . . After her and my mom, you guys are all I have. I wouldn't want to mess that up."

I know what it's like to give something a try and have it go cataclysmically awful. In fact, I have my pick: attempting to date Reid, trying to solve the mysteries of this place, losing the job I kind of actually liked . . .

"Shit." I stand up and grab my phone and bag.

"What is it?"

"I was supposed to get my things from the Windsor before they close for Thanksgiving." I check the time. It's nearly six. "I'll just gateway in and be right back."

"All good. Me and about six thousand pages of notes will be here waiting for you."

I study Peter and his kind eyes, and I find I mean it when I say, "Lucky me."

I TRUDGE THROUGH campus in nothing but an oversized sweater and a short skirt, shivering until my teeth's clacking annoys me so much I leave my mouth open like I've got a bad cold. I left my long coat in the commons, but I'm in too much of a rush to go get it. And, candidly, feeling a little too masochistic. I deserve the biting air on my legs. I want to feel as miserable physically as I do in my hollow center. An image of Fiona, leaving for the night, passing my cluttered desk on her way out, twists my stomach. I can only imagine her inner monologue: *Viv can't even make it on time to get her things after she's been fired. Good riddance.* The thought of her disappointment makes my eyes burn. Or maybe that's the howling wind.

When I get up to the sixth floor of the Windsor, prickly, anxious sweat beads at the back of my neck. All the office lights are off but one. I should've known.

"She finally shows," Fiona calls out. I have no idea how she knows it's me. Perhaps she's memorized what the labored, panicky breaths of a disappointing assistant/sister-in-law sound like. Would be niche, but I wouldn't put it past her.

I just want to get this over with.

"Hey," I say, stepping into her office.

But to my deepest displeasure, my mom's sitting on Fiona's leather couch, and Nora's perched on her desk.

"Viv," my mom says in greeting. Her entire face shifts when she sees the black eye Deacon gave me. It's better now than it was days ago, but the swollen, tender flesh around my eye socket is still as colorful as a peacock's feather. "What *happened* to you?"

"I tripped on a curb."

My mother shakes her head, fingers pressed to her lips. "I wish you'd take better care of yourself."

"You look like a Hells Angel," Nora says, studying my eye. "Or a bounty hunter."

Fiona's sitting at her desk, closing out a few windows on her computer. She doesn't even look up at me.

"Hey, Fiona," I try.

She doesn't budge. It's like a gut punch.

I know how upset all three of them are with me for missing the exhibit. There's a part of me that wishes I could just come clean. Something about my conversation with Peter—the way he blames his eight-year-old self for not saving his mom, all that he's too afraid to tell Sophia—makes me want to be brave. To tell my family everything. From why losing my dad hurt in more ways than anyone ever understood up to how I wasn't at the exhibit because I was too busy fighting the wrong battles, alienating my closest friend, and taking out years of anger on the only person who has ever understood why it's so damn difficult to be what I am.

Since Fiona refuses to acknowledge me, I redirect to my mom and Nora. "What are you guys doing here?"

"We're taking Fiona to dinner at Maison. To celebrate the success of the exhibit."

I nod, pursing my lips. "Congratulations, Fiona."

Nada.

And for whatever reason, it's the hurt in her eyes that gets me. Not the disappointment, not the expectation, not the anger. I didn't just let the Windsor down, or my mom, or Nora. I let Fiona down. I always got the sense Fiona kind of believed in me.

"Fiona," I say, ignoring my mom's and Nora's curious eyes. "I'm really sorry. The night of the exhibit I was trying to help someone who I thought was in danger. It's no excuse, but you can rest easy knowing I've been sufficiently punished."

Finally, she looks up. "That's kind of the point of being fired."

"Yeah, and I basically got dumped too, and Penny won't talk to me . . ."

"Dumped?" my mom echoes. "I thought you and James broke up last month?"

Whoops. I'll tackle that nightmare conversation later.

Fiona takes her oversized glasses off and rubs her temples until her eyes close. "I don't ask much of you, Viv. I was fine with the break you needed, even if it was a lie. I've never dinged you for coming in late or leaving early."

My mom scoffs at that, and I set my teeth against the sound.

"I know how much pressure sits on your shoulders. You're doing the best you can, and for me, Viv, that's enough. Really, it is. And you can joke all you want and say this job was a waste of time, but I think you enjoyed it."

I fight the unfamiliar pang in my chest. "I do—I did."

"Part of growing up is understanding there are consequences to our actions."

At that, my mom can't help herself. "I fear Viv may never understand that concept."

It's a gut-wrenching combination—baring my soul to Fiona only to have my mother mock me and knowing she's right and I just keep messing up and never learning. And still, I've tried so hard for years to make up for the consequences of *one* action—or inaction, I should say—that upended my entire life and made my mother look at me the way she is right now. Maybe Reid was right. Maybe my desire to save Harker was rooted in thinking it might somehow make up for not saving my father. In that ridiculous pursuit, I lost almost everything that mattered to me.

And I'm fed up. And tired. And sick of dancing around it all. I turn to my mom and ask her point-blank. "What have I done to make you hate me so fucking much?"

Nora's jaw practically unhinges from her mouth. Fiona's eyes snap to mine. My mother's face twists—just a split second of pain—before she schools her features, stands from the couch, and says with utter, perilous calm, "Will you two give us a moment?"

Nora and Fiona—adult women—file out of *Fiona's own office* like scolded schoolchildren.

Their absence makes the entire room feel like it's yawned open wider than the Chasm itself. My mother might as well be light-years away, but I don't take a single step toward her.

For long, torturous moments, we just stand there. Her in her winter-white dress pants and cashmere cardigan. Her neatly cut nails with their cream polish. Her razor-blunt bob and dermatologist-friendly skin.

And me in a miniskirt and no coat. Black eye. Heart bared on my sleeve.

"How could you think that I hate you?"

I don't say anything, though my hands have begun to tremble. Something about this conversation is scarier than any deviant I've fought.

"If I am hard on you, it's because I love you. If I pushed you toward James, it's because he can take care of you. I don't see you keeping a steady job, Viv, do you?" She gestures to the very office where we stand as if I don't know why I'm here to collect my things.

"He told me what you said," I manage. "That he could do better."

She purses her lips at that. I can tell from her weighing eyes that she's debating whether to cop to it or not. My mother is many things, but a liar is not one of them. "James asked me for advice when your relationship was rocky. He said he could have his pick of women in this city, and I agreed with him."

A cruel, hurt laugh snaps out of me. "That's really nice, Mom."

"But . . ." she says. "But I reminded him that you are fiercer and smarter and more protective of those you love than any debutante in Astera. And he stayed with you until you broke his heart."

"Oh, please."

"You don't believe he loved you, or you don't believe I championed you with him?"

"Neither one, actually."

Her brows pull together. "Everything I have done in my life, Viv, I've done for you and your sister to have the best."

Through clenched teeth I say, "That's a load."

"Watch your tongue."

"You're dating a soulless billionaire for my sister and me to have the best? Funny, it feels like that one's for your career, no?"

"I am not *dating* Caspar Harlock. He's backing my mayoral—"

"Campaign, I know. I didn't realize donors took their candidates to Maison for dinner."

My mother's face tightens in anger. "He and I are friends. He has a difficult child too. He's given me great advice, actually, on—"

"A *difficult* child?" A nasty laugh blasts out of me. "Nora, I'm assuming?"

"Vivienne! You're going to stand here and tell me you haven't made my life difficult? All the injuries and bruises?" She gestures to my ruined eye. "The missed classes at Belaire and skipping college and the chronic tardiness and the mood swings? Sullen and cold one moment, bursting with anger the next—I'm a human too, Viv. Being your mother didn't come with a rule book. I'm doing the best I can."

Her words hurt so much more than she intends. She's outlining every reason it's hard to be my mom, but worse, every reason it's hard to be *me*. I didn't pick this. I don't want to be this person. In fact, I was willing to brave a deadly spell to change myself completely until . . .

Until everything happened. With Kitty. With Lyra. With Reid.

My mother sighs, sitting down on the edge of Fiona's desk. But I don't say a thing. I'm scared that if I do, I'll cry.

"I have worked hard—harder than you can imagine—to be a decent mother to you. To give you both a better life. To get you out of the neighborhood that took your father from us."

I don't want to argue. Really, I don't. I may want to fight—to drive my fists or daggers into something—but I don't want to argue with my mother. Especially about this. Still, I find myself saying, "That wasn't for us. That was for *you*. Your ambition. Your political career. Nora and I didn't want to leave Lethe."

"I couldn't be in that house another minute!"

I take in a breath. Silence pounds through the room.

My mother's lips are trembling as she says, "Not after we lost David. And you—you were children. You didn't know what you wanted. You were children mourning a tremendous loss, and I did what I felt was right. That's part of being a mother, and I don't expect you to understand."

"At least we actually mourned."

The look on her face might have been priceless to me at one time. Right now, it carves my heart in two. "What did you just say?"

I set my jaw as if bracing for a punch. Tears brim in my eyes. "You didn't miss him. You never cried."

"I worked *tirelessly* to find the men that killed him, Viv—"

"You made me take all his things—"

"I couldn't look at them!" My mom presses her fingers to the bridge of her nose. For a moment she just inhales. Only then do I have the horrifying realization that she's tearing up too. "I couldn't look at them for years. Avoiding photos in my own house... Vivienne, I can't hear *music*. I can listen to it, but I can't *hear* it. Losing your father *broke* something in me."

"And you blame me for that. I know you do."

"No, Viv," she says, stepping toward me.

"Yes," I say through my tears. "You wish it had been me, not him."

My mom's face crumples. "No—"

But her words are swallowed up by the Windsor security alarm—a jarring, repetitive blast that blares overhead as red lights flash down the hall.

"What's going on?" she breathes.

A rumble and the unmistakable noise of crashing glass sound in a wing down the hall. Too far for my mom's mortal ears to hear, but I can tell—someone's broken into the museum. And with the way my body buzzes, the way my skin grows taut along my bones—I know that someone is a deviant.

CHAPTER 43

"EVERYONE OUT," I yell, dragging my mother from Fiona's office.

In the darkened hallway, Nora's pacing on the phone, but Fiona is nowhere to be found. Nora's eyes find mine, waves of fear cresting in them. "She just took off—"

"You have to leave," I tell Nora. "Now."

"What about you?" my mother says.

"I'm going to find Fiona."

"Me too," Nora says, pocketing her phone. "She's not answering my calls. But Astera PD is on their way."

Somewhere, one story below, I can hear a group moving across the marbled halls. Not Fiona's clacky heels or other archivists working late. Heavy boots thumping toward the new wing. The Chasm exhibit.

"Nora," I say, grasping her arms. "Get Mom out of here. Let me find Fiona. I know this place better than you do. She's probably turning on the emergency lockdown system and is safe in a panic room. I'll be okay, I promise."

Nora kisses me on the head and mutters, "Please find her."

"I will," I say. "Go. Both of you."

My mother looks back at me once, tears still fresh in her eyes, before Nora drags her toward the emergency exit stairwell. Once they're safely through, I bolt in the other direction. There's another set of stairs that will take me down to the Chasm exhibit.

Bloodlust echoes through my bones. For a herd of deviants to break into the Windsor . . .

That requires time and energy and organization. It's got to be the Brood. And if they took Fiona . . . As much as I may want to, I cannot fight them alone.

I could call Sophia or Elliot. Even Peter, but—

The realization hits like a sledgehammer: There's no one I want to fight alongside more than Reid. He's older and wiser. Better versed in deviants than any of us students could ever be, because he is one. I think back to last week, when he saved me from his own brother. The steely resolve in his eyes. The juggernaut force of his strength. He's the only one I want to charge into battle with.

My fingers are already dialing his number when I hear the sound of glass shattering. I slip through the doors and into the darkened exhibit lit only by the red streaks of the flashing alarm light.

He answers on the first ring. "Hey."

"Reid—"

"Where are you?" There's an urgency in his voice. He sounds like he could chew through iron. He must be able to hear the alarms, or my fear.

"The Windsor. The Brood is here." I move silently through the exhibit like an alley cat in the night. Mounted maps of the Chasm and infographics of its many layers have been left untouched. Artistic renditions by eighteenth-century neoclassical painters safe behind their double-paned plastic casings. But the displays filled with artifacts found within Chasm sediment have been destroyed.

"Get out of there," he instructs. I can hear him pushing through a door and out into whipping winter wind. "*Now*, Viv."

But I'm trying to understand what I'm looking at. Priceless jewels and vaguely Byzantine scrolls scatter the floor. Texts rife with demonic symbols historians still think are Sumerian—torn to shreds. Fiona is going to be apoplectic. But then other sections—the photography and the busts of the archaeologists who discovered Astera—are completely unharmed. The Brood isn't here to destroy but rather to find something. But what? Low murmurs sound from the next room. "They might have my sister-in-law."

Reid's hushed curse is a deadly sound. "I'm two minutes from the gateway."

"I'll meet you by the volcanic rock," I whisper.

I hang up and flatten myself against the wall of igneous particles found in the depths of the Chasm. Trembling, I peer around the corner. Illuminated only by the bare-bones after-hours light and the flashes of pale red are five burly, lethal-looking men, each with the brand of the Brood. I don't spy Fiona, which I tell myself is a relief, not a death sentence. No scent of human blood, either—if there were overnight security guards in this room, it seems they ran in time.

I pray the NTC police are slow tonight. If they arrive now, they'll be slaughtered in seconds.

"Do you know what it looks like, Your Highness?" one demon asks.

I clench my teeth against a sudden, unwelcome chill. There's a sound like ice cracking on a frigid pond. When I look down, frost has swept across the floor where I stand, over my shoes, and up the glass cases that house the artifacts. It clings to my bare, goose-bumped legs. I can taste it on my tongue—a bitter, barren cold.

A hooded figure in a decadent wool cloak slips into the room before me, moving across the exhibit so seamlessly, it's as if he's floating, carried on an icy, malicious wind.

"There," replies his distorted tone, low and sharp as a stab wound. "Fetch it for me."

The voice does more than send prickles beneath my skin. It threatens to knock me to my knees. A voice filled with more power—more *cruelty*—than anything I've ever heard. It's not human. It's barely demonic. It's something else entirely—

The High Thane.

I know it in my bones. Bracing myself against the aching need to tear his head from his body is like weathering a storm.

When a new vibration courses through my skin, I spin, daggers out, and press them to Reid's pulsing throat. His skin singes with the contact, but he doesn't step away from me.

"Shit," I whisper, yanking my weapons back. There's a burn mark on his Adam's apple. "Sorry."

"You're okay," he murmurs, relief shining in his shadowed eyes. His hand moves to cup my face, but he lowers it before making contact. Only then do I remember we're supposed to be done. So dumb, all of it.

"The High Thane's in there," I tell him. "And five of his men. They're here to steal something. I need to find Fiona . . . She ran when they broke in. I'd guess to protect the relics and the art."

"Let me handle them."

"I'm never going to run from a fight." It comes out like an apology. "I know that terrifies you."

He shakes his head, jaw ticking. "You have no idea."

"I'll go in first. Cover me?"

He nods, grim, and when I look down, I see his hands have been replaced with those treacherous, bloodred claws. Pointed nails as black as oblivion tip his gnarled fingers. A part of me wants to reach out and take one in my hand.

At the sound of glass cascading down to the marble floor, I peek out to get one more look at what I'm going into. The High Thane's eyes—yellow and slitted—glow like a viper's beneath his heavy hood. Beside him, another hulking figure conjures a door in the middle of the gallery. A gateway—

Adrenaline sluices through me as I rush for them, but the Brood's warlock and the High Thane have already stepped through. The door vanishes and becomes a wall just as the remaining four Broods turn to me and glare.

Menacing faces. Fiendish claws. Punishing grins.

There's no time to waste.

I drive my daggers into arms and leather and the odd marble podium when they're too quick for me. Reid's right on my tail, slashing and grunting with each blow. Roaring as the men dodge and weave past him.

I nearly drive my dagger into the neck of a thick-bearded Brood when he whirls around and shoves me to the floor. He lands atop me, breathing raggedly in my ear. I lash out with my knees and fists, using his weight against him as best I can, but his mouth is too close to mine. I can feel the shift—the moment he's decided to drink my soul rather than kill me instantly. The way his body goes rigid with perverse, murderous want.

In the distance, Reid's tearing one of them up, ripping demon flesh to strips between his claws. I try to call for him, but the Brood is on my windpipe. I can't make a noise. Can't shove him off me. I'm pinned. Not strong enough, not able to breathe—

No. No—

The Brood's laugh is insidious as it curls over my mouth. I try to turn away, but his claws hold me by the cheeks. "Stay still, hunter girl."

"Like hell she will," a woman's voice calls before a spear of silver plunges through his heart and splatters me in bright red demon blood.

I'm sputtering, scraping the iron-rich liquid from my tongue, when I finally look up and see—

"Professor Lisette?"

"Up," she instructs. Her thin blond hair is pulled back, and she's in fighting leathers more commonly worn by hunters back in the day. She fights with a two-sided spear, driving its silver points into demons on either side of her.

Still catching my breath, I store my confusion away for later and plunge my dagger into a demon who's about to sink his fanged teeth into Reid's neck. When I whip around to see who's behind me, I realize the three of us are alone.

Four demon bodies lie on the floor of the Chasm exhibit, blood leaking slowly across the shiny granite floor. Our breaths sound ragged under the alarm that continues to blare. My head aches from the noise.

"Are you hurt?" Reid's voice is a rasp. He's standing before me, shirt shredded, doused in demon blood. After a quick scan of his body, I know, thankfully, very little of it is his own.

I shake my head. "I'm fine. You called Lisette?"

Now it's his eyes that narrow in confusion.

"He didn't," a familiar voice says behind me. "I was here already, Viv."

When I turn toward the sound, I find Fiona. She's wearing Professor Lisette's hunter leathers, her hand clutched around that same double-ended spear.

"What the fuck?"

CHAPTER 44

"I KNOW THIS is a lot to take in," Fiona says.

"What the fuck?" I repeat. My heart is so high up my throat I could puke it out. "What is going on?"

Reid is equally shocked beside me. "Gemeline, you're . . . a shifter?"

"A dichotomous shifter, to be precise."

Two forms only, if I recall from Peter's Lymantrian Beings flash cards. "So when you're Fiona—"

"I'm mortal," she says. "But when I'm Gemeline, I'm a hunter, yes."

"Does Nora know?"

Fiona shakes her head. "I never intended to fall in love with a mortal. It just happened. I still haven't figured out how to tell her what I am."

All those jokes I made about Fiona being old . . . Shifters live a lot longer than regular hunters. She's probably been around for fifty or sixty years. And the strange feelings I had whenever we spoke, like she was keeping something from me . . . The laugh that breaks from me is verging on delirious. "The sugary coffee, the bare feet, the bad glasses . . ."

"Excuse me?"

But I can't stop the thoughts now. She allowed me to take that break from the Windsor. She never asked follow-up questions about my senseless, made-up campaign job with my mom. She tried to keep me out of trouble at Harker more times than I can count—I thought she had it out for me, when all along it's been the very opposite. Though I didn't realize it then, she was even encouraging me to attend Harker that first day before orientation when we spoke in her office.

"That's why you work such insane hours. You aren't traveling for work—you're teaching at Harker. You're living a double life too." I've spent my entire life thinking I was alone, when another hunter has been right under my nose. "You knew this whole time I was a student at Harker . . ."

"Long before that." She tuts. "I got you your job here at the Windsor as soon as I figured out you were a hunter. I knew firsthand how much easier it would make enrolling at Harker."

A year ago, when she saw me with the chalice and the amulet. When I lied about praying for Penny . . . She offered me the job here only a few days afterward. Not knowing I was an aeon, she probably thought I'd just begun to come into my abilities. "I thought you believed my Penny breakup story."

A small smile perks up on her face. "I teach Underworld Studies. I know what a ritual for succubus entrapment looks like."

I turn to Reid. "So I wasn't recruited by coincidence . . . Lisette told you there was a rogue hunter in Astera?"

Reid nods, still in his own shock. "I get tips from professors like that all the time. Didn't think anything of it." He looks to Fiona. "How does nobody at Harker know?"

"Some of the Elders are aware that I work at the Windsor in my mortal form. They entrusted me to keep an eye on this place.

There are lymantrians on the board, important artifacts stored here for safekeeping . . . I've successfully protected this place for years. Until tonight . . ."

My eyes crawl over the demon ash and spilled blood. "The High Thane was here."

"Yes," Fiona says faintly.

"Surveillance cameras?" Reid asks.

"We can doctor them. One of the perks of the Elders owning the institution."

"The High Thane and a turned warlock of his got away," I say.

Fiona nods. "And with the censer."

"Fucking hell," Reid groans, bringing his hand to the bridge of his nose.

"What's the censer?"

"I had it in my office the day you first went to Harker. That antique brass vessel? It was only just discovered a few days before then. It burns ritual herbs and incense. If the right blend is used on the new moon, it can ward off spells cast on demons."

The new moon . . . "When is that?"

Fiona's expression hardens. "Tomorrow."

And suddenly everything slams into shocking, gut-wrenching place. I turn to Reid. "That's why whoever took the asphodels and Lyra was in such a rush. Whatever the High Thane is planning . . . he's going to try to do it by tomorrow."

But it's more than that. All of this—the wraith attack, the zombie spell, the missing dagger—began after the censer was found at the end of the summer. Right around my first day at Harker, like Fiona said. A censer that protects demons from spells . . . I try to remember the steps of casting a syrabraxa: finding the ingredients to brew the spell, imbuing that concoction into the host, and then killing them. But after that, once the endless power has been granted to the killer ... madness descends. Drowned armadas, raw livers.

"Could the censer be the High Thane's contingency plan to stay sane after casting the syrabraxa? A way to ward off the madness caused by using the spell's power?"

Reid's face is a shadowed wreck. "Possibly."

"So it's true." Fiona's expression could strip paint from the Windsor's walls. "Someone is trying to brew a syrabraxa? That's why you went looking for the asphodels?" When I nod, she swallows thickly. "Dark magic like that in the hands of the High Thane would be ..."

"Dangerous." Reid supplies.

But Fiona's eyes have gone haunted. "Cataclysmic."

"And," I add, "he has help from someone at Harker."

I was right that night at Fever Dream. Whoever at Harker is plotting to brew the spell has been working with the High Thane all along. I just wasn't right about *who* the High Thane was. Not Deacon. Not anyone we have any leads on.

"You really never met him when you were in the Brood?" I ask Reid. "You don't have any way to find him?"

Reid shakes his head, eyes on all the broken wood and glass. "The current High Thane isn't the deadliest one deviants have ever knelt before, but he is the most cunning. He knew he couldn't best his predecessor physically, so he waited until the High Thane would least suspect it and killed him one afternoon during a casual game of chess. Had an entire mutiny ready and seized the Throne of Bael in half an hour. That was about two centuries ago." A shocking flash of demon blood splattering a castle wall sparks in my mind, and I shudder away from the sick thrill that curls low inside me. "Point is, he's not the type to let just anyone in his Brood know his identity."

That must be what the hooded cloak is for. But something doesn't add up. I know how monarchies work. "The High Thane before him had no children to take the throne?"

Reid's eyes are dark when they find mine. "He did."

Even though they were demons, the thought is chilling.

"I need to contact the Citadel and the dean with all this," Fiona interrupts. "And make sure Nora is all right." She's already sliding her spear down to its compact size and slotting it into the holster at her hip. "Can you two clean this up?"

"What about Astera PD?" I ask. "Nora said she called them, but they never came. Even if she hadn't, the whole neighborhood must have heard that alarm."

"Half of Astera's police are deviants on the payroll of the Brood. I doubt they're coming. But I'll make sure the neighbors know it was a false alarm, and I'll tell your mother and Nor the same. And that I asked you to stay behind and help me with some things before we close for the holiday."

Something small flutters in my chest. Silly, despite everything. Still, I can't help but ask, "Does that mean I get my job back?"

Fiona sighs. "I didn't fire you just to keep up appearances, Viv. It's a lesson I owe to you as both your teacher and your family to help you learn: To live a successful life as a hunter, you can't neglect who you are as a human. I don't want to see you forfeit your relationship with your mother and sister for the hunt. It's a balance."

My eyes find my feet. She's right. She's managed both for years.

"But . . . let's call it probation?"

When I look up, she isn't smiling, but her eyes are warm. She gives Reid and me one last nod before disappearing around the corner. A minute later, the alarm finally shuts off, as well as the red emergency glow, drowning the trashed exhibit hall in low, after-hours lighting.

"Well," Reid says with a sigh. "Your sister-in-law is a tenured professor at Harker."

"Yeah," I mutter. "And that's not even the biggest bombshell of the night."

Reid's voice is tight as he takes in the carnage. "We'll stop him."

I don't say what I'm thinking: *How can we?*

Reid bends down and begins to scoop up broken shards of glass. I go to the storage closet where I spent so many months grabbing coffee beans and rulers and paper towels for Fiona and the other executives—all the while there was an entire world of information I was missing about almost everything in my life. Harker, Fiona, the High Thane's plans, how my mom felt about losing my dad . . . It's been a night of revelations, to say the least.

I return with plastic trash bags, a mop, and a bucket. Reid does the dirty work, cleaning up ash and blood, while I use a pair of gloves to carefully collect as many relics, photos, and artifacts as I can. Just as I've watched Fiona do, I handle each one with care, placing them back into what remains of their cases. Fiona's going to have to put together quite the cover-up to explain the damage that Reid and I can't fix tonight.

When the exhibit looks less like there was a demonic battle and more like a rabid bird got trapped inside, Reid and I take exhausted seats side by side on the marble floor. Bathed in near pitch-darkness, illuminated only by the low safety lights along the walkways and the moonlight gilding the stained glass above, his strong jaw and masculine nose take on an otherworldly beauty I can barely look right at.

He wipes his hands down the front of his pants, and I'm hit so hard with the fact that he's about to stand up and walk away that I grow dizzy. Any second now he'll go back to Harker, contact the dean, and work with the Citadel to track down the High Thane.

We'll spend winter break apart, and the world will keep on turning, and someone will execute their diabolical plot that we couldn't prevent, and I'll spend every night I'm left alive not looking into Reid's storm-drenched eyes or hearing his dry wit or feeling seen and known and cared for.

"Wait," I blurt.

He turns to me, brows pinched. "I wasn't going anywhere."

All this time, I've told Reid he's stubborn, but I'm not sure anyone's been stronger-willed than me. Maybe it's like Fiona said earlier in her office—maybe I've got some consequences to accept and some growing up to do.

"Thank you," I say. "For coming tonight." The skylight above is closed tight to keep out the bitter chill, but I can still hear crickets chirping through the glass. "I know we weren't really talking."

"Viv . . ." He shakes his head like I'm missing something obvious. "We had an argument. I was giving you the space you asked for. But your safety . . ." He draws a hand over his mouth. "I'll always come for you. No questions asked."

"Thank you," I say again. I put my hand on his knee for emphasis and then lift it just as quickly. Too intimate. Too familiar. Reid's eyes linger on the spot where I touched him as if it were scalding.

It hits me like a mallet over the head how badly I wish things were different. It's like we're back in the planetarium, only this time I just want to pretend we're still Viv and Reid—hunter and demon—not the Viv who's fucked everything up between us.

"I was wrong. To push you away and . . ." I swallow my racing pulse.

"I was the one—"

"No, I never should have gone to Fever Dream without you. We're better as a team. Remember the strzyga?"

His hand slips over mine, warm and strong. "Remember it?"

Reid's fingers tighten, his thumb brushing over the curves of my knuckles until I shiver. "That was the night I realized I was falling in love with you."

The words still my mind. I open my mouth and close it again. Silence drowns the room, dotted only by the thud of my pulse.

"Relax," he says softly, eyes on our interlaced fingers. "I don't expect you to feel the same." I swear I can hear his heart beating through the thin cotton of his shirt. "I just wanted you to know."

I do feel the same, though. And it's like a wave crashing over me. Knocking me down and dragging me out to sea. A force I can't fight. One I don't even want to. That undertow is too strong, too knowing, too powerful. It rolls out of me like the first breath after drowning.

"I'm the loneliest person I know." It's not what I was expecting to say, but somehow it feels right. "I see movies and TV shows about loneliness and think, *Those assholes have nothing on me.* It's the worst kind of loneliness too. It's self-imposed and self-pitying." I shake my head. "After my dad died, I didn't think there was a soul on earth who knew what it felt like to be me. And not just because of the hunting—I have hunter friends now." Reid's grim expression softens, and I know images of Sophia and Peter and Elliot fill both our minds. "But it's not just them. It's not just Harker. For a while I was lonely even there, because everyone belonged, and I never did. They'd been raised by hunters . . . In fact, when I got to Harker, I was certain I didn't belong anywhere."

We're the same, Reid and me. Even though we were born on opposing sides of an eternal battle between good and evil, I've found as much volatile evil within myself and as I have good within Reid. Everything he wishes for, I do too. All the qualities that make him doubt and hate and judge himself, I have too. We're two puzzle pieces that never seem to fit.

"Viv—"

"But I belong with you, Reid."

He doesn't say anything for a moment. Only stares at me as if contemplating something weighty and wrecking. I almost tell him I'm an aeon. How nobody knows the self-loathing he struggles with like I do. But then Reid's hand slinks across my cheek and cups my face, and all I can do is lean into his palm. It's like coming home. Like crawling between fresh sheets after a long, hard day. I close my eyes against his warmth.

"Who knew a demon and a huntress could have so much in common?" he says with a sorrowful grin. "When we're together, Viv . . . I don't know. I feel reborn—I see myself in your eyes, and I like the reflection."

"You should always see yourself that way. You're not a monster. You don't take souls. You've been shunned by your own family . . . all to do what's right. That's heroic."

Reid's fingers graze the bruise around my eye. His face twists with regret. "You know I'd never hurt you, right?"

I study his pained face and nod with everything in me.

And I should tell him right now that I'm falling in love with him too. Not only that—that I've never been in love before. That meeting him and fighting with him and arguing and working together and kissing until my lips are raw has changed my brain chemistry so fundamentally that I have become capable of something I never thought was possible for me. Now, where there was just a rotting core like an apple left in the Astera subway grates, there lies a ripe, plum-red beating heart. He's solved me, this demon, with his heroism and his goodness and his mouthwatering half grin. And the world may be on the verge of ending, but I have just started to live, knowing him.

I should tell him exactly that. That he's shown me how to fall in love. And maybe more important, that I've developed feelings for someone with all my same afflictions—he's self-loathing, stubborn, isolated. He'd give anything to be someone else—and I'm falling for him just the same. He's helped me accept myself.

I should tell him all of it.

But I can't.

There's a block where my brain meets my tongue. A synapse that just isn't firing. It feels a lot like self-preservation. That hunter instinct to dodge when something's careening right at you. To jump before you even know a creature's at your feet.

In an effort to shut my brain up once and for all, I press my lips to Reid's.

CHAPTER 45

REID DOESN'T KISS me back immediately. I can feel his breath shudder out against my lips—a tether fraying somewhere inside him. I lace my hands through his soft hair and press my mouth to the curve of his jaw.

"We should"—he growls a little as my tongue traces down the side of his neck—"get back to Harker."

"Not yet," I beg him, lips against his skin. "Not yet."

Before he can respond, I climb on top of him and lower myself into his lap. His hands find my waist, slipping under the hem of my shirt. He's staring at me, eyes lit by only the silver glow of moonlight and the dim exhibit lights.

"And when we do leave"—I dig my hands into his shoulders in emphasis—"we leave together."

His hands tighten on my skin. "Viv . . ."

"I'd follow you anywhere. Harker or otherwise." I study the slope of his nose, the emotion welling in his eyes . . . "You don't have to be alone."

"I don't deserve you." His voice is rough.

"You do. We both deserve happiness, Reid."

He leans close, and I expect his ridiculously drugging lips on mine, but he surprises me by pressing his lips to my forehead. It's such a simple, gentle act that I find tears brimming in my eyes. Forget never having felt this way before. I've never been loved like this. Not by anyone.

We're so close I can feel his heart pound against my own. I can feel the warmth of his chest, smell the lemongrass on his skin, hear the ragged breaths sawing in and out of him. When he pulls away, his cheeks are flushed and his lips are warm. He kisses my cheek and the edge of my jaw. His hands slip easily below the hem of my skirt, where his fingertips graze my hip bones. My core heats and liquifies. I grind myself against his lap like a needy animal.

He closes his eyes. *"Viv."*

I can't even hear past my own heartbeat. The energy between us is as taut as a bowstring. Stretching, stretching elastic about to snap. My legs widen an inch more, pushing me closer, pressing my chest flush against his, my nipples tight and aching. His forehead finds mine, and our lips are so close, and I could cry myself hoarse begging for his mouth on mine.

"Kiss me," I whisper.

All our other kisses—the ones I've fallen asleep thinking of or woken up still tasting—are mild breezes compared to the gale force of this kiss. Desire crests in me higher and higher with every lick and stroke and nip. His hands are everywhere—low on my back, cradling my jaw, touching my hair, my ribs, my fingers. Every inch he pulls me closer sends my body further into overdrive, each nerve lighting up like the star-filled sky outside. My desire for him could rip right through me.

With every brush of our lips, I'm telling Reid, *I've never felt this way before.* My breath, hitching and catching with his groans, a message in morse code: *You. Make. Me. Belong.* I can't think of anything else when he moves against me like this. When he mumbles how beautiful I am. How perfect. How I was made for him. I can't think of why I don't tell him I'm falling in love. Maybe he already knows. I kiss him that much deeper to be sure.

It's wet and breathy, messy and urgent. Clumsy like we're teenagers in the back seat of a car. No fusing of our bodies will be close enough. Every single inch of skin against skin won't be sufficient. And that's fine by me. I'm lit up like a bonfire, crackling and scorching with a need so primal I can't believe my heart hasn't beaten clean out of my chest. I could swear this longing, this burning, is all I've ever known.

Without breaking the kiss, I pull fruitlessly at his shirt. *Off*, I try to tell him. *I need to feel the heat of your skin.* He yanks the offending material over his back and tosses it across the room. For a moment, he stares at my mouth, and I lick my lips, trying and failing to catch my breath.

Until I'm distracted by the swath of tan muscle that ripples below me. He's lean but carved like a marble statue I'd find down the hall. Muscles stacked like bricks. Pecs and abs and forearms. My mouth waters. My hands trace slowly down the swells and divots. Perfect. Spellbinding. Not of this world.

He grunts, allowing me to grope and touch in awe. My hand splays low across his abdomen, feeling the fine hairs beneath his belly button. His fingers slide down to my ass and knead the flesh there. I roll forward involuntarily and feel the hard length he's sporting between my spread legs. Like a crowbar.

"Oh god," I breathe.

He kisses me again, possessive, needy, dragging me across his length over and over. The friction on my clit is dizzyingly good. His huge, warm hands slide beneath my thong and grasp my ass. My fingers curl at his collarbone and around his shoulders. I whine a little when his cock under his pants hits just right, and he responds with a gruff "Yeah. Yeah."

His voice is an accelerator. I rub myself against him. Kissing has become too hard—requiring too much focus—so our lips are just brushing as we share breath, exchanging pleading, plaintive noises. My nipples are too sensitive against his chest, and I wish I'd worn a bra to protect myself from this kind of torment.

"Maybe we—" He cuts himself off with a throaty groan. He sounds like he's losing it a bit, but I'm too focused on the orgasm that's building from the friction alone. His tongue slides down my neck until his teeth capture my sweater. I rip it off and moan helplessly when his hands cup my breasts and squeeze.

"Jesus," he gasps. "Your body—" He winces, slamming himself back into the wall behind us. Only then do I notice that without my sweater as a buffer, my silver locket has scalded his skin.

"Oh," I breathe. "I'm so sorry,"

He rubs at his chest. "Don't be."

Carefully, I pull the necklace over my head and drop it safely atop my sweater on the floor beneath us. It's the first time I've taken it off in months.

Reid's mouth captures my own again, and his hips buck upward as if he's not even aware of the motion. His thumbs brush across my nipples until I squirm. Wriggling closer, needing more, panting like a dog in heat. Filthy. This is *filthy*. To fuck where we've just killed. I wish it didn't ignite me the way it does, but my vision has melted into sparks and stars, my body fused into one long current of pure electricity, and the cacophony of my swallowed whimpers and his muted growls is becoming deafening.

"Reid," I whine when his mouth sucks beneath my ear. His hands haven't left my breasts, cupping, massaging. Flicking my nipples until the ache between my legs is unbearable. "Reid," I repeat.

"Shh," he soothes. Another slow lick at my neck. "We can slow down."

I don't know how to tell him that's not what I want. That I want him to wreck me inside and out. I try to breathe through his leisurely ministrations. To let him take his time with me.

"I've never been able to get you out of my head," he murmurs. "It's like torture."

"I know the feeling," I whine as his cock pulses against my core.

Some merciful instinct has him scooping me up and laying me down on the cold museum floor, caging his arms over me.

"More," I plead.

He laughs lightly. "I'll crush you."

"Do it."

I pull at him, trying to get him to press all that delicious weight onto every pulsing part of me. Closer, closer, closer. I don't want any space between us. Where he ends, I begin. I arch my back, fusing us together until he releases a low, throaty noise that I feel in my stomach.

He reaches behind me and grabs his shirt, shoving it under my head like a makeshift pillow. He yanks my skirt and my thong down in one swift, confident motion, and I kick them out from under us, then lie bare beneath him. He swears as his eyes travel down my body. Then he sits back on his heels.

I watch him through lowered lashes. His hands are braced on his thighs, his chest rising and falling with choppy, rushed breaths. His abdomen contracting as the painful bulge beneath his pants twitches.

But it's his eyes I can't stop coming back to. They're darker.

Ringed in red. Half-gone with lust and need. And I'm wet. Shamelessly so. The way he's looking at me sends a trickle of it down my thigh. Motivated by something I've never felt, I bend my knees, planting my feet on the floor, and spread my legs for him. Heat blooms across my cheeks and down my chest, but I don't care. I need him to see what he's doing to me.

"Fuck," Reid chokes out, eyes rolling back in his head. His hands turn to fists along his thighs. A muted growl rumbles in his chest . . . and two curled ram's horns sprout from the crown of his head.

Oh my god.

The ridges glow in the moonlight, glossy and black and ancient.

"You said they weren't real." My voice is barely audible.

I've never seen a demon's horns. Monstrous, violent things. And yet . . . so beautiful. I blink at him in shameless, terrified wonder.

"Shit," Reid curses, shutting his eyes. His hand fists his cock over his pants. "I just need a minute . . . I'm sorry—"

"Don't be," I rasp. It's as loud as my voice will go. I sit up to reach a hand out carefully. "Can I?"

Reid's brows lift in guarded surprise. I nod once to tell him I'm serious, and he crawls over me until the horns reach my outstretched palm. Only then do I realize my hand is shaking. But he says nothing, and neither do I as I brush my fingers over the curved bone. Reid shudders out a groan.

"Sensitive?"

He only nods, his head bowing lower over my stomach. My fingers touch lightly, and he makes a sound like he's punctured a lung.

"I lied." His voice is so low I barely hear him. "When you asked if I wanted your soul."

My heart stalls in my chest. Somehow I've forgotten in my yearning that the man I've fallen for isn't a man at all. And I couldn't be more vulnerable: utterly naked, flushed, and breathless. I don't even have my daggers on me.

But Reid's words echo in my head: *You know I'd never hurt you, right?*

"Is it very hard?" I ask shakily. "To fight it?"

He nods, eyes still downcast. "I want all of you. Everything you've got, I want."

"Take me, then," I tell him. "Make me yours."

I stroke his horn once more with the pads of my fingers, and Reid brings his mouth hungrily to the inside of my thigh. His tongue sweeps closer and closer to my core as I lay back down, unable to hold myself up a second longer.

My eyes shut tightly when his lips brush over my core. "Yes." A sharp intake of breath. "Oh. Right there—"

Please don't ever stop. Never take your mouth off me.

He laps at me until I'm on the edge. I scrape my fingers over the cool marble, mewling and pleading until he sinks a finger inside me. My body fills with heat, so much I can't keep still—twitching and squirming. Convulsing with need. He adds another and clutches me tightly around the waist while he fucks me with his fingers.

"Oh god," I babble. "Oh god. Oh god."

"I need to be inside you," he murmurs, almost more to himself than to me. He lifts his head, and I find eyes that are wild, shoulders rippling, horns as sharp as spears. "Can I?"

I nod so eagerly my neck strains. He pushes his fingers in and out of me once more and a whimper catches in my throat. The sound of my own arousal is loud in the empty museum wing, but I'm too needy to care.

"Shit," he says with dark realization, palming his cock under his pants. He is furiously hard. Ferociously so. "I don't have anything."

"That's okay," I whisper. "It's not like you can get me pregnant."

"I haven't been with anyone—"

"I know," I tell him. "Come here." My hands itch to touch him. To feel his heat and smell his skin. I fear a horrible addiction has been born tonight. Some far-off corner of my mind wonders how I'll spend a single minute away from him after this.

"You can't imagine how long I've been thinking about this," he says, taking off his pants and boxers. In the half-light I make out a weighty length between his legs, and my limbs go boneless. Nothing demonic about him there but his size. I sit up to wrap my hand around the velvety skin. Reid grunts, jaw grinding shut. His hips jerk forward and a little drop of moisture beads at the head of his cock.

"Since that night we set fire to Maria's?" I ask, dazed.

His voice is strangled. "Long before that."

"Since you saved me from becoming werewolf dinner?" I'm babbling because I'm nervous and I know he can tell. This means something, what we're about to do.

Reid shakes his head, pushing us both back down to the floor until he's caged over me once more. He angles my knee up and apart to seat himself between my legs. "I could have killed him in a dozen ways for how he looked at you."

"Oh." I swallow hard. My hands are loose around his neck. "When, then?"

"Viv," he says, pulling back so I can see the full picture of his night-blue eyes and mussed hair and deadly demon horns. "We don't have to do this."

"I want to," I breathe. "Badly." Need is pulsing between my legs.

"Well, it may be faster than I'm proud of."

He eases himself inside me. I'm caught somewhere between the acute pleasure of hearing Reid's groans and the pain of being stretched larger than I'm quite ready for. When I wince a bit, Reid goes still. "Viv—"

"Don't stop," I stutter.

"But—"

I'm aching when I plead, "I'm serious."

Reid frowns at me before sitting up to grip my shaking thighs. Abs clenching, horns thrusting from his head, he jerks in another inch with a low, rumbling groan. I wonder how much of that pained noise is him fighting his baser demon instincts. Fighting the urge to swallow my soul.

His fingers dig into the flesh of my leg until they go white. The image is so profoundly erotic, made even less bearable by his thumb coaxing over my clit to soften me. I grow wetter as he soothes, relieving the strain, and he slides in to the hilt, releasing nearly inaudible praise as he does. "Good. Yeah. Don't move . . . *Fuck*, Viv—"

When I moan and buck up toward him, nearing that edge, Reid comes down over me to lick the column of my neck and the dip of my collarbone. Obscene sounds echo through the cavernous room. Wet and messy, liquid hot. Grunts and gasps of pleasure. We're both sweating, trembling, writhing along each other, and that ache in my core is building and building every time he hits that spot inside me in time with his fingers at the apex of my thighs . . . The pressure is unimaginable. Low in my stomach, fluttering down my thighs and into my belly. Like a soda bottle in an earthquake.

"Shit," he groans desperately against my neck. "Wait—stop for just—"

I clench around him, feeling him in every inch of me, heart hammering, sweat dripping, teeth clenched, and then a sweep of pleasure so tremendous it's nearly frightening cuts through my entire body.

It's not dainty or subtle like the orgasms I've faked in the past or even the rare few I've had. This is a wrecking, dirty, screeching thing. Reid's hand comes down over my mouth as he fucks me, grinding and desperate, hips rolling, groaning my name over and over again as he endures a devastating climax of his own.

We both float back down to earth. His horns have receded, and we're sticky, sweaty messes, panting naked on the floor of the Windsor, lit by that same low exhibit light. The last thought I have before I fall asleep in Reid's arms is that if everything were different, I might finally be happy.

CHAPTER 46

I PRESS MY face to the metal to try to hear more and find a crack in the container wall. A sliver I can see through—

Blood. Flashes of silver. Twelve demons against my dad. It's not a fair fight. And they all carry the mark of the Brood.

He's screaming as he drives his sword, bleeding from his ribs and neck . . .

I know he needs me. But no matter how hard I pry at the container door, it doesn't budge—

One rugged man whose face I can't see in the dark swings at him. I can hear the muffled recognition in my dad's voice. He isn't surprised. "You," he says. "After all this time . . . At least tell me why."

I don't hear the man's response. I see only a flash of light. Fire, maybe? Lightning? It isn't raining. The men converge. My dad's silver sword shrieks against claws.

"Come on, Dad," I whisper. I know the demons have hearing as good as my own. It doesn't stop me from chanting, "Come on, come on."

I press my hands together in some kind of useless prayer. I beg whoever is listening to make sure my dad survives. Why did so many Broods follow us tonight? What do they want with him?

They're slicing him down. Pushing him toward the railing of the docks. They have him cornered. If I'm going to help, it has to be now. I don't care how the container door bangs. Now, now, now—

But I can't get free.

He doesn't let the demons take him. Not his soul, not his life. He utters something I can't hear and flings himself over the docks into the churning water below.

My fist finds my mouth to stanch a scream. I sob into my hands.

A few of the demons curse. They're angry. They wanted to kill him. The burly man he recognized tips his head over the edge to stare at the ocean water.

When the Broods have left and I've cried everything I have inside of me onto the rusting base of the shipping container, the police come. I yell until they find me, and when they shove the door open, I land hard on the wooden dock. My bones ache from weeping. My eyes are dry and raw. I hurtle past them toward the railing, and there, floating in the raging, roiling sea, is my father's lifeless body.

I scream for him until my voice has left me.

Then I scream more, new, fresh tears cresting in my eyes and dripping down my face as I watch his body bob in the choppy water. The pain is unbearable. The thought of never being able to turn to him when I'm afraid.

I scream for my dad until I'm certain I'll pass out from the way it rips at my throat.

And even then, I can't stop—

"VIV!"

I jolt upright, sucking in huge gulps of air, my throat rasping as I fight to swallow.

"Viv," Reid repeats. His hands are on me, grasping tightly, cupping my shoulders, holding me upright. "You were having a nightmare." His face is a mask of worry, blue eyes wide as he searches my face for the source of my pain. "You're okay," he murmurs, his fingertips brushing over my wet cheek. "You're here, at the Windsor. With me."

My heart is pounding as my eyes adjust to the dark and I remember where I am. Where we fell asleep. His shirt is still under my head.

"I'm sorry," I mutter weakly. Shame fills my chest. And a decaying, empty grief.

"It's fine." He rubs a hand down my spine and back up until I can breathe naturally again.

"We should probably get going." My voice echoes through the exhibit hall.

Reid nods, clearing sleep from his eyes. When I've slid on my shoes, he asks quietly, "What are your nightmares about?"

"My father. The night he died."

Reid nods as if he assumed as much. "You said it was the Brood?"

"They killed him at the docks. He'd hid me somewhere safe so they wouldn't find me. But I saw everything." The words still hurt all these years later. "I was ten."

Reid's eyes widen at the realization, as if something new has hit him. Something horrifying. "I remember hearing about that . . . About a decade ago, a pack of Broods took out one of the best hunters in Astera. You were there?" It twists my stomach to think of how they might have bragged to him about the kill. I only nod.

"Viv . . ." He's really reeling. "I'm so sorry."

"Hey. It's okay." I press one soft kiss to his mouth, but he barely kisses me back. "It wasn't your fault."

He sucks in a breath. "I know, but—"

"I don't have them that often anymore. Lately, I don't dream at all."

"Really?" Reid shakes his head. "Most nights I dream of you."

I try to swallow the cartoony things that does to my heart. "You never did tell me when your lurid fantasies began."

The intensity when he finds my eyes takes my breath away. "The moment I saw you. You saved that mom and her kids. The most beautiful woman I'd ever seen, beating a demon to a pulp in a tiny black dress . . . I'm not proud of what I did that night when I got home."

A tired laugh breezes from me as I lace my locket back around my neck, and Reid throws his shirt back on. I study him in the moonlight and unexpectedly find that I miss the horns he so despises. "I think I found the first thing we don't have in common."

"Besides you being a demon-slaying angel and me a hellion?"

His words bring a small smile to my face. "I love your horns," I say, before a new thought sparks. Then, "Hey, that's it."

Reid blinks at me. "What is?"

"I've been trying to figure out what to name my daggers. Angel and Hellion."

Reid considers this as he stands. "I like it."

"I'm going to take a couple of these broken artifacts up to Fiona's office. Meet you at the gateway?"

"Sure." His eyes look sad. I wonder if he, too, is thinking about how much is about to change when we go back to Harker. The impossible fight that looms before us.

Upstairs, I've brought the few most damaged pieces into Fiona's office for safekeeping, only to find her sitting on the floor in classic Fiona fashion: poring over paperwork, shoes off, mocha latte steaming in a huge mug by her side. Her glasses are carving a dent into the side of her nose, lithe limbs folded primly under her pencil skirt.

"Viv." Fiona's round eyes glint in the soft desk light when she looks up. "What are you still doing here?"

I put the artifacts on the floor beside her. "I didn't want to leave these on the museum floor."

"Thank you," she says quietly, eyes back on her work.

"What did the Elders say?"

Fiona's lips purse. "Contacting them isn't quite so easy. I got word to the Citadel hunters. Now we wait."

I nod, prepared to leave, when something new bubbles to the surface. "You know, you could have told me what you were."

"Actually, I couldn't. That's why I keep my distance at school. One of the Elders' conditions of my role here at the Windsor is that no mortal nor lymantrian know of my double life. This museum houses more than just history, Viv. If someone knew my human identity, it might open the Windsor up to great vulnerabilities." I imagine a vampire holding Nora hostage to get Fiona's master key and shudder. "I broke a substantial rule this evening, which I don't plan on revealing to the Elders. I trust you and Reid can keep the knowledge to yourselves?"

"Of course."

When I turn to leave, she adds, "I did want to help. I didn't want you to be alone, Viv. After I saw you do that ritual, I looked for your records—wanted to know why you hadn't been enrolled . . . but you weren't in them. Not even marked *dead* or *whereabouts unknown* . . . just missing completely. I figured your father had been the hunter in your family line. He hadn't gone to Harker, either, I guess. There was no David Abbot in any of the records."

Just as I saw that day in the archives.

"But I did look into his death to confirm my suspicions," she continues. "To see if there was anything obviously deviant about it. Couldn't find much besides that twenty-six."

My muscles tense. "What twenty-six?"

Her eyes widen behind her glasses. "You never looked at his autopsy report?"

I shake my head, heart beginning to pound. "He drowned. I watched it happen. I tried to find the Brood demons who killed him, but . . . No, I didn't look at the report." Why would I have wanted to read about the sharks that had devoured him or the way the frigid ocean had bloated his corpse? Even now, the thought sends my stomach into revolt.

Fiona's mouth twists as if she doesn't know if I can handle whatever she's about to say.

"Tell me."

She takes a breath. "He carved the number twenty-six into his own hand. I did as much research as I could"—she gestures to the Windsor around her—"mortal and otherwise. For you, for Nor . . . Never came up with anything that made sense."

Twenty-six.

Twenty-six.

It hits me like a freight train.

The betrayal. The sickness.

"Viv?" Fiona asks. "What is it?"

But I can't breathe, let alone speak. I sprint back down the emergency exit stairs and through the mirrored glass of the Windsor lobby, Fiona chasing after me. I nearly barrel right through Reid.

"Come on," I gasp. "Now."

He doesn't ask what's happened. He trusts me, taking my fingers in his hand.

We leap through the gateway, my heart between my teeth.

CHAPTER 47

I BOLT ACROSS the night-dark, snow-laden campus. It's nearly dawn. If I'd thought Harker was cold and off-putting yesterday, that hollow, snow-tinged evening in the commons has nothing on the hanging darkness that creeps toward me now. There's not even a sliver of white in the sky. There will be a new moon today.

Reid races after me, and Fiona, back in her hunter form, runs after him. I bolt through the Old Campus courtyard, past all the hunting trophies and trinkets and over to that winning photo of my dad. I knew, somewhere in the corners of my mind, that I'd be back here. It's become one of my favorite parts of going to Harker, walking by his smiling face every time I make the journey from Elkfore Hall to the gateway or to class. Tonight it feels like I was waiting for this moment all along.

"What's going on?" Reid huffs behind me.

I read the plaque below the photo once more:

DAVID CADDEL WINS HARKER LACROSSE CHAMPIONSHIP FOR THE MARKSMEN, 1994. ALSO PICTURED: NUMBER FIFTEEN, TIM HAWKINS; NUMBER TWENTY-SIX, EDGAR DRISCOLL.

I read it twice more to be sure. **NUMBER TWENTY-SIX, EDGAR DRISCOLL.**

Edgar Driscoll.

A shock to the system. The warlock dean of Harker, my father's friend . . . and his killer. The one he recognized. *You. After all this time . . . At least tell me why.*

It all clicks together now, as if before I was looking at the jigsaw upside down. Edgar was the one collecting the ingredients for the High Thane all along. Of course the dean was able to find the object of origin the night of the lacrosse game. He'd *cast* the spell. He'd had access to the locked case in the armory and the hidden garden for the asphodels . . . Probably faked the emails to Reid about Kitty's hunting abroad. He had every reason to send me on a deadly, purposeless goose chase after the White Stag. I bet he even left the bag of poppy for me in the first place as soon as he caught wind that Reid and I were looking into the hidden garden. I was so foolish—I begged Reid to ask the dean for help. I could pummel myself for my own stupidity.

"Oh god," I breathe. "Kitty. And Lyra."

"You need to tell me what's happening," Reid says.

"The dean. It's been the dean all this time. He's turned, Reid. He's working for the High Thane. He killed—" A sob escapes me. "Oh god, he killed my dad."

Reid pulls me close against his chest as the tears of horror break free and spill onto his shirt. If my dad had learned the dean of Harker had joined the Brood, that would have been a decent enough reason to change his name and hide me from Harker. He'd probably had my records destroyed long before the night they came after him.

That night. My father had told me he couldn't run forever. But why was Edgar hunting him down in the first place? Every time I loose one thread, another knots itself tighter. I finger the worn grooves of my locket as the tears flow.

"I can't believe . . ." Fiona's voice fades into the night.

"He doesn't have a brand," Reid says quietly. I can't imagine the betrayal.

"I'm sorry, Reid." Then I remember the scar I noticed on Edgar's neck before he purposely sent me on a death march to Reid's own brother. "He has a horrible scar on his neck. Like he sliced off a chunk of skin." I eye Reid's brand. "About the size of your brand."

"God damn it," Reid bites out.

I don't tell him or Fiona the last bit I've worked out. That as an aeon, I should have been able to feel that he'd turned. I can sense all deviants, even warlocks and witches who cross to the dark side. But Peter inadvertently answered that for me when I thought it was Lisette who was behind all this. *A powerful turned witch could mask themselves or others*, he said. I had no way of knowing.

"You need to go to the Citadel," Fiona says. "Right away. It'll be safer than remaining on campus. I'll alert the other faculty."

"I'll get her there," Reid tells her. "Then I'll come help."

Fiona gives me one last worried look before she hurries off toward Mortimer Tower. When Reid casts his eyes back down to me, they are deadly focused. No more pain. No more hurt. "You need to leave campus."

Something inside me stills. It might be my heartbeat. "What? What about the Citadel?"

"I know Edgar better than anyone. As soon as we tell the Elders and he learns we're after him . . . he'll tell the High Thane. That means war. I can't have you in the middle of that."

"Okay. Okay . . ." My brain is turning over a new course of events. "We can go to my apartment, I'll tell Penny—"

"There is no *we*." Reid shakes his head, irritated. "You are going to keep out of this mess, and I will take it up with the Citadel."

"Let me go with you."

"*No*. I already—" He grinds his jaw so hard I hear the enamel of his teeth scraping. "I almost lost you, Viv. I think about that night at Fever Dream constantly. I wake up sick in the middle of the night."

"Reid . . ." But I have no words. I'm not allowing him and Fiona to do this without me.

Reid steps closer and cradles my chin in his hand. "I can't fight Edgar, much less the High Thane, unless I know you're safe."

But I'm already backing toward Elkfore. "And I can't sit by and do nothing." Not after my dad. Not ever again. "You can either meet me at the gates of Old Campus in five minutes or meet me in front of the Citadel when I beat you there."

Reid looks physically pained. "Is there anything I can say to convince you to let me do this alone?"

I cross my arms only to realize I'm shivering. "Would you let me do this by myself?"

Reid's jaw tics. "Not a chance."

"That's what I thought. Gates in five."

BACK IN THE commons, I find Peter asleep on top of our notebooks. There's a steady string of drool slipping from his mouth onto a page marked *Rare Venoms*. The fire's retreated into cooling embers, the jazz we put on long since faded away.

I debate waking him to tell him what's going on but think better of it. Something like this will only terrify him. Sophia can decide if she wants to fill him in. Same with Elliot.

Upstairs, the wood beneath the carpet creaks under my feet.

The fibers are old and weathered and a little gray in spots. I guess no amount of cleaning or magic can get wraith blood out of wool. It's impossible to reconcile who I was the night they attacked with who I am today.

Inside our dorm, Sophia's fast asleep. One heel still on, minidress hiked up, empty bottle of some electrolyte-heavy sports drink clutched in her hand. The periwinkle dawn paints her copper hair in hues of blue. *Like an angel*, I think. Despite her reckless side, Sophia really is as pure as they get. As a friend, as a hunter.

I'm a foot away, hand outstretched to wake her, when I realize how much danger I'd be putting her in by doing so. Telling her that our dean is a member of the Brood and we're going to the Citadel to take him down? That he let wraiths in to distract everyone from his taking Kitty and covered up her absence? That he did the same with the zombie spell so he could steal the dagger from the armory? Those are complicated plots to pull off. He could have students working for him. Professors too. For all I know, the entire commons is bugged.

Reid and I have Lisette on our side. Soon we'll have the Elders. I don't need to put anyone else in harm's way.

I throw on a pair of black jeans, a black tank, and my favorite black boots. An OG Viv Abbot ensemble for a day when I'll need to feel the most like myself. A warrior. A hunter. An aeon. A courageous take-no-prisoners bitch. I slip my winter coat on and head for the door.

"Where are you off to so early?"

I turn to find Sophia, half-awake and rubbing sleep out of her eyes.

Shit. "Nowhere." Sophia raises a brow. I guess *nowhere* doesn't really scream *unsuspicious*. "I'm meeting Reid," I amend, because it's not a lie.

Sophia kicks off her remaining heel and pulls the covers up and over her body. "I'm glad you two crazy kids worked it out. Penny's going to come around too. And your mom, I'm sure."

My heart surges up toward my throat with how badly I want her words to be true. "You really believe that?"

"'Course," she slurs, and I can tell she's drifting off again. "We're hunters. We take care of people."

And she's right. That's always been what we do.

"I really love you," I tell her.

Sophia rolls over and a mess of tangled hair covers her face. Her response is barely audible against her pillow, but I think she says, "I know."

CHAPTER 48

REID AND I are both at the gates in seven minutes, not five, because another thing we seem to have in common is chronic lateness. We hurry across the snow-tipped campus lawn, the sun looming over the hunched mountains in the distance. Through the brickwork wall denoting Old Campus and over the rocky shores of Lake Hellebore.

We don't speak a word as we pass a hollow, eerie greenhouse where a figure moves inside before we come to the edge of campus. A vast, gnarled wood spreads in every direction, thick ponderosas and towering spruces draped in fresh white snow. In the distance, the spires of the Citadel loom.

We're feet from the Citadel hunters who stand before the Fickle Thicket, stoic guards fitted with silver weaponry of every kind, when Reid's hand wraps around my wrist, grave concern twisting in those blue eyes. "Viv, there's something I . . ."

But his words are lost to me as a watery, echoing voice sounds in my ears. Someone screaming for help. I hear it like a record on a loop, blasted at full volume.

"What the—" I whirl, looking for the source. Reid only stares strangely at me as the screams warble in my mind. My blood freezes along my bones.

"*Let go of me!*" Penny shrieks. "*Don't you— What are you doing— HELP!*" Sobs break from her in ravaged waves, as clear as if she were standing right before us.

My legs nearly give out in the middle of the snow. Reid's jaw goes rigid as he watches me press my hands to my head. *What is it?* he mouths. He can't hear her. Only me.

He might even ask the question aloud, but all I can hear are the sounds of a struggle, men grunting, and Penny screaming bloody murder until someone muffles her mouth with something soft.

"They took Penny," I breathe to Reid over the transmission in my head. "I gave her the lure. I can hear everything. They *took* her."

Reid looks like he's going to be sick. "What? Is she—"

"She's alive. We have to go."

Now, now, now—

Nothing else matters. Not the Citadel, not Harker, not Reid.

Reid's shoulders stiffen. "We have to go to the Citadel first. We need the Elders."

Amid more muffled cries from Penny, I hear the crash of waves against wood and the desperate squawking of seagulls drawn to the scuffle. If my blood was frozen solid before, it shatters at the sound. "The docks. They have her at the docks."

By the time the sounds subside, my heart is slamming in my chest. It has to be Edgar who's gotten to Penny. But how did he know we were onto him?

"They can help us. They can . . ." Reid's jaw tightens as he thinks. He runs a hand through his hair, dusted with snow.

"There's no time!" I'm already moving back in the direction of Old Campus. "You're either with me or you're not."

"*Fuck.*" But whatever he sees in my face—resolve, terror, riotous unchecked aeon fury—seals the deal. "I'm always with you, Viv."

I CAN HARDLY think around the searing panic as we leap from the cab. My feet are moving, legs pumping, before an onslaught of horrible memories sends me stumbling.

Reid catches me around the waist. "You all right?"

This place—somewhere I vowed to return to only in my nightmares—hasn't changed at all. What hits me first is the scent of the sea. Astera's peninsula juts into the unruly pitch-black ocean, and I tense against the particular blend of brine, oil, and old, wet wood.

Reid looks around at the stretch of rickety dock. Moored yachts and ocean liners hem the pier, some spewing hot exhaust into the frigid morning air, others long dormant—relics of the old passenger ship terminal this place once was. Ghosts of a different kind of Astera. Now massive industrial structures have been built along the run-down waterfront marina: grim covered piers that have been turned into warehouses and decrepit stages for productions, and a maritime center that I'm certain is a front for some South of the Chasm gambling ring.

No wonder the Brood loves the spot. It's down below the Chasm, surrounded on all edges by a merciless, untraceable sea . . .

"She's here," I tell Reid. "If Penny's alive, she's here."

Reid scans the docks, winter wind whipping at his curls of chestnut hair. "It's a big place."

"This way." I stalk past those large industrial shipping containers I've avoided for more than a decade and allow my hunter instincts to guide me. The sound of the ocean beating against the pier fades away, as does the howl of the morning wind and the honking horns of the city in the distance. I close my eyes as I walk and listen for something, anything, that could help me find—

There, in the distance—a handful of deviants, smoking cigarettes and playing cards around a weather-beaten bench. Guarding a white shipping container. And inside it, a muffled shout.

It's as if I've stepped back in time. It could be me inside that shipping container, wailing for my dad. "Did you hear that?"

"Go get Penny." Reid looks pale and uneasy. "I'll draw them away."

"You can't fight ten Broods. They'll kill you."

Reid's voice is rough as he says, "They can try."

I open my mouth to protest, but he presses his lips against mine in a searing, pained kiss. It feels like an apology—the worst kiss we've shared, because I know there's a chance it's goodbye. I can *hear* the agony in his heartbeat. Can feel the panic in his hands as he wastes precious time touching the skin of my cheek, the length of my neck.

It's over before I can memorize every curve of his lips, every point of pressure. Whatever was twining us together is being split like shears tearing through vines. It's enough to crack me open. That, and the wetness in his eyes when he pulls away, fingers still lovingly wrapped around a lock of my hair. But then he's hurtling toward the group, black claws bared.

I know they're Broods and not just sailors or crooks because of the way about seven sets of eyes blink bloodred when they spot him. Demons, all of them. Except for one I assume is a vamp, were, or turned warlock, lower in stature and cast to the side, cleaning the other demons' knives. Even he looks up and snarls at Reid before taking off in his direction.

Which means I've got to move too.

I race around the other side of the dock to reach the back of the white container where Penny's held. I shove the door up and open with my shoulder until it burns.

Footsteps thud on the rickety wood of the pier from the other side. I know I have less than a minute to get Penny out. Reid can't keep them away from us forever. I slam the door back down, and only then do I realize why there was no dead bolt on the outside. I hear the *snick* of an automatic lock. The shipping container locks from the outside. Same way it kept me inside all those years ago.

I'm drowned in darkness, adrenaline coursing through me, begging me to *get out, get out, get out*—

But I need to stay calm. I've been here before. I've *lost* someone here before.

And I won't again.

Fishing in my pocket, I yank out my phone and turn on the flashlight. The sight before me twists my stomach into hideous knots.

Amid a clutter of wooden boxes and crates, a woman sits against the wall, tied at the wrists and ankles, black hood over her head. I mutter prayers to everything and anything in gratitude that those shaking Keds sneakers and blond curls are indeed Penny's.

"Penny," I hush, dropping to my knees beside her. "It's Viv. I'm here."

I yank the dark canvas off her head and exhale in a mighty rush. She's alive. Uninjured. Gagged but in pretty decent shape, all things considered. My fingers pull the cloth from her lips and begin to work at the knots at her wrists.

"Viv," Penny gasps. Her voice is a mere husk of her usual singsong tune. "Thank god. Oh my god—"

"What happened?"

"These men, they"—she sucks in a huge breath—"grabbed me

on my way to work." Another breath. "I thought they were going to—"

"I know." These knots are too fucking tight and the footsteps are thudding closer and closer. "But nobody is going to hurt you. You're going to have to trust me."

"How are you here? Where are the police?"

I whip out my dagger and begin to saw at her restraints.

Penny's eyes nearly fall out of their sockets. "Is that a knife?"

"Have you seen any other girls?"

"No," Penny says, watching me untangle her.

My brain is trying to piece a lot together in mere wisps of time. Driscoll must have found out somehow that I was onto him and took Penny to lure me here. But how did he even know who she was or what she meant to me? And worse, where are Lyra and Kitty? I swallow against the grief that's seized my limbs. My body knows the answer.

Finally, Penny's hands snap free, but not fast enough to avoid whatever Broods are looking for us. Voices call to one another right outside the crate. I can't protect her and fight them at the same time.

This is the worst plan I've ever thought up, but it's all I've got. "Tie me up," I instruct as quietly as I can, holding out the sliced rope. Despite the season, a fine mist of sweat has gathered at my brow and in the crooks of my knees. There's no fucking air in here.

Penny rubs her wrists in disbelief. "What? Are you crazy?"

"Do what I'm telling you to," I say as quietly as I can. "Tie me up lightly and put the gag in my mouth and the hood on my head." I take a seat against the wall where she was and thrust my wrists out. "Hurry, and then go hide under the crates."

She shakes her head. "You can't take my place. I won't let you."

"Penny. I know I've told you a lot of bullshit over the years, but I just need you to do what I'm saying. I have a better shot of protecting myself than you do. I'm trained for it."

Her sweat-coated brows meet in bewildered confusion, but she must understand on some level that if I'm the one who showed up to save her, and I'm wielding weapons like Lara Croft, maybe I've got a point. She sniffles, lip wobbling, but I can see snippets of all my lies over the years starting to make some kind of sense in her mind as she ties my wrists together.

"Stay put until I come back for you," I tell her. "Unless you get the chance to run. If you do, take it."

Horror slices in Penny's eyes. She places her gag in my mouth with a wince and a nod. The door begins to slide up. Penny shoves the hood over my head, and I hear her throw herself behind the boxes as I instructed.

Two pairs of footsteps stop right before me. Since I don't hear the sound of claws in flesh, I take it they haven't noticed that Penny and I have swapped. Triumph sings in my veins.

"Come on, blondie," says one Brood.

"Mmph!" I shout into my gag. I kick my legs and bang my back against the metal of the container until a blow lands across my cheek that sends my eyes pulsing in their sockets. I move my jaw in circles to make sure it's not broken. Nose might be, but I can't tell.

"Mortals are so whiny," the other grunts.

I'm hoisted up by my arms and dragged outside as the door is slammed shut behind us. The icy air whips at my tied hands and the thin fabric of my tank when my coat flies open. Against every instinct in my body, I don't break free. I can't risk escaping before I can go back and save Penny. And, shocker: I don't love my odds against two members of the Brood. So I allow myself to be carried somewhere marginally warmer—definitely inside—where I can no longer hear the push and pull of the sea.

When I'm forced to my knees and the hood is ripped off, I blink until I understand I'm in an empty warehouse. Wide, scuffed floor. High ceilings over a space that once stored yachts and shipping machinery, now long since abandoned. Wide glass windows that look out onto the angry, oil-slicked ocean.

The two men behind me are clearly run-of-the-mill Brood demons. Their brands give them away, and their clear skin, nice teeth, and various muscles tell me they're taking enough souls to live long and well.

"That's not the mortal," the demon at my side balks.

To my right stands Dean Driscoll, a patch slapped over his right eye. I narrow my gaze at him with enough vitriol to peel the skin from his bones.

"No, it's not." His expression is one of grim delight. His voice echoes off the cavernous walls. "It's David Cadell's little girl. The aeon we'd been looking for, under my nose the whole damn time."

And there it is. The reason my dad changed his name, kept me from Harker, and was on the run from Edgar. Not just because he discovered Edgar was turned, but for the same reason he always warned me against sharing that I was an aeon with anyone. Sure, the Elders would come after us to end our bloodline, but his own turned friend had been hunting for aeons too. He didn't want either of us to be an ingredient in the High Thane's syrabraxa.

I try to respond, but the gag is still lodged in my mouth. Where is Reid? A vision of his perfect jaw mangled into an unrecognizable shape sends panic into my veins.

He's fine. He has to be.

"You look just like him," Edgar muses.

I thrash and spit until the gag flies from my mouth. "Don't you dare speak about him. You *betrayed* him."

Driscoll only glowers at me. "All that bravado and you're still just a little girl who thinks her daddy could do no wrong. You didn't know the David I knew. We fought all the same battles. Bested all the same beasts, and I *never* felt like he looked at me with the respect I deserved. Because he was a hunter. And I wasn't. Can you imagine my shock when he told me what he was? A dirty, bloodthirsty *aeon*. And still, he had all the glory."

"So you joined the Brood because you were jealous of one person?" He's out of his fucking mind.

But Driscoll's grin is grim and satisfied. "I joined the Brood because they *accepted me.* Saw my value, even though I wasn't a demon. The High Thane offered me a place at the table that even the Elders never could."

That's wrong, I want to say. The *demons* are the ones who marginalize beings for what they are. Not the Elders. Not my dad.

"And in turn," Driscoll continues, "I gave him the name of the last remaining aeon bloodline and the chance to make the syrabraxa he's always wanted."

My father knew he was being hunted. Maybe for years. And all in pursuit of his aeon blood, so he could be used for some spell. It's not like he could have even gone to the Citadel—he would have had to reveal Driscoll's motive for hunting him, and the Elders would have killed him for what he was instead. Probably me too . . .

So he changed his name and erased me from their records. All to keep me safe. To keep the Brood from using me to make their syrabraxa, as they'd hoped to use him. He threw himself to his own death to avoid letting them complete their insidious spell with his blood.

But the records—

Driscoll knew my father's real identity. And those records said he had two daughters.

And I managed to end up here, in his clutches. Bound and gagged like a lobster for dinner. But I wasn't the first. "Kitty and Lyra. Your own students. You tried to use their blood for your spell, and it didn't work."

Driscoll's one remaining eye is cold. Remorseless.

It wasn't just that they seemed like aeons. It's even more obvious to me now: They also looked like they could be my father's daughter. Pitch-black hair. Light eyes. Pale skin. We could have been sisters, the three of us. The Brood was trying to find a viable aeon for the spell. Their only lead for the last decade... They were trying to find *me*. Kitty and Lyra died in *my* place. The shame and sorrow are enough to drown me. "They were *innocent*."

"You're right. They weren't you," Driscoll says as if I should carry the burden of their lost lives.

"How did you put together that I was the one you wanted?" I bite out. It's the last piece of the story I don't have. Try as I might to rack my brain, I don't know how he could have figured out I was David's daughter. And from there, my entire life in Astera—my family, my home, *Penny*. He didn't know it when I was in his cabin, or he would have captured me then. At that point he only knew I was a nuisance, looking into his plans. He set me on a path to the White Stag, hoping it would end in my death and stop me poking around. But he didn't know I was the aeon he sought until today when he kidnapped Penny as leverage. What changed?

I don't allow myself to doubt Sophia, Elliot, or Peter. None of them would have told a soul. I know it in my bones. But nobody outside of those three knows what I am.

Driscoll ignores the question. He nods to the demons, who shove the gag back into my mouth. Then he pulls out his phone to make a call. "She's here." Silence as someone asks something on the other line. "We didn't have to ransom the mortal. She made it to us on her own somehow." More silence. "Does it matter? You can tell your father you did it. You found her. Now we can begin."

Begin. To take my blood. To brew his spell. Place it in a human vessel . . .

My restraints are still loose enough for me to break free, but the demons at my sides have me in an iron grip. I don't allow myself to look around. I can't give any indication I'm not alone. If nobody knows Reid's here, he must have succeeded in killing all the Broods outside . . . But then *where is he?* I'm running out of—

Licks of ice ripple across the warehouse floor, and frost prickles my eyelashes. I convulse against the unwelcome chill as a darker, more harrowing sensation than I've felt before undulates beneath my skin. It thrums with the need to kill. I can only watch as icicles form on the vents and pipes above us. On the fingers of the demons who hold me down.

Footsteps sound behind me. Two sets. Driscoll looks up with a grim nod and walks to greet them.

"Well done." I can't see him, but I know that distorted voice from the Windsor. They're behind me, and though I thrash, the demons hold me still. But even behind the reverberating noise, there's something smooth to his voice.

Smooth and . . . familiar.

In the dirt-flecked glass of the windows before me, I can just make out the reflection of a man in a long dark cloak placing a hand on the shoulder of a demon with dark hair. That hand—claws of withered gray, wrinkled slightly with age, but sturdy, strong, and tipped in shining silver.

"See to it that she is viable," the High Thane says. "I won't be brought back here again. No mistakes this time."

"Yes, Father," another voice says. But I already figured out this dark-haired demon is the High Thane's son. That's the kind of chastising you only get from a fed-up, disappointed parent. Takes one to know one.

And then the High Thane retreats, his icy chill leaving with him, and his son and Driscoll stalk back toward me. I strain to get a better look at the High Thane before he leaves the warehouse, but I can't see much in the glassy reflection except his dark hood and his venomous snake eyes.

When the two of them draw near, so does the sound of enamel tapping. My breaths come nearly as fast as my heartbeat.

Strolling into my vision is a demon who looks like the lead in a *Grease* revival musical. Slicked-back hair, thunderbird jaw, leather jacket. He's got a mean glint in his eyes, and I'd bet all of Stan Pine's money that he tortured his childhood puppy and plucked the wings off flies. He taps his light gray claws together like it's a nervous tic. The clacking sound reverberates through the warehouse.

"Aeon," says the Brood demon heir, eyes lit with warped glee. "Finally."

CHAPTER 49

FURY CONSUMES ME, and the desire to fight takes over. I free my tethered hands faster than I can take my next breath and am almost standing when the Brood demons at my sides yank me back. I grunt into my gag, lashing out against them. Greased Lightnin' merely gives Dean Driscoll an eager nod. "Let's begin."

Driscoll prowls over. I kick and bite and spit. I manage to get the gag out of my mouth and yell, "Get your fucking hands *off me*," which, to the surprise of nobody, doesn't do shit.

"I'd be happy to remove her vocal cords with my teeth," the High Thane's son offers, eyes lit with something primordial and sick.

Driscoll frowns. "*Finn.*"

"What?" His grin is impish.

"That won't be necessary." The dean digs into his pocket, and I try to steel myself for a knife or some other bloodletting instrument. My heart bolts in place—it wouldn't be the first time I've fought something sadistic, but I've never been tortured outright. I think of my side being sliced open, or my carotid artery . . .

All bloody, gut-heaving images are replaced by a tepid relief when Driscoll reveals a simple glass vial. Sure, it could be a potion that makes me bleed from all my orifices, but for now, I tell my nervous system, it's just not a damn knife.

"What is that?" I ask, still trying to wrench myself from the demons' grasp.

"And here I thought you'd figured it all out," Driscoll says, something angry simmering in his eyes. He really hated my dad. I can feel it in his glare.

I scramble to run through the syrabraxa ingredients in my mind.

Liquified blade of the third, the stolen Aeon's Dagger.

Celestial bloom, the asphodel.

Eye of the conjuring witch—my gaze lands on Edgar's right eye socket, covered by that bandage. He must have gouged out his own eyeball for the syrabraxa, just as the recipe required. *Aeon's blood* is the last thing they need to complete the spell . . . but if it's already been brewed . . .

I fight through foggy memories of my last handful of months at Harker, trying to remember the day Peter first told us about the syrabraxa. How badly I wanted to brew one of my own. The only spell that might offer me freedom from what I am . . .

The deviant witch needs a host to put the spell into. The brewed potion is imbued into their skin . . . The power of the spell is granted to whoever kills the host . . . There's only one recorded instance of this even being possible . . . A syrabraxa was implemented into an aeon.

My entire body freezes solid as understanding sinks in.

Aeon's blood never meant the literal blood of me or my father.

The last ingredient is the *host*. They've needed an aeon all along to carry the spell within their skin.

Dean Driscoll doesn't even look at me as he unscrews the top of the vial.

"Aeons never killed mortals, did they?" My fear crests and sweeps, adrenaline pulsing.

Greased Lightnin'—or, Finn—releases a low, chilling laugh as he regards me. His claws tap together with nervous excitement. "Your Elders thought that might excuse their culling. They couldn't have aeons running around who could be utilized for power like this." He nods toward Edgar's vial, that same thrilled glow in his beady eyes. "Not after the Chasm was split and their realm crumbled."

"I believe they thought themselves very noble," Driscoll says. "The irony . . ."

I was told I was capable of as much indiscriminate savagery as a deviant for so long—by my father, at Harker—and I always believed it. Now it feels like a betrayal of myself—of my own body and my own heart—to have thought I could have killed innocents. Shame coats my tongue.

But Finn's words drip through me slowly, gathering low in my gut as I turn them around. The part I never focused on this entire semester, because I've been blinded by determination to stop what's been happening—to save Kitty and Lyra and prove myself *good*. I never stopped to ask *why*. In my undiluted horror, it's Professor Lisette's—Fiona's—horn-rimmed glasses that fill my mind: *Until the High Thane used the darkest form of magic to split the earth.*

Suddenly, a terrible click sounds in my head. Parts snapping together. Slicing through me like a guillotine. The most ferocious magic that can be cast. Capable of breaking the planes of existence. The reason the Elders crafted this elaborate lie to take out all aeons, so nobody can brew a spell like this ever again.

"Your father is going to break the Chasm open," I manage.

"Freedom for deviants to emerge and make the world their own," Finn lilts. "Don't tell me you dislike freedom, aeon."

He's going to release literal hell on earth. Deviants will destroy the mortal plane and likely the entire lymantrian order. And they'll use *me* to do so. I can't breathe. I can't *breathe*.

"As long as you don't die on us too." Finn grins at me, clicking his sickly gray claws. "All the other hunters Edgar brought me kept breaking."

I failed Kitty and Lyra. And now all of Astera too—the carnage of a split-open Chasm is nearly too much to bear. "They'll kill every human within a week."

"The strong will survive," Driscoll says, low and rough.

"And the weak will feed them with their flesh and blood like one powerful organism." Finn sounds awed. "My father says that will be how this city finally comes together."

"That is the most backward, outrageous—"

Finn ignores me. "Is the spell ready?"

Driscoll nods once.

I thrash and spit. Scream until one of the demons punches me hard in the mouth. But I can't stop. If they tether this spell to my soul, the High Thane will kill me. He'll be protected from the ensuing madness with his stolen censer, and then he'll rip open the Chasm right through Astera.

The demons at my side force me to my knees, and my body seizes with the need to escape. "Wait, wait—"

Tears crest in my eyes as Driscoll opens the vial with the brewed spell. He walks behind me until I can't turn my head far enough to see what he's doing. There's something even more terrifying about not knowing what will happen next. The demons strip me of my winter coat. Everything tenses and throbs. My body has begun to shake uncontrollably.

Driscoll begins to chant in a language of the old world. Not gnostic, Sanskrit, or Latin. Something primordial. Something sinister . . . *Where is Reid? Where is Reid? Where is—*

"Please, just wait, *please.*" I never thought I'd be the type to beg for my life, but it gurgles out of me nonetheless.

Nobody answers me. My stomach sours. My mind blanks.

Driscoll's muttered spell grows louder. The scent of burning herbs stings my nose. Finn's demonic eyes are ringed in red light as I hear the vial being unscrewed.

Reid is probably dead. I'm never going to see my friends again. I couldn't save anyone. The city will be rubble. The one thing I ever—

Pain unlike anything I could have fathomed cracks into my spine. It radiates through my back, between every rib, through each tendon and vein in my body. I scream the kind of scream that keeps on coming even when I can't make any more noise and it's just a silent, broken gasp. Somewhere, high above myself, I'm aware that the back of my shirt is burning from the sheer force of the spell. Cheap nylon is melting into my skin. It's a sponge bath compared to the agony of the syrabraxa twining deeper—around the very fibers of my soul.

Finn watches me silently, a flicker of pleasure in his shadowed eyes.

The pain builds and crests. A writhing, scattering agony. Time slows to a crawl over hot coals. I no longer hope to live through this. I want to be ended. I stop fighting. I pray for merciful oblivion.

I think of my father and the pain he suffered when he died. Carving the number twenty-six into his own palm in the bitterly cold ocean waves as he drowned. I think of Kitty and Lyra enduring the same pain I am now—failed hosts. Limp bodies finally at peace on the warehouse floor. I think of my mother and Nora and Penny and Sophia and Fiona and Peter and Elliot and Hound and all those I will leave broken when I'm gone. I think of Reid.

And then . . . it stops.

I sag into the arms of the demons at my sides as tears stream down my face. The warehouse is silent and cooler than it was minutes ago. Only my sobs rend the air.

Driscoll backs away. Clears his throat. Mutters in awe and horror and victory, "It's done."

"Congratulations, aeon," Finn purrs, prowling closer. "You've just become the bearer of the most powerful dark magic in the world."

CHAPTER 50

FINN'S WORDS BARELY sink in. I'm in such pain, it's all I can do not to vomit on the scuffed warehouse floor. I can smell the sizzling flesh on my back. There are gashes down both my arms where the Brood demons held me so tightly that I tore my own flesh against their claws.

And something else too. A lushly luminous power stalking beneath my skin. Not sinister or virtuous. Not belonging to any realm or creed. Just *power*. Crackling within my body. Curving around my spine like a serpent. Slumbering inside me like a doe. Impossible for me to harness but living within me just the same.

Finn comes to stand before me. He bends down to get a better look, lifting my chin with his smooth finger as he does. No more need for those claws. I am no threat to him in my current state. A wicked chill spreads from the point of contact, down my neck, and up to my ears. I'm too weak to even spit in his cruelly carved face.

"You've endured quite the ordeal." He sounds almost awed. "Do you know how long we've been searching for you? How long my father has awaited this?" He's flushed like he's just seen something revelatory. I realize with revulsion that it was my blaring agony.

"Shall I fetch him?" Driscoll grunts. When I turn my head to get a good look at the dean, I notice blood dripping from both his ears. *Darkest magic in the world* is right. I hope it fucking kills him.

"Yes. Get the censer and let's finish this." Finn continues to examine me like I'm a successful specimen in a lab. "Aren't you a pretty thing? I wish we could have played longer."

My head throbs behind my eyes. "Fuck you."

Finn laughs, his eyes red and wide. All I can do is grind my teeth as Finn caresses my throat.

I'm listening to my own heartbeat weakening in my chest when the demon to my left is suddenly wrenched from me and eviscerated. Claws rip through his gut, heart, and throat in one murderous slice. He collapses to the floor in a pulpy, gurgling mess.

My pulse picks up a notch.

I don't see him or hear his voice, but I know.

I *know*.

The demon to my right releases his hold on me to protect himself from my unseen savior, and I barely manage to scuttle away. My heart slams so hard in my chest that when I stand, I find I'm swaying with the force of it. I've lost a lot of blood. And when my eyes find my gouged arms, I realize I still am. *Shit*.

"*Viv*," Reid bellows, voice booming off the walls of the warehouse. "*Run!*"

I have to whirl to see him. Claws flying as he lunges for Finn. A snarling, growling creature born from hell. My heart clenches at the sight of his injuries. There's blood along his arms and down his cheek, and he's limping. I wonder how many dead Brood demons are littered around these docks. The thought brings a sick grin to my face.

I move toward him—not so much a run as Reid instructed, but

more of a weak, broken stumble. My daggers are still strapped to my body, and I brandish them, even as my hands shake and my vision blurs. Out of the corner of my eye, I see Driscoll take in the mayhem and bolt from the warehouse just as a swarm of Broods rush in.

"Reid," Finn says with the familiarity of an old boss. "About time you showed up."

But Reid ignores him, sinking his claws masterfully into another henchman's chest. The demon wheezes out a final breath before falling to the ground in a puff of ash. Reid is left standing over him, the demon's heart impaled on his claws. He glares at Finn as he crushes the creature's still-beating organ and lets it fall to the ground with a wet squelch. "Your father is not going to kill her."

He's strong. Stronger than any demon who doesn't take souls has any right to be. I almost wonder if something has changed—he *shouldn't* be this strong without human souls powering him. But I can't think of that right now. Not when more and more Broods are prowling into the warehouse to protect the heir.

"Reid," I rasp. He cannot fight them all.

"I told you to *go*," he commands, his brutal eyes still pinned on Finn as he fights through a cloud of Brood henchmen.

They're coming for me now too. I back away slowly, putting distance between myself and two snarling demons. "I'm not leaving you."

Reid finally turns to look at me, and sorrow lays itself bare in his eyes as he takes me in. "Huntress . . ." he breathes, so low only I can hear it. "It's okay. It's time I pay for my sins."

My heart lurches for him. I want to hold his clawed hands, to kiss the ravaged skin of his arms, to stitch the gash along his cheek.

Finn frowns at us both. More pitying than anything. "Even if she runs"—his eyes rove over me—"in that shape, she won't get far."

When Finn takes a tentative step closer, Reid's menacing horns sprout from his head, curling back. "Viv!" he roars. "Get the fuck out of here!"

And I don't want to leave him—I *can't* leave him. If I do, he will die. I'm sure of it.

But Penny's trapped in a shipping crate a few feet away. And Driscoll has run off, which means he's either gathering more backup or finishing off his blond loose end. If I stay and these demons bring me to the High Thane, he'll kill me and harness the power churning beneath my skin, and so many more will suffer.

So, for the first time in all the times he's begged me to let him fight alone, I listen to Reid. I take off running before the guilt can hold me back.

But I do turn and get one final look at him: blood drying under his nose, bruises blooming on his strong, muscled body. A body that held me so closely just this morning when I woke from that nightmare. This . . . this is the real nightmare. Leaving him like this. Watching him barely hold off the High Thane's son and all these men for me. For Penny. Their claws slashing through his skin. Tearing at him. Piercing. And Reid—taking blow after blow.

Tears crest in my eyes at the sounds of his pain echoing through the warehouse. They only fade as my feet slam outside on slats of sea-weathered wood. I don't allow myself to think of what they'll do to him when he falls. Not *if* but *when*. A demon who's left the Brood to teach hunters? Caught in the teeth of a sadist like Finn? Death would be a mercy. My stomach rises into my throat. That and the iron-rich taste of blood. I swallow and keep fucking running.

When I reach the shipping crate, the door's already been wrenched open.

Shit, shit, shit—

Inside, I find Driscoll, knife raised, inching toward a sobbing Penny.

"Edgar!" I shout.

He whirls on me, face gray and bleeding. Casting that spell has drained him. "You're as irritating as your whistleblowing father was, you know that?"

"That's the nicest thing you've ever said to me," I bite out, launching myself at him.

The two of us go flying. Pain sings in my blistered back and along the side of my head.

Driscoll lands one punch in my stomach, and I roll to the side before I can absorb another. All I can hear are Penny's muffled cries and Edgar's grunts as he begins to mutter the words of a spell. The crate shakes with the force of his brewing magic—

But I'm faster.

My daggers fly out, and I land one square in his back before he can finish the words. He shouts in agony and collapses to the floor. I kneel over him with my other dagger raised, snarling and dizzy with pain of my own.

Before I can bring it down, he spits, "You need me, Viv. To get that out of you."

He's right, of course. I don't need to strain to remember the rest of Peter's lesson from that day in the courtyard. I've thought of it plenty in the weeks since. *The syrabraxa can only be removed by the same witch who cast it in the first place.* If I have any hope of not being the most valuable pawn in a cataclysmic battle for the survival of the mortal plane, I need Driscoll to remove the syrabraxa that's been welded to my spine.

And maybe with it, he'll take my hunter's gene too.

It's shameful.

Rotten and darker than the killer inside me. How I want so desperately to be free of my bloodlust, and my anger, and my otherness. To be normal and pleasant and happy. The daughter my mom always envisioned. The friend Penny deserves. That photographer on a date with a planetarium expert.

And I won't get this chance again . . . Here, gurgling blood beneath me, is the man who killed my father, the only person alive who can ever set me free.

I study Driscoll's hefty, twitching frame and the tension coiled in his square jaw.

And maybe in the deepest, truest corners of my heart I debate it. I almost let this man—who's abused his sworn duty as a protector of students, who murdered my dad—live for my own selfish, cowardly gain. So he can remove this spell from me and, with it, all my hunter abilities, instincts, and duties.

But then I hear Penny's sniffling, muffled cries. I think of all the lives I've saved. My friends, strangers, that mom on the subway. I think of what Reid told me. How it's a privilege and an honor to hunt. And that it's about time I make peace with who I am.

We take care of people.

My heart cracks wide open. My eyes burn.

"This is for my dad," I say before I plunge my dagger into Edgar Driscoll's heart.

He gurgles and sputters, first in fury, then in fear. I move to climb off him when his meaty hand grasps my shirt, pulling me back.

"You're a fool." Blood coats his teeth and dribbles from the side of his mouth. "Reid—" He hacks a wet cough.

"Reid what?"

"He's . . . He's not—" And then his eyes fade from furious to nothing at all.

My breathing is tight as I scramble off him. There's no time for deathbed mind games right now. He lived a liar and died as one too. I hurtle over to Penny without a second thought.

"You killed—" Penny gasps. "You *killed*—"

"I'm going to explain everything," I tell her, out of breath. "For real this time. But first we need to get out of here, okay?" I fish my phone out of my pocket and shoot Fiona a frantic text: High Thane at docks. Edgar dead. They have Reid—HURRY.

"We have to move fast," I manage. "There are others."

Penny sobs. "Oh god."

"We're going to be fine. Come on."

The sun outside is beginning to descend in the sky, painting the licorice-black sea with caps and spindrifts of sparkling gold. Unless Reid pulls off a miracle and executes the High Thane's son and all of his men, we have very little time before they're all after us.

And Reid—

I cannot think about Reid.

When we take off running, I realize I'm in even worse shape than I thought. Each time my legs pump me farther down the dock, currents of pain spasm up and into my shredded, scorched back. The tendrils of the spell tingle in my bones like a beetle underneath my skin.

When we cross from the docks into the buzz of Half City, I can hardly stand upright, but I can hear the rapid footfalls of at least three Brood demons chasing after us. Steam rises from subway grates into the crisp air. Car horns blare, and I nearly careen into a couple sharing a foamy latte.

"*Faster*," I urge Penny, her hand in mine, my boots squelching in dirty melted snow.

When I spy the STC police station, I tug us behind a snow-capped dumpster and press us against the chilled alley wall. It sizzles against my back like an egg in a frying pan.

"When I say go"—I wince—"you need to run to the police station."

"What are those things? They have *claws*, Viv."

I muster any strength I have left to tell her, "You never saw your captors and I was never here. It was a botched ransom for your dad's money, and you escaped on foot, okay?"

Penny nods vigorously. Her eyes are bloodshot, her hands shaking with adrenaline. "What about you?"

The Brood doesn't care about Penny—they don't even know who she is. Only Edgar knew who I was—who my friend was—and his only use for her was to lure me to them. They'll let her go. At least for now.

But with the syrabraxa in my back . . . Finn will follow me to the ends of the earth.

And despite the way my vision's dotted with black spots, one thing is crystal clear: I have nowhere to go. I cannot save Reid in the state I'm in. Not alone, that's for certain. And I can't go back to Harker, where I have no idea who I can trust. Nor can I go to my friends or family and put them in the crosshairs of the most dangerous deviants in existence. Anywhere I go, I'm jeopardizing everyone around me.

I'm thoroughly, completely, and desperately alone.

But I know this city. I just need to think. We're pretty deep South of the Chasm. In fact, we're not too far from—

Demon voices echo around the corner. Muttered words about where we might have run.

"I'll figure something out," I whisper, eyeing them on the bustling street. The demons are scanning the sidewalk, nostrils flaring, scenting the air. When they turn their backs, I urge her on. "Go now."

"Stay safe, please." She grasps my hand, which is gripping my dagger. "I love you."

I look down at my father's blade between us. The swirling serpent, now caked in blood, coiling itself around the hilt.

Hellion.

When I look back up, Penny's already crossing the busy intersection to the police department, out of sight of the stumped demons. But beyond her, looming in the distance, nine stories high, with lights already blinking, lies Fever Dream.

IT'S A LITTLE warmer down here. Snow melts into gray slush at my feet as I drag my limp body to the wide stone entry. Pale violet light slants against the towering building, telling me it's nearly dusk. Too early for the club's usual line around the block and too late in the day for the building to be empty.

Baz, the same vampire bouncer who tossed us out a week ago, is sitting on his rickety stool outside the eerily quiet nightclub. He's thumbing through his phone, a modern act that feels so at odds with the ancient darkness that emanates from him. He could have been Bram Stoker's inspiration for *Dracula*, and here he is scrolling Grindr.

"I need to see Deacon," I say to him. Only my voice is almost entirely gone, and it comes out a mere whisper that even his vamp hearing doesn't pick up on.

Though my limbs are numb from the cold and my teeth are chattering, I slink closer. "I need"—I cough, blood on my tongue—"Deacon."

As gut-wrenching as it is to admit, Reid's brother is my only hope. Fever Dream is heavily protected and not owned, run, or operated by the Brood, Harker, or the Elders. An outlier in the battle at hand. A neutral zone. A strobe-lit, techno-filled safe haven.

But more importantly, Deacon could have killed Reid and me that night I broke into his office. He could have, but he didn't. I have to believe the fact that he spared Reid's life once means he'll care enough to save it again.

"Please," I choke.

Finally Baz looks up at me with an unimpressed frown. "Fuck. You look awful."

I brandish my daggers as best I can, wiping sweat from my brow with my forearm. "Get me your boss."

Baz only lifts a brow, still perched on his stool like a crow. "You're that hunter we kicked out last week . . . He's going to drink your soul like a beer on tap."

"I'd kill him first," I snarl.

At that, Baz's lips curl with the hint of a lazy grin. "Good fucking luck killing Deacon Graveheart."

"Listen to me. I need his *help*." Baz's gaze is back on his phone, but I press onward. "I'm not leaving here without speaking to him."

"Doesn't look to me like you're leaving here at all." That voice . . . like razor blades and honey. Goes down smooth and rips you up.

Baz and I both turn to see Deacon strolling around the corner. He stubs a cigarette out on the wall of his club and lets it fall into the snow with a wet sizzle. I forgot how hulking he is. How deadly that roguish smile is, aimed right at me.

"Jesus, Vivienne." His eyes gobble me up with pure, fiendish delight. "What happened to you?"

"The High Thane's twisted son." I'm seized by a violent cough that splatters blood on the snow at our feet.

Deacon eyes me curiously, his gaze sliding over all my wounds and stretches of bare skin. It's almost as violating as it is humiliating. He tsks. "How dare they break my favorite doll . . ."

"I need your *help*, Deacon."

"You shouldn't have come back here."

I stare into his glacial eyes and try not to cower. "I had nowhere else to go."

Deacon pouts at me facetiously. "How sad."

Baz looses the first chuckle I've heard out of him.

"But I did tell you I'd kill you if I saw you again," Deacon says. "And I'm nothing if not a man of my word."

Before I can respond, Deacon's got his massive hand tangled in my hair and is dragging me toward the club's entrance. My scalp blares in pain while I fight to wrench free. My legs burn as he tugs me along rough, icy asphalt. "You don't"—I cry out—"want to kill me."

"Wrong," he purrs. "I really do."

He tries to haul me inside, but I twist in his grasp to show him the back of my ruined shirt. "No, *you don't*."

Baz jolts up from his stool in awe. The fibers that have fused to my skin rip, and I wince, catching my breath, allowing Deacon and Baz to study the wound down my spine. The clear and sinister wound from the syrabraxa. Like I'm a fluorescent frog warning predators of the poison running through my blood.

Deacon releases me instantly and I fall to the ground.

"Interesting," he drawls.

I whimper in the snow, every synapse in my body failing. Seconds from unconsciousness. I can hardly inhale.

Deacon lowers to a crouch before me. Wicked curiosity dances in those depthless blue eyes as they fill my vision. "Why are you here, Vivienne?"

The low sun gilds his ice-white hair and the menacing tattoos on his neck as I get a whiff of tobacco and human souls on his breath.

I steel my stomach. This can only go one of two ways.

"It's about your brother..."

I barely get the words out before Deacon yanks me up and hurls me inside his club, the cavernous doors slamming shut behind us.

ACKNOWLEDGMENTS

First and foremost, thank you to my brilliant editor, Kristine. She is the light at the end of every drafting tunnel. When anything is hard to write, plot, or string together, I just tell myself, *Kristine will know what to do*, and she always does. She lets me push my deadlines, write back to emails in all caps, and DM her far too often about baked goods. She's excellent and I adore her.

Thank you just as enthusiastically to my agents, Taylor and Sam. They put up with an ungodly number of questions, comments, concerns, thoughts, ideas, quick Q's, and the rest. Their patience, support, and enthusiasm make me feel all gooey inside. I love you guys.

While I'm at it, thank you to Gab and Jasmine at Root, who take such good care of everything from my blurb schedule—sorry I'm always behind—to my merch deals. I am so grateful to have you both on my team.

And *that's* a decent segue (I'm on a roll!) to all the amazing brands, book boxes, concept artists, and special editions I've had the pleasure of partnering with these past few years. Briarwick Candles, Threaded by Sabrina, Blissfully Bookish, FairyLoot,

Probably Smut, Midnight Whispers, Coco Merwild, Anna Svab, Maria Makovetskaya, Sasha Lee Coleman, Elithien, Wictoria Nordgård, Kei Ella, and the Bookish Shop: Thank you for putting your creative heart and soul into my work and helping to bring my stories to life for readers.

Thank you to the incomparable Anika and Kristin, my marketing and publicity gurus, for making sure people even know about these books in the first place. Thank you to Heather Baror-Shapiro, who does all my wonderful foreign translation deals. And thank you to those foreign publishers who share my work all over the world, especially Anne Perry at Arcadia, who I've had the pleasure of working with on every title I've written; I hope to continue doing so for as long as she'll have me. Thank you also to the audiobook team who brought Viv and Reid to life and to Iris McElroy for producing another banger.

Thank you to my tireless betas, who work under increasingly ridiculous timelines for longer and longer books and still offer incredibly valuable feedback. Especially those who really dove into the deep end with me on this one. If you saw the doc titled "BIG Q's" *shudders*, I'm talking about you.

Thank you to all my inspiring fellow authors who have supported me through the entire writing process on this book and all my others, such as my forever soulmate, Lana Ferguson; double-date besties Emily Wibberley and Austin Siegemund-Broka; and AO3/IWTV educators Julie Soto and Ali Hazelwood, as well as all the other wonderful authors who make the solitary job of writing a little less lonely.

Thank you to the remarkable friends I've made in the bookish community who have championed, posted about, and reviewed my books or even just put up with long, rambling text messages and voice notes in which I complained about love interests and world-building for hours on end. Special shout-outs to Tina, Jac, Amy, Lila, Dayna, Kristen, Vanessa, and so many more.

Thank you to my wildly supportive friends and family, who always ask me how my books are coming along even though they know they've got a manic, overly detailed answer coming their way. To my mom especially: Thank you for reading every draft; giving such thoughtful, necessary, and brilliant feedback; and never commenting on the sex scenes. We just pretend those aren't there, right?

Thank you to my incredible husband, Jack, who shows me every day what happily ever after looks like. There's a piece of you and me in all these books, and that piece is always my favorite part. And to our puppy, Milo, thank you for keeping me company on long writing days and for being the overall light of my life.

And last but never, ever least, thank you to my readers. Your support and enthusiasm have changed my life. I'll never have the right language to thank you properly, so I'll just say this: Every word I write is for you. Please don't hate me for the cliffhangers.

KEEP READING FOR A PREVIEW OF

A DAWN OF ONYX,

FROM KATE GOLDEN'S HEART-POUNDING ROMANTASY SERIES, AVAILABLE NOW!

RYDER AND HALDEN were probably dead.

I wasn't sure what was making me feel sicker, finally admitting that truth to myself or my aching, burning lungs. The misery of the latter was, admittedly, self-induced—this section of my morning run was always the most brutal—but today marked one year since the letters had stopped coming, and while I'd sworn not to think the worst until there was reason to, the epistolary silence was hard to argue with.

My heart gave a miserable thump.

Attempting to slip the unpleasant thoughts under the floorboards of my mind, I focused on making it to the edge of the clearing without vomiting. I pumped my legs, swung my elbows back, and felt my braid land between my shoulder blades, as rhythmic as a drumbeat. Just a few more feet—

Finally reaching the expanse of cool grass, I staggered to a halt, bracing my hands on my knees and inhaling deeply. It smelled like the Kingdom of Amber always did—of morning dew, woodfire from a nearby hearth, and the crisp, earthy notes of slowly decaying leaves.

But deep breaths weren't enough to keep my vision from blurring, and I collapsed backward onto the ground, the weight of my body crushing the leaves beneath me with a satisfying crunch. The clearing was littered with them—the last remnants of winter.

Eighteen months ago, the night before all the men in our town were conscripted to fight for our kingdom, my family had gathered on the grassy knoll just behind our home. We had watched the pink-hued sunset fade like a bruise behind our town of Abbington all together, one last time. Then, Halden and I had snuck away to this very glade and pretended he and my brother, Ryder, weren't leaving.

That they'd be back one day.

The bells chimed in the town square, distant but clear enough to jar me from the melancholy memory. I eased up to sitting, my tangled hair now littered with leaves and twigs. I was going to be late. Again.

Bleeding Stones.

Or—*shit.* I winced as I stood. I was trying to swear less on the nine Holy Gemstones that made up the continent's core. I didn't care so much about damning the divinity of Evendell's creation, but I hated the force of habit that came from growing up in Amber, the kingdom that worshipped the Stones most devoutly.

I jogged back through the glade, down the path behind our cottage, and toward a town just waking up. As I hurried through alleyways that could barely accommodate two people heading in opposite directions, a depressing thought filtered in. *Abbington really used to have more charm.*

At least it was charming in my memories. Cobblestone streets once swept clean and sprinkled with street musicians and idle merchants were now strewn with garbage and abandoned. Mismatched brick buildings covered with vines and warmed by flickering lanterns had been reduced to crumbling decay—abandoned, burned, or broken down, if not all three. It was like watching an apple core rot, slowly turning less and less vibrant over time until, one day, it was just gone.

I shivered, both at the thoughts and the weather. Hopefully, the chilly air had dried some of the dampness from my forehead; Nora did not like a sweaty apprentice. As I pushed the creaky door open, ethanol and astringent mint assaulted my nostrils. My favorite scent.

"Arwen, is that you?" Nora called, her voice echoing through the infirmary's hallway. "You're late. Mr. Doyle's gangrene is getting worse. He might lose the finger."

"Lose my *what?*" a male voice squawked from behind a curtain.

I shot Nora a withering look and slipped inside the makeshift room separated by cotton sheets.

Bleeding Stones.

Mr. Doyle, an elderly bald man who was all forehead and earlobes, was in his bed, cradling his damaged hand like a stolen dessert that someone aimed to take from him.

"Nora's only kidding," I said, pulling up a chair. "That's her fun and very professional sense of humor. I'll make sure all fingers remain attached, I promise."

With a skeptical huff, Mr. Doyle relinquished his hand, and I got to work carefully peeling away the layers of rotting skin.

My ability twitched at my fingertips, eager to help. I wasn't sure I needed it today; I liked the meticulous work, and gangrene was fairly routine.

But I would never forgive myself if I broke my promise to cranky Mr. Doyle.

I covered one hand with the other, as if I didn't want him to see how gruesome his injury was—I had gotten very good at finding ways to sneak my powers into patients. Mr. Doyle closed his eyes and leaned his head back, and I allowed a flicker of pure light to seep from my fingers like juice from a lemon.

The decaying flesh warmed and blushed pink once more, healing before my eyes.

I was a good healer. I had a steady hand, was calm under pressure, and never got squeamish at the sight of someone's insides. But I could also heal in ways that couldn't be taught. My power was a pulsing, erratic light that poured out of my hands and seeped into others, spreading through their veins and vessels. I could fuse a broken bone, give color back to a flu-ravaged face, or stitch a gash closed with no needle.

But it wasn't common witchcraft. I had no witches or warlocks in my family heritage, and even if I had, when I used my powers, there was no uttered spell followed by a flurry of wind and static. Instead, my gift seeped from my body, draining my energy and mind each time. Witches could do endless magic with the right grimoires and tutelage. My abilities would fizzle out if worked too hard, leaving me depleted. Sometimes it could even take days for the power to come back fully.

The first time I exhausted myself on a particularly brutal burn victim, I thought my gift was actually gone for good, leaving me with an inexplicable mix of relief and horror. When it finally returned, I told myself I was grateful. Grateful that when I was growing up and was covered in welts or had limbs cracked at odd angles, I could heal myself before my mother or siblings could notice what my stepfather had done. Grateful that I could help those around me who were suffering. And grateful that I could make a decent amount of coin doing it when times were as tough as they were now.

"All right, Mr. Doyle, good as new."

The older man shot me a toothless grin. "Thank you," he said, before leaning in conspiratorially. "I didn't think you'd be able to save it."

"The lack of faith hurts," I joked.

He moved gingerly out of the room, and I followed him into the hall. Once he was through the front doors, Nora shook her head at me.

"What?"

"Too chipper," she said, but her mouth lifted in a smile.

"It's a relief to have a patient who isn't on death's door." I cringed. Mr. Doyle was actually quite old.

Nora just snorted and refocused on the gauze in her hands. I slunk back over to the cots and busied myself sanitizing some surgical tools. I should have been thrilled with how few patients we had today, but the quiet was making my stomach twist.

Healing took my mind off of my brother and Halden. Helped to quell the misery that churned in my gut at their absence. Like running, there was a meditative quality to healing people that calmed my chattering brain.

Silence did the opposite.

I'd never expected to be thrilled about a case of gangrene, but it seemed like anything that wasn't certain death was a win these days. Most of our patients were soldiers—bloody, bruised, and broken from battle—or neighbors I'd known my entire life, shriveling away from parasites found in the meager food scraps they could get their hands on. That, at least, was a better fate than starvation. Parasites could be healed in the infirmary. Endless hunger, not so much.

And through all this pain and suffering, loved ones lost, homes destroyed—it was still a mystery why the Onyx Kingdom had started a war with us in the first place. Our King Gareth was not one for the historical tomes, and Amber land was not known for anything but its harvest. Meanwhile, kingdoms like Garnet were rich with coin and jewels. The Pearl Mountains had their ancient scrolls and the continent's most sought-after scholars. Even the Opal Territories, with their distilleries and untouched land, or the Peridot Provinces, with their glittering coves filled with hidden treasure, would all have been better places to begin the gradual crawl toward power over all of Evendell. But so far, every other kingdom had been left unscathed, and lone Amber was trying to keep it that way.

Still, no other kingdom fought beside us.

Meanwhile, Onyx was dripping in riches, jewels, and gold. They had the most land, the most stunning cities—or so I had heard—and the biggest army. Even that wasn't enough for them. Onyx's king, Kane Ravenwood, was both imperialistic and insatiable. Worst of all, he was senselessly cruel. Our generals were often found strung up by their limbs, sometimes flayed or crucified. He took and took and took until our meager kingdom had little left to fight with, and then inflicted pain for the sport of it. Cutting us off at the knees, then the elbows, then the ears just for fun.

The only option was to keep looking on the bright side. Even if it was a dim, blurry kind of bright side that you had to bribe and coax to come out. That, Nora had claimed, was why she kept me around. *"You have a knack for this, you're optimistic to a fault, and your tits entice the local boys to donate blood."*

Thank you, Nora. You're a peach.

I peered up at her, putting away a basket filled with bandages and ointments.

She wasn't the warmest associate, but Nora was one of my mother's closest friends, and despite her prickly exterior, she'd been thoughtful enough to give me this job so I could take care of our family once Ryder left. She even helped with my sister, Leigh, when Mother was too sick to take her to classes.

My smile at Nora's kindness faded as I thought of my mother—she had been too frail to even open her eyes this morning. The irony that I worked as a healer and my mother was slowly dying from an ailment none of us could identify was not lost on me.

Even worse—and maybe more ironic—my abilities had never worked on her. Not even if all she had was a paper cut. Yet another sign that my powers were not those of a common witch, but something far stranger.

My mother had been sick since I was old enough to talk, but it had worsened these past few years. The only things that helped were the little remedies Nora and I put together—concoctions made of the white canna lilies and rhodanthe flowers native to Amber, blended with Ravensara oil and sandalwood. But the relief was temporary, and her pain grew worse each day.

I physically shook my head to rattle the unpleasantness away.

I couldn't focus on that now. The only thing that mattered was taking care of her and my sister as best I could, now that Ryder was gone.

And might never be coming back.

"NO, YOU DIDN'T hear me right! I didn't say he was *cute*, I said he was *astute*. Like, smart or worldly," Leigh said, throwing a log on the dwindling hearth fire. I bit back a laugh and pulled three small bowls from the cupboard.

"Mhm, right. I just think you have a little crush, that's all."

Leigh rolled her pale blue eyes as she turned around in our tiny kitchen gathering cutlery and mugs. Our house was small and rickety, but I loved it with my whole heart. It smelled like Ryder's tobacco, the vanilla we used for baking, and fragrant white lilies. Leigh's sketches hung on almost every wall. Every time I walked in our front door, a smile tugged at my lips. Perched on a little hill overlooking most of Abbington and with three well-insulated, cozy rooms, it was one of the nicer houses in our village. My stepfather, Powell, had built it for my mother and me before my siblings were born. The kitchen was my favorite place to sit, the wooden table put together by Powell and Ryder one summer back when we were all young and Mother was healthier.

It was uncanny, the warm memories tied to the bones of our home in such contrast to those that swam in my head, in my stomach, when I thought of Powell's stern face and clenched jaw. The scars on my back from his belt.

I shuddered.

Leigh squeezed in beside me, jarring me from cobwebbed memories and handing over a bundle of roots and herbs for Mother's medication.

"Here. We don't have any rosemary left."

I peered down at her blonde head and a warmth bloomed in me—she was always radiant, even with the misery of wartime that surrounded us. Joyful, funny, bold.

"What?" she asked, narrowing her eyes at me.

"Nothing," I said, biting back a smile. She was just starting to see herself as a grown-up and no longer tolerated being treated like a kid. Loving stares of adoration from her older sister were clearly not allowed. She liked it even less when I tried to protect her.

I swallowed hard, throwing the herbs into the bubbling pot over our hearth.

Recently, rumors had been swirling in the taverns, schools, and markets. The men were all gone now—Ryder and Halden had likely given their lives—and we were still losing to the wicked kingdom in the north.

The women would have to be next.

It wasn't that we couldn't do what the men could. I had heard the Onyx Kingdom's army was filled with strong, ruthless women who fought alongside the men. *I* just couldn't do it. Couldn't take someone's life for my kingdom, couldn't fight for my own. The thought of leaving Abbington at all raised the hair on the back of my neck.

It was Leigh I worried about. She was too fearless.

Her youth made her think she was invincible, and her hunger for attention made her loud, risky, and brave to the point of recklessness. The thought of her golden curls bouncing onto the front lines made my stomach twist.

If that wasn't bad enough, both of us being carted off to fight against Onyx meant Mother would be left alone. Too old and frail to fight, she might avoid the draft but wouldn't be able to take care of herself. With all three of her children gone, she wouldn't last a week.

How was I supposed to protect either of them then?

"You couldn't be more wrong about Jace," Leigh said, pointing a fork at me with faux assuredness. "I've never had a crush in my life. Especially not on him."

"Fine," I said, searching through a cupboard for carrots. I wondered if Leigh had purposely distracted me—if she could tell I was worrying.

"Honestly," she continued, plopping down at our kitchen table and folding her feet underneath her. "I don't care what you think. Look at your taste! You're in love with Halden Brownfield." Leigh made a disgusted face.

My pulse rose at his name, remembering the date and my anxiety from this morning. I shook my head at Leigh's accusation.

"I am not *in love* with him. I like him. As a person. We're just friends, actually."

"Mhm, right," she said, mocking my earlier sentiments about her and Jace.

I popped the carrots in a separate pot for dinner, beside Mother's medication. Multitasking had become one of my strong suits since Ryder left. I opened the window above the hearth, letting some of the heat from both pots billow outside. The cool evening breeze washed over my sticky face.

"What's wrong with Halden anyway?" I asked, curiosity getting to me.

"Nothing, really. He was just boring. And fussy. And he wasn't silly at all."

"Stop saying 'was,'" I said, with more bite than I intended. "He's all right. They both are."

Not a lie. Just that same bright-side thinking that could occasionally border on denial. Leigh stood to set the table, gathering mismatched mugs for our cider.

"And Halden is silly and interesting . . . and fussy," I conceded. "I'll give you that one. He's a little tightly wound." Leigh smiled, knowing she'd gotten me.

I considered my sister. She had grown up so much in so little time that I wasn't sure what information I was protecting her from anymore.

"Fine," I said, stirring the two pots simultaneously. "We were seeing each other."

Leigh raised her brows suggestively.

"But truthfully, there was no 'in love' to speak of. By the Stones."

"Why not? Because you knew he would have to leave?"

My gaze landed on the hearth, watching the meager flames flicker as I thought about her question in earnest.

It was shallow, but the first thing that came to mind when I heard his name was Halden's hair. Sometimes, especially in the moonlight, his blond curls looked so pale they nearly glowed. It was actually what first drew me to him—he was the only boy in our town with fair hair. Amber mainly produced chocolatey brunettes like me or dirty blonds like Leigh and Ryder.

I had fallen for that ice-blond hair at the determined age of seven. He and Ryder had become inseparable right around then. Certain I was going to marry him, I didn't mind trailing their every adventure and clinging to their scraped-knee-inducing games. Halden had a smile that made me feel safe. I would have followed it anywhere. The day word of conscription came to Abbington was the only time I ever saw his smile falter.

That, and the day he first saw my scars.

But if I'd been enamored with Halden since I was little, why didn't it feel like love when he finally saw in me what I had seen in him for so long?

I didn't have a good answer, and certainly not one fit for a ten-year-old. Had I not loved him because I'd never seen it go well for anyone, namely our mother? Or because sometimes I'd ask him what he thought of Onyx's expansion of their already sprawling land and his dismissive responses would make me feel prickly for some reason I couldn't quite place? Maybe the answer was far worse. The one I hoped wasn't true but feared the most—that I wasn't capable of such a feeling.

There was nobody more deserving of it than Halden. Nobody else whom Mother, Ryder, or Powell would have wished me to be with.

"I don't know, Leigh."

I swept my attention back to the dinner preparation and sliced vegetables in silence. Leigh, sensing I was finished with that particular line of questioning, returned to setting the table. When Mother's medicine was done boiling, I moved it to the counter to steep. Once it cooled, I would fill a new vial and place it in the pouch by the cupboard as always.

Maybe I could do this—take care of them all on my own.

The savory aroma of stewing vegetables mixed with the medicinal notes of Mother's medication drifted through the home. It was a familiar scent. A comfortable one. Amber was surrounded by mountains, which meant the valley we were nestled in always had chilly mornings, crisp days, and cold nights. Every tree wilted brown leaves year-round. Every dinner was always corn, squash, pumpkin, carrots. Even the harshest of winters brought only rain and bare branches, and the hottest summer I could remember had a mere two trees of green. For the most part, it was brown and blustery here every day of the year.

And after twenty of them, there were days when it felt like I'd had enough corn and squash for a lifetime. I tried to imagine my life filled with other flavors, landscapes, people . . . But I'd seen so little, the fantasies were blurred and vague—a cluttered constellation of books I'd read and stories I'd heard over the years.

"It smells divine in here."

My eyes found my mother as she hobbled in. A bit worse for wear today, her hair was tied back in a damp braid at the nape of her neck. She was only forty, but her thin body and sallow cheeks aged her.

"Here, let me help you," I said, walking to her.

Leigh hopped off the table, leaving one candle unlit, to come to her other side.

"I'm fine, I promise." She clucked at us. But we ignored her. It had become a well-choreographed dance at this point.

"Roses and thorns?" she said, once we had seated her at the table.

My sweet mother, who, despite her chronic fatigue, pain, and suffering, always genuinely cared about what happened in our days. Whose love of flowers had made its way into our nightly routine.

My mother had come to Abbington with me when I was nearly one. I never knew my father, but Powell was willing to wed her and take me in as his own. They had Ryder less than a year later, and Leigh seven after that. It was rare in our traditional town to be a woman with three children, one with a different father than the rest. But she never let unkind words cloud the sunshine she radiated daily. She worked tirelessly her whole life to give us a home with a roof, food in our bellies, and more laughter and love each day than most children get in a lifetime.

"My rose was saving Mr. Doyle's finger from being amputated," I offered. Leigh made a retching sound. I left my thorn out. If they hadn't realized it yet, I was not going to be the one to share that our brother hadn't written to us in a year.

"Mine was when Jace told me—"

"Jace is the boy Leigh thinks is cute," I interrupted, and gave my mother a conspiratorial nod. She shot back a dramatic wink, and Leigh's eyes became slits aimed at both of us.

"His cousin is a messenger in the army, delivering plans directly from King Gareth to his generals where even ravens can't reach them," Leigh said. "The cousin told him that she saw a man with wings in the Onyx capital." Her eyes went big and blue as the sea.

I looked to my mother at the absurdity, but she just nodded politely at Leigh. I tried to do the same. We shouldn't poke so much fun at her.

"How curious. Do you believe him?" Mother asked, resting her head on her hand in thought.

Leigh contemplated this as I sipped my stew.

"No, I don't," she said after deliberating. "I guess still-living Fae are a possibility, but I think it was more likely some kind of witchcraft. Right?"

"Right," I agreed, even though I knew better. The Fae had been completely extinct for years—if they had ever been real at all. But I didn't want to burst her imaginative bubble.

I smiled at Leigh. "I see why you're so in love with Jace. He's got all the good intel."

My mother bit back a smile. So much for not poking fun. Force of habit.

Leigh frowned and launched into a tirade about how she *obviously* didn't have *any* romantic feelings for this boy. I grinned, knowing that song and dance all too well.

Stories like Jace's cousin's were always floating around. Especially in relation to Willowridge, Onyx's mysterious capital city. The night before Halden left, he had told me it was rumored to be filled with all kinds of monstrous creatures. Dragons, goblins, ogres—I could tell he was trying to spook me, hoping I might nestle myself into the safety of his embrace and allow him to protect me from whatever was beyond our kingdom's barriers.

But it hadn't frightened me at all. I knew how those tales went. Men, built up in story after story, twisted by retellings into some horrific beasts, wielding unknown powers and capable of untold torment. In reality, they were just . . . men. Evil, power-hungry, corrupt, debauched *men*. Nothing more, nothing less, and none worse than the one who had lived in my own home. My stepfather was more vicious and cruel than any monster from a story.

I didn't know if that truth would have brought Halden more or less fear on the day he and Ryder were sent off to war. It definitely wouldn't help me if Leigh and I were forced into battle next.

Truth was, our King Gareth was doing the best he could, but Onyx had a far superior army, better weapons, stronger allies, and I'm sure countless other advantages I knew nothing about. I could promise that Onyx wasn't winning this war because of some big bad that went bump in the night.

My mother's sigh brought my thoughts back from wicked, winged creatures to our warm, wooden kitchen. The last dregs of daylight were slipping across the room, leaving the dancing flames of the hearth to cast her sallow face in shadow.

"My rose is this stew, and my two beautiful girls sitting in front of me. My kind, responsible Arwen." She turned to Leigh. "My bold, brave Leigh."

Ice ran through my veins. I knew what was coming next.

"And my thorn is my son, who I miss so, so dearly. But it's been a year since we've heard from him. I think . . ." She breathed. "I think it's time we accepted that he—"

"Is fine," I interrupted her. "Ryder is fine. I can't imagine how hard it must be to get a letter out in the conditions he could be in."

"Arwen," my mother started, her voice warm and comforting and making my skin itch with its gentleness.

I babbled over her. "Can you imagine trying to send a letter to a small town like ours from a jungle? Or, or . . . a forest? From the middle of an ocean? Who knows where he is?" I was starting to sound hysterical.

"It makes me so sad, too, Arwen." Leigh's little voice was even harder to bear. "But I think Mother may be right."

"It's healthy to talk about it," Mother said, taking my hand in hers. "How much we miss him, how hard it will be to continue on without him."

I bit my lip; their serious faces were cleaving me in two. I knew they were right. But saying it out loud . . .

As soothing as her touch was, I pulled my hand away and turned to face the window, letting the evening breeze whisper over my face and closing my eyes to the cool sensation.

My lungs filled with dusk air.

I couldn't be the one to make this harder for them.

Wrapping my hands around my bowl to quell their shaking, I turned back to face my only remaining family.

"You're right. It's unlikely he's—"

The deafening sound of our front door slamming open caused the bowl I was holding to jump from my hands and shatter on the floor. Bright orange splattered everywhere like fresh blood. I spun and saw my mother's face go slack with shock. In front of us, breathing heavily, face bloodied, and leaning into the doorframe to support a twisted arm, stood my brother, Ryder.

ABOUT THE AUTHOR

KATE GOLDEN is the *USA Today* bestselling author of the Sacred Stones trilogy. She lives in Los Angeles, where she works in the film industry developing movies with screenwriters and filmmakers. When she isn't telling stories, Kate is an avid book reader, puzzle addict, and game night enthusiast, which she hosts with her husband and puppy, Milo.

VISIT KATE GOLDEN ONLINE

KateGoldenBooks.com
◉ KateGoldenAuthor
♪ Kate_Golden_Author

RAISING READERS
Books Build Bright Futures

Dear Reader,

We'd love your attention for one more page to tell you about the crisis in children's reading, and what we can all do.

Studies have shown that reading for fun is the **single biggest predictor of a child's future success** – more than family circumstance, parents' educational background or income. It improves academic results, mental health, wealth, communication skills and ambition.

The number of children reading for fun is in rapid decline. Young people have a lot of competition for their time, and a worryingly high number do not have a single book at home.

Our business works extensively with schools, libraries and literacy charities, but here are some ways we can all raise more readers:

- Reading to children for just 10 minutes a day makes a difference
- Don't give up if your children aren't regular readers – there will be books for them!
- Visit bookshops and libraries to get recommendations
- Encourage them to listen to audiobooks
- Support school libraries
- Give books as gifts

Thank you for reading.
www.JoinRaisingReaders.com